'Scudder is on... ...around' *LA Times*

'Bull's-eye dialogue and laser-image description . . . any search for false notes will prove futile . . . [Block's] eye for detail is as sharp as ever, and characters almost real enough to touch abound' *New York Times Book Review*

'Fast-paced, insightful, and so suspenseful it zings like a high-tension wire' Stephen King

'Absolutely riveting . . . Block is terrific' *Washington Post*

'What he does best – writing popular fiction that always respects his readers' desire to be entertained but never insults their intelligence' *GQ*

'There with the best . . . The real McCoy with a shocking twist and stylish too' *Observer*

Hit List

'*Hit List* rattles along like a runaway express on the downhill section and gives a damn good ride' *Time Out*

'*Hit List* is an astonishing book; beautifully written, as deeply enjoyable as it is fundamentally upsetting. Block is not only one of the great technicians of the form; with this book he reveals himself as a writer capable of ripping your moral compass right out of your chest, smashing it to pieces on your forehead, and then leaving you to glue it back together' *Independen...*

Wholly absorbing, enti... you have time to finish. ... unattended' *Literary Re...*

Lawrence Block is a Grand Master of the Mystery Writers of America. His novels and short stories have won the Edgar Allan Poe and Shamus awards four times each. He is the creator of Matt Scudder, who features in a series of his books, and of other great characters such as Bernie Rhodenbarr, Evan Tanner and Chip Harrison. Lawrence Block lives in New York City, and maintains a website at www.lawrenceblock.com.

BY LAWRENCE BLOCK

The Sins of the Fathers
Time to Murder and Create
In the Midst of Death
A Stab in the Dark
When the Sacred Ginmill Closes
Eight Million Ways to Die
Out on the Cutting Edge
A Ticket to the Boneyard
A Dance at the Slaughterhouse
A Walk Among the Tombstones
The Devil Knows You're Dead
A Long Line of Dead Men
Even the Wicked
Everybody Dies
Hit Man
The Collected Mystery Stories
Hit List
Hope to Die

HIT LIST

Lawrence Block

HIT LIST

An Orion paperback

First published in Great Britain in 2000
by Orion Books
This paperback edition published in 2001
by Orion Books,
an imprint of The Orion Publishing Group Ltd,
Carmelite House, 50 Victoria Embankment,
London EC4Y 0DZ

A CIP catalogue record for this book is available
from the British Library.

ISBN 978 0 7528 4424 4

Printed and bound in Great Britain by
Clays Ltd, St Ives plc

www.orionbooks.co.uk

This one's for
Justin Scott

ACKNOWLEDGEMENTS

The author is pleased to acknowledge The Writers Room, Caffè Borgia, Caffè San Marco, and The Players, all in New York City, where portions of this book were written.

CHAPTER ONE

Keller, fresh off the plane from Newark, followed the signs marked Baggage Claim. He hadn't checked a bag, he never did, but the airport signage more or less assumed that everybody checked their luggage, because you got to the exit by heading for the baggage claim. You couldn't count on a series of signs that said *This is the way to get out of this goddam place*.

There was a down escalator after you cleared security, and ten or a dozen men stood around at the foot of it, some in uniform, most holding hand-lettered signs. Keller found himself drawn to one man, a droopy guy in khakis and a leather jacket. He was the guy, Keller decided, and his eyes went to the sign the man was holding.

But you couldn't read the damn thing. Keller walked closer, squinting at it. Did it say Archibald? Keller couldn't tell.

He turned, and there was the name he was looking for, on a card held by another man, this one taller and heavier and wearing a suit and tie. Keller veered away from the man with the illegible sign—what was the point of a sign that nobody could read?—and walked up to the man with the Archibald sign. "I'm Mr. Archibald," he said.

"Mr. Richard Archibald?"

What possible difference could it make? He started to nod, then remembered the name Dot had given him. "Nathan Archibald," he said.

"That's the ticket," the man said. "Welcome to Louisville, Mr. Archibald. Carry that for you?"

"Never mind," Keller said, and held on to his carry-on bag. He followed the man out of the terminal and across a couple of lanes of traffic to the short-term parking lot.

"About the name," the man said. "What I figured, anybody can read a name off a card. Some clown's got to figure, why take a cab when I can say I'm Archibald and ride for free? I mean, it's not like they gave me a picture of you. Nobody here even knows what you look like."

"I don't come here often," Keller said.

"Well, it's a pretty nice town," the man said, "but that's beside the point. Which is I want to make sure I'm driving the right person, so I throw out a first name, and it's a wrong first name. 'Richard Archibald?' Guy says yeah, that's me, Richard Archibald, right away I know he's full of crap."

"Unless that's his real name."

"Yeah, but what's the odds of that? Two men fresh off a plane and they both got the name Archibald?"

"Only one."

"How's that?"

"My name's not really Archibald," Keller said, figuring he wasn't exactly letting state secrets slip by the admission. "So it's only one man named Archibald, so how much of a long shot is it?"

The man set his jaw. "Guy claims to be Richard Archibald," he said, "he's not my guy. Whether it's his name or not."

"You're right about that."

"But you came up with Nathan, so we're in business. Case closed. It's the Toyota there, the blue one. Get in and we'll take a run over to long-term parking. Your car's there, full tank of gas, registration in the glove box. When you're done, just put her back in the same spot, tuck the keys and the claim check in the ashtray. Somebody'll pick it up."

The car turned out to be a mid-size Olds, dark green in color. The man unlocked it and handed Keller the keys and a cardboard claim check. "Cost you a few dollars," he said apologetically. "We brought her over last night. On the passenger seat there you got a street map of the area. Open it up, you'll see two spots marked, home and office. I don't know how much you been told."

"Name and address," Keller said.

"What was the name?"

"It wasn't Archibald."

"You don't want to say? I don't blame you. You seen a photo?"

Keller shook his head. The man drew a small envelope from his inside pocket, retrieved a card from it. The card's face displayed a family photograph, a man, a woman, two children and a dog. The humans were all smiling, and looked as though they'd been smiling for days, waiting for someone to figure out how to work the camera. The dog, a golden retriever, wasn't smiling, but he looked happy enough. "Season's Greetings . . ." it said below the photo.

Keller opened the card. He read: ". . . from the Hirschhorns—Walt, Betsy, Jason, Tamara, and Powhatan."

"I guess Powhatan's the dog," he said.

"Powhatan? What's that, an Indian name?"

"Pocahontas's father."

"Unusual name for a dog."

"It's a fairly unusual name for a human being," Keller said. "As far as I know it's only been used once. Was this the only picture they could come up with?"

"What's the matter with it? Nice clear shot, and I'm here to tell you it looks just like the man."

"Nice that you could get them to pose for you."

"It's from a Christmas card. Musta been taken during the summer, though. How they're dressed, and the background. You know where I bet this was taken? He's got a summer place out by McNeely Lake."

Wherever that was.

"So it woulda been taken in the summer, which'd make it what, fifteen months old? He still looks the same, so what's the problem?"

"It shows the whole family."

3

"Right," the man said. "Oh, I see where you're going. No, it's just him, Walter Hirschhorn. Just the man himself."

That was Keller's understanding, but it was good to have it confirmed. Still, he'd have been happier with a solo headshot of Hirschhorn, eyes narrowed and mouth set in a line. Not surrounded by his nearest and dearest, all of them with fixed smiles.

He didn't much like the way this felt. Hadn't liked it since he walked off the plane.

"I don't know if you'll want it," the man was saying, "but there's a piece in the glove box."

A piece of what, Keller wondered, and then realized what the man meant. "Along with the registration," he said.

"Except the piece ain't registered. It's a nice little twenty-two auto with a spare clip, not that you're gonna need it. The clip, I mean. Whether you need the piece altogether is not for me to say."

"Well," Keller said.

"That's what you guys like, isn't it? A twenty-two?"

If you shot a man in the head with a .22, the slug would generally stay within the skull, bouncing around in there, doing no good to the skull's owner. The small-calibre weapon was supposed to be more accurate, and had less recoil, and would presumably be the weapon of choice for an assassin who prided himself in his artistry.

Keller didn't spend much time thinking about guns. When he had to use one, he chose whatever was at hand. Why make it complicated? It was like photography. You could learn all about f-stops and shutter speeds, or you could pick up a Japanese camera and just point and shoot.

"Just use it and lose it," the man was saying. "Or if you don't use it just leave it in the glove box. Otherwise it goes in a Dumpster or down a storm drain, but why am I telling you this? You're the man." He pursed his lips and whistled without making a sound. "I have to say I envy a man like you."

4

"Oh?"

"You ride into town, do what you do, and ride on out. Well, fly on out, but you get the picture. In and out with no hassles, no complications, no dealing with the same assholes day in and day out."

You dealt with different ones every time, Keller thought. Was that supposed to be better?

"But I couldn't do it. Could I pull a trigger? Maybe I could. Maybe I already done that, one time or another. But your way is different, isn't it?"

Was it?

The man didn't wait for an answer. "By the baggage claim," he said, "you didn't see me right away. You were headed for one of the other guys."

"I couldn't make out the sign he was holding," Keller said. "The letters were all jammed together. And I had the sense that he was waiting for somebody."

"They're all of them waiting for somebody. Point is, I was watching you, before you took notice of me. And I pictured myself living the life you lead. I mean, what do I know about your life? But based on my own ideas of it. And I realized something."

"Oh?"

"It's just not for me," the man said. "I couldn't do it."

It cost Keller eight dollars to get his car out of the long-term lot, which struck him as reasonable enough. He got on the interstate going south, got off at Eastern Parkway, and found a place to have coffee and a sandwich. It called itself a family restaurant, which was a term Keller had never entirely understood. It seemed to embody low prices, Middle American food, and a casual atmosphere, but where did family come into the picture? There were no families there this afternoon, just single diners.

Like Keller himself, sitting in a booth and studying his

map. He had no trouble finding Hirschhorn's downtown office (on Fourth Street between Main and Jefferson, just a few blocks from the river) and his home in Norbourne Estates, a suburb a dozen miles to the east.

He could look for a hotel downtown, possibly within walking distance of the man's office. Or—he studied the map—or he could continue east on Eastern Parkway, and there would almost certainly be a cluster of motels where it crossed I-64. That would give him easy access to the residence and, afterward, to the airport. He could get downtown from there as well, but he might not have to go there at all, because it would almost certainly be easier and simpler to deal with Hirschhorn at home.

Except for the damned picture.

Betsy, Jason, Tamara, and Powhatan. He'd have been happier not knowing their names, and happier still not knowing what they looked like. There were certain bare facts about the quarry it was useful to have, but everything else, all the personal stuff, just got in the way. It could be valuable to know that a man owned a dog—whether or not you chose to break into his home might hinge upon the knowledge—but you didn't have to know the breed, let alone the animal's name.

It made it personal, and it wasn't supposed to be personal. Suppose the best way to do it was in a room in the man's house, a home office in the basement, say. Well, somebody would find him there, and it would probably be a family member, and that was just the way it went. You couldn't go around killing people if you were going to agonize over the potential traumatic effect on whoever discovered the body.

But it was easier if you didn't know too much about the people. You could live easier with the prospect of a wife recoiling in horror if you didn't know her name, or that she had close-cropped blond hair and bright blue eyes and cute little chipmunk cheeks. It didn't take too much in the

6

way of imagination to picture that face when she walked in on the death scene.

So it was unfortunate that the man with the Archibald sign had shown him that particular photograph. But it wouldn't keep him from doing the job at Hirschhorn's residence any more than it would lead him to abort the mission altogether. He might not care what calibre gun he used, and he didn't know that he took a craftsman's pride in his work, but he was a professional. He used what came to hand, and he got the job done.

"Now I can offer you a couple of choices," the desk clerk said. "Smoking or non, up or down, front or back."

The motel was a Super 8. Keller went for nonsmoking, rear of the building, first floor.

"No choice on beds," the clerk said. "All the units are the same. Two double beds."

"That still gives me a choice."

"How do you figure that?"

"I can choose which bed to sleep in."

"Clear-cut choice," the clerk said. "First thing you'll do is drop your suitcase on one of the beds."

"So?"

"So sleep in the other one. You'll have more room."

There were, as promised, two double beds in Room 147. Keller considered them in turn before setting his bag on top of the dresser.

Keeping his options open, he thought.

From a pay phone, he called Dot in White Plains. He said, "Refresh my memory. Didn't you say something about an accident?"

"Or natural causes," she said, "though who's to say what's a natural cause in this day and age? Outside of choking to death on an organic carrot, I'd say you're about as natural a cause of death as there is."

7

"They provided a gun."

"Oh?"

"A twenty-two auto, because that's the kind guys like me prefer."

"That's a far cry from an organic carrot."

" 'Use it and lose it.' "

"Catchy," Dot said. "Sounds like a failure to communicate, doesn't it? Guy who furnished the gun didn't know it was supposed to be natural."

"Leaving us where? Does it still have to be natural?"

"It never *had* to, Keller. It was just a preference, but they gave you a gun, so I'd say they've got no kick coming if you use it."

"And lose it."

"In that order. Customer satisfaction's always a plus, so if you can arrange for him to have a heart attack or get his throat torn out by the family dog, I'd say go for it. On the other hand—"

"How did you know about the dog?"

"What dog?"

"The one you just mentioned."

"It was just an expression, Keller. I don't know if he has a dog. I don't know for sure if he's got a heart, but—"

"It's a golden retriever."

"Oh?"

"Named Powhatan."

"Well, it's all news to me, Keller, and not the most fascinating news I ever heard, either. Where is all of this coming from?"

He explained about the photo on the Christmas card.

"What a jerk," she said. "He couldn't find a head and shoulders shot, the kind the papers run when you get a promotion or they arrest you for embezzlement? My God, the people you have to work with. Be grateful you were spared the annual Christmas letter, or you'd know how Aunt Mary's doing great since she got her appendix trans-

8

plant and little Timmy got his first tattoo."

"Little Jason."

"God, you know the kids' names? Well, they wouldn't put the dog's name on the card and leave the kids off, would they? What a mess."

"The guy was holding a sign. 'Archibald.' "

"At least they got that part right."

"And I said that's me, and he said, 'Richard Archibald?'"

"So."

"You told me they said Nathan."

"Come to think of it, they did. They screw that up too, huh?"

"Not exactly. It was a test, to make sure I wasn't some smartass looking for a free ride."

"So if you forgot the first name, or just didn't want to make waves . . ."

"He'd have figured me for a phony and told me to get lost."

"This gets better and better," she said. "Look, do you want to forget the whole thing? I can tell you're getting a bad feeling about it. Just come on home and we'll tell them to shit in their hat."

"Well, I'm already here," he said. "It could turn out to be easy. And I don't know about you, but I can use the money."

"I can always find a use for it," she said, "even if all I use it for is to hold on to. The dollars have to be someplace, and White Plains is as good a place as any for them."

"That sounds like something he would have said."

"He probably did."

They were referring to the old man, for whom they had both worked, Dot living with him and running his household, Keller doing what he did. The old man was gone now—his mind had gone first, little by little, and then his body went all at once—but things went on essentially unchanged. Dot took the phone calls, set the fees, made

9

the arrangements, and disbursed the money. Keller went out there, checked out the territory, closed the sale, and came home.

"Thing is," Dot said, "they paid half in advance. I hate to send money back once I've got it in hand. It's the same money, but it feels different."

"I know what you mean. Dot, they're not in a hurry on this, are they?"

"Well, who knows? They didn't say so, but they also said natural causes and gave you a gun so you could get close to nature. To answer your question, no, I don't see why you can't take your time. Been to any stamp dealers, Keller?"

"I just got here."

"But you checked, right? In the Yellow Pages?"

"It passes the time," he said. "I don't think I've ever been in Louisville before."

"Well, make the most of it. Take the elevator up to the top of the Empire State Building, catch a Broadway show. Ride the cable cars, take a boat ride on the Seine. Do all the usual tourist things. Because who knows when you'll get back there again."

"I'll have a look around."

"Do that," she said. "But don't even think about moving there, Keller. The pace, the traffic, the noise, the sheer human energy—it'd drive you nuts."

It was late afternoon when he spoke to Dot, and twilight by the time he followed the map to Winding Acres Drive, in Norbourne Estates. The street was every bit as suburban as it sounded, with good-sized one- and two-story homes set on spacious landscaped lots. The street had been developed long enough ago for the foundation plantings to have filled in and the trees to have gained some size. If you were going to raise a family, Keller thought, this was probably not a bad place to do it.

Hirschhorn's house was a two-story center-hall colonial

with the front door flanked by a symmetrical planting of what looked to Keller like rhododendron. There was a clump of weeping birch on the left, a driveway on the right leading to a garage with a basketball hoop and backboard centered over the door. It was, he noted, a two-and-a-half-car garage. Which was handy, he thought, if you happened to have two and a half cars.

There were lights on inside the house, but Keller couldn't see anybody, and that was fine with him. He drove around, familiarizing himself with the neighborhood, getting slightly lost in the tangle of winding streets, but getting straightened out without much trouble. He drove past the house another couple of times, then headed back to the Super 8.

On the way back he stopped for dinner at a franchised steak house named for a recently deceased cowboy film star. There were probably better meals to be had in Louisville, but he didn't feel like hunting for them. He was back at the motel by nine o'clock, and he had his key in the door when he remembered the gun. Leave it in the glove compartment? He went back to the car for it.

The room was as he'd left it. He stowed the gun in his open suitcase and pulled up an armchair in front of the television set. The remote control was a little different from the one he had at home, but wasn't that one of the pleasures of travel? If everything was going to be exactly the same, why go anywhere?

A little before ten there was a knock on the door.

His reaction was immediate and dramatic. He snatched up the gun, chambered a round, flicked off the safety, and flattened himself against the wall alongside the door. He waited, his index finger on the trigger, until the knock came a second time.

He said, "Who is it?"

A man said, "Maybe I got the wrong room. Ralph, izzat you?"

"You've got the wrong room."

"Yeah, you sure don't sound nothin' like Ralph." The man's voice was thick, and some of his consonants were a little off-center. "Now where the hell's Ralph? Sorry to disturb you, mister."

"No problem," Keller said. He hadn't moved, and his finger was still on the trigger. He listened, and he could hear footsteps receding. Then they stopped, and he heard the man knocking on another door—Ralph's, one could but hope. Keller let out the breath he'd been holding and took in some fresh air.

He stared at the gun in his hand. That wasn't like him, grabbing a gun and pressing up against a wall. And he'd just gone and done it, he hadn't even stopped to think.

Very strange.

He ejected the chambered round, returned it to the clip, and turned the gun over in his hands. It was supposed to be the weapon of choice in his line of work, but it was more useful on offense than defense, handy for putting a bullet in the back of an unsuspecting head, but not nearly so handy when someone was coming at you with a gun of his own. In a situation like that you wanted something with stopping power, something that fired a big heavy slug that would knock a man down and keep him there.

On the other hand, when your biggest threat was some drunk looking for Ralph, anything beyond a rolled-up newspaper amounted to overkill.

But why the panic? Why the gun, why the held breath, why the racing pulse?

Why indeed? He waited until his heartbeat calmed down, then shucked his clothes and took a shower. Drying off, he realized how tired he was. Maybe that explained it.

He went right to sleep. But before he got into bed he made sure the door was locked, and he placed the little .22 on the bedside table.

CHAPTER TWO

The first thing he saw when he woke up was the gun on the bedside table. Shaving, he tried to figure out what to do with it. He ruled out leaving it in the room, where the chambermaid could draw her own conclusions, but what were the alternatives? He didn't want to carry it on his person.

That left the glove compartment, and that's where he put it when he drove out to Winding Acres Drive. They gave you a free continental breakfast at the motel—a cup of coffee and a doughnut, and he wasn't sure what continent they had in mind—but he skipped it in order to get out to Hirschhorn's house as early as possible.

And was rewarded with the sight of the man himself, walking his dog.

Keller came up on them from the rear, and the man could have been anybody dressed for a day at the office, but the dog was unmistakably a golden retriever.

Keller had owned a dog for a while, an Australian cattle dog named Nelson. Nelson was long gone—the young woman whose job it was to walk him had, ultimately, walked off with him—and Keller had no intention of replacing either of them. But he was still a dog person. When February rolled around, he watched the American Kennel Club show on television, and figured one of these years he'd go over to Madison Square Garden and see it in person. He knew the different breeds, but even if he didn't, well, how tough was it to recognize a golden retriever?

Of course, a street like Winding Acres Drive could support more than one golden retriever. The breed, oafishly endearing and good with children, was deservedly popular, especially in suburban neighborhoods with large homes on ample lots. So just because this particular dog was a golden didn't mean it was necessarily Powhatan.

All this was going through Keller's mind even as he was overtaking man and dog from the rear. He passed them, and one glance as he did so was all it took. That was the man in the photograph, walking the dog in the photograph.

Keller circled the block, and so, eventually, did the man and the dog. Keller, parked a few houses away on the other side of the street, watched them head up the walk to the front door. Hirschhorn unlocked the door and let the dog in. He stayed outside himself, and a moment later he was joined by his children.

Jason and Tamara. Keller was too far away to recognize them, but he could put two and two together as well as the next man. The man and two children went to the garage, entering through the side door, and Keller keyed the ignition and timed things so that he passed the Hirschhorn driveway just as the garage door went up. There were two cars in the two-and-a-half-car garage, one a squareback sedan he couldn't identify and the other a Jeep Cherokee.

Hirschhorn left the Jeep for his wife and drove the kids to school in the squareback, which turned out to be a Subaru. Keller stayed with the Subaru after Hirschhorn dropped off the kids, then let it go when Hirschhorn got on the interstate. Why follow the man to his office? Keller knew where the office was, and he didn't need to fight commuter traffic to go have a look at it now.

He found another family restaurant and ordered orange juice and a western omelet with hash browns and a cup of coffee. The orange juice was supposed to be fresh-squeezed, but one sip told you it wasn't. Keller thought about saying something, but what was the point?

"Bring your own catalog?"

"I use it as a checklist," Keller explained. "It's simpler

than trying to carry around a lot of sheets of paper."

"Some use a notebook."

"I thought of that," he said, "but I figured it would be simpler to make a notation in the catalog every time I buy a stamp. The downside is it's heavy to carry around and it gets beat up."

"At least you've only got the one volume. That the Scott Classic? What do you collect?"

"Worldwide before 1952."

"That's ambitious," the man said. "Collecting the whole world."

The man was around fifty, with thin arms and legs and narrow shoulders and an enormous belly. He sat in an armchair on wheels, and a pair of high-tech aluminum crutches propped against the wall suggested that he only got out of the chair when he had to. Keller had found him in the Yellow Pages and had had no trouble locating his shop, in a strip mall on the Bardstown Road. His name was Hy Schaffner, and his place of business was Hy's Stamp Shoppe, and he was sure he could keep Keller busy looking at stamps. What countries would he like to start with?

"Maybe Portugal," Keller said. "Portugal and Colonies."

"Angra and Angola," Schaffner intoned. "Kionga. Madeira, Funchal. Horta, Lourenço Marques. Tete and Timor. Macao and Quelimane." He cleared his throat, swung his chair around to the left, and took three small black loose-leaf notebooks from a shelf, passing them over the counter to Keller. "Have a look," he said. "Tongs and a magnifier right there in front of you. Prices are marked, unless I didn't get around to it. They run around a third off catalog, more or less depending on condition, and the more you buy the more of a break I'll give you. You from around here?"

Keller shook his head. "New York."

"City or state?"

"Both."

"I guess if you're from the city you'd have to be from the state as well, wouldn't you? Here on business?"

"Just passing through," Keller said. That didn't really answer the question, but it seemed to be good enough for Schaffner.

"Well, take your time," the man said. "Relax and enjoy yourself."

Keller's mind darted around. Should he have said he was from someplace other than New York? Should he have invented a more specific reason for being in Louisville? Then he got caught up in what he was doing, and all of that mental chatter ceased as he gave himself up entirely to the business of looking at stamps.

He had collected as a boy, and had scarcely thought of his collection until one day when he found himself considering retirement. The old man in White Plains was still alive then, but he was clearly losing his grip, and Keller had wondered if it might be time to pack it in. He tried to imagine how he'd pass the hours, and he thought of hobbies, and that got him thinking about stamps.

His boyhood collection was long gone, of course, with the rest of his youth. But the hobby was still there, and it was remarkable how much he remembered. It struck him, too, that most of the miscellaneous information in his head had got there via stamp collecting.

So he'd gone around and talked to dealers and looked at some magazines, dipping a toe in the waters of philately, then held his breath and plunged right in. He bought a collection and remounted it in fancy new albums, which took hours each day for months on end. And he bought stamps over the counter from dealers in New York, and ordered them from ads other dealers placed in *Linn's Stamp News*. Other dealers sent him price lists, or selections on approval. He went to stamp shows, where dozens of dealers offered their wares at bourse tables, and he bid in stamp auctions, by mail or in person.

16

It was funny how it worked out. Stamp collecting was supposed to give him something to do in retirement, but he'd embraced it with such enthusiasm and put so much money into it that retirement had ceased to be an option. Then the old man had died while Keller was at a stamp auction in Kansas City, and Dot had decided to stay on and run the operation out of the big house on Taunton Place. Keller took the jobs she found for him and spent a healthy share of the proceeds on stamps.

The philatelic winds blew hot and cold. There were weeks when he read every article in *Linn's*, others when he barely scanned the front page. But he never lost interest, and the pursuit—he no longer thought of it as a hobby—never failed to divert him.

Today was no exception. He went through the three notebooks of Portugal and Colonies, then looked at some British Commonwealth issues, then moved on to Latin America. Whenever he found a stamp that was missing from his collection he noted the centering, examined the gum on the reverse, held it to the light to check for thins. He deliberated as intensely over a thirty-five-cent stamp as over one priced at thirty-five dollars. Should he buy this used specimen or wait for a more costly mint one? Should he buy this complete set, even though he already had the two low values? He didn't have this stamp, but it was a minor variety, and his album didn't have a place for it. Should he buy it anyway?

Hours went by.

After he left Hy's Stamp Shoppe, Keller spent another couple of hours driving aimlessly around Greater Louisville. He thought about heading downtown for a look at Hirschhorn's office, but he decided he didn't feel like it. Why bother? Hirschhorn could wait.

Besides, he'd have to leave the car in a parking lot, and he'd have to make sure it was the kind where you parked it and locked it yourself. Otherwise the attendant would have the key, and suppose he opened the glove compartment just to see what it held? He might not be looking for a gun, but that's what he'd find, and Keller didn't figure that was the best thing that could happen.

It was a great comfort, having a gun. Took your mind off your troubles. You spent all your time trying to figure out where to keep it.

He'd missed lunch, so he had an early dinner and went back to his room at the Super 8. He watched the news, then sat down at the desk with his catalog and the stamps he'd bought. He went through the book, circling the number of each stamp he'd acquired that day, keeping his inventory up-to-date.

He could have done this at home, at the same time that he mounted the stamps in his albums, but suppose he dropped in on another stamp dealer between now and then? If your records weren't right, it was all too easy to buy the same stamp twice.

Anyway, he welcomed the task, and took his time with it. There was something almost meditative about the process, and it wasn't as though he had anything better to do.

He was almost finished when the noise started overhead. God, who could it be, carrying on like that? And what could they be doing up there?

He stood it for a while, then reached for the phone, then changed his mind. He left the room and walked around the building to the lobby, where a young man with a wispy blond beard and wire-rimmed glasses was manning the desk. He looked up at Keller's approach, an apologetic expression on his face.

"I'm sorry to say we're full up," he said. "So are the folks across the road. The Clarion Inn at the next interchange going north still had rooms as of half an hour ago, and I'll be glad to call ahead for you if you want."

"I've already got a room," Keller said. "That's not the problem."

The young man's face showed relief, but only for a moment. *That's not the problem*—if it wasn't, something else was, and now he was going to hear about it, and be called upon to deal with it.

"Uh," he said.

"I'm in One forty-seven," Keller said, "and whoever's in the room directly upstairs of me, which I guess would be Two forty-seven—"

"Yes, that's how it works."

"I think they're having a party," Keller said. "Or butchering a steer, or something."

"Butchering a steer?"

"Probably not that," Keller allowed, "but the point is they're being noisy about it, whatever it is they're doing. I mean really noisy."

"Oh." The clerk's gaze fell to the counter, where he seemed to find something fascinating on the few inches of Formica between his two hands. "There haven't been any other complaints," he said.

"Well, I hate to be first," Keller said, "but then I'm probably the only guest with a room directly under theirs, and that might have something to do with it."

The fellow was nodding. "The walls between the units are concrete block," he said, "and you never hear a peep through them. But I can't say the same for the floors. If you've got a noisy party upstairs, some sound does filter through."

"This is a noisy party, all right. It wouldn't be out of line to call it a riot."

"Oh."

"Or a civil disturbance, anyway. And filter's not the word for it. It comes through unfiltered, loud and clear."

"Have you, uh, spoken to them about it?"

19

"I thought I'd speak to you."

"Oh."

"And you could speak to them."

The clerk swallowed, and his Adam's apple bobbed up and down. "Two forty-seven," he said, and thumbed a box of file cards, and nodded, and swallowed again. "I thought so. They have a car."

"This is a motel," Keller said. "Who comes here on foot?"

"What I mean, I took one look at them and thought they were bikers. Like Hell's Angels? But they came in a car."

He was silent, and Keller could tell how much he wanted to ask a roomful of outlaw bikers to keep it down. "Look," he said, "nobody has to talk to them. Just put me in another room."

"Didn't I say, when you first walked in? We're full up. The No Vacancy sign's been lit for hours."

"Oh, right."

"So I don't know what to tell you. Unless . . ."

"Unless what?"

"Well, unless you wanted to call in a complaint to the police. Those guys might pay a little more attention to the cops than to you or me."

Just what he wanted. Officer, could you tell the Hell's Angels upstairs to pipe down? I've got urgent business in your town and I need my rest. My name? Well, it's different from the one I'm registered under. The nature of my business? Well, I'd rather not say. And the gun on the bedside table is unregistered, and that's why I didn't leave it in the car, and don't ask me whose car it is, but the registration's in the glove compartment.

"That's a little abrupt," he said. "Think how you'd feel if somebody called the cops on you without any warning."

"Oh."

"And if they figured out who called them—"

20

"I could call the Clarion," the clerk offered. "At the next interchange? But my guess is they're full up by now."

It was a little late to be driving around looking for a room. Keller told him not to bother. "Maybe they'll make it an early night," he said, "or maybe I'll get used to it. You wouldn't happen to have some ear plugs in one of those drawers, would you?"

The bikers didn't make it an early night, nor did Keller have much success getting used to the noise. The clerk hadn't had ear plugs, or known where they might be available. The nearest drugstore was closed for the night, and he didn't know where Keller might find one open. Would a 7-Eleven be likely to stock ear plugs? He didn't know, and neither did Keller.

After another hour of biker bedlam, Keller was about ready to find out for himself. He'd finished recording his new stamps in his catalog, but found the operation less diverting than usual. The noise from above kept intruding. With the job done and the stamps and catalog tucked away, he found a movie on television and kicked the volume up a notch. It didn't drown out the din from upstairs, but it did let him make out what William Holden was saying to Debra Paget.

There was no point, he found, in hitting the Mute button during the commercials, because he needed the TV sound to cancel out the bikers. And what good was TV if you couldn't mute the commercials?

He watched as much of the movie as he could bear, then got into bed. Eventually he got up, moistened scraps of toilet paper, made balls of them, and stuffed them in his ears. His ears felt strange—why wouldn't they, for God's sake? But he got used to it, and the near silence was almost thrilling.

CHAPTER THREE

Keller awoke to the faint sound of a phone ringing in the apartment next to his. Funny, he thought, because he couldn't usually hear anything next door. His was a prewar building, and the walls were good and thick, and—

He sat up, shook off the mantle of sleep, and realized he wasn't in his apartment, and that the telephone ringing ever so faintly was right there on the bedside table, its little red bubble lighting up every time it rang. And just what, he wondered, was the point of that? So that deaf guests would be aware that the phone was ringing? What good would it do them? What could they do about it, pick up the receiver and wiggle their fingers at the mouthpiece?

He answered the phone and couldn't hear a thing. "Speak up," he said. "Is anybody there?" Then he realized he had little balls of toilet paper in his ears. "Hell," he said. "Just hold on a minute, will you?" He put the receiver down next to the gun and dug the wads of paper out of his ears. They had dried, of course, rather like papier mâché, and it took some doing to get them out. He thought whoever it was would have hung up by then, but no, his caller was still there.

"Sorry to disturb you," she said, "but we've got you down for a room change. A second-floor unit? Housekeeping just finished with your new room, and I thought you might want to pick up the key and transfer your luggage."

He looked at his watch and was astonished to note that it was past ten. The noise had kept him up late and the toilet-paper-induced silence had kept him sleeping. He showered and shaved, and it was eleven o'clock by the time he'd packed his things and moved to Room 210.

Once you were inside it with the door closed, the new room was indistinguishable from the one he'd just vacated. The same twin double beds, the same desk and dresser, the same two prints—a fisherman wading in a stream, a boy herding sheep—on the same concrete-block walls. Its second-floor front location, on the other hand, was the precise opposite of where he'd been.

Years ago a Cuban had told him always to room on the ground floor, in case he had to jump out the window. The Cuban, it turned out, was acting less on tradecraft than on a fairly severe case of acrophobia, so Keller had largely discounted the advice. Still, old habits died hard, and when offered a choice he usually took the ground floor.

Way his luck was running, this would be the time he had to go out the window.

After breakfast he drove into downtown Louisville and left the car in a parking ramp, the gun locked in the glove compartment. There was a security desk in the lobby of Hirschhorn's office building. Keller didn't figure it would be too much of a challenge, but he couldn't see the point. There would be other people in Hirschhorn's office, and then he'd have to ride down on the elevator and fetch the car from where he'd parked it. He exited the lobby, walked around for twenty minutes, then collected his car and drove over the bridge into Indiana. He rode around long enough to get lost and straightened out again, then stopped at a convenience store to top up the gas tank and use the phone.

"This fellow I've got to see," he said. "What do we know about him?"

"We know the name of his damn dog," Dot said. "How much more do you need to know about anybody?"

"I went looking for his office," he said, "and I didn't know what name to hunt for in the directory."

"Wasn't his name there?"

"I don't know," he said, "because I didn't go in for a close look, not knowing what to look for. Aside from his own name, I mean. Like if there's a company name listed, I wouldn't know what company."

"Unless it was the Hirschhorn Company."

"Well," he said.

"Does it matter, Keller?"

"Probably not," he said, "or I would have figured out a way to learn what I had to know. Anyway, I ruled out going to the office."

"So why are you calling me, Keller?"

"Well," he said.

"Not that I don't welcome the sound of your voice, but is there a point to all this?"

"Probably not. I had trouble getting to sleep, there were Hell's Angels partying upstairs."

"What kind of place are you staying at, Keller?"

"They gave me a new room. Dot, do we know anything about the guy?"

"If I know it, so do you. Where he lives, where he works—"

"Because he seems so white-bread suburban, and yet he's got enemies who give you a car with a gun in the glove compartment. And a spare clip."

"So you can shoot him over and over again. I don't know, Keller, and I'm not even sure the person who called me knows, but if I had to come up with one word it would be gambling."

"He owes money? They fly in a shooter over a gambling debt?"

"That's not where I was going. Are there casinos there?"

"There's a race track," he said.

"No kidding, Keller. The Kentucky Derby, di dah di dah di dah, but that's in the spring. City's on a river, isn't it? Have they got one of those riverboat casinos?"

"Maybe. Why?"

"Well, maybe they've got casino gambling and he wants to get rid of it, or they want to have it and he's in the way."

"Oh."

"Or it's something entirely different, because this sort of thing's generally on a need-to-know basis, and I don't." She sighed. "And neither do you, all things considered."

"You're right," he said. "You want to know what it is, Dot? I'm out of synch."

"Out of synch."

"Ever since I got off the goddam plane and walked up to the wrong guy. Tell me something. Why would anyone meet a plane carrying an unreadable sign?"

"Maybe they told him to pick up a dyslexic."

"It's the same as the little red light on the phone."

"Now you've lost me, Keller. What little red light on the phone?"

"Never mind. You know what I just decided? I'm going to cut through all this crap and just do the job and come home."

"Jesus," she said. "What a concept."

The convenience store clerk was sure they had ear plugs. "They're here somewhere," she said, her nose twitching like a rabbit's. Keller wanted to tell her not to bother, but he sensed she was already committed to the hunt. And, wouldn't you know it, she found them. Sterile foam ear plugs, two pairs to the packet, $1.19 plus tax.

After all she'd gone through, how could he tell her he'd changed his room and didn't need them, that he'd just asked out of curiosity? Oh, these are foam, he considered saying. I wanted the titanium ones. But that would just set her off on a twenty-minute hunt for titanium ear plugs, and who could say she wouldn't find some?

He paid for them and told her he wouldn't need a bag. "It's a good thing they're sterile," he said, pointing to the copy on the packet. "If they started breeding we'd have 'em coming out of our ears."

She avoided his eyes as she gave him his change.

He drove back to Kentucky, then out to Norbourne Estates and Winding Acres Drive. He passed Hirschhorn's house and couldn't tell if anyone was home. He circled the block and parked where he could keep an eye on the place.

On his way there he'd seen school buses on their afternoon run, and, shortly after he parked and killed the engine, one evidently made a stop nearby, because kids in ones and twos and threes began to show up on Winding Acres Drive, walking along until they either turned down side streets or disappeared into houses. One pair of boys stopped at the Hirschhorn driveway, and the shorter of the two went into the garage and emerged dribbling a basketball. They dropped their book bags at the side of the driveway, shucked their jackets, and began playing a game which seemed to involve shooting in turn from different squares of the driveway. Keller wasn't sure how the game worked, but he could tell they weren't very good at it.

But as long as they were there, he could forget about getting into the garage. He didn't know if the Jeep was there or if Betsy Hirschhorn was out stocking up at the Safeway, but for now it hardly mattered. And he couldn't stay where he was, not for very long, or somebody would call 911 to report a suspicious man lurking on a block full of children.

He got out of there. The development had been laid out by someone with a profound disdain for straight lines and right angles, balanced by a special fondness for dead-end streets. It was hard to keep one's bearings, but he found his way out, and had a cup of coffee at the suburb's equivalent of Starbucks. The other customers were mostly women, and they looked restless. If you wanted to pick up a caffeinated housewife with attitude to spare, this was the place to do it.

He found his way back to Winding Acres Drive, where the two boys were still playing basketball. They had switched games and were now doing a White Guys Can't Jump version of driving layups. He parked in a different spot and decided he could stay there for ten minutes.

When the ten minutes were up, he decided to give it five minutes more, and just before they ran out Betsy Hirschhorn came home, honking the Cherokee's horn to clear the boys from the driveway. The garage door ascended even as they dribbled out of her path, and she drove in. Before the door closed, Keller drove by the driveway himself. Her Jeep was the only vehicle in the garage, unless you wanted to count the power lawn mower. Walter Hirschhorn's Subaru squareback hadn't come home yet.

Keller drove away and came back, drove away and came back, passing the Hirschhorn house at five- to ten-minute intervals. The idea was to be waiting inside the garage when Hirschhorn came home, but first the boys had to finish their game. For Christ's sake, how long could two unathletic kids keep this up? Why weren't they inside playing video games or visiting Internet porn sites? Why didn't Jason take the family dog for a walk? Why didn't his friend go home?

Then the door opened, and Jason's sister emerged with Powhatan on his leash. (Tiffany? No, something else. Tamara!) How had she gotten home? On the bus with her brother? Or had she been in the Jeep just now with her mother? And what possible difference could it make to Keller?

None that he could make out, but off she went, walking the dog, and the boys went on with their interminable game. Weren't kids these days supposed to be turning into couch potatoes? Somebody ought to tell these two they were bucking a trend.

They were still at it the next time he passed, and now time was starting to work against him. It was past five.

Hirschhorn might well have left his office by now, and might get home any minute. Suppose he arrived before the boys ended their game? Maybe that's how they knew to quit for the day. When Daddy comes home, Jason goes in for dinner and his friend Zachary goes home.

He drove out of the development—no wrong turns this time, he was getting the hang of it, and beginning to feel as though he lived there himself. He left the car at a strip mall, parked in front of a discount shoe outlet, and returned on foot, with the .22 in a pocket.

On his way out he'd counted houses, and now he circled halfway around the block, trying to estimate which house backed up on the Hirschhorn property. He narrowed it down to two and settled on the one with no lights burning, walked the length of its driveway, skirted the garage, and stood in the backyard, looking around, trying to get his bearings. The house directly opposite him was one story tall with an attached garage, so it wasn't Hirschhorn's, but he knew he wasn't off by much. He walked through the yards—they didn't have fences here, thank God for small favors—and he knew when he was in the right place because he could hear the sound of the basketball being dribbled.

In addition to the big garage door that rose when you triggered the remote, there was a door on the side to let humans in and out. You couldn't see it from the street, but Keller had watched the boy come out of it with a basketball, so he knew it was there. It was, he now saw, about a third of the way back on the left wall of the garage, facing the house, at the end of an overhang that let you get from the house to the garage without getting rained on.

Which wasn't a problem today, because it wasn't raining. Not that he wouldn't welcome rain, which would put an end to the basketball game and give him access to the garage.

He flattened out against the garage wall and moved quickly if stealthily toward the door, staying in the shadows and wishing they were deeper. The boys, dribbling and shooting, moved in and out of his field of vision. If he could see them, they could see him.

But they didn't. He reached the door and stood beside it with a hand on the knob until the boys dribbled to a spot where the garage blocked his view of them and theirs of him. He waited until their voices were raised in argument. You never had to wait long for this, they argued as much as they dribbled and far more than they jumped, they'd make better lawyers than NBA all-stars, but the argument never got serious enough to send one of them inside and the other one home for dinner. At last, to the strains of *Did not! Did too! Did not! Did too!* he opened the door and ducked inside.

Where, with the door safely shut, it was pitch dark and, aside from the dribbling and bickering, quiet as the tomb. Keller stood perfectly still while his eyes adjusted to the dimness. He got so he could make out shapes and move around without bumping into things. The Jeep Cherokee was there, where Betsy Hirschhorn had parked it, and, he was pleased to note, the Subaru was not. He'd been gone for almost twenty minutes, finding a place to leave the car and coming back on foot, and there was always the chance that Hirschhorn would make it home while he was sneaking into strangers' backyards. In which case he could either sneak out and go home or curl up on the car seat and wait for morning.

Which it looked as though he might have to do anyway. Because suppose Hirschhorn came home now, while the basketball players were still at it. The boys would stand aside respectfully, the garage door would pop up like toast in a toaster, the Subaru would slide into its slot next to the Cherokee, and its driver would emerge, striding out to greet his son. The kids would be right there, and Keller wouldn't be able to do a thing before they were all tucked away for the night.

And if he did stay cooped up in the garage all night, then what? When Hirschhorn got in the car the next morning, he'd have the goddam kids with him, all set to be driven to school. Why couldn't the little bastards take the bus? If it was good enough to bring them home from school, why wasn't it good enough to take them there?

Not that it mattered, he thought savagely. After a night in the garage, he'd be ready to kill the father and toss in both kids as a bonus. And the wife, if she showed her face. No one was safe, not even the goddam dog.

Seriously, he thought, suppose it did play out that way, with the boys still at their game when the man arrived. He couldn't do anything in front of the boys, let alone make it look like an accident. And he couldn't see himself hanging around all night, either.

What did that leave? Could he break into the house while everybody was asleep? Hold off and sandbag Hirschhorn during the dog's morning constitutional?

What he'd probably do, he decided, was go back to the Super 8 and work on Plan B. Which might not be better than Plan A, but couldn't be much worse. And if that didn't work he had the whole rest of the alphabet, and . . .

They'd stopped dribbling.

Stopped shooting baskets, too. Stopped talking. While he'd been building ruined castles in the air, the boys had finally called it a day.

Back to Plan A.

Waiting wasn't all that easy, with or without the sounds of basketball for company. At first he just stood there in the dark, but eventually he found ways to make himself more comfortable. There was a Peg Board on one wall, he discovered, with tools hanging on it, and among them he found a flashlight. He flicked it rapidly on and off and found other tools he could envision a use for, including a pair of thin cotton gloves to keep what he touched free of

30

fingerprints. Duct tape, pruning shears, garden hose—Hirschhorn had it all. And there were a couple of folding patio chairs, aluminum frames and nylon webbing, and he unfolded one of them and parked himself in it.

He was bored and edgy. The job still didn't feel right, hadn't felt right since he got off the plane. But at least he was sitting in a comfortable chair. That was something.

Day or night, Winding Acres Drive didn't get a lot of traffic. He could hear what there was of it from where he sat, and his ears would perk up when a car approached. Then it would drive on by and his ears would do whatever it was they did. Unperk? Whatever.

He checked his watch from time to time. At 7:20 he decided Hirschhorn wasn't going to make it home in time for dinner. At 8:14 he started wondering if the man might have left town on a business trip. He was weighing the possibility, and then a car approached, and he drew a short breath. The car kept on going and he let it out.

He thought about the stamps he'd bought the previous day. When he got back to New York, whenever that might be, he could look forward to several hours at his desk, mounting them in his albums. It was curiously satisfying, adding the first stamp to a hitherto blank page, then watching the spaces fill in over the months. Schaffner's stock had been spotty, strong in some areas and weak in others, but Keller had been particularly interested in Portugal, that was the first thing he'd asked to see, and he'd done well in that area. Funny how you were drawn to some countries and not to others. It didn't have anything to do with the nations themselves, as political or geographic entities. It was just something about their stamps, and how you responded to them.

Another car. He perked up, and prepared to perk down. But no, it was turning into the driveway, and the garage door was on its way up.

By the time the headlights were filling the garage with light, Keller was hunkered down behind the Jeep. The Subaru pulled into the garage. Hirschhorn, alone in the car, cut the engine, doused the headlights. The garage went dark, and then the dome light came on as Hirschhorn opened the car door.

When he stepped out, Keller was waiting for him.

There was an outdoor pay phone at the strip mall where he'd left the car, but the mall stores had all closed for the night, and the Olds was the only car still parked there. Keller felt too visible, and too close to Winding Acres Drive. He got into the car and on and off the interstate and called Dot from a pay phone at an Exxon station.

"All done," he said.

"That was quick."

"It didn't seem quick," he said, "but I suppose it was. All I know is it's done. I'd like to get off the phone and hop on a plane."

"Why don't you?"

"It's too late," he said. "I have to figure the last flight's in the air by now, and I still have to go back to the motel for my stuff. Anyway, the room's paid for."

"And maybe the Hell's Angels are in a mellow mood tonight."

"They're probably in a different time zone by now," he said, "but all the same they put me in another room. On the top floor, so nobody's going to raise hell overhead."

"Suppose you get a carload of Satan's Slaves down below?"

"Unless they can figure out a way to dance on the ceiling," he said, "I think I'll be all right. Anyway, I've got ear plugs. You can buy them at the 7-Eleven."

"What a country."

"You said it."

"Keller? Did it go all right?"

32

"Yeah, it was fine," he said. "Anyway, it's done, and I'll be on the first flight out tomorrow morning. It's not a bad town—"

"Keller, that's what you always say. You said it about Roseburg, Oregon."

"—but I'll be damn glad to see the last of it," he finished, "and that's something you never heard me say about Roseburg. I can't wait to get out of here."

He had the Olds tucked away in his usual slot at the rear of the Super 8 before he remembered his new room was at the front. He left it there, reasoning that it might as well stay where it couldn't be seen from the street, even if no one was looking for it. He didn't have to decide what to do with the gun. That, like Walter Hirschhorn, was something he no longer had to worry about.

He soaked in the tub, then watched a little TV, including a half hour of local news. A black woman and a white man shared the anchor desk, and it was hard to tell them apart. Color and gender somehow disappeared, and all you were aware of were their happy voices and big bright teeth.

It was consequently hard to pay attention to what they were saying, but Hirschhorn wasn't in any of the stories they reported. Keller hadn't figured he would be.

He got into bed. The traffic noise from outside wasn't too bad, and Keller was a New Yorker, rarely bothered by horns or sirens or screeching brakes, rarely even subliminally aware of them. But he tried the ear plugs anyway, just to see how they felt, and fell asleep before he could get around to taking them out.

He woke up around ten-thirty, coming awake abruptly, sitting up in bed with his heart pounding. He couldn't hear a thing, of course, and it took him a minute to figure out why. Then he glanced at the phone, expecting to see the red light flashing, but it wasn't. He checked his watch and

33

was amazed he'd slept so long. Plug up your ears and you slept like the dead.

He unplugged his ears and put the plugs, no longer sterile, in with the unsullied pair. Was that okay? Did you have to throw away ear plugs after you'd used them once? Or could you reuse them? They weren't sterile anymore, he understood that much, but did they have to be? It wasn't as though somebody else was going to be exposed to your ear wax. If they'd never been anywhere but your own ears, and if that was their sole future destination, how unsanitary was it to use them again? Was it like reusing a Q-Tip, or more like getting a second shave out of a disposable razor?

He packed his bag and carried it to the car, and as he rounded the building he saw the rear parking lot filled with police cars and emergency vehicles, some with lights flashing on their tops. Yellow crime scene tape was stretched here and there, and, while he stood watching, two men in teal jumpsuits emerged from one room carrying a stretcher between them. There was an olive-drab body bag on the stretcher, and it was zipped up tight.

Keller, suitcase in hand, went to the office to check out. "What a horrible thing!" the girl at the desk said, clearly loving every minute of it. "The maid, the Mexican girl? No doughnut on the door, so she knocked, and—"

"No doughnut?"

"Like the sign? Do Not Disturb, only my boyfriend calls it Doughnut Disturb, on account of there's a hole where you slip it over the doorknob? Anyway, where was I?"

"No doughnut."

"Right, so she knocked, and when nobody answered she used her key. And she saw they were in bed, and when this happens you're supposed to just leave and close the door without saying anything? So you won't disturb them more than you already did?"

Why did she make an ordinary statement of fact come out sounding like a question? She paused, too, as if waiting for an answer. Keller nodded, which seemed to be what was required to get her going again.

"But she must have noticed something. Maybe the smell? Anyway, she went in, and when she got a good look she started screaming. Both of them shot dead in their bed, and blood on the bed linen, and . . ."

He let her go on for a while. Then he said, "Say, my car's back there. Are the cops letting people drive their cars out?"

"Oh, sure. It's been like hours since Rosalita found the bodies. Hasn't she got a pretty name?"

"Very pretty."

"It means Little Rose, which is kind of sweet, but imagine naming someone Little Rose in English. It would sound like she was an Indian. Or like her mother's name was Rose, too. Big Rose and Little Rose?"

Jesus, Keller thought.

"Anyway, the police have been here for hours, and they've been letting people come and go. Just so you don't need to go in the room where it happened."

But he'd already been there. Why would he want to go back?

CHAPTER FOUR

"Room One forty-seven," he told Dot. "My original room. I moved out in the morning, and that night a man and woman checked in."

"They checked in but they never checked out," she said. "Where were you staying, Keller? The Roach Motel?"

They were in the kitchen of the big house on Taunton Place. There was a pitcher of iced tea on the table between them, and Dot helped herself to a second glass. Keller's was still more than half full.

He said, "I got the hell out of there. I was driving to the airport, and don't ask me why, but I turned around and got on I-71 and drove straight to Cincinnati." He frowned. "Well, Cincinnati Airport. It's actually across the river in Kentucky."

"I'll be glad you told me that," she said, "one of these nights when it comes up on *Jeopardy*. You didn't want to fly out of Louisville?"

"I figured it would probably be all right, but what if it wasn't? I didn't really know what to think. All I knew was I took care of Hirschhorn and a couple of hours later somebody took care of the people in my old room."

"Took good care of them, it sounds like. And if they realized their mistake, maybe they're waiting at the airport."

"That was my thinking. Plus the drive to Cincinnati would give me time to think things out, and maybe listen to the news."

"And make sure that wasn't you in the body bag after all. Just a little surrealism, Keller. Don't look so confused."

"I've been confused a lot," he said.

36

"Ever since you got off the plane in Louisville, I seem to recall your saying."

"Ever since then. Here's how it evidently went down, Dot. I did Hirschhorn around nine and went straight to the motel, and—"

"First you called me."

"Called you en route, and then went back to my room—"

"Your new room."

"My new room, and I was in bed by midnight, and around the time I was putting in ear plugs, somebody was killing the lovely couple in One forty-seven. What's the first thought comes to mind?"

"The client."

"Right, the client."

"Tying off loose ends. You did it, and now we make sure you don't talk."

"Right."

"Except we *know* you won't talk. That's why we hire somebody like you. You won't get caught, and if you do you won't say anything, because what the hell would you say? You don't know who the client is."

"Or what he had against Hirschhorn, or anything about him."

"They could have decided that killing you was cheaper than paying the balance due," she said, "but that's ridiculous. They paid half in front, remember? If they were that eager to save money, they could have saved the whole fee and done Hirschhorn themselves."

"Dot," he said, "how would they even know the job was done?"

"Because the man was dead. Oh, you mean the time element."

"The body could have been discovered anytime after I did the job. I watched the late news on the chance that I might hear something, but there was nothing to hear."

37

"Just because it didn't make the news—"

"Doesn't mean it didn't happen. Exactly what I thought. But that's not what happened. I found out later the body wasn't discovered until morning. I don't know how worried Mrs. Hirschhorn may have been when her husband didn't come home, and I don't know if she called anybody, but what I do know is nobody went out to the garage until it was time to drive the kids to school."

She drank some iced tea. "So the people in One forty-seven died hours before anybody knew Hirschhorn was dead."

"Well, I knew, and you knew because I told you. But you're the only person I told, and I have a feeling you didn't spread it around."

"I figured it was our little secret."

"Besides not knowing I'd done what I was brought in to do," he said, "how would they know where to find me?"

"Unless they followed you there from Windy Hill."

"Winding Acres."

"Whatever."

"Nobody followed me," he said. "And if they had they'd have followed me to the new room, not the old one. I didn't go anywhere near One forty-seven."

"The people in One forty-seven. A man and a woman?"

"A man and a woman. The room had two beds, they all do, but they were only using one of them."

"Let me take a wild guess. Married, but not to each other?"

He nodded. "Guy at the Louisville paper told me the cops are talking to the dead woman's husband. Who denies all knowledge, but right now they like him for it."

"All you have to do is call up and they tell you all that?"

"If you're polite and well-spoken," he said, "and if they somehow get the impression you're a researcher at *Inside Edition*."

38

"Oh."

"I told him it sounded pretty open and shut, and he said that's how it looked up close. He's going to update me if there's a big break in the case."

"How's he going to do that? You didn't leave him a number."

"Sure I did."

"Not yours, I hope."

"*Inside Edition*'s. 'Hang on,' I said. 'I can never remember the number here.' And I looked it up and read it off. I could have just made something up. He's never going to call. The husband did it, and what does *Inside Edition* care?"

"If he strikes out there," she said, "he can always try *Hard Copy*. The husband did it, huh? That's your best guess?"

"Or his wife, or somebody one of them hired. Or he was two-timing somebody else, or she was. There were empty bottles and full ashtrays all over the room, they'd been drinking and smoking since they checked in . . ."

"In a nonsmoking room? The bastards. And on top of that they were committing adultery?" She shook her head. "Triple sinners, it sounds like to me. Well, they deserved to die, and may God have mercy on their souls."

She was reaching for her iced tea but drew her hand back as the door chime sounded. "Now who could that be?" she wondered aloud, and went to find out. He had a brief moment of panic, sure he ought to do something, unable to think what it was. He was still working on it when she came back brandishing a package.

"FedEx," she said, and gave the parcel a shake. It didn't make a sound. She pulled the strip to open it and drew out banded packets of currency. She slipped the wrapper off one of them and riffled the bills. "I hate to admit it," she said, "but I'm starting to get used to the way the new bills look. Not the twenties, they still look like play money to me, but the fifties and hundreds are beginning to look just fine. You buy any stamps in Louisville?"

"A few."

"Well," she said, counting out stacks of bills, making piles on the table. "Now you can go buy some more."

"I guess the customer's satisfied."

"Looks that way, doesn't it?"

"You just gave them the address and they put the cash in the mail?"

"No, I told them I work for *Inside Edition*. It's not the mail, anyway. It's Federal Express."

"Whatever."

"There's a cutoff man between me and the client, Keller. This particular one is a guy in—well, it doesn't matter where, but it's not Louisville and it's not New York. We've done business for years, even before I was part of the picture."

She gestured toward the ceiling, and Keller understood the reference to the old man, who'd never come down from the second floor in the final years of his life. You'd think he was up there still, the way they referred to him.

"So he knows where to send the money," she said, "and the client knows how to get it to him. No business of ours how much of it stays with him, as long as we get our price. And the client doesn't know anything about you, or me either." She patted the piles of money. "All he knows is we do good work. Well, a happy customer is our best advertisement, and I'd say this one's happy. How did you do it, Keller? How'd you manage natural causes?"

"I didn't, not exactly. It was suicide."

"Well, that's close enough, isn't it? It's not as though they had their hearts set on a lingering illness." She drained her glass, put it down on the table. "Let's hear it. How'd you do it?"

"When he got out of the car," he said, "I got him in a choke hold."

40

"It's good you're not a cop, Keller. These days that comes under the heading of police brutality."

"I kept the pressure on until he went limp. And it would have been the most natural thing to finish the job, you know? Cut off his air a little longer. Or just break his neck."

"Whatever."

"And I could have left him looking like he had a heart attack and hurt himself when he fell down. Something like that. But I figured any coroner who looked twice would see it didn't happen that way, and then it looks staged, which is probably worse from the client's point of view than a straightforward homicide."

"I suppose."

"So I put him behind the wheel," he said, "and I got out the gun they gave me—"

"The twenty-two auto, first choice of professionals from coast to coast."

"And overseas as well, for all I know. I wrapped his hand around it and stuck the business end in his mouth."

"And squeezed off a round."

"No," he said, "because who knows how far the sound is going to carry?"

" 'Hark, I hear the cannon's roar.' "

"And suppose one bullet doesn't do it? It's a small calibre, it's not going to splatter his brains all over the roof liner."

"And I guess it's a pretty severe case of suicide if the guy has to shoot himself twice. Although you could argue that it shows determination."

"I stayed with what I'd worked up while I was waiting for him to come home. I had a length of garden hose already cut, and I taped one end to the exhaust pipe and stuck the other end in the car window."

"And started the engine."

"I had to do that to get the window down. Anyway, I

41

left him there, in a closed garage with the engine running."

"And got the hell out."

"Not right away," he said. "Suppose somebody heard him drive in? They might come out to check. Or suppose he came to before the carbon monoxide level built up enough to keep him under?"

"Or suppose the engine stalled."

"Also a possibility. I waited by the side of the car, and then I started to worry about how much exhaust I was breathing myself."

" 'Two Men Gassed in Suicide Pact.' "

"So I let myself out the side door and stood there for ten minutes. I don't know what I would have done if I heard the engine cut out."

"Gone in and fixed it."

"Which is fine if it stalled, but suppose he came to and turned it off himself? And I rush in, and he's sitting there with a gun in his hand?"

"You left him the gun?"

"Left it in his hand, and his hand in his lap. Like he was ready to shoot himself if the gas didn't work, or if he got up the nerve."

"Cute."

"Well, they gave me the gun. I had to do something with it."

"Chekhov," she said.

"Check off what?"

She rolled her eyes. "Anton Chekhov, Keller. The Russian writer. I'll bet you anything he's got his picture on a stamp."

"I know who he is," he said. "I just misheard you, because I didn't know we were having a literary discussion. He was a physician as well as a writer, and he wrote plays and short stories. What about him?"

"He said if you show a gun in Act One, you'd better have it go off before the final curtain." She frowned. "At least I think it was Chekhov. Maybe it was somebody else."

"Well, it didn't go off," he said, "but at least I found a use for it. He had it in his hand with his finger on the trigger, and he had a round in the chamber, and if they happen to look they'll find traces of gun oil on his lips."

"Now that's a nice touch."

"It's great," he agreed, "as long as there's a body to examine, but what if he wakes up? He realizes he's got a gun in his hand, and he looks up, and there I am." He shrugged. "As jumpy as I was, I didn't have a lot of trouble imagining it that way. But it didn't happen."

"You checked him and he was nice and dead."

"I didn't check. I gave him ten minutes with the engine running, and I figured that was enough. The engine wasn't going to stall and he wasn't going to wake up."

"And he evidently didn't," she said, motioning at the money. "And everybody's happy." She cocked her head. "Wouldn't there be marks on his neck from the choke hold?"

"Maybe. Would they even notice? He's in a car, he's got a hose hooked up, he's holding a gun, his bloodstream's bubbling over with carbon monoxide . . ."

"If I found marks on his neck, Keller, I'd just figure he tried to hang himself earlier."

"Or choke himself to death with his own hands."

"Is that possible?"

"Maybe for an advanced student of the martial arts."

"Ninja roulette," she said.

He said, "That guy I talked to, thought he was talking to *Inside Edition*? I asked if there were any other colorful murders in town."

"Something worthy of national coverage."

"He told me more than I needed to know about some cocaine dealer who got gunned down a few days before I got to town, and about some poor sonofabitch who killed his terminally ill wife, called it in to 911, then shot himself

43

before the cops could get there."

"Never a dull moment in Louisville."

"He didn't even mention Hirschhorn. So I guess it's going in the books as a suicide."

"Fine with me," she said, "and the client's happy, and we got paid, so I'm happy. And the business at the Super Duper wasn't an attempt on your life . . ."

"The Super 8."

"Whatever. It was a couple of cheaters suffering divine retribution."

"Or bad luck."

"Aren't they the same thing? But here's my question. Everybody else is happy. Why not you, Keller?"

"I'm happy enough."

"Yeah, I've never seen anybody happier. What did it, the pictures of the kids? And the dog?"

He shook his head. "Once it's done," he said, "what's the difference? It just gets in your way while you're doing it, but when it's over, well, dead is dead."

"Right."

"One reason I didn't shoot was I didn't want them walking in on a mess, but it's the same shock either way, isn't it? And don't people blame themselves when there's a suicide? 'How could he have felt that bad and not let on?'"

"And so on."

"But none of that's important. The important thing is to get it done and get away clean."

"And you did, and that's why you're so happy."

"You know what it is, Dot? I knew something was wrong."

"What do you mean?"

"I sensed something. I had a feeling. When I get off the plane, when I can't read the first sign, when I go through a song and dance with the moron who meets me. And later on some drunk turns up at my door and I grab the gun and I'm ready to start blasting away through the door. And it's just some poor slob who can't find the right room. He staggers off and never comes back, and I have to lie down and wait for my heart to quit doing the tango."

"And then the bikers."

"And then the bikers, and toilet paper in my ears, and the kids with the basketball. Everything was out of synch, and it felt worse than that, it felt dangerous."

"Like you were in danger?"

"Uh-huh. But I wasn't. It was the room."

"The room?"

"Room One forty-seven. Something bad was scheduled to take place there. And I sensed it."

She gave him a look.

"Dot, I know how it sounds."

"You don't," she said. "Or you wouldn't have said it."

"Well, I wouldn't say it to anybody but you. Remember that girl I was seeing a while ago?"

"As far as I know, you haven't been seeing anybody since Andria."

"That's the one."

"The dog walker, the one with all the earrings."

"She used to talk about karma," he said, "and energy, and vibrations, and things like that. I didn't always understand what she was saying."

"Thank God for that."

"But I think sometimes a person senses things."

"And you sensed something was wrong."

"And that something was going to happen."

"Keller, something always happens."

"Something violent."

"When you take a business trip," she said, "something violent is par for the course."

"You know what I mean, Dot."

"You had a premonition."

"I guess that's what it was."

"You checked into a room and just got the feeling that

somebody was going to get killed there."

"Not exactly, because the room felt fine to me."

"So?"

He looked away for a moment. "I went over all this in my mind," he said. "Last night, and again coming up here on the train today. And it made sense, but now it's not coming out right."

"That's what they call a reality check, Keller. Keep going."

"I sensed something bad coming," he said, "and I was somehow drawn to the place where it was going to happen."

"Like a moth to a flame."

"I picked the motel, Dot. I looked at the map, I said here's where I am, here's where he lives, here's the airport, here's the interstate, and there ought to be a motel right here. And I drove right to it and there it was and I asked for a ground-floor room in the rear. I *asked* for it!"

" 'Give me the death room,' you said. 'I'm a man. I can take it.' "

"And I panicked when the drunk came knocking, because I knew I was in a dangerous place, even if I didn't know I knew it. That's why I grabbed the gun, that's why I reacted the way I did."

"But it was only a drunk."

"It was a warning."

"A warning?"

He drew a breath. "Maybe it was just a drunk looking for Ralph," he said, "and maybe it was someone sent to get my attention."

"Sent," she said.

"I know it sounds crazy."

"Sent, like an angel?"

"Dot, I'm not sure I even believe in angels."

"How can you not believe in them? They're on television where everybody can see them. My favorite's the

46

young one with the bad Irish accent. Though she's probably not as young as she looks. She's probably a thousand years old."

"Dot . . ."

"Or whatever that comes to in dog years. You don't believe in angels? What about the bikers partying upstairs? Angels from Hell, Keller. Pure and simple."

"Simple," he said, "but probably not pure. But that's the whole thing, that's why they were there."

"So that you would change your room."

"Well, it worked, didn't it?"

"And you changed your room first thing in the morning."

"To one in front," he said. "On the second floor."

"Out of harm's way. And later on who came along but two people out of a bad country song, and what room did they get?" She hummed the opening bars of the *Dragnet* theme. "Dum-de-dum-dum. Dum-de-dum-dum-dah! One forty-seven! The death room!"

"All I know," he said doggedly, "is a couple of hours later they were dead."

"While you lived to bear witness."

"I guess it really does sound weird, doesn't it?"

"Weirder than weird."

"It made sense on the train."

"Well, that's trains for you."

"What you said earlier, about a reality check?"

"You want my take on it?"

"Absolutely."

"Okay," she said. "Now you have to bear in mind that I don't know squat about karma or angels or any of that *Twilight Zone* stuff. You got a bad feeling when the pickup at the airport came off a little raggedy-ass, and then the guy they sent to meet you turned out to be a turkey. And seeing the family photo didn't help, either."

"I already said all that."

"Then the drunk knocked on your door, and you were edgy to begin with, and you reacted the way you did. And your own reaction made you edgier than ever."

"Exactly how it was."

"But all *he* was," she said, "was a drunk knocking on doors. He probably knocked on every door he came to until he found Ralph. You don't need angel's wings to do that."

"Go on."

"The noisy party upstairs? Bikers aren't exactly famous for their silent vigils. A motel's dumb enough to rent to people like that, they're going to have some loud parties. Somebody's got to be downstairs from them, and this time it was you, and as soon as you could you got your room changed."

"But if I hadn't—"

"If you hadn't," she said, patiently but firmly, "then the loving couple would have wound up in some other room when they decided they couldn't keep their hands off each other another minute. Not One forty-seven but, oh, I don't know. Say Two oh eight."

"But then when the husband turned up—"

"He'd have gone to Two oh eight, Keller, because that's where they were. He was looking for them, not whatever damn fool happened to be in One forty-seven. He followed them to their room and wreaked his horrible revenge, and it had nothing to do with what room they were in and even less to do with you."

"Oh," he said.

"That's your take on it? 'Oh?' "

"I had this whole elaborate theory," he said, "and it was all crap, wasn't it?"

"It was certainly out there on the crap side of the spectrum."

"But you thought it was a coincidence. That was your first thought."

"No, my first thought was it couldn't be a coincidence. That it was the client, or somebody the client sent."

"But it wasn't."

"No, because the client's satisfied, and he couldn't have found you even if he wasn't. But that doesn't mean it had to be angels. What it means is it really was a coincidence after all."

"Oh."

"And it was a coincidence for everybody in the motel, Keller, not just you. They were all there while the couple in One forty-seven were getting killed."

"But they hadn't just checked out of the room."

"So? That means they had an even narrower escape. They might have checked into One forty-seven. But you couldn't do that, because you'd already checked out of it."

He wasn't sure he followed that, but he let it go. "I guess it was a coincidence," he said.

"Don't sound so disappointed."

"But I sensed something. I knew something was going to happen."

"And it did," she said. "To Mr. Hirschhorn, may he rest in peace. Go home, Keller. Those stamps you bought? Go paste them in your album. What's the matter? Did I say something wrong?"

"You don't paste them," he said. "You use hinges."

"I stand corrected."

"Or mounts, sometimes you use mounts."

"Whatever."

"Anyway," he said, "I already mounted them. Last night. I was up until three in the morning."

"Well, isn't that a coincidence? You're all done mounting your stamps, and you coincidentally just came into some money." She beamed at him. "That means you can go buy some more."

49

CHAPTER FIVE

Keller speared a cube of cheese with a toothpick, helped himself to a glass of dry white wine. To his left, two young women clad entirely in black were chatting. "I can't believe he really said that," one announced. "I mean, just because you're postmodern doesn't mean you absolutely have to be an asshole."

"Chad would be just as big an asshole if he was a Dadaist," the other replied. "He could be a Pre-Raphaelite, and you know what he'd be? He'd be a Pre-Raphaelite asshole."

"I know," the first one said. "But I still can't believe he said that."

They wandered off, leaving Keller to wonder who Chad was (aside from being an asshole) and what he'd said that was so hard to believe. If Chad had said it to him, he thought, he probably wouldn't have understood it. He hadn't understood most of the words the two women used, and he hadn't understood anything of what Declan Niswander himself had had to say about the paintings on display.

The show's brochure contained photographs of several of the works, along with a brief biography of the artist, a chronological listing of his one-man and group shows, and another list of the museums and private collections in which he was represented. The last two pages were given over to Niswander's own explanation of what he'd been trying to do, and Keller knew what most of the words meant, but he couldn't make head or tail out of the sentences. The man didn't seem to be writing about art at all, but about philosophical determinism and the evanescence of imagery and casuistry as a transcendent phenomenon. Words Keller recognized, every one of them, but what were they doing all jumbled together like that?

The paintings, on the other hand, weren't at all hard to understand. Unless there was something to them that he wasn't getting, something that the two pages in the brochure might clarify for someone who spoke the language. That was possible, because Keller didn't feel he himself understood art in a particularly profound way.

He hardly ever went to galleries, and only once before had he attended an opening. That had been a few years back, when he went to one in SoHo with a woman he'd seen a couple of times. The opening was her idea. The artist was an old friend of hers—an ex-lover, Keller figured— and she hadn't wanted to show up unescorted. Keller had been introduced to the artist, a scruffy guy with a potbelly, whose paintings were drab and murky seas of brown and olive drab. He hadn't wanted to say as much to the artist, and didn't know what you were supposed to say, so he'd just smiled and kept his mouth shut. He figured that got you through most situations.

He tried the wine. It wasn't very good, and it reminded him of the wine they'd served at that other opening. Maybe bad wine was part of the mystique, bad wine and rubbery cheese and people dressed in black. Black jeans, black T-shirts, black chinos, black turtlenecks and sweat-shirts, and the occasional black sport jacket. Here and there a black beret.

Not everyone was wearing black. Keller had shown up in a suit and tie, and he wasn't the only one. There was a variety of other attire, including a few women in dresses and a young man in white overalls spattered with paint. But there was, on balance, a great deal of black, and it was the men and women in black who looked most at home here.

Maybe there was a good reason for it. Maybe you wore black to an art gallery for the same reason you turned off

51

your pager at a concert, so as to avoid distracting others from what had brought them there. That made a kind of sense, but Keller had the feeling there was more to it than that. He somehow knew that these people wore black all the time, even when they gathered in dimly lit coffee-houses with nothing on the walls but exposed brick. It was a statement, he knew, even if he wasn't sure what was being stated.

You didn't see nearly as much black at the museums. Keller went to museums now and then, and felt more at ease there than at private galleries. No one was lurking in the hope that you'd buy something, or waiting for you to express an opinion of the work. They just collected the admission fee and left you alone.

Declan Niswander's paintings were representational. All things considered, Keller preferred it that way. There was plenty of abstract art he liked, and he tended to favor those artists he could recognize right off the bat. If you were going to make paintings that didn't look like anything, at least you ought to shoot for an identifiable style. That way a person had something to grab hold of. One glance and you knew you were looking at a Mondrian or a Miró or a Rothko or a Pollock. You might not have a clue what Mondrian or Miró or Rothko or Pollock had in mind, but you wound up regarding them as old friends, familiar in their quirkiness.

Niswander's work was realistic, but you didn't feel like you were looking at color photographs. The paintings looked painted, and that seemed right to Keller. Niswander evidently liked trees, and that's what he painted—slender young saplings, gnarled old survivors, and everything in between. There was a similarity—no question that you were looking at the work of a single artist, and not a group show in celebration of Arbor Day—but the paintings, united by their theme and by Niswander's distinctive style, nevertheless varied considerably one from the next. It was as if each tree had its own essential nature, and that's what came through and rendered the painting distinctive.

Keller stood in front of one of the larger canvases. It showed an old tree in winter, its leaves barely a memory, a few limbs broken, a portion of the trunk scarred by a lightning strike. You could sense the tree's entire life history, he thought, and you could feel the power it drew from the earth, diminished over the years but still strongly present.

Of course you wouldn't get any of that in Niswander's little essay. The man had managed to fill two whole pages without once using the word *tree*. Keller was willing to believe the paintings weren't just about trees—they were about light and form and color and arrangement, and they might even be about what Niswander claimed they were about—but the trees weren't there by accident. You couldn't paint them like that unless you honest-to-God knew what a tree was all about.

A woman said, "You can't see the forest for them, can you?"

"You can imagine it," Keller said.

"Now *that's* very interesting," she said, and he turned and looked at her. She was short and thin, and—surprise!—dressed all in black. Baggy black sweater and short black shirt, black panty hose and black suede slippers, a black beret concealing most of her short black hair. The beret was wrong for her, he decided. What she needed was a pointed hat. She looked like a witch, no question, but not an unattractive witch.

She cocked her head—now she looked like a witch trying to look like a bird—and looked frankly at Keller, then at the painting.

"There are a few artists who paint trees," she said, "but it's generally the same tree over and over again. But in Declan's work they're all different trees. So you really can imagine the forest. Is that what you meant?"

"I couldn't have put it better myself."

"Oh, sure you could," she said, and a grin transformed her witch's face. "Margaret Griscomb," she said. "They call me Maggie."

"John Keller."

"And do they call you John?"

"Mostly they call me Keller."

"Keller," she said. "I kind of like that. Maybe that's what I'll call you. But don't call me Griscomb."

"I wouldn't dream of it."

"Not until we know each other a great deal better than we do now. And probably not even then. But I wonder if we will."

"Know each other better?"

"Because I'm good at this," she said. "Chatting ever so engagingly with a fellow tree-lover. But I'm not very good at getting to know someone, or getting known in return. I seem to do better in superficial relationships."

"Maybe that's the kind we'll have."

"No depth. Everything on the surface."

"Like a thin skin of ice on a pond in winter," he said.

"Or the scum that forms on the top of a mug of hot chocolate," she said. "Why do you suppose it does that? And don't bother working out an answer, because Regis is about to introduce Declan, who will then Say Something Profound."

Someone was tapping a spoon against a wineglass, trying to get the room's attention. A few people caught on and in turn shushed the rest. Things quieted down, and the glass-tapper, a willowy young man in gray flannel slacks and a maroon velvet blazer, began telling everyone how pleased he was to see them all here.

"Regis Buell," Maggie murmured. "It's his gallery. No wonder he's pleased."

Buell kept his own remarks brief and introduced Declan Niswander. Keller had known what the artist looked like—there was a photo in the brochure,

Niswander with his arms folded, glaring—but the man had a presence beyond what the camera revealed. Perhaps the paintings might have suggested it, because there was a passive strength to him that was almost arboreal in nature. Keller thought of the old hymn. Like a tree standing by the water, Niswander would not be moved.

Keller looked at him and took in the wiry black hair graying at the temples, the blunt-featured square-jawed face, the thick body, the square shoulders. Niswander was wearing a suit, and it was a black suit, and his shirt was black, and so was his necktie. And was that a black hanky in his pocket? It was hard to tell from this distance, but Keller was fairly sure it was.

He looked like his paintings, Keller decided, but his appearance was also somehow of a piece with the two pages of artsy twaddle in the brochure. The twaddle and the paintings hadn't seemed to go together, but Niswander managed to bridge the gap between the two. Like a tree, Keller thought, tying together the earth and the sky.

And wasn't that an artsy-fartsy way of looking at it? That's what happened when you put him in a place like this, he thought. Next thing you knew he'd be wearing black.

Mourning, if all went well.

"I don't know about this," Dot had said the other day. "I probably shouldn't even run this by you, Keller. I should stop right now and send you home."

"I just got here," he said.

"I know."

"You called me, said you had something."

"I do, but I had no business calling you."

"It's not the kind of work I do? What is it, addressing envelopes at home? Telemarketing?"

"Now there's something you'd be great at," she said. " 'Hello, Mrs. Clutterpan? How are you today?' "

55

"They always say that, don't they? 'How are you today?' Right away you know it's somebody trying to sell you something you don't want."

"I guess they figure it's an icebreaker," she said. "They ask you a question and you answer it, they're halfway home."

"It doesn't work with me."

"Or me either, but would you ever buy anything from some mope who called you on the phone?"

"The last time *I* got a phone call," he said, "I hopped on a train to White Plains, and now I'm supposed to turn around and go home."

"I'm sorry," she said. "Can we back up and start over? A job came in, and it's what you do, and there's no problem with the fee."

"And I'll bet the next sentence starts with *but*."

"But it's here in New York."

"Oh."

"It happens, Keller. People in New York are like people everywhere else, and sometimes they want somebody taken out. It's hard to believe there are New Yorkers with the same callous disregard for the sanctity of human life that you get in Roseburg, Oregon, and Martingale, Wyoming. But there it is, Keller. What can I tell you?"

"I don't know. What can you tell me?"

"Obviously," she said, "this has happened before. When a New York job comes in, I don't call you. I call somebody else and he comes in from somewhere else and does it."

"But this time you called me."

"There are two people I'd ordinarily call. One of them does what I do, he makes arrangements, and when I've got something I can't handle I call him and sub it out to him. But I couldn't call him this time, because he was the one who called me."

"And who did that leave?"

"A fellow out on the West Coast, who does the same sort of work you do. I wouldn't say he's got your flair,

56

Keller, but he's solid and professional. I've used him before in New York, and once or twice when you were busy on another assignment. He's my backup man, you might say."

"So you called him."

"I tried."

"He wasn't home?"

"Phone's been disconnected."

"What does that mean?"

"It means he's not going to hear me unless I shout at the top of my lungs. I don't know what else it means, Keller. Plain and simple, his phone's been disconnected. Did he change his number for security reasons? Did he move? You'd think he'd give me his new number, but I don't send him much work and I'm probably not one of the low numbers on his Speed Dial. In fact . . ."

"What?"

"Well, I'm not even positive he has this number. He must have had it once, but if he lost it he wouldn't know how to reach me."

"Either way—"

"Either way he hasn't called and I can't call him, and here's this job, and I thought of you. Except it's in New York, and you know what they say about crapping where you eat."

"They don't recommend it."

"They don't," she said, "and I have to say I agree with the conventional wisdom this time around. The whole idea is you go in where you don't know anybody and nobody knows you, and when you're done you go home. You're out of there before the body is cold."

"Not always. Sometimes you can't get a flight out right away."

"You know what I mean."

"Sure."

"I'm a big believer in keeping things separate."

"Like crapping and eating."

57

"Like crapping and eating. New York's for you to live in. That leaves the whole rest of the world to work in, and isn't that enough?"

"Of course three-quarters of the earth's surface is water," he said.

"Keller . . ."

"And how much work do you get up around the North Pole, or down in Antarctica? But you're right, there's a lot left."

"I'll call the man back and tell him we pass."

"Hang on a minute."

"What for?"

"I came all this way," he said. "I might as well hear about it. Just tell me it's a connected guy, has a couple of no-neck bodyguards with him night and day, and I can go home."

"He's an artist."

"At what, mayhem? Extortion?"

"At art," she said. "He paints pictures."

"No kidding."

"He's got a show coming up. In Chelsea."

"I heard there were galleries opening over there. Way west, by the river. Is that where he lives?"

"Uh-uh. Williamsburg."

"That's in Brooklyn."

"So?"

"Practically another city."

"What are you doing, Keller? Talking yourself into something?"

He was silent for a moment. Then he said, "The thing is, Dot, it's been a while."

"Tell me about it."

"And the last one, that business in Louisville . . ."

"Not a walk in the park, as I recall."

"It actually went pretty smoothly," he said, "when you look back on it, but it didn't seem so smooth while it was going on. We got paid and everybody was happy, but even so it left a bad taste."

"So you'd like to rinse your mouth out?"

"Is there a lot of fine print in the contract, Dot? Does it have to look like a heart attack or an accident?"

She shook her head. "Homicide's fine, and as noisy as you want it."

"Oh?"

"So I'm told. I don't know what it's supposed to be, unless it's an object lesson for a player to be named later, but if you can arrange for the guy to get decapitated at high noon in Macy's window, nobody would be the least bit upset."

"Except for the artist."

"Keller," she said, "you can't please everybody. What do you think? You want to do this?"

"I could use the money."

"Well, who couldn't? The first payment's on its way, because I said yes first and then looked for someone to do it. I don't have to tell you how I hate to send money back once I have it in hand."

"Not your favorite thing."

"I get attached to it," she said, "and I think of it as my money, so returning it feels like spending it, and without getting anything for it. Do you want a day or two to think about this?"

He shook his head. "I'm in."

"Really? Brooklyn or no, it's still New York. He's in Williamsburg, you're on First Avenue, you can just about see his house from your window."

"Not really."

"All the same . . ."

"It won't be the first time in New York, Dot. Never on a job, but personal business, and what's the difference?" He straightened up in his chair. "I'm in," he said. "Now tell me about the guy."

★

"I used to paint," Maggie Griscomb said. "Now I make jewelry."

"I was noticing your earrings."

"These? They're my work. I only wear my own pieces, because that way I get to be a walking showcase. Unless I'm sitting down, in which case I'm a sitting showcase."

They were sitting now, in a booth at a Cuban coffee shop on Eighth Avenue, drinking café con leche.

"It's odd," she said, "because I like jewelry, and not just my own. I buy other people's jewelry and it just sits in the drawer."

"How come you stopped painting?"

"I stopped being twenty-nine."

"I didn't know there was an age limit."

"I spent my twenties painting moody abstract oils and sleeping with strangers," she said. "I figure my twenties lasted until my thirty-fourth birthday, when I got out of some guy's bed, threw up in his bathroom, and tried to get out of there without looking at him or the mirror. It struck me that I was older than Jesus Christ, and it was time to quit being twenty-nine and grow up. I looked at all my paintings and I thought, Jesus, what crap. Nobody ever bought any of them. Nobody even went so far as to admire them, unless it was some guy desperate to get laid. A horny man will pretend an enthusiasm for just about anything. But aside from that, about the best most people would do was say my work was interesting. Listen, I've got a tip for you. Don't ever tell an artist his work is interesting."

"I won't."

"Or different. 'Did you like the movie?' 'It was different.' What the hell does that mean? Different from what?" She stirred her coffee and left the spoon in the cup. "I don't know if my paintings were different," she said. "Whatever that means. But they weren't interesting, to me or anybody else. They weren't even pretty to look at. I was going to burn the canvases, but that seemed too dramatic. So I

60

stacked them at the curb, and somebody hauled them away."

"That sounds so sad."

"Well, it felt liberating. I thought, What do I like? And I thought, Jewelry, and I went out and took a class. I had a flair right from the beginning. These are pretty, aren't they?"

"Very pretty."

"And it's okay for them to be pretty," she said. "I had to work to keep my paintings from being pretty, because pretty art is facile and decorative and doesn't wind up in museums. So I did everything I could to turn out pictures that no one would ever get any pleasure out of, and I succeeded beyond my wildest dreams. Now I make rings and bracelets and necklaces and earrings, and I purposely make them attractive, and people buy my work and wear it and enjoy it. And it's really a pleasure not being twenty-nine anymore."

"You changed your whole life."

"Well, I still live downtown," she said, "and I still wear black. But I don't drink myself stupid, and I don't hurt my ears listening to loud music . . ."

"Or go to bed with strangers?"

"It depends," she said. "How strange are you?"

CHAPTER SIX

She was still sleeping when he left around daybreak. It was a crisp clear morning, and he set out to walk a few blocks and wound up walking all the way home. She lived in a loft on the top floor of a converted warehouse on Crosby Street, and he'd been living for years now in a prewar apartment building on First Avenue, just a few blocks up from the United Nations. He stopped for breakfast along the way, and he lingered in Union Square to look at the trees. Closer to home he ducked into a bookstore and flipped through a pocket guide to the trees of North America. The book was designed to enable you to identify a tree, and then told you everything you might want to know about it. More, he decided, than he needed to know, and he left without buying the book.

But he went on noticing the trees the rest of the way home. Midtown Manhattan wasn't exactly the Bois de Boulogne, but most of the side streets in Kips Bay and Murray Hill had some trees planted at curbside, and he found himself looking at them like somebody who'd never seen a tree before.

He'd always been aware of the city's trees, and never more so than during the months when he'd owned a dog. But a dog owner tends to see a tree as an essentially utilitarian object. Keller, dogless now, was able to see the trees as—what? Art objects, possessed of special properties of form and color and density? Evidence of God's handiwork on earth? Powerful beings in their own right? Keller wasn't sure, but he couldn't take his eyes off them.

At home in his tidy one-bedroom apartment, Keller found himself struck by the emptiness of his walls. He had a pair of Japanese prints in his bedroom, neatly framed in bamboo, the Christmas gift of a girlfriend who'd long since married and moved away. The only artwork in the living room was a poster Keller had bought on his own, after he'd viewed a Hopper retrospective a few years ago at the Whitney.

The poster showed one of the artist's most recognizable works, solitary diners at a café counter, and its mood was unutterably lonely. Keller found it cheering. Its message for him was that he was not alone in his solitude, that the city (and by extension the world) was full of lonely guys, sitting on stools in some sad café, drinking their cups of coffee and getting through the days and nights.

The Japanese prints were unobjectionable, but he hadn't paid any attention to them in years. The poster was different, he enjoyed looking at it, but it was just a poster. What it did, really, was refresh his memory of the original oil painting it depicted. If he'd never seen the painting itself, well, he'd probably still respond to the poster, but it wouldn't have anywhere near the same impact on him.

As far as owning an original Hopper, well, that was out of the question. Keller's work was profitable, he could afford to live comfortably and still sink a good deal of money into his stamp collection, but he was light-years away from being able to hang Edward Hopper on his wall. The painting shown on his poster—well, it wasn't for sale, but if it ever did come up at auction it would bring a seven-figure price. Keller figured he might be able to pay seven figures for a piece of art, but only if two of those figures came after the decimal point.

Keller had lunch at a Vietnamese restaurant on Third Avenue, then stopped at a florist. From there he walked up to Fifty-seventh Street, where he found a building he'd noticed in passing, with one or more art galleries on each of its ten floors. All but a couple were open, and he walked through them in turn, having a look at the works on display. At first he was wary that the gallery attendants would give him a sales pitch, or that he'd feel like an interloper, looking at work he had no intention of buying. But nobody even nodded at him, or gave any sign of caring what he looked at or how long he looked at it, and by the time he'd walked in and out of three galleries he was entirely at ease.

It was like going to a museum, he realized. It was exactly like going to a museum, except for two things. You didn't have to pay to get in, and there were no groups of restless children, with their teachers desperate to explain things to them.

How were you supposed to know how much the stuff cost? There was a number stuck to the wall beside each painting, but there were no dollar signs, and the numbers ran in sequence, 1-2-3-4-5-6-7, and couldn't possibly have anything to do with the price. Evidently it was considered loutish to post the price publicly, but didn't they want sales? What were you supposed to do, ask the price of anything that caught your eye?

Then at one gallery he noticed another patron carrying a plastic-laminated sheet of paper, referring to it occasionally, dropping it at the front table on her way out. Keller retrieved it, and damned if it didn't contain a numbered list of all the works on display, along with the title, the dimensions, the medium (oil, watercolor, acrylic, and gouache, whatever that was), and the year it was completed.

One work had NFS for a price, which he supposed meant Not For Sale. And two had little red dots next to the price, and he remembered that some of the paintings had displayed similar red dots alongside their numbers. Of course—the red dots meant the paintings had been sold! They wouldn't just wrap one up and send you home with it. The paintings had to hang for the duration of the show, so when you bought something, they tagged it with a red

64

dot and left it right where it was.

He congratulated himself for figuring it all out, then was taken aback by the thought that everyone else no doubt already knew it. In all the galleries in New York, he was probably the only person who'd lacked this particular bit of knowledge. Well, at least he'd been able to work it out on his own. He hadn't made a fool of himself, asking what the dots were for.

By the time he got home the mail was in. Keller had never cared much about the mail, collecting it and dealing with it as it came, tossing the junk mail and paying the bills. Then he took up stamp collecting, and now every day's mail held treasures.

Dealers throughout the country, and a few overseas, sent him the stamps he'd ordered from their lists, or won in mail auctions. Others sent him selections on approval, to examine at leisure and keep what pleased him. And there were the monthly stamp magazines, and a weekly stamp newspaper, and no end of auction catalogs and price lists and special offers.

Today, along with the usual lists and catalogs, Keller received his monthly selection from a woman in Maine. "Dear John," he read. "Here's a nice lot of German Colonies, plus a few others for your inspection. Enclosed are 26 glassines totaling $194.43. Hope you find some to your liking. Sincerely, Beatrice."

Keller had been dealing with Beatrice Rundstadt for almost two years now. She enclosed a similar note with each shipment, and he always wrote back along the same lines: "Dear Beatrice, Thanks for a nice selection, much of which has found a home here on First Avenue. I'm enclosing my check for $83.57 and look forward to next month's assortment. Yours, John." It had taken well over a year of Dear Mr. Keller and Dear Ms. Rundstadt, but now they were John and Beatrice, which gave the correspondence a nice illusion of intimacy.

Just an illusion, though. He didn't know if Beatrice Rundstadt was married or single, old or young, tall or short, fat or thin, didn't know if she collected stamps herself (as many dealers did) or thought collecting stamps was a fool's errand (as many other dealers did). For her part, all she knew about him was what he collected.

And that was how he hoped it would remain. Oh, he couldn't avoid the occasional fantasy, in which Bea Rundstadt (or some other lady philatelist) turned out to be a soul mate with the face of an angel and the build of a Barbie doll. Fantasies were harmless, as long as you kept them in their place. His notes remained as steadfastly perfunctory as hers. She sent him stamps, he sent her checks. Why mess with something that worked?

You could generally hold a selection of approvals for up to a month, but Keller rarely kept them around for more than a day or two. This time all he needed was an hour to pick out the stamps he wanted. He could mount them later on; for now he wrote out a check and a three-line note and went downstairs to the mailbox. Then he took a bus to Fourteenth Street and rode the L train under the East River to Bedford Avenue.

Keller knew Manhattan reasonably well, but his mental map of the outer boroughs was like a medieval mariner's map of the world. There were little floating pockets of known land and vast stretches inscribed "Beyond this point there be monsters." He had a glancing familiarity with parts of Brooklyn—Cobble Hill, because he'd had a girlfriend there once, and Marine Park, from the time years ago when he'd belonged to a bowling team that competed (if you could call it that) in a league out there. He didn't really know Williamsburg at all, but recalled that the dominant ethnic groups were Puerto Ricans and Hasidic Jews in the southern portion and Poles and Italians farther north. In recent years, artists seeking low-cost loft space had been moving in. ("There goes the neighborhood" went the cry—in Spanish and Yiddish, Polish and Italian.)

Declan Niswander lived on Berry Street, on Williamsburg's north side, just a ten-minute walk from the subway stop. Keller found the address, one of a row of modest three-story brick houses on the east side of the street. There were three bells at the side of the front door, which suggested that there was one apartment to a floor. Whether that was a lot of space or a little depended on how deep the Niswander house was, and you couldn't tell from the street.

The block, and indeed the whole neighborhood, was in the process of gentrification, but it had a ways to go yet, and hadn't yet reached the tree-planting stage. Thus Declan Niswander, who painted trees so evocatively as to make a termite change his diet, lived on a block without a single tree. Keller wondered if it bothered him, or if he even noticed. Maybe trees were just something to paint, and Niswander put them out of his mind the minute he packed up his paints and brushes.

Keller walked around, got a sense of the area. A block away he found a little Polish restaurant where he had a bowl of borscht and a big plate of pierogis, drank the large glass of grape Kool-Aid they brought without his asking, and, after a generous tip, still had change left from a ten-dollar bill. Dinner out here was quite a bargain, even when you counted the subway fare.

He was nursing a glass of dark beer in a bar called The Broken Clock when Niswander walked in. He hadn't been expecting the man, but he wasn't greatly surprised at the sight of him. The Broken Clock (and why did they call it that? There wasn't a clock to be seen, broken or not) was the only bar in the vicinity that looked to be a likely watering hole for artists. The others were straightforward working-class saloons, better suited to a painter of houses than one of elms and maples. Niswander might visit them now and then for a shot and a beer, but if he was going to hang out anywhere in the neighborhood it would be at The Broken Clock.

Niswander strode in, accompanied by a woman who was plainly his, and who bore papoose-style a baby that was plainly theirs. He passed out greetings to people left and right. Keller heard someone congratulate him on a review, heard another ask how the opening had gone. They knew Declan Niswander here, and they evidently liked him well enough.

For his part, Niswander looked right at home, but Keller figured he'd look okay in any of the local bars. He had the form and features to fit in anywhere, and, in his red and black plaid shirt and button-fly Levi's, he looked more likely to chop down a tree than paint its picture. He wasn't wearing a drop of black today, but then neither were the bar's other patrons. Black, Keller guessed, was for Lower Manhattan, where regular people dressed like artists. On this side of the river, artists dressed like regular people.

Keller finished his beer and went home.

There were no phone messages when he got home that night, and nobody called the next morning while he was around the corner having breakfast. He looked up a number and picked up the phone.

When she answered he said, "Hi, it's Keller."

"There you are."

"Here I am," he agreed.

"And no wonder people tend to call you Keller. It's what you call yourself."

"It is?"

" 'Hi, it's Keller.' Your very words. Your roses are beautiful. Completely unexpected and wholly welcome."

"I was wondering if they got there."

"What you're too polite to say is you were wondering if I was ever going to call."

"Not at all," he said. "I know you're busy, and—"

"And maybe the florist lost the card, and I didn't know who sent them."

"That occurred to me."

"I'll just bet it did. You think I didn't call? Believe me, I called. Do you happen to know how many Kellers there are in the Manhattan book?"

"There's something like two columns of them, if I remember correctly."

"Two columns is right. And there are two John Kellers and two Jonathans, not to mention seven or eight J Kellers. And not one of them is you."

"No, I'm not in the book."

"No shit, Sherlock."

"Oh," he said. "I guess you didn't have my number."

"I guess not, but I do now, Mr. Smarty, because I've got Caller ID on this phone, so your secret's not a secret anymore. I can call you anytime I want to, big boy. What do you think about that?"

"I haven't thought about it yet," he said, "so it's hard to say. But here's what I was thinking. Suppose I come by for you around seven tonight and we have dinner."

"Won't work."

"Oh."

"But I've got a better idea. Suppose you come over around nine-thirty and we have sex."

"That would work," he allowed. "But don't you want to have dinner?"

"I'm a lousy cook."

"At a restaurant," he said. "I meant for us to go out."

"I have revolting table manners," she said. "I also have a shrink appointment at five."

"Aren't they usually done in an hour?"

"Fifty minutes, generally."

69

"We could have dinner after."

"What I always do," she said, "is pick up a banana smoothie on the way to the shrink's, with added wheat germ and protein powder and spirulina, whatever that is, and I sip it while we talk. It's the perfect time to be nourished, you know? And then I'll go right home and work, because I've got an order I have to get out, and I'll knock off at nine and bathe and wash my hair and make myself irresistible, and at nine-thirty you'll show up and we'll have an inventive and highly satisfying sexual encounter. To which, I might add, I'll be looking forward all day. Nine-thirty, Keller. See ya."

Early that afternoon, Keller took a bus across Twenty-third and found his way to the Regis Buell gallery. There were other art galleries on the same block, and he stopped in a couple of them for a brief look. Prices were lower on average than in the Fifty-seventh Street galleries, but not by much. Art could get expensive in a hurry, once you got past museum show posters and mass-produced prints of kabuki dancers.

On opening night the Buell gallery had been jammed with people. Now it was empty, except for Keller and the young woman at the desk, a self-assured blonde who'd recently graduated from a good college and would soon be some commuter's wife. She gave Keller a low-wattage smile and went back to her book. Keller picked up one of the price lists. They must have had them at the opening, but at the time he hadn't known to look for one.

He spent two full hours at the gallery, going from canvas to canvas.

Back at his apartment, he gave Dot a call. "I've been thinking," he said.

"You want to bail. Pull the plug. Cut and run. Well, I can't say I blame you."

"No."

"No?"

He shook his head, then remembered he was on the phone. "No," he said, "that's not it. I was wondering about the client."

"What about him?"

"It's a him?"

"It's a generic pronoun, Keller. What do you want me to say, 'them'? 'It'? 'I was wondering about the client.' 'The client? What about him or her?' I'm an old-fashioned girl, Keller. I do like my eighth-grade English teacher taught me."

"As," he said.

"Huh?"

"You do *as* your teacher taught you."

"The suggestion that comes to mind," she said, "is not one I learned from Mrs. Jepson, and anyway I don't think it's physically possible. So never mind. What about the client?"

"Who is he?"

"Or she? No idea."

"Because I'm having trouble figuring out why anybody would want to kill this guy. Except maybe someone from the logging industry."

"Huh?"

"He paints pictures of trees, and after you've looked at them you wouldn't want to cut one down."

"So what is it you're turning into, Keller? A tree hugger or an art lover?"

"I went out to Williamsburg last night, and—"

"You think that was wise?"

"Well, I might want to close the sale out there. So I had to do a little reconnaissance."

"I guess."

"It's a nice neighborhood, artsy but honest. Place has a good feel to it."

"And you want to move there."

71

"I don't want to move anywhere, Dot. But do you think you could find out anything about the client? Call the guy who called you, nose around a little?"

"Why?"

"Why?"

"Yeah, why? It's tricky enough, working in your hometown. Why muck it up more?"

"Well . . ."

"He won't tell me anything. He's a pro. And so am I, so I won't even ask. And you're a pro yourself, Keller. Need I say more?"

"No, never mind. You know what he gets for a painting?"

"The subject?"

"Ten thousand dollars. That's on the average. The bigger ones are a little more, the smaller ones are a little less."

"Like diamonds," she said, "or, I don't know. Apartments. What's it matter what he gets? You don't want to buy one, do you?"

He didn't say anything.

"Oh, Lord have mercy," she said. "That's brilliant, Keller. You do the guy and you hammer a nail in your wall and hang up one of his paintings. Nothing quite so professional as keeping a little memento of the occasion."

"Dot . . ."

"If you absolutely have to have a souvenir," she said, "why don't you cut off one of his ears? You'll save yourself ten grand just like that. Anyone asks, you can tell 'em it was Van Gogh's."

"There," Maggie Griscomb said. "Now wasn't that nice?"

Keller would have said something, but he wasn't sure he was capable of forming sentences.

"As I worked my way through the Kellers," she went on, "the Johns and the Jonathans and the mere Js, I wanted to kill the man who invented the Touch-Tone phone. With an old-fashioned rotary dial I never would have bothered in the first place. Because I knew you weren't going to be in the book. Not the Manhattan book, anyway. I figured you lived in Scarsdale."

"Why Scarsdale?"

"Well, someplace like it. Westchester or Long Island, or maybe Connecticut. Well-to-do suburban."

"I live in Manhattan."

"Why would you want to bring up kids in Manhattan?"

"I don't have any. I'm not married."

"I thought of seeing what John Kellers I could find in Westchester," she said, "but you'd be at the office and I'd get your wife."

"I don't have a wife."

"So then I thought of calling your office."

He didn't have an office, either. "How? I never said where I worked."

"I was going to work my way through the Fortune 500 companies until I got you. But then you called me and saved me the trouble."

"I guess you see me as a corporate type."

"And why would I jump to a conclusion like that?" She put her hand on him. "Pegged you at a glance, Keller. Did you show up at the opening in basic black? Were you making a statement in paint-splattered jeans and a red bandanna? No, there you were in a suit and tie. Now where would I get the idea you were a corporate kind of guy?"

"I'm retired."

"Aren't you a little young for that? Or did you make such a pile of money that there's no point in working anymore?"

"I still work once in a while."

"Doing what?"

"Consulting."

"Consulting for whom?"

"Corporations."

"Bingo," she said.

"So once in a while I have to go out of town for a few days or a week."

"To consult."

"Well, I'm a sort of consultant-slash-troubleshooter. And a couple of jobs a year is all I get, so it's not that far from being completely retired."

"And you're all right for money."

"I manage okay. I saved money over the years, and I inherited some, and I was lucky in my investments."

"Doesn't alimony and child support eat up a lot of it?"

"I've never been married."

"Honestly? I know you're not married now, I was just yanking on your chain a little, but you've never been married at all? How did you escape?"

"I don't know."

"I dragged a guy home once," she said, "back when I was still painting ugly pictures and sleeping with strangers. He was about your age and incredibly good-looking and just sensational in bed, and he'd never been married, either. I couldn't figure it until I found out he was a priest."

"I'm not a priest."

"That's a shame. You could be a troubleshooter for God. You know something? We shouldn't be talking like this. In the first place, I want to keep this relationship superficial."

"Then I'd say this conversation is a step in the right direction."

"No, it's too personal. We can talk about things, but not about ourselves. Nothing ruins everything like getting to know each other."

"Oh."

"Anyway, you're almost as cute as the priest, and even better in bed. And you're right here, and God only knows where *he* is, which, when you think about it, is perfectly appropriate. But why are we wasting time talking?"

*

74

A little later he said, "I went back to that gallery today."

"Which gallery?"

"Where we met. Regis Buell? I wanted to see how the paintings looked without wine and cheese."

"And a few hundred people. What did you think?"

"I liked them," he said. "The man can paint the day-lights out of a tree. But they're not exactly flying off the walls. I only spotted two paintings with red dots."

"That's two more than Declan would prefer."

"How's that?"

"Well, all I know is what people are saying. It seems he called several people who've been collecting his work, and a few museum officials who've shown an interest, and he told them all the same thing. Come to the show, have a look at what I've been doing lately, but for God's sake don't buy anything."

"Why?"

"Because Declan can't stand Regis Buell."

"The gallery owner? Then why doesn't he show his paintings somewhere else?"

"He's going to, now that he's out from under his contract with Regis. This is his last show there, and as of the first of the month he'll be represented by Ottinger Galleries. So Declan wants everybody to wait, so that Jimmy Ottinger gets the commission on his work and not Regis Buell."

"Will the prices be the same at Ottinger?"

"Jimmy may nudge them up a notch or so," she said. "If he thinks the traffic will bear it. He thinks a great deal of Declan's work."

"And Regis Buell doesn't?"

"What Regis knows is that this is his last chance to make money off Declan's work. So he'd want to keep prices low enough to make the maximum number of sales. Jimmy Ottinger can afford to think long-term. It may be better to establish a higher price for the artist now than to sell everything at a lower level."

"I guess it's all more complicated than it looks."

"Like everything else," she agreed. "And what about you? Why the interest? Are you thinking of investing in one of Declan's mighty oaks?"

"There are a few that might work in my apartment," he said. "One in particular, but don't ask me to describe it."

"A tree is a tree is a tree."

"This is an old one, and it's a winter setting, but that fits quite a few of them. The thing is they're all different, but when you describe them the descriptions all come out the same."

"I know. Listen, don't tell Declan I said this, but what do you care who gets the commission? If you've found one you really love, and if you're sure you'll still want to look at it a month or a year from now . . ."

"Buy it?"

"You'll never get it cheaper. And somebody else might buy it out from under you."

Around one-fifteen, Maggie walked him to the door and stood on her tiptoes to give him a kiss. "No more flowers," she cautioned him. "Once was perfect, but once is enough. Call me every now and then, say once a week, and we'll get together like this for an hour or two."

"A couple of hours," he said. "Every week or so."

"Is that too much?" She patted his cheek. "More often than that and we might wear it out."

More often than that, he thought, as the cab carried him home, and we might wear *me* out.

CHAPTER SEVEN

At home, he paged through one of his stamp albums. Many of his fellow hobbyists were topical or thematic philatelists, collecting stamps not of a particular country or time period but united by what they portrayed. Stamps showing trains, say, or butterflies, or penguins. A doctor might choose stamps with a medical connection, while a musician could seek out stamps showing musical instruments, or those with portraits of the great composers. Or you could collect rabbit stamps for no more abiding reason than that you just plain liked to look at rabbits.

Art on stamps was an increasingly popular topic. Early on, when postage stamps were commonly of a single color, reproducing a great painting on a scrap of paper was easier said than done. A monochromatic miniature of the *Mona Lisa* might be recognizable for what it was, but it lacked a certain something.

Those early stamps, skillfully engraved and beautifully printed, were to Keller's mind far more attractive than what they turned out these days, when virtually every stamp from every country was printed in full color, and any stamp-issuing entity could spew out gemlike reproductions of the world's art treasures. Collectors made such endeavors profitable, and, unlike animation art from Disney or Warner Brothers, the works of Rembrandt and Rubens were unprotected by trademark or copyright. Anyone could copy them, and many did.

Keller's 1952 cutoff date put most of the world's art stamps out of his reach. But some countries had issued such stamps back in the old one-color days, more out of pride in their artistic heritage than in a grab for the collector's dollar. The French were particularly eager to show off their culture, portraying writers and painters and composers at the slightest provocation, and Keller looked now at a set of French semipostals that gave you a real sense of the artists' power.

And of course there was the Spanish set honoring Goya. One of the stamps showed his nude portrait of the Duchess of Alba. The painting had caused a stir when first displayed, and, years later, the stamp had proven every bit as stirring to a generation of young male philatelists. Keller remembered owning the stamp decades ago, and scrutinizing it through a pocket magnifier, wishing fervently that the stamp were larger and the glass stronger.

In the current issue of *Linn's*, as in almost every issue, there was a spirited exchange in the letters column on the best way to attract youngsters to the hobby. Evidently boys and girls were less strongly drawn to philately in a world full of computers and Nintendo and MTV. If kids stopped collecting stamps, where would the next generation of adult collectors come from?

Keller, having considered the question, had decided that he didn't care. All he wanted to do was add to his own collection, and he didn't really give a damn how many other men and women were working on theirs. Without new collectors joining the fold, stamps might eventually decline in value, but he didn't care about that, either. He wasn't going to sell his collection, and what difference did it make what became of it upon his death? If he couldn't take it with him, then somebody else could figure out what to do with it.

But others clearly did care about the hobby's future. The U.S. Post Office evidently saw a very profitable sideline threatened, and had responded by issuing stamps designed specifically to appeal to the young collector. When Keller was a boy, stamps showed great American writers and inventors and statesmen, people he mostly hadn't heard of, and in the course of collecting their images he had in fact learned a great deal about them, and about the history in which they'd played a part.

Nowadays, stamp collecting was a great way for young Americans to learn about Bugs Bunny and Daffy Duck.

Keller thought it over and decided they were doing it wrong. He'd collected avidly as a boy not because stamp collecting was designed for kids but because it was something undeniably grown-up that he could enjoy. If it had felt like kid stuff he wouldn't have had any part of it.

Would a stamp with Bugs Bunny's picture on it have prompted a young Keller to whip out his magnifying glass for a closer look?

Not a chance. If they wanted to get the kids interested, he thought, let them start putting naked ladies on them.

He called Dot first thing in the morning. "I hope it's not too early," he said.

"Five minutes ago you'd have been interrupting my breakfast," she told him. "Now all you're interrupting is the washing up, and that's fine with me."

"I was wondering," he said. "About the client."

"Refresh my memory, Keller. Didn't we already have this conversation?"

"Suppose you were to call whoever called you," he said. "Suppose you ask how the client feels about mushrooms."

"You going into the catering business, Keller?"

"Innocent bystanders," he said. "Drug dealers call them mushrooms because they just sort of pop up and get caught in the crossfire."

"That's charming. When did you take to hanging out with drug dealers?"

"I read an article in the paper."

"That's where you get your figures of speech, Keller? From newspaper articles?"

79

He drew a breath. "What I'm getting at," he said, "is suppose something happened to a guy in Brooklyn, and his wife and kid got in the way."

"Oh, I see where you're going."

"And the art gallery's another possibility, but there too you might have people around."

"So I should run it past my guy so he can get in a huddle with the client."

"Right."

"And I report back to you, and then what? Don't tell me the job gets done and we can all move on."

"Sure," he said. "What else?"

Keller sat in front of the Hopper poster, taking it in. If you wanted to hang something on the wall, you couldn't beat a poster. Ten or twenty bucks plus framing and you had a real piece of art in your living room.

On the other hand, how many posters could you hang before you ran out of wall space? No, if you were going to collect art in a small apartment, stamps were the way to go. One album, a few inches of shelf space, and you could put together a tiny Louvre all your own.

He could go either way. He could start a topical collection, art on stamps, or he could look for a few more posters that hit him the way Hopper's did.

He put on a tie and jacket and got on a crosstown bus.

It was ridiculous, he thought, walking from the bus stop to the gallery. The painting he liked best, #19 on the laminated price list, was one of the larger ones, and the price they were asking was $12,000. It would be nice to be able to look at it whenever he felt like it, but he could walk over to Central Park anytime he wanted and look at thousands of trees. He could get as close as he wanted and it wouldn't cost him a dime.

The same Vassar graduate sat behind the desk, reading

the same Jane Smiley novel and waiting for her Wall Street prince to come. She nodded at Keller without moving her head—he wasn't sure how she managed that—and went back to her book while he crossed the room to the painting.

And there it was, as vivid and powerful as ever. He felt himself drawn into the picture, sucked into the trunk and up the branches. He let himself sink into the canvas. This had never happened to him before and he wondered if it happened to other people. He stayed in front of the painting for a long time, knowing that there was no question of passing it up. He had the money, he could spend it on a painting if he wanted.

He'd tell the girl he wanted to buy it, and they'd take his name and perhaps a deposit—he wasn't sure how that part worked. Then they'd record it as sold, and when the show came down at the end of the month he'd pay the balance and take it home.

And have it framed? It was minimally framed now with flat strips of dark wood, and that worked okay, but he suspected a professional framer could improve on it. Something simple, though. Something that enclosed the painting without drawing attention to itself. Those carved and gilded frames looked great around a portrait of a codger with muttonchop whiskers, but they were all wrong for something like this, and—

There was a red dot on the wall beside the painting.

He stared at it, and it was there, all right, next to the number 19. He extended a forefinger, as if to flick the dot away, then let his hand fall to his side.

Well, he'd left it too long. Remembering to look before he leapt, he'd hesitated, and was lost.

And so was the painting, lost to him.

Disappointment washed over him, along with a paradoxical sense of relief. He wouldn't have to part with twelve thousand dollars, wouldn't have to seek out a framer, wouldn't have to pick a spot and hammer a nail into the wall.

But, dammit to hell, he wouldn't own the painting.

Of course there were others. This was the one he'd picked, the old tree trying to get through one more winter, but the choice hadn't been all that clear-cut, because he'd responded strongly to all of Declan Niswander's work. If he couldn't have his favorite, well, it wasn't the end of the world. How hard would it be to find one he liked almost as well?

Not hard at all, as it turned out. But it would be equally impossible to buy any of the other works, no matter how much he liked them, because every single painting in the gallery had been given the red dot treatment.

He stared at the desk until the girl looked up from her book. "Everything's been sold," he said.

"Yes," she agreed. "Isn't it marvelous?"

"It's great for you people," he said, "and I suppose it's great for Mr. Niswander, but it's not so great for me."

"You were in yesterday afternoon, weren't you?"

"And I should have bought the painting then, but I wanted to sleep on it. And now it's too late."

"Things happen overnight in this business," she said. "I always heard that, and here's an example. When I went home last night there were only two paintings sold, the ones that were purchased the night of the opening. And when I came in this morning there were so many red dots I thought the walls had measles."

"Well," he said, "at least I've got the rest of the month to look at the paintings. Who bought them, anyway?"

"I wasn't here. Look, suppose I get Mr. Buell? Maybe he can help you."

She went away and Keller returned to Niswander's trees, trying not to notice the plague of red dots. Then a man appeared, the willowy young chap who'd introduced Niswander at the opening. Up close, Keller could see that

Regis Buell wasn't really as young as he appeared. He looked like an aging boy, and Keller wondered if he might have had a face-lift.

"Regis Buell," he said. "Jenna informs me we've disappointed you by selling out to the bare walls."

"I'm the one with the bare walls," Keller told him.

Buell laughed politely. "What painting was it? That you had your heart set on."

"Number nineteen."

"The old horse chestnut? A splendid choice. You have a good eye. But I have to say they're all good choices."

"And they've already been chosen. Who bought them?"

"Ah," Buell said, and clasped his hands. "Mystery buyers."

"More than one?"

"Several, and I'm afraid I can't disclose any of their names."

"And they all came through at the same time? I was here yesterday and there were only two paintings sold."

"Yes, just the two."

"And today they're all gone."

"Ah. Well, I had a private showing last night, after we'd officially closed. And, as a matter of fact, some of the work was already sold when you saw it yesterday. The red dots weren't in place yet, but several paintings had in fact been spoken for." He smiled winningly. "I don't believe Jenna told me your name."

"I never gave it to her," Keller said. "It's Forrest."

Buell smiled prettily, and Keller immediately regretted the name. "Mr. Forrest," Buell said. "No wonder you respond to trees."

"Well," Keller said.

"You know, there's always the chance a purchaser will change his mind."

"And back out of the deal?"

"Or consent to an immediate resale, especially if he's offered an incentive."

83

"You mean if he can make a profit?"

"It happens all the time. If you wanted to make an offer, on the horse chestnut or indeed any of the works, I could relay it and see what response it receives." And how much of an incentive would it take? Buell thought it would have to be substantial. "The man's a private buyer, not a dealer, so he wasn't planning on this, but who doesn't like to turn a quick profit? The prospect of a ten percent gain wouldn't move him, but if he could double his money, well, that might be a difficult temptation to resist."

"In other words, offer him twenty-four thousand?"

Buell gnawed on a fingernail. "May I make a suggestion? Round it up to twenty-five. It's a far more impressive number."

"It's impressive," Keller allowed.

"And I daresay you're impressed with it yourself, having expected to take home the painting for twelve. Still, you could pay twenty-five or even *thirty*-five thousand for that painting and still come out well ahead."

"You really think so?"

"Absolutely." Regis Buell leaned in close, let his voice drop. "Look how rapidly the entire show sold out. Declan Niswander's price is about to shoot through the roof. If you were to ask my advice, I'd tell you to offer the twenty-five and go higher if you have to. And, if the *buyer* were to ask my advice, I'd have to tell him not to sell." He smiled conspiratorially. "But he may not ask. Would you like me to sound him out?"

Keller said he'd have to think about it.

"First I had to reach the guy," Dot said, "and then he had to reach his guy, and then he had to get back to me."

"It's always something," Keller said.

"The questions surprised him, but he came back with answers. The client thinks Williamsburg's perfect, and he doesn't care how many people come to the party. If you

84

want to make an omelet you've got to break some eggs, and you might as well cap a few mushrooms while you're at it."

"And if the wife's around—"

"Fine with him. Remember how he wanted it dramatic? I guess that comes under the heading of drama." She cleared her throat. "Other hand, Keller, it doesn't sound much like your kind of thing."

"No, it doesn't. What about the gallery? He have anything to say about that?"

"He didn't like the idea."

"What didn't he like about it? Never mind, I don't want an answer."

"Then you're not going to get one," she said. "What do you think of that?"

Monday morning he went over his bid sheet, then addressed an envelope to a dealer in Hanford, Oklahoma. Lately the ads were full of Internet auctions. You could buy and sell online, and when your stamps came you could use special philatelic software to design your album pages and other software to maintain an inventory of your holdings.

Keller didn't have a computer and didn't want one. He figured he was spending enough money already.

He mailed the letter on the way to Grand Central and caught a train to White Plains. When he got to Taunton Place Dot opened the door for him and he followed her to the kitchen. The TV was on, tuned to a game show, but the sound was off.

"You took me by surprise," she said. "What's wrong, Keller? Why are you looking at me like that?"

"I, uh, phoned."

She rolled her eyes. "I know that. You phoned and I said come on up. Oh, that explains the look. You thought I'd forgotten our phone conversation. You figured I was starting to go ga-ga, just like the late lamented. No, I think I've got a few more years yet before my brain turns to jelly. All I meant was I didn't hear your cab drive up. Or pull away, either, as far as that goes. What did you do, make him drop you at the corner?"

"No, I—"

"Remember when he had everybody doing that? He got it in his head it drew attention, people coming here all the time, so everybody had to walk a block or two, and that really drew attention. Did you walk a block or two?"

"I walked from the station."

"All the way from the station?"

"It's a nice day."

"It's never that nice," she said. "You must have been in a big hurry to see me."

"If I'd been in a hurry, I'd have taken a cab."

"Keller, I was being sarcastic."

"Oh."

"For all the good it did me. Let me look at you. I guess it's not much fun, working in your own city. Bright side, you're not dead or in jail. You think there's a chance of wrapping this up while that's still true of both of us?"

"It's all settled."

"You're kidding."

"I'm not the sarcastic one," he said. "I handled it over the weekend. It's all taken care of."

"Account closed."

"Yes."

"End of story."

"Right."

"You never said a word on the phone, and you always do."

"I'm usually calling from out of town. I figured I'd be here soon enough, I'd tell you in person."

"And you usually seem, oh, what's the word I want? Triumphant? Not bursting into song necessarily, and maybe even a little reserved, but like you're the cat bringing in the dead mouse. Pleased with yourself."

"I'm pleased."

"Any minute now you're going to do handsprings. I can tell."

"Well, it was complicated," he said, "and it took a while. And when it was done I didn't get to pack up and go home."

"Nothing to pack. And you were already home. How'd you do it?"

"The subway."

"Is that how you got out to Williamsburg? Oh, the subway's how you did it."

"An oncoming train."

"And a body on the tracks. 'Did he jump or was he pushed?' You know what's funny? So many times they want an accident, and it's not always possible to stage it so it gets past forensics. But this guy wanted a big splash, and what you gave him is something that'll go in the books as an accident." She frowned. "Although when a whole subway train runs over you, 'big splash' is not an entirely inappropriate phrase."

"The client won't complain."

"I don't even care if he does," she said, "because we're not working for him again, or for anybody else in New York. So I'd just as soon he doesn't ask us."

"He won't."

She gave him a sharp look. "There's something you're trying to tell me," she said, "and I have a horrible idea I know what it is. Am I right?"

"How do I know?"

"Keller, do I have to send the money back?"

"No."

"And when can I expect the rest of it? I can't, can I?"

"No."

"Because the client's had trouble writing checks ever since he took the A train."

"It wasn't the A train."

"Keller, I don't care if it was the Atchison, Topeka, and the Santa Fe." She sighed heavily. "You might as well tell me all about it."

Where to start? "I figured out who the client was."

"And a good thing, too, or you wouldn't have known who to kill."

"It was the gallery owner," he said, and explained how Niswander had changed allegiances. "Galleries get fifty percent of sales. Buell had worked hard and spent a lot of money building Niswander up, and now the guy was going with somebody else, and on top of that he was telling his friends and patrons not to buy anything from his last show with Buell. They should wait and spend their money with the new dealer."

"So Buell was angry," she said, "but angry enough to kill? And it's not as if you work for minimum wage. He was throwing good money after bad."

"What he was throwing was bread upon the waters. Do you know what happens when an artist dies?"

"They give him an enema," she said, "and bury him in a matchbox."

"His price goes up. They know he's not going to flood the market with new pictures, and that he doesn't have his best work ahead of him. So there's a scramble for what he managed to complete before his death."

"So every artist is worth more dead than alive?"

"No," he said, "but Niswander is a rising star, just beginning to hit his stride. That's why Buell was so upset at the prospect of losing him. And, if Niswander happened to be murdered in some dramatic fashion, that would give things a major boost."

"But what would Buell get out of it? He was losing Niswander after the show, and didn't you tell me everything in the show was already sold?"

He nodded. "Niswander told everybody not to buy. And

Buell sold out the entire show overnight."

"Got it. He sold them to himself."

"Plastered the walls with red dots the minute his assistant went home for the night. Four hundred thousand dollars is what the prices added up to, but he would have only had to pay half of that to Niswander. And, if the artist happened to be dead, he could probably take his sweet time settling with the estate."

"And if Mrs. Niswander got killed, too, he might never get called to account. No wonder he didn't care how many mushrooms wound up in the omelet."

"More publicity, too. *Artist, Whole Family Slain in Brooklyn Rampage*. More hype for the Niswander mystique."

"And he'd be sitting on forty paintings, with the price set to go through the roof." She frowned. "That's a pretty extreme thing, killing off your own artists so you can make more money on them. I don't know much about ethics in the gallery business, but I'd call that pretty low."

"Most people would."

"On the other hand," she said, "did you happen to notice what kind of a house we're in?"

"Victorian, isn't it? I don't know a whole lot about architecture."

"I'm talking metaphorically, Keller, and that makes it a glass house, and what do you think we shouldn't do?"

"Throw stones?"

"Especially at our own clients."

"I know."

"Because they tend to be moral lepers, but what the hell do you expect? Albert Schweitzer never hired a hit man, and neither did the guy in the loincloth, and—"

"The guy in the loincloth?"

"They made a movie about him. He was little and he talked funny and at the end he got shot. You know who I mean."

"It sounds like Edward G. Robinson in *Little Caesar*," he said, "but are you sure he never hired a hit man? Because it seems to me——"

"Christ almighty," she said. "Gandhi, all right? Mahatma Gandhi, from India. Okay?"

"Whatever you say."

"Edward G. Robinson," she said. "Edward G. Robinson in *Little Caesar*. When the hell did Edward G. Robinson ever wear a loincloth?"

"I was wondering about the loincloth."

"Jesus, Keller. Where was I?"

"They never hired a hit man."

"Schweitzer and Gandhi. Well, they never did. You don't have to be a good human being to be a good client. All you have to do is play straight with us and pay what you owe. Which Regis Buell might or might not have done, but how will we ever know?"

"I really liked Niswander's paintings, Dot."

"Look, I'll take your word for it he's the real thing. What the hell, Buell must have thought so himself. That's what made him worth killing."

"It's not just that he's good. I responded to his work."

"You wanted to hang him on your wall."

"Dot, I wanted to climb right up into one of his trees and hide in the branches. A man who can paint something that does that to me, how can I kill him?"

"We could have resigned the account."

"So? Then someone else does it."

"At least the blood's not on your hands."

"The man's just as dead. He's not going to be painting any more trees. What do I care about blood on my hands?"

She was silent for a long moment. Then she said, "Look, what's done is done, and I'm not even going to say you were wrong to do it. What do I know about right and wrong? I'm in the same glass house, Keller. I'm not going to be heaving boulders at you."

"But?"

"But this isn't the first time one of our clients purchased the agricultural real estate."

"Huh? Oh, bought the farm."

"Acre by acre."

"There was that cutie pie in Iowa, played games with us and tried to screw us out of the final payment."

"And the one in Washington, had you convinced your orders came straight from the White House. Forget those two, Keller. They had it coming."

"And one other time," he admitted, "when two clowns each hired us to do the other. And he"—his eyes rose to the ceiling—"said yes to both jobs. What choice did I have? How could I do the job without tagging a client?"

"The way I remember it, you tagged them both."

"All I can say is it seemed like a good idea at the time."

"And maybe it was. You know, a lot of people must have had it in for Regis Buell. It's a shame you couldn't get one of them to hire you, because this way there was no money in killing him."

"No."

"In fact," she said, "his death means we don't get paid for Niswander. Who's still alive and well, so why should we?"

"On the other hand, we got half in front from Buell and he's not going to ask for it back."

"He's not, and half a loaf is better than a poke in the eye with a sharp stick. Look at it one way, it was money I should have sent back at the beginning, and now I don't have to."

"And it's all yours," he said.

"How do you figure that?"

"I screwed up," he said. "No way I'm entitled to my share. So you keep it all, and you wind up the same as if I did the job and we collected the second payment and split down the middle. You look puzzled, Dot. All of half is half of all."

91

" 'All of half is half of all.' You know who you sound like, Keller? The Three Musketeers."

"It's true, though, and—"

"It's crap," she said. "Keller, you and I are the Two Musketeers, get it? You earned your share when you made sure Buell didn't miss his train."

"I don't know, Dot."

"I do. Knock knock."

"Huh?"

"Weren't you ever a kid, Keller? Come on. Knock knock."

"Who's there?"

"Sharon."

"Huh?"

"Keller, play the game."

"Sharon who?"

"Sharon share alike. We each did something we should-n't have done, and we both came out of it okay. But I'll make you a deal, Keller. You stop killing our clients and I'll stop accepting jobs in New York. Deal?"

"Deal. Only . . ."

"Only what?"

"Well, you can still book local assignments. Just don't book them for me."

"Assuming I can find someone from out of town that I can work with."

"You've already got somebody."

"Used to."

"Just because his phone's out doesn't mean he's gone for good."

"In this case it does," she said. "Seeing as he's dead."

"Dead?"

"I made a few calls," she said, "and I checked with people who checked with other people. A little over a month ago the police kicked his door in after a neighbor complained about the smell."

"I don't suppose it was clogged drains."

"They found him in bed. Except for the decomposition, you'd have thought he was sleeping. Which he was, I guess. He went to sleep and never woke up."

"Heart attack?"

"I guess. Nobody showed me the death certificate."

"How old?"

"Somebody said but I forget. Younger than either of us, I remember that much."

"Jesus."

"Maybe he used drugs, Keller."

"In this business? You screw around with drugs and you don't last."

"Well," she said, "he didn't. And don't tell me there aren't plenty of guys who use something when they're not working. Or even when they are. Not everyone lives as clean as you, Keller."

"Maybe he had a congenital heart condition."

"Maybe. People die, Keller, and not all of them get a hand from a helpful guy like yourself. Far as that goes, people fall in front of subway trains."

"Or jump."

"Or jump. They don't all get pushed." She got to her feet. "But let me get your share of the fee from one who did, and you can go home. Say, what about that tree you fell in love with? What happens to it now?"

"Niswander will get it back, along with the rest of his paintings, since the mystery buyers represented by all those little red dots will fail to materialize. And I guess his new dealer will offer it for sale sooner or later."

"At a much higher price."

"Not necessarily, since the artist is still alive."

"So he is. Will you buy it?"

"I don't know. I really like the painting, I liked all of his paintings."

"But?"

He frowned. "But I'm not sure I want to get into all that, Dot. The whole art scene. I think maybe I'm better off sticking with stamps."

She pinched his cheek. "Perfect," she said. "You know what they say, Keller. You stick to your stamps and your stamps will stick to you."

CHAPTER EIGHT

Keller got out of the taxi at Bleecker and Broadway
because that was easier than trying to tell the Haitian cabdriver how to find Crosby Street. He walked to Maggie's
building, a former warehouse with a forbidding exterior,
and rode up to her fifth-floor loft. She was waiting for him,
wearing a black canvas coat of the sort you saw in western
movies. It was called a duster, probably because it was cut
long to keep the dust off. Maggie was a small woman—
elfin, he had decided, was a good word for her—and this
particular duster reached clear to the floor.

"Surprise," she said, and flung it open, and there was
nothing under it but her.

Keller, who'd met Maggie Griscomb at an art gallery, had
been keeping infrequent company with her for a while
now. Just the other day a chance remark of his had led Dot
to ask if he was seeing anybody, and he'd been stuck for an
answer. Was he? It was hard to say.

"It's a superficial relationship," he'd explained.

"Keller, what other kind is there?"

"The thing is," he said, "she wants it that way. We get
together once a week, if that. And we go to bed."

"Don't you at least go out for dinner first?"

"I've given up suggesting it. She's tiny, she probably
doesn't eat much. Maybe eating is something she can only
do in private."

"You'd be surprised how many people feel that way
about sex," Dot said. "But I'd have to say she sounds like
the proverbial sailor's dream. Does she own a liquor store?"

She was a failed painter, he explained, who'd reinvented

herself as a jewelry maker. "You bought earrings for the last woman in your life," Dot reminded him. "This one makes her own. What are you going to buy for her?"

"Nothing."

"That's economical. Between not giving her gifts and not taking her out to dinner, I can't see this one putting much of a strain on your budget. Can you at least send the woman flowers?"

"I already did."

"Well, it's something you can do more than once, Keller. That's one of the nice things about flowers. The little buggers die, so you get to throw them out and make room for fresh ones."

"She liked the flowers," he said, "but she told me once was enough. Don't do it again, she said."

"Because she wants to keep things superficial."

"That's the idea."

"Keller," she said, "I've got to hand it to you. You don't find that many of them, but you sure pick the strange ones."

"Now that was intense," Maggie said. "Was it just my imagination, or was that a major earth-shaking experience?"

"High up there on the Richter scale," he said.

"I thought tonight would be special. Full moon tomorrow."

"Does that mean we should have waited?"

"In my experience," she said, "it's the day *before* the full moon that I feel it the strongest."

"Feel what?"

"The moon."

"But what is it you feel? What effect does it have on you?"

"Gets me all moony."

"Moony?"

96

"Makes me restless. Heightens my moods. Sort of intensifies things. Same as everybody else, I guess. What about you, Keller? What does the moon do for you?"

As far as Keller could tell, all the moon did for him was light up the sky a little. Living in the city, where there were plenty of streetlights to take up the slack, he paid little attention to the moon, and might not have noticed if someone took it away. New moon, half moon, full moon—only when he caught an occasional glimpse of it between the buildings did he know what phase it was in.

Maggie evidently paid more attention to the moon, and attached more significance to it. Well, if the moon had had anything to do with the pleasure they'd just shared, he was grateful to it, and glad to have it around.

"Besides," she was saying, "my horoscope says I'm going through a very sexy time."

"Your horoscope."

"Uh-huh."

"What do you do, read it every morning?"

"You mean in the newspaper? Well, I'm not saying I never look, but I wouldn't rely on a newspaper horoscope for advice and counsel any more than I'd need Ann Landers to tell me if I have to pet to be popular."

"On that subject," he said, "I'd say you don't absolutely have to, but what could it hurt?"

"And who knows," she said, reaching out for him. "I might even enjoy it."

A while later she said, "Newspaper astrology columns are fun, like *Peanuts* and *Doonesbury*, but they're not very accurate. But I got my chart done, and I go in once a year for a tune-up. So I have an idea what to expect over the coming twelve months."

"You believe in all that?"

"Astrology? Well, it's like gravity, isn't it?"

"It keeps things from flying off in space?"

"It works whether I believe in it or not," she said. "So I

97

might as well. Besides, I believe in everything."

"Like Santa Claus?"

"And the Tooth Fairy. No, all the occult stuff, like tarot and numerology and palmistry and phrenology and—"

"What's that?"

"Head bumps," she said, and capped his skull with her hand. "You've got some."

"I've got head bumps?"

"Uh-huh, but don't ask me what they mean. I've never even been to a phrenologist."

"Would you?"

"Go to one? Sure, if somebody steered me to a good one. In all of these areas, some practitioners are better than others. There are the storefront gypsies who are really just running a scam, but after that you've still got different levels of proficiency. Some people have a knack and some just hack away at it. But that's true in every line of work, isn't it?"

It was certainly true in his.

"What I don't get," he said, "is how any of it works. What difference does it make where the stars are when you're born? What has that got to do with anything?"

"I don't know how anything works," she said, "or why it should. Why does the light go on when I throw the switch? Why do I get wet when you touch me? It's all a mystery."

"But head bumps, for Christ's sake. Tarot cards."

"Sometimes it's just a way for a person to access her intuition," she said. "I used to know a woman who could read shoes."

"The labels? I don't follow you."

"She'd look at a pair of shoes that you'd owned for a while, and she could tell you things about yourself."

" 'You need half-soles.' "

"No, like you eat too much starchy food, and you need to express the feminine side of your personality, and the relationship you're in is stifling your creativity. Things like that."

"All by looking at your shoes. And that makes sense to you?"

"Does sense make sense? Look, do you know what holism is?"

"Like eating brown rice?"

"No, that's whole foods. Holism is like with holograms, the principle's that any cell in the body represents the entire life in microcosm. That's why I can rub your feet and make your headache go away."

"You can?"

"Well, not me personally, but a foot reflexologist could. That's why a palmist can look at your hand and see evidence of physical conditions that have nothing to do with your hands. They show up there, and in the irises of your eyes, and the bumps on your head."

"And the heels of your shoes," Keller said. "I had my palm read once."

"Oh?"

"A year or two ago. I was at this party, and they had a palmist for entertainment."

"Probably not a very good one, if she was hiring out for parties. How good a reading did she give you?"

"She didn't."

"I thought you said you had your palm read."

"I was willing. She wasn't. I sat down at the table with her and gave her my hand, and she took a good look and gave it back to me."

"That's awful. You must have been terrified."

"Of what?"

"That she saw imminent death in your hand."

"It crossed my mind," he admitted. "But I figured she was just a performer, and this was part of the performance. I was a little edgy the next time I got on a plane—"

"I'll bet."

99

"—but it was a routine flight, and time passed and nothing happened, and I forgot about it. I couldn't tell you the last time I even thought about it."

She reached out a hand. "Gimme."

"Huh?"

"Give me your hand. Let's see what got the bitch in a tizzy."

"You can read palms?"

"Not quite, but I can claim a smattering of ignorance on the subject. Let's see now, I don't want to know too much, because it might jeopardize the superficiality of our relationship. There's your head line, there's your heart line, there's your life line. And no marriage lines. Well, you said you've never been married, and your hand says you were telling the truth. I can't say I can see anything here that would make me tell you not to sign any long-term leases."

"That's a relief."

"So I bet I know what spooked her. You've got a murderer's thumb."

Keller, working on his stamp collection, kept interrupting himself to look at his thumb. There it was, teaming up with his forefinger to grip a pair of tongs, to pick up a glassine envelope, to hold a magnifying glass. There it was, his own personal mark of Cain. His murderer's thumb.

"It's the particular way your thumb is configured," Maggie had told him. "See how it goes here? And look at my thumb, or your left thumb, as far as that goes. See the difference?"

She was able to recognize the murderer's thumb, he learned, because a childhood friend of hers, a perfectly gentle and nonviolent person, had one just like it. A palmist had told her friend it was a murderer's thumb, and the two of them had looked it up in a book on the subject. And there it was, pictured life size and in color, the Murderer's Thumb, and it was just like her friend

Jacqui's thumb, and, now, just like Keller's.

"But she never should have given you your hand back the way she did," Maggie had assured him. "I don't know if anybody's keeping statistics, but I'm sure most of the murderers walking around have two perfectly normal thumbs, while most people who do happen to have a murderer's thumb have never killed anybody in their life, and never will."

"That's a comfort."

"How many people have you killed, Keller?"

"What kind of a question is that?"

"And do you sense a burst of homicidal rage in your future?"

"Not really."

"Then I'd say you can relax. You may have a murderer's thumb, but I don't think you have to worry about it."

He wasn't worried, not exactly. But he would have to say he was puzzled. How could a man have a murderer's thumb all his life and be unaware of it? And, when all was said and done, what did it mean?

He had certainly never paid any particular attention to his thumb. He had been aware that his two thumbs were not identical, that there was something slightly atypical about his right thumb, but it was not eye-catchingly idiosyncratic, not the sort of thing other kids would notice, much less taunt you about. He'd given it about as much thought over the years as he gave to the nail on the big toe of his left foot, which was marked with ridges.

Hit man's toe, he thought.

He was poring over a price list, France & Colonies, wrestling with some of the little decisions a stamp collector was called upon to make, when the phone rang. He picked it up, and it was Dot.

He made the usual round-trip by train, Grand Central to White Plains and back again. He packed a bag before he went to bed that night, and in the morning he caught a cab to JFK and a plane to Tampa. He rented a Ford Escort and drove to Indian Rocks Beach, which sounded more like a headline in *Variety* than a place to live. But that's what it was, and, though he didn't see any Indians or rocks, it would have been hard to miss the beach. It was a beauty, and he could see why they had all these condos on it, and vacation time-shares.

The man Keller was looking for, an Ohioan named Stillman, had just moved in for a week's stay in a beach-front apartment on the fourth floor of Gulf Water Towers. There was an attendant in the lobby, Keller noticed, but he didn't figure to be as hard to get past as the Maginot Line.

But would he even need to find out? Stillman had just arrived from sunless Cincinnati, and how much time was he going to spend inside? No more than he had to, Keller figured. He'd want to get out there and soak up some rays, maybe splash in the Gulf a little, then zone out some more in the sun.

Keller's packing had included swim trunks, and he found a men's room and put them on. He didn't have a towel to lie on—he hadn't taken a room yet—but he could always lie on the sand.

It turned out he didn't have to. As he was walking along the public beach, he saw a woman approach a man, her hands cupped. She was holding water, and she threw it on the man, who sprang to his feet. They laughed joyously as he chased her into the surf. There they frolicked, perfect examples of young hormone-driven energy, and Keller figured they'd be frolicking for a while. They'd left two towels on the sand, anonymous unidentifiable white beach towels, and Keller decided one was all they needed. It would easily accommodate the two of them when they tired of splashing and ducking one another.

He picked up the other towel and walked off with it. He spread it out on the sand at the private beach for Gulf

Water Towers residents. A glance left and right revealed no one who in any way resembled George Stillman, so Keller stretched out on his back and closed his eyes. The sun, a real stranger to New York of late, was evidently wholly at home in Florida, and felt wonderful on his skin. If it took a while to find Stillman, that was okay with him.

But it didn't.

Keller opened his eyes after half an hour or so. He sat up and looked around, feeling a little like Punxsutawney Phil on Groundhog Day. When he failed to see either Stillman or his own shadow, he lay down and closed his eyes again.

The next time he opened them was when he heard a man cursing. He sat up, and not twenty yards away was a barrel-chested man, balding and jowly, calling his right hand every name in the book.

How could the fellow be that mad at his own hand? Of course he might have a murderer's thumb, but what if he did? Keller had one himself, and had never felt the need to talk to it in those terms.

Oh, hell, of course. The man was on a cell phone. And, by God, he was Stillman. The face had barely registered on Keller at first, his attention held by the angry voice and the keg-shaped torso thickly pelted with black hair. None of that had been visible in the head-and-shoulders shot Dot had shown him, and it was what you noticed, but it was the same face, and here he was, and wasn't that handy?

While Stillman took the sun, Keller did the same. When Stillman got up and walked to the water's edge, so did Keller. When Stillman waded in, to test his mettle in the surf, Keller followed in his wake.

When Keller came ashore, Stillman stayed behind. And, by the time Keller left the beach, carrying two towels and a cellular phone, Stillman had still not emerged from the water.

CHAPTER NINE

Why a thumb?

Keller, back in New York, pondered the question. He couldn't see what a thumb had to do with murder. When you used a gun, it was your index finger that gave the trigger a squeeze. When you used a knife, you held it in your palm with your fingers curled around the handle. Your thumb might press the hilt, as a sort of guide, but a man could have no thumbs at all and still get the business end of a knife to go where he wanted it.

Did you use your thumbs when you garroted somebody? He mimed the motion, letting his hands remember, and he didn't see where the thumbs had much of a part to play. Manual strangulation, now that was different, and you did use your thumbs, you used all of both hands, and would have a hard time otherwise.

Still, why a murderer's *thumb*?

"**H**ere's what I don't get," Dot said. "You go off to some half-a-horse town at the ass end of nowhere special and you poke around for a week or two. Then you go to a vacation paradise in the middle of a New York winter and you're back the same day. The same day!"

"I had an opening and I took it," he said. "I wait and maybe I never get that good a shot at him again."

"I realize that, Keller, and God knows I'm not complaining. It just seems like a shame, that's all. Here you are, the two of you, fresh off a couple of planes from the frozen North, and before either one of you gets the chill out of your bones, you're on a flight to New York and he's rapidly approaching room temperature."

"Water temperature."

"I stand corrected."

"And it was like a bathtub."

"That's nice," she said. "He could have opened his veins in it, but after you held his head underwater for a few minutes he no longer felt the need to. But couldn't you have waited a few days? You'd have come home with a tan and he'd have gone into the ground with one. You meet your Maker, you want to look your best."

He glanced over at the television set, where a thin young man and a fat young woman were having a food fight. Intermittently a couple of burly men in jumpsuits restrained one or both of them, only to let them resume pelting one another with bowls of salad.

"Jerry Springer," Dot said. "It's sort of a combination of *Family Court* and *WWF Wrestling*."

"How come you've got the sound off?"

"Believe me, it's worse if you can hear them."

"I can see how it would be," he said. "But lately you've always got the sound off. The picture on and the sound off."

"I know."

"If you had it the other way around I'd say you invented the radio. This way, what? The silent film?"

"I hardly look at it, Keller. Then what's it doing on—is that what you were going to ask?"

"I might have."

"For years," she said, "I only put the set on to watch something. I had my afternoon programs, and then for a while I got hooked on those home shopping channels."

"I remember."

"I never bought anything, but I would stare at the screen for hours. Part of it was there were no commercials to break your concentration."

"Whole thing's a commercial."

"Well, no kidding," she said. "I didn't delude myself that

I was watching PBS. Anyway, I watched QVC for a while, and then I got over it before I could spend my life savings on Diamonique."

"Close call."

"And then he died," she said, with a glance at the ceiling. "And he wasn't much company, especially toward the end, but the house all of a sudden felt empty without him. It's not like I was getting choked up all the time. And I didn't feel myself longing for the comfort of his presence, because when was he ever a comfort?"

"Even so."

"Even so," she said. "What I did, I took to keeping the radio going all the time. Just to have the sound of a human voice. Does that sound strange to you?"

"Not at all."

"But I'll tell you what's the trouble with radio. You can't mute the commercials."

"I had the same thought myself not long ago. You can, by turning it off, but you don't know when to turn it back on again."

"TV spoils you. Somebody starts yammering at you, telling you their flashlight batteries keep going and going and going . . ."

"I kind of like that rabbit, though."

"So do I, but I don't want to hear about it. Watching it's another matter. I tried NPR, but it's not just commercials, it's all the other crap you don't want to hear. Traffic, weather, and please-send-us-money-so-we-won't-have-to-keep-asking-you-for-money. So I started playing the TV all the time, muting it whenever it got on my nerves, and the commercials aren't so bad when you can't hear what they're saying. Some of them, with the sound off you can't even tell what they're selling."

"But you've got it mute all the time, Dot."

"What I found out," she said, "is that damn near everything on television is better with the sound off. And that

106

way it doesn't interfere with the rest of your life. You can read the paper or talk on the phone and the TV doesn't distract you. If you don't look at it, you get so that you forget it's on."

"Then why not turn it off?"

"Because it gives me the illusion that I'm not all alone in a big old barn of a house waiting for my arteries to harden. Keller, do you suppose we could change the channel? Not on the TV, on this conversation. Will you do me a big favor and change the subject?"

"Sure," he said. "Dot, have you ever noticed anything odd about my thumb?"

"Your thumb?"

"This one. Does it look strange to you?"

"You know," she said, "I've got to hand it to you, Keller. That's the most complete change of subject I've ever encountered in my life. I'd be hard put to remember what we were talking about before we started talking about your thumb."

"Well?"

"Don't tell me you're serious? Let me see. I'd have to say it looks like a plain old thumb to me, but you know what they say. You've seen one thumb . . ."

"But look, Dot. That's the whole point, that they're not identical. See how this one goes?"

"Oh, right. It's got that little . . ."

"Uh-huh."

"Are mine both the same? Like two peas in a pod, as far as I can make out. This one's got a little scar at the base, but don't ask me how I got it because I can't remember. Keller, you made your point. You've got an unusual thumb."

"Do you believe in destiny, Dot?"

"Whoa! Keller, you just switched channels again. I thought we were discussing thumbs."

"I was thinking about Louisville."

"I'm going to take the remote control away from you,

Keller. It's not safe in your hands. Louisville?"

"You remember when I went there."

"Vividly. Kids playing basketball, guy in a garage, and, if I remember correctly, the subtle magic of carbon monoxide."

"Right."

"So?"

"Remember how I had a bad feeling about it, and then a couple got killed in my old room, and—"

"I remember the whole business, Keller. What about it?"

"I guess I've just been wondering how much of life is destined and preordained. How much choice do people really have?"

"If *we* had a choice," she said, "we could be having some other conversation."

"I never set out to be what I've become. It's not like I took an aptitude test in high school and my guidance counselor took me aside and recommended a career as a killer for hire."

"You drifted into it, didn't you?"

"That's what I always thought. That's certainly what it felt like. But suppose I was just fulfilling my destiny?"

"I don't know," she said, cocking her head. "Shouldn't there be music playing in the background? There always is when they have conversations like this in one of my soap operas."

"Dot, I've got a murderer's thumb."

"Oh, for the love of God, we're back to your thumb. How did you manage that, and what in the hell are you talking about?"

"Palmistry," he said. "In palmistry, a thumb like mine is called a murderer's thumb."

"In palmistry."

"Right."

"I grant you it's an unusual-looking thumb," she said,

"although I never noticed it in all the years I've known you, and never would have noticed it if you hadn't pointed it out. But where does the murderer part come in? What do you do, kill people by running your thumb across their life line?"

"I don't think you actually do anything with your thumb."

"I don't see what you *could* do, aside from hitching a ride. Or making a rude gesture."

"All I know," he said, "is I had a murderer's thumb and I grew up to be a murderer."

" 'His Thumb Made Him Do It.' "

"Or was it the other way around? Maybe my thumb was normal at birth, and it changed as my character changed."

"That sounds crazy," she said, "but you ought to be able to clear it up, because you've been carrying that thumb around all your life. *Was* it always like that?"

"How do I know? I never paid much attention to it."

"Keller, it's your thumb."

"But did I notice it was different from other thumbs? I don't know, Dot. Maybe I should see somebody."

"That's not necessarily a bad idea," she said, "but I'd think twice before I let them put me on any medication."

"That's not what I mean," he said.

The astrologer was not what he'd expected.

Hard to say just what he'd been expecting. Someone with a lot of eye makeup, say, and long hair bound up in a scarf, and big hoop earrings—some sort of cross between a Gypsy fortune-teller and a hippie chick. What he got in Louise Carpenter was a pleasant woman in her forties who had long since thrown in the towel in the battle to maintain her figure. She had big blue-green eyes and a low-maintenance haircut, and she lived in an apartment on West End Avenue full of comfortable furniture, and she wore loose clothing and read romance novels and ate chocolate, all of which seemed to agree with her.

"It would help," she told Keller, "if we knew the precise time of your birth."

"I don't think there's any way to find out."

"Your mother has passed?"

Passed. It might be more accurate, he thought, to say that she'd failed. He said, "She died a long time ago."

"And your father . . ."

"Died before I was born," Keller said, wondering if it was true. "You asked me over the phone if there was anyone who might remember. I'm the only one who's still around, and I don't remember a thing."

"There are ways to recover a lot of early memory," she said, and popped a chocolate into her mouth. "All the way back to birth, in some instances, and I've known people who claim they can remember their own conception. But I don't know how much to credit all of that. Is it memory or is it Memorex? Besides, you probably weren't wearing a watch at the time."

"I've been thinking," he said. "I don't know the doctor's name, and he might be dead himself by this time, but I've got a copy of my birth certificate. It doesn't have the time of birth, just the date, but do you suppose the Bureau of Vital Statistics would have the information on file somewhere?"

"Possibly," she said, "but don't worry about it. I can check it."

"On the Internet? Something like that?"

She laughed. "No, not that. You said your mother mentioned getting up early in the morning to go to the hospital."

"That's what she said."

"And you were a fairly easy birth."

"Once her labor started, I came right out."

"You wanted to be here. Now you happen to be a

Gemini, John, and . . . shall I call you John?"

"If you want."

"Well, what do people generally call you?"

"Keller."

"Very well, Mr. Keller. I'm comfortable keeping it formal if you prefer it that way, and—"

"Not Mr. Keller," he said. "Just plain Keller."

"Oh."

"That's what people generally call me."

"I see. Well, Keller . . . no, I don't think that's going to work. I'm going to have to call you John."

"Okay."

"In high school kids used to call each other by their last names. It was a way to feel grown up. 'Hey, Carpenter, you finish the algebra homework?' I can't call you Keller."

"Don't worry about it."

"I'm being neurotic, I realize that, but—"

"John is fine."

"Well then," she said, and rearranged herself in the chair. "You're a Gemini, John, as I'm sure you know. A late Gemini, June nineteenth, which puts you right on the cusp of Cancer."

"Is that good?"

"Nothing's necessarily good or bad in astrology, John. But it's good in that I enjoy working with Geminis. I find it to be an extremely interesting sign."

"How so?"

"The duality. Gemini is the sign of the twins, you see." She went on talking about the properties of the sign, and he nodded, agreeing but not really taking it all in. And then she was saying, "I suppose the most interesting thing about Geminis is their relationship to the truth. Geminis are naturally duplicitous, yet they have an inner reverence for the truth that echoes their opposite number across the Zodiac. That's Sagittarius, of course, and your typical Sadge couldn't tell a lie to save his soul. Gemini can lie without a second thought, while being occasionally capable of this startling Sagittarean candor."

"I see."

He was influenced as well by Cancer, she continued, having his sun on its cusp, along with a couple of planets in that sign. And he had a Taurus moon, she told him, and that was the best possible place for the moon to be. "The moon is exalted in Taurus," she said. "Have you noticed in the course of your life how things generally turn out all right for you, even when they don't? And don't you have an inner core, a sort of bedrock stability that lets you always know who you are?"

"I don't know about that last part," he said. "I'm here, aren't I?"

"Maybe it's your Taurus moon that got you here." She reached for another chocolate. "Your time of birth determines your rising sign, and that's important in any number of ways, but in the absence of available information I'm willing to make the determination intuitively. My discipline is astrology, John, but it's not the only tool I use. I'm psychic, I sense things. My intuition tells me you have Cancer rising."

"If you say so."

"And I prepared a chart for you on that basis. I could tell you a lot of technical things about your chart, but I can't believe you're interested in all that, are you?"

"You're psychic, all right."

"So instead of nattering on about trines and squares and oppositions, let me just say it's an interesting chart. You're an extremely gentle person, John."

Oh?

"But there's so much violence in your life."

Oh.

"That's the famous Gemini duality," she was saying. "On the one hand, you're thoughtful and sensitive and calm, exceedingly calm. John, do you ever get angry?"

"Not very often."

"No, and I don't think you stifle your anger, either. I get that it's just not a part of the equation. But there's violence all around you, isn't there?"

"It's a violent world we live in."

"There's been violence swirling around you all your life. You're very much a part of it, and yet you're somehow untouched by it." She tapped the sheet of paper, with his stars and planets all marked out. "You don't have an easy chart," she said.

"I don't?"

"Actually, that's something to be grateful for. I've seen charts of people who came into the world with no serious oppositions, no difficult aspects. And they wind up with lives where nothing much happens. They're never challenged, they never have to draw upon inner resources, and so they wind up leading reasonably comfortable lives and holding secure jobs and raising their kids in a nice safe, clean suburb. And they never make anything terribly interesting of themselves."

"I haven't made much of myself," he said. "I've never married or fathered a child. Or started a business, or run for office, or planted a garden, or written a play, or . . . or . . ."

"Yes?"

"I'm sorry," he said. "I never expected to get . . ."

"Emotional?"

"Yes."

"It happens all the time."

"It does?"

"Just the other day I told a woman she's got Jupiter squaring her sun, but that her Jupiter and Mars are trined, and she burst into tears."

"I don't even know what that means."

"Neither did she."

"Oh."

"I see so much in your chart, John. This is a difficult time for you, isn't it?"

"I guess it must be."

"Not financially. Your Jupiter—well, you're not rich, and you're never going to be rich, but the money always seems to be there when you need it, doesn't it?"

"It's never been a problem."

"No, and it won't be. You've found ways to spend it in the past couple of years"—stamps, he thought—"and that's good, because now you're getting some pleasure out of your money. But you won't overspend, and you'll always be able to get more."

"That's good."

"But you didn't come here because you were concerned about money."

"No."

"You don't care that much about it. You always liked to get it and now you like to spend it, but you never cared deeply about it."

"No."

"I've prepared a solar return," she said, "to give you an idea what to expect in the next twelve months. Some astrologers are very specific—'July seventeenth is the perfect time to start a new project, and don't even think about being on water on the fifth of September.' My approach is more general, and . . . John? Why are you holding your right hand like that?"

"I beg your pardon?"

"With the thumb tucked inside. Is there something about your thumb that bothers you?"

"Not really."

"I've already seen your thumb, John."

"Oh."

"Did someone once tell you something about your thumb?"

"Yes."

"That it's a murderer's thumb?" She rolled her eyes. "Palmistry," she said heavily.

"You don't believe in it?"

"Of course I believe in it, but it does lend itself to some gross oversimplification." She reached out and took his hand in both of hers. Hers were soft, he noted, and pudgy, but not unpleasantly so. She ran a fingertip over his thumb, his homicidal thumb.

"To take a single anatomical characteristic," she said, "and fasten such a dramatic name to it. No one's thumb ever made him kill a fellow human being."

"Then why do they call it that?"

"I'm afraid I haven't studied the history of palmistry. I suppose someone spotted the peculiarity in a few notorious murderers and spread the word. I'm not even certain it's statistically more common among murderers than the general population. I doubt anyone really knows. John, it's an insignificant phenomenon and not worth noticing."

"But you noticed it," he said.

"I happened to see it."

"And you recognized it. You didn't say anything until you noticed me hiding it in my fist. That was unconscious, I didn't even know I was doing it."

"I see."

"So it must mean something," he said, "or why would it stay in your mind?"

She was still holding his hand. Keller had noticed that this was one of the ways a woman let you know she was interested in you. Women touched you a lot in completely innocent ways, on the hand or the arm or the shoulder, or held your hand longer than they had to. If a man did that it was sexual harassment, but it was a woman's way of letting you know she wouldn't mind being harassed herself.

But this was different. There was no sexual charge with this woman. If he'd been made of chocolate he might have had something to worry about, but mere flesh and blood was safe in her presence.

"John," she said gently, "I was looking for it."

"For . . ."

"The thumb. Or anything else that might confirm what I already knew about you."

She was gazing into his eyes as she spoke, and he wondered how much shock registered in them. He tried not to react, but how did you keep what you felt from showing up in your eyes?

"And what's that, Louise?"

"That I know about you?"

He nodded.

"That your life has been filled with violence, but I think I already mentioned that."

"You said I was gentle and not full of anger."

"But you've had to kill people, John."

"Who told you that?" She was no longer holding his hand. Had she released it? Or had he taken it away from her?

"Who told me?"

Maggie, he thought. Who else could it have been? Maggie was the only person they knew in common. But how did Maggie know? In her eyes he was a corporate suburbanite, even if he lived alone in the heart of the city.

"Actually," she was saying, "I had several informants."

His heart was hammering. What was she saying? How could it be true?

"Let me see, John. There was Saturn, and Mars, and we don't want to forget Mercury." Her tone was soft, her gaze so gentle. "John," she said, "it's in your chart."

"My chart."

"I picked up on it right away. I got a very strong hit while I was working on your chart, and when you rang the bell I knew I would be opening the door to a man who had done a great deal of killing."

"I'm surprised you didn't cancel the appointment."

"I considered it. Something told me not to."

"A little bird?"

"An inner prompting. Or maybe it was curiosity. I wanted to see what you looked like."

"And?"

"Well, I knew right away I hadn't made a mistake with your chart."

"Because of my thumb?"

"No, though it was interesting to have that extra bit of confirmation. And the most revealing thing about your thumb was the effort you made to conceal it. But the vibration I picked up from you was far more revealing than anything about your thumb."

"The vibration."

"I don't know a better way to put it. Sometimes the intuitive part of the mind picks up things the five senses are blind and deaf to. Sometimes a person just knows something."

"Yes."

"I knew you were . . ."

"A killer," he supplied.

"Well, a man who has killed. And in a very dispassionate way, too. It's not personal for you, is it, John?"

"Sometimes a personal element comes into it."

"But not often."

"No."

"It's business."

"Yes."

"John? You don't have to be afraid of me."

Could she read his mind? He hoped not. Because what came to him now was that he was not afraid of her, but of what he might have to do to her.

And he didn't want to. She was a nice woman, and he sensed she would be able to tell him things it would be good for him to hear.

"You don't have to fear that I'll do anything, or say

anything to anyone. You don't even need to fear my disapproval."

"Oh?"

"I don't make many moral judgments, John. The more I see, the less I'm sure I know what's right and what's wrong. Once I accepted myself "—she reached, grinning, for a chocolate—"I found it easier to accept other people. Thumbs and all."

He looked at his thumb, then raised his eyes to meet hers.

"Besides," she said, very gently, "I think you've done wonderfully in life, John." She tapped his chart. "I know what you started with. I think you've turned out just fine."

He tried to say something, but the words got stuck in his throat.

"It's all right," she said. "Go right ahead and cry. Never be ashamed to cry, John. It's all right."

And she drew his head to her breast and held him while, astonished, he sobbed his heart out.

CHAPTER TEN

"Well, that's a first," he said. "I don't know what I expected from astrology, but it wasn't tears."

"They wanted to come out. You've had them stored up for a while, haven't you?"

"Forever. I was in therapy for a while and never even got choked up."

"That would have been when? Three years ago?"

"How did you . . . It's in my chart?"

"Not therapy per se, but I saw there was a period when you were ready for self-exploration. But I don't believe you stayed with it for very long."

"A few months. I got a lot of insight out of it, but in the end I felt I had to put an end to it."

Dr. Breen, the therapist, had had his own agenda, and it had conflicted seriously with Keller's. The therapy had ended abruptly, and so, not coincidentally, had Breen.

He wouldn't let that happen with Louise Carpenter.

"This isn't therapy," she told him now, "but it can be a powerful experience. As you just found out."

"I'll say. But we must have used up our fifty minutes." He looked at his watch. "We went way over. I'm sorry. I didn't realize."

"I told you it's not therapy, John. We don't worry about the clock. And I never book more than two clients a day, one in the morning and one in the afternoon. We have all the time we need."

"Oh."

"And we need to talk about what you're going through. This is a difficult time for you, isn't it?"

Was it?

"I'm afraid the coming twelve months will continue to be difficult," she went on, "as long as Saturn's where it is. Difficult and dangerous. But I suppose danger is something you've learned to live with."

"It's not that dangerous," he said. "What I do."

"Really?"

Dangerous to others, he thought. "Not to me," he said. "Not particularly. There's always a risk, and you have to keep your guard up, but it's not as though you have to be on edge all the time."

"What, John?"

"I beg your pardon?"

"You had a thought, it just flashed across your face."

"I'm surprised you can't tell me what it was."

"If I had to guess," she said, "I'd say you thought of something that contradicted the sentence you just spoke. About not having to be on edge all the time."

"That's what it was, all right."

"This would have been fairly recent."

"You can really tell all that? I'm sorry, I keep doing that. Yes, it was recent. A few months ago."

"Because the period of danger would have begun during the fall."

"That's when it was." And, without getting into specifics at all, he talked about his trip to Louisville, and how everything had seemed to be going wrong. "And there was a knock on the door of my room," he said, "and I panicked, which is not like me at all."

"No."

"I grabbed something"—a gun—"and stood next to the door, and my heart was hammering, and it was nothing but some drunk who couldn't find his friend. I was all set to kill him in self-defense, and all he did was knock on the wrong door."

"It must have been upsetting."

"The most upsetting part was seeing how upset I got.

That didn't get my pulse racing like the knock on the door did, but the effects lasted longer. It still bothers me, to tell the truth."

"Because the reaction was unwarranted. But maybe you really were in danger, John. Not from the drunk, but from something invisible."

"Like what, anthrax spores?"

"Invisible to you, but not necessarily to the naked eye. Some unknown adversary, some secret enemy."

"That's how it felt. But it doesn't make any sense."

"Do you want to tell me about it?"

Did he?

"I changed my room," he said.

"Because of the drunk who knocked on your door?"

"No, why would I do that? But a couple of nights later I couldn't sleep because of noise from the people upstairs. I had to keep my room that night, the place was full, but I let them put me in a new room first thing the next morning. And that night . . ."

"Yes?"

"Two people checked into my old room. A man and a woman. They were murdered."

"In the room you'd just moved out of."

"It was her husband. She was there with somebody else, and the husband must have followed them. Shot them both. But I couldn't get past the fact that it was my room. Like if I hadn't changed my room, her husband would have come after me."

"But he wasn't anyone you knew."

"No, far from it."

"And yet you felt as though you'd had a narrow escape."

"But of course that's ridiculous."

She shook her head. "You could have been killed, John."

"How? I kept thinking the same thing myself, but it's just not true. The only reason the killer came to the room was because of the two people who were in it. They were

121

what drew him, not the room itself. So how could he have ever been a danger to me?"

"There was a danger, though."

"The chart tells you that?"

She nodded solemnly, holding up one hand with the thumb and forefinger half an inch apart. "You and Death," she said, "came this close to one another."

"That's how it *felt*! But—"

"Forget the husband, forget what happened in that room. The woman's husband was never a threat to you, but someone else was. You were out there where the ice was very thin, John, and that's a good metaphor, because a skater never realizes the ice is thin until it cracks."

"But—"

"But it didn't," she said. "Whatever endangered you, the danger passed. Then those two people were killed, and that got your attention."

"Like ice cracking," he said, "but on another pond. I'll have to think about this."

"I'm sure you will."

He cleared his throat. "Louise? Is it all written in the stars, and do we just walk through it down here on earth?"

"No."

"You can look at that piece of paper," he said, "and you can say, 'Well, you'll come very close to death on such and such of a day, but you'll get through it safe and sound.' "

"Only the first part. 'You'll come very close to death'— I could have looked at this and told you that much. But I wouldn't have been able to tell you that you'd survive. The stars show propensities and dictate probabilities, but the future is never entirely predictable. And we do have free will."

"If those people hadn't been killed, and if I'd just gone on home—"

"Yes?"

"Well, I'd be here having this conversation, and you'd

122

tell me what a close shave I'd had, and I'd figure it for just so much starshine. I'd had a feeling, but I would have forgotten all about it. So I'd look at you and say, 'Yeah, right,' and turn the page."

"You can be grateful to the man and woman."

"And to the guy who shot them, as far as that goes. And to the bikers who made all the noise in the first place. And to Ralph."

"Who was Ralph?"

"The drunk's friend, the one he was looking for in all the wrong places. I can be grateful to the drunk, too, except I don't know his name. But then I don't know any of their names, except for Ralph."

"Maybe the names aren't important."

"I used to know the name of the man and woman, and of the man who shot them, the husband. I can't remember them now. You're right, the names aren't important."

"No."

He looked at her. "The next year . . ."

"Will be dangerous."

"What do I have to worry about? Should I think twice before I get on an airplane? Put on an extra sweater on windy days? Can you tell me where the threat's coming from?"

She hesitated, then said, "You have an enemy, John."

"An enemy?"

"An enemy. There's someone out there who wants to kill you."

CHAPTER ELEVEN

"I don't know," he told Dot.

"You don't know? Keller, what's to know? What could be simpler? It's in Boston, for God's sake, not on the dark side of the moon. You take a cab to La Guardia, you hop on the Delta Shuttle, you don't even need a reservation, and half an hour later you're on the ground at Logan. You take a cab into the city, you do the thing you do best, and you're on the shuttle again before the day is over, and back in your own apartment in plenty of time for Jay Leno. The money's right, the client's strictly blue chip, and the job's a piece of cake."

"I understand all that, Dot."

"But?"

"I don't know."

"Keller," she said, "clearly I'm missing something. Help me out here. What part of 'I don't know' don't I understand?"

I don't know, he very nearly answered, but caught himself in time. In high school, a teacher had taken the class to task for those very words. "The way you use it," she said, " 'I don't know' is a lie. It's not what you mean at all. What you mean is 'I don't want to say' or 'I'm afraid to tell you.' "

"Hey, Keller," one of the other boys had called out. "What's the capital of South Dakota?"

"I'm afraid to tell you," he'd replied.

And what was he afraid to tell Dot? That the Boston job just wasn't in the stars? That the day the client had selected as ideal, this coming Wednesday, was a day specifically noted by his astrologer—his astrologer!—as a day fraught with danger, a day when he would be at extreme risk.

("So what do I do on those days?" he'd asked her. "Stay in bed with the door locked? Order all my meals delivered?" "The first part's not a terrible idea," she'd advised him, "but I'd be careful who was on the other side of the door before I opened it. And I'd be careful what I ate, too." The kid from the Chinese restaurant could be a Ninja assassin, he thought. The beef with oyster sauce could be laced with cyanide.)

"Keller?"

"The thing is, Wednesday's not the best day for me. There was something I'd planned on doing."

"What have you got, tickets to a matinee?"

"No."

"No, of course not. It's a stamp auction, isn't it? The thing is, Wednesday's the day the subject goes to his girl-friend's apartment in Back Bay, and he has to sneak over there, so he leaves his security people behind. Which makes it far and away the easiest time to get next to him."

"And she's part of the package, the girlfriend?"

"Your call, whatever you want. She's in or she's out, whatever works."

"And it doesn't matter how? Doesn't have to be an accident, doesn't have to look like an execution?"

"Anything you want. You can plunge the son of a bitch into a vat of lanolin and soften him to death. Anything at all, just so he doesn't have a pulse when you're through with him."

Hard job to say no to, he thought. Hard job to say *I don't know* to.

"I suppose the following Wednesday might work," Dot said. "The client would rather not wait, but my guess is he will if he has to. He said I was the first person he called, but I don't believe it. He's the type of guy's not that comfortable doing business with a woman. Our kind of business, anyway. So I think I was more like the third or fourth person he called, and I think he'll wait a week if I tell him he has to. Do you want me to see?"

Was he really going to lie in bed waiting for the bogey-man to get him?

"No, don't do that," he said. "This Wednesday's fine."

"Are you sure?"

"I'm sure," he said. He wasn't sure, he was miles short of sure, but it had a much better ring to it than *I don't know.*

Tuesday, the day before he was supposed to go to Boston, Keller had a strong urge to call Louise Carpenter. It had been a couple of weeks since she'd gone over his chart with him, and he wouldn't be seeing her again for a year. He'd thought it might turn out to be like therapy, with weekly appointments, and he knew some of her clients dropped in frequently for an astrological tune-up and oil change, but he gathered that astrology was a sort of hobby for them. He already had a hobby, and Louise seemed to think an annual checkup was sufficient, and that was fine with him.

So he'd see her in a year's time. If he was still alive.

The forecast for Wednesday was rain and more rain, and when he woke up he saw they weren't kidding. It was a bleak, gray day, and the rain was coming down hard. An apologetic announcer on New York One said the down-pour was expected to continue throughout the day and evening, accompanied by high winds and low tempera-tures. The way he was carrying on, you'd have thought it was his fault.

Keller put on a suit and tie, good protective coloration in a formal kind of city like Boston, and the standard uni-form on the air shuttle. He got his trench coat out of the closet, put it on, and wasn't crazy about what he saw in the mirror. The salesman had called it olive, and maybe it was, at least in the store under their fluorescent lights. In the cold damp light of a rainy morning, however, the damn thing looked green.

Not shamrock green, not Kelly green, not even putting green. But it was green, all right. You could slip into it on St. Patrick's Day and march up Fifth Avenue, and no one would mistake you for an Orangeman. No question about it, the sucker was green.

In the ordinary course of things, the coat's color wouldn't have bothered him. It wasn't so green as to bring on stares and catcalls, just green enough to draw the occasional appreciative glance. And there was a certain convenience in having a coat that didn't look like every other coat on the rack. You knew it on sight, and you could point it out to the cloakroom attendant when you couldn't find the check. "Right there, a little to your left," you'd say. "The green one."

But when you were flying up to Boston to kill a man, you didn't want to stand out in a crowd. You wanted to blend right in, to look like everybody else. Keller, in his unremarkable suit and tie, looked pretty much like everybody else.

In his coat, no question, he stood out.

Could he skip the coat? No, it was cold outside, and it would be colder in Boston. Wear his other topcoat, unobtrusively beige? No, it was porous, and he'd get soaked. He'd take an umbrella, but that wouldn't help much, not with a strong wind driving the rain.

What if he bought another coat?

But that was ridiculous. He'd have to wait for the stores to open, and then he'd spend an hour picking out the new coat and dropping off the old one at his apartment. And for what? There weren't going to be any witnesses in Boston, and anyone who did happen to see him go into the building would only remember the coat.

And maybe that was a plus. Like putting on a postman's uniform or a priest's collar, or dressing up as Santa Claus.

People remembered what you were wearing, but that was all they remembered. Nobody noticed anything else about you that might be distinctive. Your thumb, for instance. And, once you took off the uniform or the collar or the red suit and the beard, you became invisible.

Ordinarily he wouldn't have had to think twice. But this was an ominous day, one of the days his motherly astrologer had warned him about, and that made every little detail something to worry about.

And wasn't that silly? He had an enemy, and this enemy was trying to kill him, and on this particular day he was particularly at risk. And he had an assignment to kill a man, and that task inevitably carried risks of its own.

And, with all that going on, he was worrying about the coat he was wearing? That it was too discernibly *green*, for God's sake?

Get over it, he told himself.

A cab took him to La Guardia and a plane took him to Logan, where another cab dropped him in front of the Ritz-Carlton Hotel. He walked through the lobby, came out on Newbury Street, and walked along looking for a sporting goods store. He walked a while without seeing one, and wasn't sure Newbury Street was the place for it. Antiques, leather goods, designer clothes, Limoges boxes—that was what you bought here, not Polartec sweats and climbing gear.

Or hunting knives. If you could find such an article here in Back Bay, it would probably have an ivory handle and a sterling silver blade, along with a three-figure price tag. He was sure it would be a beautiful object, and worth every penny, but how would he feel about tossing it down a storm drain when he was done with it?

Anyway, was it a good idea to buy a hunting knife in the middle of a big city on a rainy spring day in the middle of the week? Deer season was, what, seven or eight months off? How many hunting knives would be sold in Boston today? How many of them would be bought by men in green trench coats?

In a stationery store he browsed among the desk accessories and picked out a letter opener with a sturdy chrome-plated steel blade and an inlaid onyx handle. The salesgirl put it in a gift box without asking. It evidently didn't occur to her that anyone might buy an item like that for himself.

And in a sense Keller hadn't. He'd bought it for Alvin Thurnauer, and now it was time to deliver it.

That was the subject's name, Alvin Thurnauer, and Keller had seen a photograph of a big, outdoorsy guy with a full head of light brown hair. Along with the photo, the client had supplied an address on Exeter Street and a set of keys, one for the front door and one for the second-floor apartment where Thurnauer and his girlfriend would be playing Thank God It's Wednesday.

Thurnauer generally showed up around two, Dot had told him, and Keller was planted in a doorway across the street by half past one. The air was a little colder in Boston, and the wind a little stiffer, but the rain was about the same as it had been in New York. Keller's coat was waterproof, and his umbrella had not yet been blown inside-out, but he still didn't stay a hundred percent dry. You couldn't, not when the rain came at you like God was pitching sidearm.

Maybe that was the risk. On a fateful day, you stood in the rain in Boston and caught your death of cold.

He toughed it out, and shortly before two a cab pulled up and a man got out, bundled up anonymously enough in a hat and coat, neither of them green. Keller's heart quickened. It could have been Thurnauer—it could have been anybody—and the fellow did stand looking across at the right house for a long moment before turning and heading off down the street. Keller gave up watching him when he got a couple of houses away. He retreated into the shadows, waiting for Thurnauer.

Who showed up right on time. Two on the button on Keller's watch, and there was the man himself, easy to spot as he got out of his cab because he wasn't wearing a hat. The mop of brown hair was a perfect field mark, identifiable at a glance.

Do it now?

It was doable. Just because he had keys didn't mean he had to use them. He could dart across the street and catch up with Thurnauer before the man had the front door open. Do him on the spot, shove him into the vestibule where the whole world wouldn't see him, and be out of sight himself in seconds.

That way he wouldn't have to worry about the girlfriend. But there might be other witnesses, people passing on the street, some moody citizen staring out the window at the rain. And he'd be awfully visible racing across the street in his green coat. And the letter opener was still in its box, so he'd have to use his hands.

And by the time he'd weighed all these considerations the moment had passed and Thurnauer was inside the house.

Just as well. If a roll in the hay was going to cost Thurnauer his life, let him at least have a chance to enjoy it. That was better than rushing in and doing a slapdash job. Thurnauer could have an extra thirty or forty minutes of life, and Keller could get out of the goddam rain and have a cup of coffee.

At the lunch counter, feeling only a little like one of the lonely guys in his Edward Hopper poster, Keller remembered that he hadn't eaten all day. He'd somehow missed breakfast, which was unusual for him.

Well, it was a high-risk day, wasn't it? Pneumonia, starvation—there were a lot of hazards out there.

Eating would have to wait. He didn't have the time, and he never liked to work on a full stomach. It made you sluggish, slowed your reflexes, spoiled your judgment. Better to wait and have a proper meal afterward.

While his coffee was cooling he went to the men's room and took the letter opener out of its gift box, which he discarded. He put the letter opener in his jacket pocket where he could reach it in a hurry. You couldn't cut with it, the blade's edge was rounded, but it came to a good sharp point. But was it sharp enough to penetrate several layers of cloth? Just as well he hadn't acted on the spur of the moment. Wait for Thurnauer to get out of his coat and jacket and shirt, and then the letter opener would have an easier time of it.

He drank his coffee, donned his green coat, picked up his umbrella, and went back to finish the job.

CHAPTER TWELVE

Nothing to it, really.

The keys worked. He didn't run into anybody in the entryway or on the stairs. He listened at the door of the second-floor apartment, heard music playing and water running, and let himself in.

He put down his umbrella, took off his coat, slipped off his shoes, and made his way in silence through the living room and along a hallway to the bedroom door. That was where the music was coming from, and it was where the woman, a slender dishwater blonde with translucent white skin, was sitting cross-legged on the edge of an unmade bed, smoking a cigarette.

She looked frighteningly vulnerable, and Keller hoped he wouldn't have to hurt her. If he could get Thurnauer alone, if he could do the man and get out without being seen, then he could let her live. If she saw him, well, then all bets were off.

The shower stopped running, and a moment later the bathroom door opened. A man emerged with a dark green towel around his waist. The guy was completely bald, and Keller wondered how the hell he'd managed to wind up in the wrong apartment. Then he realized it was Thurnauer after all. The guy had taken off his hair before he got in the shower.

Thurnauer walked over to the bed, made a face, and reached to take the cigarette away from the girl, stubbing it out in an ashtray. "I wish to God you'd quit," he said.

"And I wish you'd quit wishing I would quit," she said. "I've tried. I can't quit, all right? Not everybody's got your goddam willpower."

"There's the gum," he said.

"I started smoking to get out of the habit of chewing gum. I hate how it looks, grown women chewing gum, like a herd of cows."

"Or the patch," he said. "Why can't you wear a patch?"

"That was my last cigarette," she said.

"You know, you've said that before, and much as I'd like to believe it—"

"No, you moron," she snapped. "It was the last one I've got with me, not the last one I'm ever going to smoke. If you had to play the stern daddy and take a cigarette away from me, did it have to be my last one?"

"You can buy more."

"No kidding," she said. "You're damn right I can buy more."

"Go take a shower," Thurnauer said.

"I don't want to take a shower."

"You'll cool off and feel better."

"You mean I'll cool off and *you'll* feel better. Anyway, you just took a shower and you came out grumpy as a bear with a sore foot. The hell with taking a shower."

"Take one."

"Why? What's the matter, do I stink? Or do you just want to get me out of the room so you can make a phone call?"

"Mavis, for Christ's sake . . ."

"You can call some other girl who doesn't smoke and doesn't sweat and—"

"Mavis—"

"Oh, go to hell," Mavis said. "I'm gonna go take a shower. And put your hair on, will you? You look like a damn cue ball."

The shower was running and Thurnauer was hunched over her makeup mirror, adjusting his hairpiece, when Keller got a hand over his mouth and plunged the letter opener into his back, fitting it deftly between two ribs and driving it home into his heart. The big man had no time to struggle; by the time he knew what was happening, it had already happened. His body convulsed once, then went slack, and Keller lowered him to the floor.

The shower was still running. Keller could be out the door before she was out of the shower. But as soon as she did come out she would see Thurnauer, and she'd know at a glance that he was dead, and she'd scream and yell and carry on and call 911, and who needed that?

Besides, the pity he'd felt for her had dried up during her argument with her lover. He'd responded to a sense of her vulnerability, a fragile quality that he'd since decided was conveyed by that see-through skin of hers. She was actually a whining, sniping, carping nag of a woman, and about as fragile as an army boot.

So, when she stepped out of the bathroom, he took her from behind and broke her neck. He left her where she fell, just as he'd left Thurnauer on the bedroom floor. You could try to set a scene, make it look as though she had stabbed him and then broke her neck in a fall, but it would never fool anybody, so why bother? The client had merely stipulated that the man be dead, and that's what Keller had delivered.

It was sort of a shame about the girl, but it wasn't all that much of a shame. She was no Mother Teresa. And you couldn't let sentiment get in the way. That was always a bad idea, and especially on a high-risk day.

There were good restaurants in Boston, and Keller thought about going to Locke-Ober's, say, and treating himself to a really good meal. But the timing was wrong. It was just after three, too late for lunch and too early for dinner. If he went someplace decent they would just stare at him.

He could kill a couple of hours. He hadn't brought his catalog, so there was no point making the rounds of the stamp shops, but he could see a movie, or go to a museum.

It couldn't be that hard to find a way to get through an afternoon, not in a city like Boston, for God's sake.

On a nicer day he'd have been happy enough just walking around Back Bay or Beacon Hill. Boston was a good city for walking, not as good as New York, but better than most cities. With the rain still coming down, though, walking was no pleasure, and cabs were hard to come by.

Keller, back on Newbury Street, walked until he found an upscale coffee shop that looked okay. It wasn't going to remind anybody of Locke-Ober, but it was here and they would serve him now, and he was too hungry to wait.

The waitress wanted to know what the problem was. "It's my coat," Keller told her.

"What happened to your coat?"

"Well, that's the problem," he said. "I hung it on the hook over there, and it's gone."

"You sure it's not there?"

"Positive."

"Because coats tend to look alike, and there's coats hanging there, and—"

"Mine is green."

"Green green? Or more like an olive green?"

What difference did it make? There were three coats over there, all of them shades of beige, none at all like his. "The salesman called it olive," he said, "but it was pretty green. And it's not here."

"Are you sure you had it when you came in?"

Keller pointed at the window. "It's been like that all day," he said. "What kind of an idiot would go out without a coat?"

"Maybe you left it somewhere else."

Was it possible? He'd shucked the coat in the Exeter Street living room. Could he have left it there?

No, not a chance. He remembered putting it on, remembered opening his umbrella when he hit the street,

135

remembered hanging both coat and umbrella on the peg before he slid into the booth and reached for the menu. And where was the umbrella? Gone, just like the coat.

"I didn't leave it anywhere else," he said firmly. "I was wearing the coat when I came in, and I hung it up right there, and it's not there now. And neither is my umbrella."

"Somebody must of taken it by mistake."

"How? It's green."

"Maybe they're color-blind," she suggested. "Or they got a green coat at home, and they forgot they were wearing the tan one today, so they took yours by mistake. When they bring it back—"

"Nobody's going to bring it back. Somebody stole my coat."

"Why would anybody steal a coat?"

"Probably because he didn't have a coat of his own," Keller said patiently, "and it's pouring out there, and he didn't want to get wet any more than I do. The three coats on the wall belong to your three other customers, and I'm not going to steal a coat from one of them, and the guy who stole my coat's not going to bring it back, so what am I supposed to do?"

"We're not responsible," she said, and pointed to a sign that agreed with her. Keller wasn't convinced the sign was enough to get the restaurant off the hook, but it didn't matter. He wasn't about to sue them.

"If you want me to call the police so you can report it . . ."

"I just want to get out of here," he said. "I need a cab, but I could drown out there waiting for an empty one to come along."

She brightened, able at last to suggest something. "Right over there," she said. "The hotel? There's a canopy'll keep you dry, and there's cabs pulling up and dropping people off all day long. And you know what? I'll bet Angela at the register's got an umbrella you can take. People leave them here all the time, and unless it's raining they never think to come back for them."

The girl at the cash register supplied a black folding umbrella, flimsy but serviceable. "I remember that coat," she said. "Green. I saw it come in and I saw it go out, but I never realized it was two different people coming and going. It was what you would call a very distinctive garment. Do you think you'll be able to replace it?"

"It won't be easy," he said.

"**Y**ou didn't want to do this one," Dot said, "and I couldn't figure out why. It looked like a walk in the park, and it turns out that's exactly what it was."

"A walk in the rain," he said. "I had my coat stolen."

"And your umbrella. Well, there are some unscrupulous people out there, Keller, even in a decent town like Boston. You can buy a new coat."

"I never should have bought that one in the first place."

"It was green, you said."

"Too green."

"What were you doing, waiting for it to ripen?"

"It's somebody else's problem now," he said. "The next one's going to be beige."

"You can't go wrong with beige," she said. "Not too light, though, or it shows everything. My advice would be to lean toward the Desert Sand end of the spectrum."

"Whatever." He looked at her television set. "I wonder what they're talking about."

"Nothing as interesting as raincoats, would be my guess. I could unmute the thing, but I think we're better off wondering."

"You're probably right. I wonder if that was it. Losing the raincoat, I mean."

"You wonder if what was what?"

"The feeling I had."

"You did have a feeling about Boston, didn't you? It

wasn't a stamp auction. You didn't want to take the job."

"I took it, didn't I?"

"But you didn't want to. Tell me more about this feeling, Keller."

"It was just a feeling," he said. He wasn't ready to tell her about his horoscope. He could imagine how she'd react, and he didn't want to hear it.

"You had a feeling another time," she said. "In Louisville."

"That was a little different."

"And both times the jobs went fine."

"That's true."

"So where do you suppose these feelings are coming from? Any idea?"

"Not really. It wasn't that strong a feeling this time, anyway. And I took the job, and I did it."

"And it went smooth as silk."

"More or less," he said.

"More or less?"

"I used a letter opener."

"What for? Sorry, dumb question. What did you do, pick it up off his desk?"

"Bought it on the way there."

"In Boston?"

"Well, I didn't want to take it through the metals detector. I bought it in Boston, and I took it with me when I left."

"Naturally. And chucked it in a Dumpster or down a sewer. Except you didn't or you wouldn't have brought up the subject. Oh, for Christ's sake, Keller. The coat pocket?"

"Along with the keys."

"What keys? Oh, hell, the keys to the apartment. A set of keys and a murder weapon and you're carrying them around in your coat pocket."

"They were going down a storm drain before I went to the airport," he said, "but first I wanted to get something

138

to eat, and the next thing I knew my coat was gone."

"And the thief got more than just a coat."

"And an umbrella."

"Forget the umbrella, will you? Besides the coat he got keys and a letter opener. There's no little tag on the keys, tells the address, or is there?"

"Just two keys on a plain wire ring."

"And I hope you didn't let them engrave your initials on the letter opener."

"No, and I wiped it clean," he said. "But still."

"Nothing to lead to you."

"No."

"But still," she said.

"That's what I said. 'But still.' "

Back in the city, Keller picked up the Boston papers. Both covered the murder in detail. Alvin Thurnauer, it turned out, was a prominent local businessman with connections to local political interests and, the papers hinted, to less savory elements as well. That he'd died violently in a Back Bay love nest, along with a blonde to whom he was not married, did nothing to diminish the news value of his death.

Both papers assured him that the police were pursuing various leads. Keller, reading between the lines, concluded that they didn't have a clue. They might guess that someone had contracted to have Thurnauer hit, and they might be able to guess who that someone was, but they wouldn't be able to go anywhere with it. There were no witnesses, no useful physical evidence.

He almost missed the second murder.

The *Globe* didn't have it. But there it was in the *Herald*, a small story on a back page, a man found dead on Boston Common, shot twice in the head with a small-calibre weapon.

Keller could picture the poor bastard, lying facedown

on the grass, the rain washing relentlessly down on him. He could picture the dead man's coat, too. The *Herald* didn't say anything about a coat, but that didn't matter. Keller could picture it all the same.

He went home and made some phone calls. The next morning he went out first thing and bought the *Globe* and the *Herald* and read them both over breakfast. Then he made one more phone call and caught a train.

CHAPTER THIRTEEN

"His name was Louis 'Why Not?' Minot," he told Dot. "No ID on the body, but his prints were on file. He had a dozen arrests on charges ranging from petty theft to bad checks."

"Well, you wondered what kind of man would steal another man's raincoat. A small-time crook, that's what kind."

"Somebody gave him two in the head with a twenty-two."

"Mathematically, that's the same as one with a forty-four."

"It was enough. Gun was silenced, would be my guess, but there's no way to tell. Minot was walking on the Common, someone waited until there was nobody nearby, not hard to manage with the weather as bad as it was. Went up to him, popped him, and walked away."

"Must have been a vigilante," Dot said. "Whenever he sees someone steal a coat, he wreaks vengeance. Charles Bronson can play him in the movie."

"What do you know about our client, Dot?"

"I can't believe this came from him. I just can't."

"What must have happened," he said, "is someone was watching the house on Exeter Street. As a matter of fact . . ."

"What?"

"There was a cab came along, dropped a guy in front of the place. I thought it was him, what's his name, Thurnauer. Not that there was a resemblance, but I was seeing him from the back, watching him take a long look at the house across the street. But he walked away. Except maybe he just walked a little ways off and waited."

"And saw you go in and come out."

"In my pretty green coat. Then he tagged me to the place where I had lunch, and then he picked me up when I left, except this time it wasn't me."

"It was Louis Minot."

"Wearing my coat. A day like that, rain coming down hard, he wouldn't get too good a look at my face. The coat would do it. He stayed with the coat. Minot walked over to the Common, the shooter followed him, picked his moment . . ."

"Bang bang."

"Or pop pop, if he used a suppressor."

"Who knew you were going to Exeter Street? Answer: the client. But I still can't believe it."

"The cops believe it."

"How's that?"

"We already know what color Minot's coat was. Do you want to guess what he had in the pockets?"

"The keys and the knife."

"Letter opener."

"Whatever. I forgot about them, Keller. The cops made the connection?"

"Well, how could they miss it? One guy's stabbed to death and another guy turns up dead less than a mile away with a letter opener in his pocket? They found blood traces on it, too."

"I thought you wiped it."

"I wiped it, I didn't run it through a car wash. They found traces. Probably not enough for a DNA match, but they can type it, and it'll be the same type as Thurnauer's."

"And the letter opener fits the wound."

"Right. And the keys fit the locks."

She nodded slowly. "Not hard to reconstruct. Minot moved up in class and took a contract, iced Thurnauer on Exeter Street and kept a date on Boston Common to get paid off. And got shot instead, bang bang or pop pop, because dead men tell no tales."

"That's how they figure it."

"But we know better, don't we, Keller? Minot said 'Why not?' to the wrong coat, and got himself killed by mistake. By somebody working for our client."

"You just got finished saying you couldn't believe it."

"Well, what choice have I got, Keller? I have to believe it, whether I want to or not."

"Not necessarily."

"Oh?"

"I was up most of the night," he said. "Thinking about things. Do you remember Louisville?"

"Do I remember Louisville? As if I could forget. The smell of bluegrass, the taste of a tall mint julep in a frosty glass. The packed stands at Churchill Downs, the horses thundering down the stretch. Keller, I've never been to Louisville, so what's to remember?"

"You know what I mean."

"Your trip there, the other time you had a bad feeling. And a husband tracked his cheating wife to your motel and killed her and her boyfriend in your old room."

"Capped them with two in the head from a twenty-two."

"Jesus Christ. But they got the husband for it, remember?"

"He didn't do it."

"You sure?"

"The cops are," he told her. "His alibi held up."

"Do they have anybody else they like for it?"

"I don't think they're looking too hard," he said, "because they still like the husband. They think he arranged it, although he doesn't seem like the kind of a guy who could arrange a three-car funeral. But they think he hired someone else to follow the wife and kill her in the act. Because it sure looked like a pro hit."

"Two in the head, di dah di dah di dah."

"Rings a bell, doesn't it?"

"Ding fucking dong. A whole carillon. Give me a minute, will you? And turn that damn thing off, I can't hear myself think."

The TV had the sound off, the way she generally had it, but he knew what she meant. He hit the Power button and the screen went dark.

After a long moment she said, "It wasn't the client in Louisville and it's not the client in Boston. It was somebody else who was after you personally."

"Only way it adds up."

"Only way I can see, Keller. It can't be some avenging angel, has to even the score for Thurnauer or the guy in Louisville—"

"Hirschhorn."

"Whatever. In Boston he staked the place out, waited for you to do it, then made his move. He didn't care if Thurnauer got killed, just so he got his shot at you."

"And in Louisville . . ."

"In Louisville he must have been watching Hirschhorn's house. After you gassed the guy in his garage, he followed you back to the motel and—"

"And?"

"Doesn't work, does it? He couldn't have followed you back to the room you already checked out of twelve hours ago."

"Keep going, Dot."

"I'll tell you, it'd be easier if I had a map and a flashlight. I'm in the dark here. If he went to the wrong room, the old room, it's because he already knew where you were staying. He knew about the room before you did Hirschhorn."

"Bingo."

"*Definitely* not the client," she said, "because how would he know where you were staying? He didn't even know

144

who you were. Keller, I'm bumping into the furniture here. Help me out, will you?"

"Remember the drunk?"

"Looking for his friend, wasn't he? What was the friend's name?"

"What difference does it make?"

"None. Forget it."

"The name was Ralph, if it matters, but—"

"How could it matter? He didn't exist, did he? Ralph, I mean. Obviously the drunk existed, except I don't suppose he was really drunk."

"Probably not."

"He knew where you were staying. How did he know? You didn't make any calls from your room, did you?"

"I don't think so. If I used the room phone at all, it was well after he came knocking on my door."

"And you didn't use your own name at the motel?"

"Of course not."

"Must have tagged you from the airport, then. Or he put a homing device on your car, but the client gave you the car, and we already established that the client didn't do this. Somebody else knew you were coming, or else, Jesus, followed you out from New York—is that possible?"

"No."

"Are you sure?"

"Sure enough. Look, I think I know who it was."

"Who, for God's sake?"

"Go back to Louisville for a minute. I get off the plane and there's a guy there to meet me."

"As arranged."

"As arranged, and there's another guy, has a sign I can't make out. I walk up to him until I'm almost in his face, trying to read what's on his sign."

"That's the guy?"

"I think so."

"Because he can't spell?"

"Because he wasn't waiting for anybody, unless you count me. Look, Dot, it has to be somebody who doesn't know who I am."

"What does he do, just kill people at random?"

"He knows what I do," he said, "but not who I am. If he knew my name and address he wouldn't have to chase all over the country after me. Why go after me when I'm working and on guard? Between jobs, what do I do? Watch a movie, take a walk, go out for a meal."

"Maybe he wants a challenge."

"No," he said, "I don't think so. I think he knew the guy who was meeting me, knew him by sight, and knew he was going to the airport to pick up the out-of-town shooter. So he made a sign of his own, one that wouldn't match anybody coming off a plane, and he stood around and waited. And then I showed up and made sure he got a good close look at me."

"And then you went to the right guy, and that confirmed the ID."

"Who followed us to the car they had for me in long-term parking. And when I drove off in it he got on my tail."

"Straight to the motel."

"I stopped for a bite on the way, and looked at a map, but then I went and found a motel, and I wouldn't have been hard to tail. I wasn't looking out for it. I didn't have any reason to."

"And he came and knocked on your door. Suppose you open up. Then what? Bang bang?"

"I don't think so."

"Why not? Be easy, wouldn't it?"

"It would have been easy any time during the next couple of days. But he waited until I did Hirschhorn. And in Boston he waited until I got Thurnauer."

"What is he, polite? He lets the other person go first?"

"Evidently."

"A real gentleman," she said. "I'm trying to sort this out, Keller. He came looking for Ralph to make sure he was right about what room you were in. Then, once he knew for sure, he sat tight."

"He probably followed me around some."

"While you bought stamps and drove over the bridge to Indiana. Is that what's on the other side of the river? Indiana?"

"That's right."

"And then you finally made your move on Hirschhorn, and he was close enough to know about it, and then what? He followed you back to the motel?"

"He wouldn't have had to follow too close. He knew where I was going."

"So you both drove there, and you went to your new room and he went to the old one."

"I parked in back, near the old room," he remembered. "Out of habit, I guess. He'd have seen the car and known I was home for the night. Then he gave me a little time to unwind and go to bed, and then he came calling."

"Had a key?"

"Or had enough tradecraft to get through a motel room lock without one. Which isn't the hardest thing in the world."

"He goes in and there's two heads on the pillow. He must figure you got lucky."

"I guess."

"It's dark, so he doesn't notice that neither head is yours. Doesn't he turn on the light afterward? You'd think he'd want the chance to admire his work."

"He might."

"But not necessarily?"

"Why bother, if he knows he nailed both parties? But if he does put the light on, then what?"

"He's been following you around all this time, Keller, he must know what you look like."

147

"The man he shot might look enough like me to pass," he said, "especially with his face in a pillow and two bullets in his head. But say he realizes his mistake. What's he going to do? Go door-to-door looking for me?"

"He can't do that."

"Odds are he figures I dumped the car, checked out, somebody drove me to the airport and I'm gone. One way or another he missed me. But my guess is he never turned on the light and never knew he screwed up until he read about it the next day in the paper."

"I'm trying to sort this out," she said, "and it's not easy. You want some iced tea?"

"Sure, but don't get up. I'll get it."

"No, it helps me think if I move around a little. What did you do after Louisville?"

"Came home and lived my life."

"In terms of work, I mean. There was the job in New York, which was the one I had the bad feeling about, because I should have turned it down. Where was our friend while you were busy with that one?"

"No idea."

"If he got on you here in the city, even if he missed you he'd wind up knowing your name and address. But nothing like that happened. Keller, what do you figure gets him off and running? What's his wake-up call?"

"It has to be he learns a contract's been put out and a hit's going down."

"So he starts off knowing who the subject is, but not the shooter."

"Has to be."

"And he stakes out the subject, or he picks up the shooter coming in, like he did with you in Louisville. New York, that artist, maybe he didn't get wind of the contract in the first place."

"Maybe not."

"Or he did, but he couldn't pick you up on the way in.

Nobody met you, nobody fingered the artist. What was his name?"

"Niswander."

"You showed up at the opening."

"Along with half the freeloaders in Lower Manhattan," he said.

"If he staked out Niswander, waiting for somebody to hit him, well, he's still waiting, because you went and knocked off the client instead. What came after that?"

"Tampa."

"Tampa. Something something beach."

"Indian Rocks Beach."

"You were down and back the same day. Even if he was ready to play, it was over and done with before he could have drawn a bead on you. And then comes Boston, and that brings us up-to-date, unless I'm forgetting something."

"I think that covers it."

"You saw him in Boston, isn't that what you said? Getting out of a cab and looking at Thurnauer's house?"

"It wasn't Thurnauer's place. I think it was the girl's."

"I'm glad you cleared that up. Point is you saw him, didn't you?"

"I saw somebody. Maybe it was him and maybe not."

"Here's the real question. Was it somebody you saw before?"

"I don't know."

"Like in Louisville, standing around with a sign."

"When I saw him get out of the cab," he said, "I assumed it was Thurnauer. What did I see? A guy in a hat and coat, all bundled up and trying not to get soaked. And I saw him from the back. I never got a look at his face."

"So maybe it was the same guy and maybe it wasn't."

"Helps a lot, doesn't it?"

"Getting back to Louisville," she said. "Did you get a good look at him then?"

"Did I look at him? Yes. Can I picture him now? No, not really. I got a better look at the sign he was holding."

"That's not much help, Keller. He's probably not still carrying it."

"He was wearing a leather jacket," he said, "and that's no help, either. He was about my height, not young, but not old, either. Not fat, not thin. Nothing terribly memorable about him."

"You could be describing yourself, Keller."

"Well, it wasn't me."

"No, you'd remember if it was. What's his angle? I'll tell you, he doesn't sound like the Caped Crusader to me, not the way he stands aside and lets you fulfill the contract before he makes his move. If all this was in aid of truth and justice and the American Way, wouldn't he go for an ounce of prevention?"

"You'd think so."

"So why does he wait? In Boston he may not have had much choice. He probably couldn't ID you until you were on your way out of the place. But in Louisville he had all the time in the world. What was he waiting for?"

"Maybe he was being considerate."

"Of whom, for Christ's sake? Not of Hirschhorn, that's for sure. Considerate of you? Like he wants to let you have your moment of triumph before he takes you off the board? Somehow I don't think so. So who does that leave?" Her eyes widened. "Jesus. He was being considerate of the *client*."

"I don't know who else there is."

"But why would he care about the client? Wait a minute. I'm actually beginning to get a glimmer here. He doesn't want to screw things up for the client, so that's why he lets the hit go down before he makes a move on the hitter. And what does he care about the client?"

"He's in the business."

"Which I suppose should have been obvious from the

150

jump. I mean, look at his trade mark. Two in the head with a twenty-two? That's not the gunfight at the OK Corral. That's a pro signing his work."

"But what's he got against me?" He got to his feet. "It can't be personal. He doesn't even know who I am. Is he trying to get me to join the union? I didn't even know there was one, but I'd pay my dues along with everybody else."

"It might be worth it," she said, "if only for the group medical coverage. Keller, maybe you're too self-centered."

"He wants to kill me because I'm too self-centered?"

"Maybe it's not about you."

"You know," he said, "it couldn't be about me, could it? Because he starts with the contract and waits for the hitter to show up. So where does that lead us? He's in the business and he's trying to kill other guys in the business? Is that possible, Dot? And wouldn't we have heard something?"

"Remember the New York job?"

"Of course I remember it. We were just talking about it."

"Remember I called the guy I generally call for work in the city?"

"His phone was disconnected."

"Right."

"And later you found out that . . ."

"Don't stop there, Keller. Finish the thought."

"That he was dead. Didn't he die in bed?"

"So did that nice couple in Louisville, remember?"

"But I thought it was his heart or something."

"His heart stopped," she said, "and so did theirs. You die, your heart stops. That's how it works."

"You think he was killed?"

"I don't think we can rule it out. If it went down as natural causes, well, how many of your jobs over the years went in the books that way?"

"A few."

"And in every case," she said, "their hearts stopped."

"So you figure your guy had a job somewhere, and he did it, and this other guy waited until he was done and followed him home and . . ."

"And made his heart stop."

"Why?"

"Why would someone do something like that? Is that your question?"

"Uh-huh, because I don't get it."

"Well, you do the same thing, Keller, so I'll ask you the same question. Why do you do it?"

He thought about it. "Andria told me it was my karma," he said, "but I'm not sure I know what that means. Maybe it's in the stars, I don't know. Maybe my thumb has something to do with it, in ways I don't begin to understand, and maybe—"

"Keller, stop it."

"What's the matter?"

"Don't go philosophical on me," she said. "I'm not asking what's a nice girl like you doing in a business like this. I'm saying here you are, you do what you do, and a job comes in, and you take it. Why do you take it?"

"What do you mean, Dot? Why do I take it? It's what I do."

"And why do you do it? What's in it for you?"

"What's in it for me? Well, you know."

"Humor me."

"Well, money," he said. "I get paid."

"Bingo."

"That's what you wanted me to say? That I get paid for it? I thought it went without saying. So what's the point? Guy who tried to kill me, he did it because somebody paid him?"

"No, he did it for the money."

"What money?"

"It's an investment," she said. "Long term. Keller, why does Coke go after Pepsi? He's killing off the competition."

CHAPTER FOURTEEN

It sounded crazy.

"Maybe it is crazy," Dot allowed. "Maybe *he's* crazy. When did sanity get to be part of the job description? As far as the dollars-and-cents logic of it is concerned, I don't see how you can argue the point. If you kill off the other people in your line of work, there's going to be more work coming your way. Either you'll increase your volume or boost your price, but one way or another you'll be putting more dollars in your pocket."

"But who thinks that way? All the years I've been doing this, all I ever did was come up here when I got a call and then go where I was sent. The old man would tell me where to go and what to do, and I went wherever and did whatever, and when I came home I got paid. I didn't try to work out how to get more money. I didn't have to, I always had more money than I needed."

"You never went looking for business."

"Of course not."

"You let it come to you."

"And it always did," he said.

"Uh-huh. Remember when I ran that ad?"

"In the magazine. Not *Soldier of Fortune*, the other one. What was the name of it?"

"Mercenary Times."

"We got one job out of it," he recalled, "and we had to sneak around to keep the old man from finding out, and then the client tried to stiff us."

"For all the good it did him. But the point is we went looking for work. I was the one who did the looking, but that's what it amounted to."

"Special circumstances. The old man was in a mood, turning jobs down left and right."

"I know."

"There was plenty of work out there. We just weren't getting it."

"I understand that, Keller. It was just an example."

"Oh."

"Remember when the call came for the Boston job? The client told me I was the first person he called, but I didn't believe him."

"Because he had problems working with women, I think you said."

"I think he made a few calls before he got to me. I think guys who do what you do are getting harder to find, and I don't think it's because of a dramatic elevation in the moral climate of the nation. I think this son of a bitch has been running around the country shooting the shooters, and I think his strategy's working. There are fewer of you guys around."

"And more work for him."

"More work and more money."

"Dot, what could he possibly need with it? There's plenty of work to go around."

"There's less than there was five years ago."

"I'm working as much as I ever did."

"Maybe because this guy's thinning the ranks. He's doing you a favor, if you want to look at it that way."

"I don't think so. Dot, how much money does he think he needs?"

"For some people, the phrase 'enough money' is as meaningless as the sign he held up in Louisville. There's no such thing as enough."

"What's he going to do with it?"

"Buy something he couldn't afford otherwise. Keller, you sink a lot of dollars into your stamp collection. Are there stamps you can't afford to buy?"

155

"Are you kidding? There are stamps, plenty of them, that run into six figures."

"And that artist you didn't kill. Niswander. Did you ever buy one of his paintings?"

"No."

"But you thought about it. You could have bought one if you wanted to, couldn't you?"

"Sure."

"Suppose you wanted a Picasso."

Or a Hopper. "Okay," he said. "I get it."

"The guy's a pig," she said. "The more he gets the more he wants. He wants to be the only hitter out there so he can get all the money. What the hell's the difference why he wants it? That's not the question. The question is what are we going to do about it."

If somebody was trying to kill you, what you did was kill him first. That much seemed obvious.

But how? Keller killed people all the time, it was what he did, but it was easier when you knew who they were and where to find them. The whole operation was fairly straightforward. It demanded resolve and ingenuity, and it helped if you could think on your feet, but it wasn't rocket science.

"I keep thinking he's from Louisville," he said, "but he probably flew there himself, same as I did. You know, that may not have been him at the baggage claim. He could have given some mope ten bucks to hold up a sign while he was over to one side, keeping his eyes open."

"There has to be a way to find him."

"How?"

They were silent, considering the question. Then Dot said, "How would you do it, Keller?"

"That's what I can't figure, and—"

"No," she said. "Suppose you were him. You want to be the Microsoft of murder and wipe out the competition.

How would you go about it?"

"Oh, I see what you mean. How would I even know where to start? I don't know anybody else who does what I do. It's not like there's an annual convention."

"That's good, because I'd hate to see all you guys in funny hats."

"He doesn't know anybody, either," he said. "That's why he has to stand around airports. But how does he know what airport to stand around in? You know what I'd do, Dot? Turn down work."

"How's that?"

"I get a call, can I do such and such a guy in Omaha. I find out all I can about the job and then I make some excuse, why I can't do it."

"Your grandmother's funeral, that's always good."

"A conflict, a prior commitment, who cares what. I tell the man he'll have to hire somebody else and then I go to Omaha and see who turns up."

"And wait until your replacement does the deed before you take him out. Why wait?"

"So nobody knows. Say he takes me out that first day in Louisville. Say instead of looking for Ralph he just plants himself outside my door, and when I show my face he gives me my two in the head. Right away, the client knows."

"And after the job?"

"The best thing to do," he said, "is follow me home."

"Which he did, but he went to the wrong room."

"No," he said. "Follow me all the way home. Follow me back to New York, find out who I am and where I live and take me out at leisure, while I'm living my life."

"Seeing a movie," she said. "Pasting stamps in your album."

"Whatever. That's how he worked it with the guy who died in his sleep. Followed him home and bided his time."

"But with you he couldn't wait."

"Evidently not, one reason or another. It's a good thing,

157

too, because he would have had me cold. I wouldn't have expected a thing. And if he tried for me in New York and killed the wrong person, he could come back the next day and try again."

"The miserable son of a bitch."

"You could call him that."

"It's not like he doesn't have enough work. The way you laid it out, he turns down a job every time."

"Well, that's the way I would do it."

"And I'll bet it's the way he does it, too, the rat bastard. Well, he made a mistake. He's in trouble."

"He's in trouble? We don't know anything about him, Dot. Not who he is or where he lives or what he looks like. How much trouble can he be in?"

"We know he's out there," she said grimly. "And that's enough. Keller, go home."

"Huh?"

"Go home, lie down, put your feet up. Play with your stamps. This guy's not a danger today. He probably thinks he got the right person when he nailed Louis Minot. And even if he knows better, he doesn't know where to look for you. So go home and live your life."

"And?"

"And I'll pick up the phone," she said, "and ask a few questions, and see what I can find out about this unprincipled son of a bitch."

"What I don't get," she was saying, "is where they get off calling this a Long Island Iced Tea. There must be half a dozen different kinds of booze in it, but is there any tea at all?"

"You're asking the wrong person."

"No tea," she decided. "Are they being ironic? Like this is what they drink for tea on Long Island? Or do you figure it's a reference to Prohibition?"

"Beats me."

"And I bet you don't care, either. Well, one of these is going to be enough, I'll say that much. I want to be sober when I shop, and the last thing I want is to sleep through *The Lion King* tonight."

They were at a restaurant on Madison Avenue. Dot didn't come to the city often, and when she did she managed to look like a suburban matron all gussied up for a day of shopping and a night at the theater. Which was reasonable enough, he thought, since that pretty much described her.

When the food came she said, "Well, let's get to it. I didn't want to do this over the phone, and why make you chase up to White Plains when I had to come in anyway? I ordered this ticket so long ago I feel as though I've already seen the play. I made some calls."

"You said you were going to."

"And I found out a thing or two about Roger."

"That's his name?"

"Probably not," she said, "but that's what he goes by. No last name, just Roger."

"Where does he live?"

"Nobody knows."

"Somebody's got to. Not his address necessarily, but the city."

"Roger the Lodger," she said. "But wherever he's lodged, it's a secret."

"If somebody wants to reach me," he said, "they go through you. Who do you call to reach Roger?"

"Any of several brokers. Or you call him direct."

"Well, there you go. His number must have an area code. What is it?"

"Three-oh-nine."

"I don't know that one."

"Peoria, Illinois. But all you get when you call the number is his voice mail at Sprint's central office, and that's nowhere near Peoria. You leave a number and he calls you back."

"You figure he lives in Peoria?"

"There's a chance," she said, "but I've probably got a better chance in the lottery, and I haven't bought a ticket. I think he went to Peoria once and bought a cell phone just so he could have the voice mail."

"He calls you back," he said. "Probably not on his cell phone, he probably just uses that for his messages. Then what?"

"You tell him about the job and he says yes or no."

"You give him the name and address, the other details."

"And anything else he's going to need."

"Suppose you want to point out the target?"

She shook her head. "No finger men for Roger. Nobody ever meets his plane."

"In other words, nobody ever sees the guy."

"Right."

"Well, that's damn smart," he said. "And from now on it's how we do business, and not because we're afraid of the client."

"But because we're afraid of Roger."

"Not afraid exactly, but—"

"But close enough. How's your veal?"

"It's fine. What's that, filet of sole?"

"And it's nice," she said, "only a Long Island Iced Tea may not be the best way in the world to pave the way for it. Very nice, though. Delicate. But you're right, no more airport pickups, no more jerks supplying a car and a gun."

"Still," he said, "he must have a way to collect his half in advance. And if you want to send him keys or a gun."

"FedEx."

"FedEx to where?"

"A FedEx office, and he calls for it."

"I don't suppose it's the same FedEx office every time."

"Never the same one twice, never the same city twice. Then afterward when it's time to pay him, it's another FedEx office in another city. And the recipient's name is different each time, too. This guy doesn't make the obvious mistakes."

"No."

"He's a pro."

"Right, a pro," he said. "You know, I got back from Boston and I couldn't stop looking over my shoulder. I was jumpy, I couldn't sit still."

"I can imagine."

"But you get used to it. At first I thought, all right, I'll pack it in. Who needs it? I was thinking about retiring that one time, and this time I'll do it."

"Neat trick, now that you've spent all your retirement fund on stamps."

"Not all of it," he said. "A good part of it, but not all of it. But even if I had the money back, even if I could afford to retire, am I going to let this son of a bitch chase me out of the business?"

"I get the sense the answer is no."

"We'll be very careful," he said. "We'll take a cue from Roger. No face-to-face with the client or any of his people. If they insist, we'll pass."

"And I'll ask some questions I don't normally ask. Like who turned this job down before you offered it to us? Sometimes a contract goes through different brokers, so the man who calls me may not know who had first refusal, but I'll make it a point to find out what I can. And if I get a whiff of Roger anywhere near it, I'll find a reason for us to take a pass."

"And I'll keep my eyes open."

"Never a bad idea."

"And somewhere down the line," he said, "we'll find a way to cut his trail."

" 'Cut his trail'? What's that mean?"

"They say it in westerns," he said. "I don't know exactly what it means. We'll double back, get behind him, something like that."

"What I more or less surmised."

"Well, we'll do it," he said. "He's a pro, but so what? I'm a pro myself, but that doesn't mean I never make a mistake. I've made plenty of them over the years."

"He'll make one."

"Damn right," he said. "And when he does . . ."

"Bang bang. Excuse me, better make that pop pop."

"No, bang bang is fine," he said. "When I get this guy, I don't care if I make a little noise."

CHAPTER FIFTEEN

Keller, chasing the last forkful of omelet with the last bite of toast, watched while the waitress filled his coffee cup. He wasn't sure he wanted more coffee, but it was easier to leave it behind than to stop the woman from pouring it for him. The restaurant had signs touting their bottomless cup of coffee. Keller, who'd been brought up to finish what was on his plate, had a problem with that. You couldn't finish your coffee, they didn't let you finish your coffee, they refilled your cup before you could empty it. He supposed that was good for people with scarcity issues, but it bothered him.

And what about the tea drinkers? It seemed to him that they got screwed royally. If you finished your tea, they'd give you more hot water to go with the same tea bag. He supposed you could get a second cup of tea out of a tea bag, if you didn't mind weak and flavorless tea, but a third cup would be a real stretch. Meanwhile, a coffee drinker could polish off gallons of coffee, each cup as strong as the last.

Then again, who ever said life was fair?

"**I**'d have to say it looks good," Dot had told him. "The man I talked to is dealing directly with the client, and according to him I'm the first person who got called. And we've got a name and address, and a photo's on its way, and there's nobody going to be waiting for you at the baggage claim at O'Hare. It's a pretty safe bet our friend Roger doesn't know zip about this one, and neither does Klinger."

"Klinger?"

"The fellow in Lake Forest you'll be saying hello and

163

goodbye to. He's not going to be looking over his shoulder. And you won't have to spend a lot of time looking over your own shoulder, either."

"Maybe an occasional glance."

Back at his apartment, Keller's first glance was at the horoscope Louise Carpenter had drawn for him. The period of great danger, peaking right around the time of his trip to Boston, had passed. Right now he had several relatively safe months ahead of him, at least as far as the stars were concerned. Things might get a bit perilous in the summer, but that was a whole season away.

Still, there was no point in being a damned fool. Lake Forest, Illinois, was on Lake Michigan north of Chicago, and you got there by flying to O'Hare Airport. Keller flew to Milwaukee instead, rented a car, and got a room at a motel fifteen minutes north of Lake Forest.

No rush. The client wasn't in a hurry, and Klinger wasn't going anywhere, except to the office and back, five days a week. Keller, keeping an eye on him, kept the other eye open for any sign of an alien presence. If Roger was around, Keller wanted to see him first.

Keller looked at his watch. He had time to finish the coffee in his cup, he decided, but what was the point? She'd only fill it up again, and he'd run out of time before the woman ran out of coffee. He paid the check, left a good tip, and went out to his car, and twenty minutes later he was parked on Rugby Road, a picture-book suburban lane lined with mature shade trees that could have come straight from a Declan Niswander painting. His eyes were focused on a white frame house with dark green shutters standing a hundred yards or so down the road. The motor was idling, and Keller had a street map unfolded and draped over the steering wheel, so that anyone passing by would assume he was trying to figure out where he was.

But he knew where he was, and he knew he wouldn't

have long to wait. Lee Klinger was a creature of habit, as likely to change his routine as the waitress was to leave a coffee cup unfilled. Five mornings a week he caught the 8:11 train to Chicago, and if the weather was halfway decent he walked to the station, leaving the house at 7:48.

You could set your watch by the guy.

Keller, who had set his own watch by the car radio, watched the side door open at the appointed hour. Klinger, wearing a dark brown suit this morning, and carrying his tan briefcase, headed down the driveway and turned left at its end. He walked to the corner, where a traffic light controlled the intersection. He crossed Culpepper Lane with the light, then turned and waited for the light to change so that he could cross Rugby Road. There were no cars coming, so he could have jaywalked safely enough. In fact, Keller thought, he could have proceeded diagonally and crossed both streets at once. But, in the three days he'd been tagging him, Keller had gotten enough of a sense of Lee Klinger to know he'd do no such thing. He'd wait for the light, and he'd cross streets the way you were supposed to cross them.

Keller wondered who wanted the man dead, and why. He didn't really want to know the answer, he'd learned over the years that he was better off not knowing, but it was impossible to avoid speculation. Some business rival? Someone who was sleeping with Mrs. Klinger? Somebody with whose wife Klinger himself was sleeping?

All of this seemed unlikely, given Keller's impression of the man. But, when you came right down to it, what did Keller actually know about Klinger? Next to nothing, really. He was punctual, he obeyed traffic laws, he wore suits, and somebody wanted him dead. There was very likely a lot more to Klinger than that, but that was all Keller knew, and all he needed to know.

Keller put the Ford in gear, pulled away from the curb.

He would let Klinger cross the street, and then when the light changed he'd drive through the intersection himself, and take another route to the suburban railway station. After that, well, he wasn't sure what he'd do. Maybe there would be an opportunity on the platform, waiting for the train. Maybe he'd find his chance on the train, or in Chicago. And maybe not. There were some stamp dealers in Chicago, right there in the Loop where you could walk to them, and he had brought along the catalog he used as a checklist. He could make the rounds, buy some stamps. Dot hadn't said anything about time being of the essence. He could give it another day or two.

The light changed. Another car, approaching the intersection, slowed. Klinger stepped off the curb, headed across the street. The other car accelerated abruptly, springing forward like a predatory animal. Klinger didn't even have time to freeze in his tracks, let alone try to get away. The car hit him in mid-stride, sending him and his briefcase flying. Keller had barely registered what was happening before it was over. Klinger never knew what hit him.

"Okay," Dot said. "I give up. How'd you do it?"

"All I did," he said, "was watch it, and I barely did that. I was following him, but I knew where he was going, so I didn't have to pay close attention."

"That fucking Roger," Dot said. "He's changed his approach. Instead of hitting the hitter, he beats you to the punch."

"It couldn't have been Roger. Rogeretta, maybe."

"It was a woman?"

"A little old lady. She was doing something like sixty miles an hour at the moment of impact. Car was an Olds, last year's model, a big sedan."

"Not your father's Oldsmobile."

"She said there was something wrong with the car. She

stepped on the brake, but all it did was go faster."

"Definitely not your father's Oldsmobile."

"It happens a lot," Keller said, "with all kinds of cars. The driver steps on the brake and the car speeds up instead of slowing down. The one common denominator is the driver's always getting along in years."

"And I don't suppose it's really the brake."

"They get confused," he said, "and they think they're stepping on the brake pedal, and it's the accelerator. So they panic and step down harder, to force the brakes to work, and the car goes faster, and, well, you see where it's going."

"Straight into Klinger."

"She took her foot off the gas," he said, "to stop for the light, and her car slowed down, and Klinger started across, and then she stepped on what was supposed to be the brake pedal. And the rest is history."

"And so is Klinger," Dot said. "And you were right there."

"I saw it happen," he said. "I have to tell you, it gave me a turn."

"You, Keller?"

"I saw a man die."

She gave him a look. "Keller," she said, "you see men die all the time, and you're generally the cause of death."

"This was different," he said. "The unexpectedness of it. And it was so violent."

"It's usually violent, Keller. It's what you do."

"But I didn't do it," he said. "I just sat there and watched it. Then the cops came and—"

"And you were still there?"

"I figured it might be riskier if I drove away. You know, leaving the scene of an accident. Even if I wasn't a part of the accident." He shrugged. "They took a statement and waved me on. I told them I didn't really see anything, and they had another witness who saw the whole thing, and it's not as though there was any dispute about what had happened. Except that the little old lady still thinks it was the car's fault and not hers."

"But we know otherwise," she said. "And so does the client."

"The client?"

"Thinks you're a genius, Keller. Thinks you arranged the whole thing, figures you found some perfectly ingenious way to get Klinger to step in front of that lady's car."

"But . . ."

"The customer," she said, "is always right. Remember? Especially when he pays up, which this one did, like a shot. The job's done and the client's happy and we've been paid. Do you see a problem, Keller? Because I don't."

He thought about it.

"Keller? What did you do after Klinger got flattened?"

"He didn't get flattened. It hit him and he went flying, and—"

"Spare me. I know you stuck around and gave a statement like a good citizen, but then what did you do?"

"I came home," he said. "But not immediately. As a matter of fact, the first thing I did was go into Milwaukee and see a couple of stamp dealers."

"You bought some stamps for your collection."

"Well, yes. I was there anyway, and I didn't figure there was any reason to hurry home."

"You were right," she said. "There wasn't. And we've been paid, and now you can buy some more stamps. Are you all right, Keller? You seem a little bit out of it, and nobody gets jet lag coming home from Milwaukee."

"I'm fine," he said. "It just seems strange. That's all."

CHAPTER SIXTEEN

Three weeks later Keller was eating huevos rancheros at Call Me Carlos, on the edge of Albuquerque's Old Town. The menu had the same logo as the sign outside, with a grinning Mexican in an oversize sombrero. You knew at a glance that the place was Mexican-owned, Keller thought, because no gringo would have dared use such a broad caricature.

If there was any doubt, the food resolved it. They served the best huevos rancheros he'd had, with the possible exception of a little café he knew in Roseburg, Oregon.

He'd said as much to Dot the previous night. "Oh, spare me, Keller," she'd replied. "Roseburg, Oregon? Keller, you wanted to move there. Remember?"

It had been a mistake to mention Roseburg, and he'd realized it the minute he said it. Usually it was Dot who mentioned the town, throwing it up at him whenever he said anything nice about any of the places he visited.

"I didn't exactly want to move there," he protested.

"You looked at houses."

"I thought about it," he said, "the way you think about things, but I didn't—"

"The way *you* think about things, Keller. Not the way *I* think about things. There's something else you could be thinking about, instead of houses in Roseburg, Oregon."

"I know," he said. "And anyway, I wasn't."

"Thinking about houses? You said . . ."

"I was thinking about that café, and all I was thinking was that it was better than where I've been having breakfast. Except it probably isn't, because memory improves things."

"It would have to," Dot said, "or we'd all kill ourselves."

"And as far as the other thing I could be thinking about, I think it's impossible."

"Doesn't surprise me."

"A few more plates of huevos rancheros," he said, "and I think it'll be time for me to come home."

"Without looking at houses?"

"They're mostly adobe," he said, "and I have to say they look pretty from the outside, but that's as much as I want to see of them. I'll stay long enough to make it look good, but then I'm coming home."

He finished his eggs, finished his second cup of coffee, and went out to his rented Toyota. The sun was bright, the air cool and dry. If you had to make a pointless trip somewhere, this wasn't the worst place for it.

A week earlier he'd taken the train to White Plains and sat across the kitchen table from Dot while she laid it all out for him. Michael Petrosian was in federal custody, guarded around the clock while he waited to testify. Without his testimony, the government didn't have much of a case. With it, they could put some important people away for a long time.

"That's why," he'd said. "The question is how."

"Sounds impossible, doesn't it?"

"That's the word that came to mind."

"It came to my mind, too. It came to my lips, too, along with the phrase 'I think we'll pass on this one.'"

"But you changed your mind."

"The minute he agreed that you get paid either way."

"How's that?"

"Half in advance, half on completion."

"So? That's standard."

"Patience," she said. "What's not standard is you can look it over, decide it's impossible, and come on home. And the half they paid is yours to keep."

170

"How'd you manage that?"

"By letting them talk me into it. It turns out I'm good at this, Keller."

"I'm not surprised."

"And I guess you could say they're pretty desperate. One hand, the job has to be done. Other hand, it can't be done. Add 'em up, it comes out desperate."

"They probably got even more desperate," he said, "when they offered the contract and got turned down."

She poured herself some more iced tea. "I know they shopped this around. They wouldn't come right out and say so, but they never would have taken my terms if they hadn't run into a few brick walls along the way."

"It'd be nice to know just who told them no."

"Roger, for instance."

"For instance," he agreed.

"Well," she said, "I think we have to assume they ran it past him. So we're taking the usual precautions. Nobody's meeting you, nobody knows who you are or where you're coming from. Even if Roger's out there in Albuquerque, even if he's sitting in Petrosian's lap, he's never going to draw a bead on you. Because all you have to do is fly out there and fly back and you get paid."

"Half," he said.

"Half if all you do is take a look. The other half if you make it happen. And there's an escalator."

"Instead of a staircase?"

"No, of course not."

"Because what's the difference? He's going to lose his footing on the escalator?"

"An escalator clause, Keller. In the contract."

"Oh."

"Big bonus if you get him before he testifies. Smaller bonus if it's after he starts but before he finishes."

"While he's on the stand?"

She rolled her eyes. "It's going to take him several days

to make all the trouble he can for our guys. Say he's on the stand one day, and that night he slips on a banana peel and falls down the escalator."

"Or finds some other way to break his neck."

"Whatever. We get a bonus, but not as big as if he broke it a day earlier." She shrugged. "That was just something to negotiate, because it's not going to happen. You'll go out there and come back, and they can console themselves by thinking how much money they just saved. Not just half the fee, but the bonus, too."

"Because it's impossible," he said. "Except it's never completely impossible. I mean, a bomb under a manhole cover on the route to the courthouse, say. Or a strike force of commandos hitting the place where he's cooped up."

"Desperate men," she said, "led by Lee Marvin, their hard-bitten colonel."

"Or a sharpshooter on a roof. But none of those are my style."

"You could strap some explosive around your waist and run up and give him a hug," she said, "but I don't suppose that's your style, either. Don't worry about it. Spend a week, ten days tops. Have they got stamp dealers in Albuquerque? They must."

"I've done business through the mails with a fellow in Roswell," he said.

"Roswell, New Mexico?"

"Wherever that is."

"Well, it's in New Mexico," she said. "We know that much, don't we?"

"But I don't know if it's near Albuquerque, and he may just deal through the mails. But sure, there'll be stamp dealers there. There'd have to be."

"So have fun," she said. "Buy some stamps."

"Or if it turns out there's a way to do it . . ."

"So much the better," she said, "but don't knock yourself out. They'll guard Petrosian like Fort Knox until he's done testifying. Then they'll stick him in the Witness Protection Program, and years from now somebody'll spot him. And, if anybody still cares, you'll get another crack at him."

Keller's motel was about a mile from the Arrowhead Inn on Candelaria where the feds were keeping Michael Petrosian. It might have been interesting to take a room in the Arrowhead himself, handy and risky at the same time, but he didn't have the option. Petrosian and the men who guarded him were the motel's only guests. The media referred to the place as an armed compound, and Keller didn't have any quarrel with the term. He'd driven past it a few times, and had seen it over and over again on television, and that's what it was, its parking lot filled with government cars, its doors manned by unsmiling men in suits and sunglasses. All it lacked was a watchtower and a few hundred yards of concertina wire.

Short of digging a tunnel, Keller couldn't see any way in—or any way out once you got in. And Petrosian never left the place. His keepers brought food in, ordering it by phone and sending a couple of the suit-and-sunglasses boys to fetch it.

If you knew where they were going to order from, and if you could get to the food order before anybody picked it up, and if you knew which dishes were destined for Petrosian, and if you could slip something appropriate into his food, and if they let him eat it without trying it out on a food taster first, and—

Forget it.

They'd keep Petrosian under lock and key until it was time for him to go to the courthouse, and Keller had already heard an overfed U.S. marshal on CNN, boasting about their security precautions. There'd be a whole convoy of armored government vehicles to shepherd him from the motel to the courthouse and back again, and nobody would be able to get anywhere near him. Guy had a double chin and a smug expression, looked nothing like Dennis Weaver as McCloud, and Keller had a strong urge to wipe the smile off his well-fed face. But how?

He drove past the courthouse a couple of times, and you couldn't get close to the place, not even in the pre-Petrosian days before they geared their security measures all the way up. You couldn't loiter in the area unless you had business there—uniformed officers made sure of that—and you couldn't get into the building without a pass. Keller supposed he could get hold of one. Find a newsman, take a press pass away from him, something like that. But then what? You had to pass through a metal detector in order to enter the building, and even if you could do the deed with your bare hands, how would you get out afterward?

No point in hanging around the courthouse. No point in loitering in the vicinity of the Arrowhead Inn, either.

It was easier to watch the whole thing on Court TV. And that's what he was doing now, sitting in his motel room and muting the commercials, trying to figure out what they were selling. Eventually he'd be intrigued enough to turn the sound back on, and then you'd have him hanging on every word. It hadn't happened to Keller yet, but he could see how it might.

He watched the commercial, his finger poised over the Mute button, and only when it ended did he put the sound back on. A commentator was saying something about the arrival at last of the much-anticipated Michael Petrosian, the government's star witness, and they cut to an outside shot as a cameraman in a helicopter filmed the arrival of the government convoy.

And, just as he'd figured, there was no way anybody could get anywhere near the son of a bitch. There were no other cars around when the government cars pulled up, and the only spectators on the courthouse steps were a small contingent of photographers and reporters. They looked frustrated, penned as they were behind a rope barrier, unable to get close to their quarry. Even from the helicopter it was hard to spot Petrosian, just another body in a herd of bodies emerging from the cars and moving briskly up the flight of marble steps.

Lee Marvin and the boys would have their work cut out for them, he thought. Unless . . . well, suppose that was Lee up there in the helicopter? And he brings the chopper in as close as he can, steering one-handed and leaning out of the thing with a machine gun. That might work, but so would a tactical nuclear weapon, and one was about as likely as the other for Keller.

You had to hand it to the cameraman, though. He'd managed to single out Petrosian, and there the guy was, head lowered, shoulders hunched forward, climbing those steps.

And then, for some reason, the men circling Petrosian drew away from him. He turned, and raised his balding head so that he was looking right at the camera. He looked terrified, Keller thought. Stricken.

And Keller watched as the government's star witness paled, clutched his hand to his chest, and pitched forward on his face.

"They think you're a genius," Dot said. "A miracle worker. And you know what, Keller? I have to say I agree with them."

"I watched it on TV," he said.

"Keller," she said, "*everybody* watched it on TV. More people saw it than saw Ruby shoot Oswald. I must have seen it twenty times myself. I wasn't watching while it happened, but who needs to in the Age of Instant Replay?"

"I saw it live."

"And a few times since then, I'll bet. Did I say twenty times? It was probably closer to fifty. And you know something, Keller? I still can't figure out how you did it."

"I didn't do anything."

"I understand they're looking for puncture marks," she said, "like the Bulgarian that got stabbed with the umbrella, or whatever the hell it was. Then two days later he died. They're looking for puncture marks and traces of a slow-acting poison."

"And when they don't find them?"

"That'll show that it's a poison without a trace, and one that was delivered without breaking the skin. A puff from an atomizer, say. He breathes it in, and a day or two later he has what looks for all the world like a heart attack."

"It looked like one," he said, "because that's what it was."

"Right, but how did you make it happen?"

"I didn't."

"It just happened."

"Right."

"Help me find a way to believe that, Keller."

"Ask yourself why I would lie to you."

She thought about it. "You wouldn't," she said. "Well, he was overweight, he was out of shape, and he was under a lot of stress."

"Must have been."

"And those stairs looked steep. In the movies when somebody gets shot on the stairs he falls all the way to the bottom, but he just sort of flopped on his face and stayed where he fell. Keller? This is even better than the guy crossing the street, and why can't I remember his name?"

"Lee Klinger."

"Right. There at least you were on the scene. When Petrosian got it you were watching TV in your motel room."

"First there was a commercial," he said, "and I couldn't tell what they were advertising. And then Petrosian dropped dead, and the first thing I thought was the guy in the helicopter shot him. But nobody shot him, or stabbed him with an umbrella, or sprayed poisoned perfume in his face."

"He just dropped dead."

"In front of God and everybody."

"Especially everybody." She took a long drink of iced tea. "We got paid," she said.

"That was quick."

"Well, you've got a real fan club in Albuquerque, Keller. There are some people there who may not know your name, but they're sure crazy about your work."

"So they paid the second half. How about the escalator?"

"It was marble steps. Oh, sorry, I got lost there. Yes, they paid the escalator. You nailed the bastard before they could even swear him in. They paid the escalator, and they paid a bonus."

"A bonus?"

"A bonus."

"Why? What for?"

"To make themselves feel good, would be my guess. I don't know what the prisons are like in New Mexico, but I gather they're grateful not to be going, and they wanted to make a grand gesture. What they said, the bonus was for dramatic effect."

"Dramatic effect?"

"On the courthouse steps, Keller? The man dies surrounded by G-men, and the whole world gets to see him do it over and over again? Believe me, they'll get their money's worth out of this one. They'll be playing that tape every time they swear in a new member. 'You think you can ever cross us and get away with it? Look what happened to Petrosian.'"

He thought about it. "Dot," he said, "I didn't *do* anything."

"You just went out every morning for a Mexican breakfast."

"Huevos rancheros."

"And here I always thought a Mexican breakfast was a cigarette and a glass of water. You ate eggs and watched television. What else? Get to a movie?"

"Once or twice."

"Buy any stamps?"

He shook his head. "Roswell's like a three- or four-hour drive from Albuquerque. The stamp dealers in town, a couple of them just work through the mails, and the one shop I went to was basically a coin dealer. He sells supplies and albums, a few packets, but he doesn't really have a stamp stock."

"Well, you can buy stamps now, Keller. Lots of them."

"I suppose so."

She frowned. "Something's bothering you," she said.

"I told you. I didn't do anything."

"I know, and that'll have to be our little secret. And who's to say it's true?"

"What do you mean?"

"Think about it," she said, and hummed the *Twilight Zone* theme. "You go to Illinois and Klinger gets hit by a car. You go to Albuquerque and Petrosian has a handy little heart attack. Coincidence?"

"But . . ."

"Maybe your thoughts are powerful, Keller. Maybe all you have to do is get to thinking about a guy and his ticket's punched."

"That's crazy," he said.

"Be that as it may," said Dot.

CHAPTER SEVENTEEN

"It's been a while," Maggie Griscomb said.

They were in her loft on Crosby Street. Keller's clothes were neatly folded on the couch, while Maggie's lay in a black heap on the floor. Music played on her stereo, something weird and electronic. Keller couldn't guess what the instruments were, let alone why they were being played like that.

"I thought you weren't going to call me anymore," she said. "And then you did. And here you are."

Here he was, in her bed, his perspiration evaporating beneath the overhead fan.

"I was out of town," he said.

"I know."

"How?" He turned to face her, worked to keep the alarm from showing on his face or in his voice. "That I was out of town," he said. "How did you know that?"

"You told me."

"I told you?"

"Two hours ago," she said, "or whenever it was that you called. 'Hi, it's me, I was out of town.'"

"Oh."

"Or words to that effect. Does it all come back to you now?"

"Sure," he said. "I was confused there for a minute, that's all."

"Addled by lovemaking."

"Must be."

She rolled over on her side, propped her pointed chin on his chest. "You thought I was checking up on you," she said.

"No."

179

"Sure you did. You thought I meant I already knew you were out of town, *before* you told me."

That was what he'd thought, all right. And that was why alarm bells had gone off.

"But I didn't," she said, "or I wouldn't have thought our superficial relationship was coming to an end. 'He'll call when he gets back to town,' I would have thought."

Maybe it was the music, he thought. If they played it in a movie, you'd be waiting for something to happen. Something scary, if it was that kind of picture. Something unexpected, whatever kind of picture it was.

"Or maybe not," she said. Her eyes were so close to his that it was impossible to read them, or even to look into them without getting a headache. He wanted to close his own eyes, but could you do that when someone was staring into them like that? Wouldn't it be impolite?

"I almost called you, Keller. A few days ago. You never gave me your number."

"You never asked for it."

"No. But I've got Caller ID on my phone, and I've got your number. Or I used to."

"You lost it?"

"I looked it up, when I almost called you. And I decided calling you was no way to maintain a superficial relationship. So I burned up your phone number."

"Burned it up?"

"Well, no. Tore it into little tiny scraps and threw them out the window like confetti. Which I guess is what they were, because confetti's just little scraps of paper, isn't it?"

His mind filled with the image of a squad of police technicians, piecing together tiny scraps of paper, deliberately assembling a tiny jigsaw puzzle until his telephone number reappeared.

"You're losing interest," she said. "Admit it—the only reason you called me tonight was you felt like having sex."

He opened his mouth, prepared to deny the charge,

then stopped and frowned. "That's all we do," he said.

"That's a point."

"So why else would I call?"

"Right," she said, drawing away. "Got to hand you that one. Why else would you call?"

"I mean—"

"I know what you mean. And I made the rules, didn't I? I'll tell you something, superficial relationships are as hard to maintain as the other kind. I'm not going to see you again, am I?"

"Well . . ."

"I'm not," she said decisively, "and I think it's better that way. You with your downtown bohemian mistress, dressed all in black and playing weird music. Me with my buttoned-down corporate lover, living uptown somewhere. I don't even know where you live."

Good, Keller thought.

"Of course I could find out if I hadn't turned your phone number into a ticker-tape parade. Just check out the number in a reverse directory. Oh, hell."

"What's the matter?"

"You called me a couple of hours ago. I don't suppose you used a pay phone, did you?"

"No."

"You called from your place."

"Well, yes."

"Damn right you did. I knew it was you before I picked up. Remember how I answered the phone? 'Well, hello there,' like I knew who it was. Or did you figure I answer all my calls that way?"

"I didn't think about it," he said.

"Maybe I should. It would confuse the telemarketers, wouldn't it? Anyway, I saw the number on the screen, and I recognized it. I never actually memorized it, but I still recognized it when I saw it."

"So?"

"So nobody called me since then, which means it's still on my called ID screen. I pick up the phone and there's your number. Listen, do me a favor? First pay phone you come to, call me. Then wherever you're calling from, *that*'ll be the number on my Caller ID screen, and I won't have to have your home number around, complicating my life."

The music, he thought, was by no means the weirdest thing going. His phone number? Complicating her life? "Sure," he said carefully. "I could do that."

"In fact, make the call from the pay phone down on the corner. So you don't forget."

"All right."

"And the best thing," she said, "would be if you put your clothes on now, and went straight out and made that call."

"If you say so," he said, "but can't it wait, and I'll do it on my way home?"

"Make the call now," she said, "on your way home."

"Oh."

"Or wherever else you want to go. Because we're history, Keller. So get your number off my phone, and lose *my* number, and we'll both get on with our lives. How does that sound?"

He wasn't sure if the question required an answer, but in any event he couldn't come up with one. He got out of bed and into his clothes and out of her loft, and he called her from a pay phone in a bar at the corner of Broadway and Bleecker.

She picked up right away, and without preamble she said, "It was great fun, but it was just one of those things." And hung up.

Keller, feeling he'd missed something, took a seat at the bar. The crowd was mixed—downtown types, uptown types, out-of-town types. The bartender was a Chinese girl with long straight hair the color of buttercups. She had a nose ring, but almost everybody did these days. Keller

182

wondered how the hell that had caught on.

He heard someone order a Black Russian. He'd had one years ago and couldn't remember if he'd liked it or not. He had the yellow-haired Chinese girl make him one, took a sip, and decided he could go years before he ordered another.

A song played on the jukebox. Keller didn't recognize it, but, listening to it, he realized Maggie's parting shot had been a line from a song. She'd delivered it like conversation, with no irony, none of the cadence you gave lines when you were quoting them, and it had taken him until now to place it. Great fun. Just one of those things.

I was out of town, he'd said. I know, she'd said.

And there'd been a tingling in his hands.

Had she sensed anything? Had she had any idea how close she'd come, how his hands had been ready to reach for her?

He thought about it and decided she hadn't, not consciously. But maybe she'd picked something up on a deeper level, and maybe that was why, still in the afterglow of their lovemaking, she'd rushed him into his clothes and out of her life.

After all, his thoughts were powerful. Why shouldn't she pick up on them?

He took another sip of his drink. Somewhere out there, the man they were calling Roger had him on a list. Not by name—Roger wouldn't know his name, any more than he knew Roger's. But Roger had tried to kill him twice, and would very likely try to kill him again.

Did Roger even know the same man had been his target both times, in Louisville and in Boston? For that matter, did Roger have a clue he'd killed the wrong person on both occasions?

If so, Keller could see how Roger might begin to take the whole thing personally, like Wile E. Coyote in a Roadrunner cartoon.

Keller knew it was nothing personal. How could it be, when you didn't know the person you were killing? Still, he seemed to be taking it personally himself, at those times when Roger took up space in his thoughts.

Which wasn't that often. The days went by, and he didn't see anything when he looked over his shoulder, and he forgot about Roger. And every once in a while Dot sent him out on a job, at which time he did do a certain amount of looking over his shoulder, a certain amount of thinking about Roger. But then he came back from the job without having done anything, to Roger or to anyone else, and the client paid him, and that was that.

And then he'd said he was out of town, and Maggie said she knew, and he'd been ready to grab her and snap her neck. Just like that.

He'd called up, as requested, to replace his home number on her Caller ID with the number of the pay phone. But was that how Caller ID worked? Did it keep track of just one number at a time? He didn't have it on his phone, he couldn't imagine why he'd want it, so he wasn't too clear on how it worked. And, even if it was the way she'd said it was, how did he know she hadn't picked up the phone the minute he was out the door? She could have copied the number off the screen before he called back to erase it.

She was, let's face it, more than a little strange. That had been part of her initial appeal, that offbeat downtown weirdness, though he had to say it had grown less appealing with time. Still, it made it impossible to guess what the woman would do.

If she had the number, she could get the address. She'd mentioned the reverse directory herself, so she knew about it, knew how to get an address to go with a phone number. If she knew all that, and of course she already knew his name, she'd known that from the beginning . . .

But that didn't mean she knew what he did for a living.

Suppose she'd picked up on his reaction, suppose she'd half-sensed that he'd been ready to reach for her and put her down. The fact remained that he hadn't done anything, hadn't even acted angry, let alone homicidal. Once he was out the door, once it was clear that she was safe, she'd talk herself out of any alarm she might have felt.

Wouldn't she?

Back home, he worked on his stamp collection for a few minutes, then put everything away and turned on the TV. He worked his way through the channels two or three times, triggering the remote until his hand was tired, then thumbing the power button and darkening the set. And sat there in what little light came in from the window, looking at the remote in his hand. Looking at his thumb.

Maggie knew he had a murderer's thumb. She'd pointed it out, called it to his attention.

Maybe she'd think about that and put it together with whatever she'd picked up when he'd been ready to reach for her. And maybe she'd factor in the way he was retired at an early age, but went out of town occasionally on special jobs for unspecified corporate employers. And maybe there'd be a hired killer in the headlines, or in some movie she saw, or some TV program. And maybe her eyes would widen, and she'd make a connection, and realize just who he was and what he was.

And then?

CHAPTER EIGHTEEN

The airport in Orange County was named after John Wayne. Keller got off the plane with a tune running through his head, and he was halfway to the baggage claim before he worked out what it was. The theme from *The High and the Mighty*.

Funny how the mind did things like that.

There were half a dozen men standing alongside the baggage claim, some in chauffeur's livery, all of them holding hand-lettered signs. Keller walked past them without a glance. No one was meeting him—that was policy, now that the mysterious Roger was out there somewhere. Anyway, no one would be expecting him to fly to Orange County, because his assignment was all the way down in La Jolla. La Jolla was a suburb of San Diego, and San Diego had a perfectly good airport of its own, larger and busier than Orange County's, and not named after anyone.

"Unless you count St. James," Dot had said. When he looked blank, she told him that San Diego was Spanish for St. James. "Or Santiago," she said. "San Diego, Santiago. Same guy."

"Then why do they have two names for him?"

"Maybe one's the equivalent of James," she said, "and the other's more like Jimmy. What's the difference? You're not flying there."

Instead he'd flown to Orange County, just in case Roger might be lurking in San Diego. He didn't really think there was much likelihood of this. They hadn't heard a peep out of Roger since he'd killed a man in Boston, a man who'd stolen Keller's green trench coat and paid dearly for his crime. That was when he and Dot had fig-

186

ured out who Roger was and what he was trying to do.

At the time, Keller had found the whole business extremely upsetting. The idea that there was someone out there, hell-bent on being the impersonal instrument of his death, had him constantly looking over his shoulder. He'd never had to do that before, and he didn't much like it.

But you got used to it. Keller supposed it was a little like having a heart condition. You worried about it at first, and then you stopped worrying. You took sensible precautions, you didn't take the stairs two at a time, you paid a kid to shovel out your driveway in the winter, but you didn't think about it all the time. You got used to it.

And he had gotten used to Roger. There was a man out there, a man who didn't know his name and might or might not recognize him by sight, a man who shared Keller's profession and wanted to thin the ranks of the competition. You quit letting clients meet you at the airport, you covered your tracks, but you didn't have to hide under the bed. You went about your business.

Flying into a less convenient airport came under the heading of sensible precautions. Keller saw it as a bonus that the airport was named for John Wayne. Approaching the Avis counter, he felt a few inches taller, a little broader in the shoulders.

The clerk—Keller wanted to call him *Pilgrim*, but suppressed the urge—checked the license and credit card Keller showed him and was halfway through the paperwork when something pulled him up short. Keller asked him if something was wrong.

"Your reservation," the man said. "It seems it's been canceled."

"Must be a mistake."

"I can reinstate it, no problem. I mean, we have cars available, and you're here."

"Right."

"So I'll just . . . oh, there's a note here. You're supposed to call your office."

"My office."

"That's what it says. Shall I go ahead with this?"

Keller told him to wait. From a pay phone, he called his own apartment in New York. While it rang he had the eerie feeling that the call would be answered, and that the voice he heard would be his own, talking to him. He shook his head, amused at the workings of his own mind, and then he did in fact hear his own voice, inviting him to leave a message. It was his answering machine, of course, but it took him a split second to realize as much, and he almost dropped the phone.

There were no messages.

He broke the connection and called Dot in White Plains, and she picked up halfway through the first ring. "Good," she said. "It worked. I thought of having you paged. 'Mr. Keller, Mr. John Keller, please pick up the white courtesy phone.' But do we really want your name booming out over a loudspeaker?"

"I wouldn't think so."

"And would you even hear it? He'll be through the airport like a shot, I thought. He won't have to stop at the baggage claim, and as soon as he picks up his rental car he's out of there. Bingo, I thought."

"So you called Avis."

"I called everybody. I remembered the name on that license and credit card of yours, but suppose you were using something else? Anyway, Avis had your reservation, and they said they'd see that you got the message, and they were as good as their word. So it worked."

"Not entirely," he said. "While they were at it, they canceled my reservation."

"*I* canceled your reservation, Keller. You don't need a car because you're not going anywhere, aside from the next plane back to New York."

"Oh?"

"Three hours ago, while you were over what? Illinois? Iowa?"

"Whatever."

"While you were experiencing slight turbulence at thirty-five thousand feet," she said, "a couple of uniforms were making vain efforts to revive Heck Palmieri, who had put his belt around his neck, closed the closet door around the free end of the belt, and kicked over the chair he was standing on. Guess what happened to him?"

"He died?"

"For our sins," Dot said, "or for his own, more likely. Either way, it leaves you with nothing to do out there. Other hand, who says you have to make a U-turn? I'll bet you can find somebody to rent you a car."

"They were all set to reinstate the reservation."

"Well, reinstate it, if you want. Have some lunch, see the sights. You're where, Orange County? Go look at some Republicans."

"Well," Keller said. "I guess I'll come home."

"It's a good way to miss jet lag," Keller said, "because I was back where I started before it could draw a bead on me."

"How were your flights?"

"All right, I guess. Pointless, but otherwise all right."

They were on the open front porch of the big house on Taunton Place, sitting in lawn chairs with a pitcher of iced tea on the table between them. It was a warm day, warmer than it had been in Southern California. Of course he'd never really felt the temperature there, because he'd never stepped outside of the air-conditioned airport.

"Not entirely pointless," Dot said. "They paid half in advance, and we get to keep that."

"I should hope so."

"They called here," she said, "to call it off, but of course your flight to California was already in the air by then.

189

They said something about a refund, and I said something about they should live so long."

"A refund!"

"They were just trying it on, Keller. They backed down right away."

"They should pay the whole thing," he said.

"How do you figure that?"

"Well, the guy's dead, isn't he?"

"By his own hand, Keller. His own belt, anyway. What did you have to do with it?"

"What did I have to do with Klinger? Or Petrosian?"

"May they rest in peace," Dot said, "but they're our little secret, remember? Far as the clients were concerned, you showed them the door, sent them on their way. With Palmieri, you were up in the air when he decided to check out the tensile strength of a one-inch strip of split cowhide. Don't look at me like that, Keller. I don't really know what kind of belt he used. The point is you were nowhere around, so how are they going to figure it was your doing?"

"Something you said last time," he said. "About how my thoughts are powerful."

"Oh, right, I'll quick pick up the phone and sell that to the client. 'My guy closed his eyes and thought real hard,' I'll tell him, 'and that's why your guy decided to hang himself. It's a suicide, but we get an assist.' How can they possibly say no?"

"They cut the deal," Keller said doggedly, "and next thing you know the guy's dead."

"Probably because he knew somebody was coming for him and he didn't want to wait." She leaned back in her chair. "For your information," she said, "I tried on something similar. 'You wanted him dead and he's dead,' I said. 'So we should get paid in full.' But it was just a negotiating technique, a counter for them asking for their initial payment back. They laughed at me, and I laughed at them, and we left it where we knew we were going to leave it."

"With us getting half."

"Right. Keller, you didn't really expect the whole thing, did you?"

"No, not really."

"And does it make a difference? I mean, are you stretched financially? It seems to me you've had a batch of decent paydays not too far apart, but maybe it's been going out faster than it's been coming in. Is that it?"

"No."

"Or maybe there's some stamp you were counting on buying with the Palmieri proceeds, and now you can't. Is it anything like that?"

"No."

"Well, don't leave a girl hanging, Keller. What is it?"

He thought for a moment. "It's not the money," he said.

"I hope you're not going to tell me it's the principle of the thing."

"No," he said. "Dot, remember when I was talking about retiring?"

"Vividly. You had enough money, and I told you you'd go nuts, that you needed a hobby. So you started collecting stamps."

"Right."

"And all of a sudden you couldn't afford to retire anymore, because you spent all your money on stamps. So we were back in business."

That was a simplification, he thought, but it was close enough. "Even without the stamps," he said, "I couldn't have retired. Well, I could have, but I couldn't have stayed retired."

"You're saying you need the work."

"I guess so, yes."

"You need to do what you do."

"Evidently."

"Some inner need."

"I suppose. I don't get a kick out of it, you know."

"I never thought you did."

"Sometimes, you know, it's tricky, and there's the satisfaction that comes from solving a problem. Like a crossword puzzle. You fill in the last square and the thing's complete."

"Stands to reason."

"But that's only some of the time. Mostly all it is is work. You go someplace, you do the job, you come home."

"And you get paid."

"Right. And I don't mind long layoffs between jobs. I find ways to keep busy, and that was true even before I started with the stamps."

"But all of a sudden something's different."

"Roger's got something to do with it," he said. "The idea that somebody's out there, you know? Lurking in the shadows, waiting to make his move. Doesn't even know who I am and he wants to kill me anyway."

"Stress," Dot said.

"Well, I suppose. And, you know, once we figured out what he was doing and why, the bastard disappeared."

"We stopped giving him opportunities," she pointed out. "Once you started flying to less obvious airports and we stopped letting the client send somebody to meet you, we shut Roger out. I'd have to call that a good thing, Keller. You're still breathing, right?"

"Right."

"And the last three jobs, well, even if he was lurking on the scene, he still couldn't get a look at you, could he? Because you didn't do anything."

"I would have," he said. "If I'd had any kind of a chance."

"But you didn't, and if Roger was around all he could do was stand there with his thumb up his nose, and you came home and got paid. I don't see a major problem here, Keller."

"It's being teased like this," he said. "Packing my bag, going someplace, figuring out what I'll do and how I'll do it, and the rug's pulled out from under me. I don't like it, that's all."

"I can understand that."

He lowered his eyes, sorted out his thoughts. Then he said, "Dot, I almost killed somebody."

"Except you couldn't, because he killed himself first."

"No, forget that. Here."

"Here?"

"Not here," he said, gesturing. "Not right here in White Plains. In New York. And not for business."

She looked at him sharply. "What's that leave, Keller? For pleasure?"

"Dot, for God's sake."

"Well, what else is there?"

"Personal reasons."

"Oh, right," she said, relaxing. "Don't take it personally, Keller, but sometimes I forget you have a personal life."

"There's this woman I was seeing," he said.

"Dresses in black."

"That's the one."

"Wants to keep it superficial, won't have dinner with you or let you buy her anything."

"Right."

"And you wanted to kill her?"

"I didn't exactly want to," he said, "but I almost did."

"No kidding," Dot said. "What did she do to piss you off, if you don't mind my asking? Was she sleeping with somebody else?"

"No," he said, and then thought about it. "Or maybe she was, for all I know. I never gave it much thought."

"I guess you're not the jealous type. So it must have been something serious, like eating crackers in bed."

"I wasn't angry."

"If I just sit here quietly," Dot said, "you'll explain."

When he'd finished, Dot took the empty pitcher inside and came back with a full one. "This weather," she said, "I drink gallons of this stuff. You suppose it's possible to drink too much iced tea?"

"No idea."

"I guess everything's bad for you if you take in enough of it."

"I guess."

"Keller," she said, "the woman's a loose end. Getting the impulse to tie her off doesn't make you a homicidal maniac."

"I never said—"

"I know what you never said. You think you're frustrated because you keep going out on jobs and fate won't let you pull the trigger. And maybe you are, but that's not why the hair stood up on the back of your neck when your girlfriend said what she did."

"It was more that I got a tingling in my hands."

"Thanks for clearing that up, Keller. I repeat, she's a loose end. You'd have had the same impulse if you'd just come back from depopulating Kosovo. And it wouldn't have just been a passing thought, either. You'd have closed the sale."

"She didn't do anything, Dot."

"And you'd have made sure she never did."

He thought about it. "Maybe," he acknowledged. "But I didn't, and I never heard anything from her. By now she's probably been in and out of half a dozen other superficial relationships. Odds are she never even thinks of me."

"You're probably right," Dot said. "Let's hope so."

Six weeks later, Keller got a phone call, made another trip to White Plains. He was back in his apartment around one in the afternoon, and two hours later he was at JFK, waiting to board a TWA flight to St. Louis.

During the flight, Keller read the SkyMall catalog.

There were articles he wanted to buy, and he knew he wouldn't have given them a second thought under other circumstances. This happened all the time when he flew, and once he was on the ground the urge to order the supervalue luggage or the handy Pocket Planner vanished forever, or at least until his next flight. Maybe it was the altitude, he thought. Maybe it undercut your sales resistance.

No one was supposed to meet him at the airport, and no one did. Keller took a slip of paper from his wallet. He'd already committed the name and address to memory, but he read them again, just to be certain. Then he went outside and got a cab.

The target was a man named Elwood Murray. He lived in Florissant, a suburb north of the city, and had an office on Olive, halfway between City Hall and the city's trademark arch.

Keller had the cab drop him at a lunch counter a block from Murray's office. A sign in the window said the daily special was Three-Alarm Chili, and that sounded good to Keller. If it was as good as it sounded, he could come back for more. There was no rush on this one, Dot had told him. He could take his time.

But instead he went directly to Murray's office building. It was six stories tall and a few years past its prime. Murray's name was listed on the board in the lobby: MURRAY, ELWOOD, #604. The self-service elevator was one of the slowest Keller had encountered, and he found himself urging it upward. If he'd known it was going to be this slow he'd have taken the stairs.

Murray had his name painted on the frosted glass of his office door, along with some initials that didn't mean anything to Keller. There was a light on, and Keller turned the knob, opened the door. A man a few years older than Keller sat behind a big oak desk. He was in shirtsleeves, and his suit jacket was hanging from a peg on the side wall.

"Elwood Murray?"

"Yes?"

"I'll just need a minute of your time," Keller said, and closed the door. That would keep them from being observed by anyone passing in the hall, but the act was enough to alert Murray, and one look at Murray's face was enough to put Keller in motion. Murray moved first, his hand darting into the desk's center drawer, and Keller threw himself forward, hurling himself against Murray's desk and shoving it all the way to the wall, pinning Murray and his chair, jamming the drawer shut on his hand.

Murray couldn't open the drawer, couldn't get his hand out, couldn't move. Keller could move, though, and did, and got his hands on the man.

"Oh, good," Dot said. "You got the message."

"What message?"

"On your machine. You didn't get it? Then why are you calling?"

"Mission accomplished," he said.

There was a pause. Then she said, "I suppose that means what I think it means."

"There aren't too many different things it could mean," he said. "Remember the errand you asked me to run this morning? Well, I ran it."

"You're not still in New York, then."

"No, of course not. I'm in . . . well, I can see the Arch from here."

"And I don't suppose it's the McDonald's across the street, is it? And you already did what you went there to do."

"Or I wouldn't be calling. Dot, what the hell's the matter?"

"They called it off," she said.

"They . . ."

"Called it off. Changed their minds. Canceled the contract."

196

"Oh."

"But you didn't know that."

"How would I know?"

"You wouldn't, not unless you happened to check your machine, and why would you do that? Well, what's your plan now, Keller?"

"I thought I'd come home."

"You're not going to visit some stamp dealers? Spend a few days, find a nice Mexican restaurant?"

"Not this time."

"Probably just as well," she said. "Come home, come see me, and we'll get this sorted out."

"On the way out," he said, "I had the urge to buy a Pocket Planner. Coming home, it was a set of college courses on video. The country's best lecturers, the ad said."

"Would you watch them?"

"Of course not," Keller said. "Any more than I'd use the Pocket Planner. What do I want to plan? It's funny how it works. You stow your carry-on in the overhead compartment, you make sure your seat belt's securely fastened, and you start wanting things you never wanted before. They have these in-flight phones, and you can call and order this stuff at no charge." He frowned. "No charge for the phone call, that is."

"What did you buy?"

"Nothing," he said. "I never do, but I always think about it."

"Keller . . ."

"Why'd they call it off?"

"I don't know," she said, "because I don't know why they called it on in the first place. Who was he, anyway?"

"He had an office," Keller said, "all by himself, and he had some initials after his name, but I don't remember what they were. I guess he was some kind of businessman, and I got the impression he wasn't doing too well at it."

"Well, maybe he owed money, and maybe he paid up after all. Which is more than they're going to do."

"The client, you mean."

"Right."

"Paid half in front, and doesn't want to pay the balance."

"Right again."

"I don't see why. I did what I was supposed to do."

"But by the time you did it," she said, "you weren't supposed to do it."

"Not my fault."

"I agree with you, Keller."

"They didn't say go out there and await further instructions. They said do the job, and I did the job. What's the problem?"

"The problem is they hate paying for a job they tried to cancel. As a matter of fact, they wanted their advance back."

"That's ridiculous."

"Exactly what I told them."

"I did the job," he said. "I should get paid in full."

"I told them that, too."

"And?"

"You could call it a Mexican standoff," she said, "if you're prepared to run the risk of being politically incorrect."

"We keep what they already paid us."

"You got it."

"And they keep what they owe us."

"If you want to call it that."

"I don't know what else to call it," he said. "Why a *Mexican* standoff, do you happen to know? What's Mexican about it?"

"You're the stamp collector, Keller. Is there a Mexican stamp with a famous standoff pictured on it?"

"A famous standoff? What's a famous standoff?"

"I don't know. The Alamo, maybe."

198

"The Alamo wasn't a standoff. It was a massacre, every-body got killed."

"If you say so."

"And the Mexicans wouldn't put it on a stamp. It's the Texans who made a shrine out of the place."

"The ones who got massacred."

"Well, not the same ones, but other Texans. The Mexicans would just as soon forget the whole thing."

"All right," she said. "Forget the Alamo. Forget the Maine, too, while you're at it. If you want to know why they call it a Mexican standoff, I'm sure you can look it up. Spend an afternoon at the library, ask the lady at the research desk to help you out. That's what she's there for, Keller."

"Dot . . ."

"Keller, it's an expression. Who cares where it came from?"

"It won't keep me up nights."

"And who cares about the money? You don't. It's not about the money, is it?"

He thought about it. "No," he said. "I guess not."

"It's about being right. They don't pay you, they're saying you're wrong. You settle for half, you're *admitting* you're wrong."

"But I did what I was supposed to do, Dot! They didn't say go there and wait for instructions. They didn't say find the guy and count to ten. They said—"

"I know what they said, Keller."

"Well."

"You were in a hurry," she said, "because of the way things have been going lately, and because there's always the shadow of Roger lurking in the wings. On the one hand you're absolutely right, you did what you were sup-posed to do, but there's something else to think about that's got nothing to do with the client."

"What's that?"

199

"Normally you take your time," she said. "A couple of days, anyway. Sometimes a week, sometimes longer."

"So?"

"Why, Keller?"

"Why was I in a hurry? You just told *me* why I was in a hurry."

She shook her head. "Why do you take your time? I'll tell you, Keller, sometimes it's frustrating for the folks on the home front. You don't just take your time. You dawdle."

"I dawdle?"

"You probably don't, but it seems that way from a distance. And it's not just because there's a good place for breakfast, or the motel television set gets HBO. You take your time so you can make sure you do the job right."

She went on talking and he found himself nodding. He got the point. Because he'd been in such a rush, Murray had seen it coming, had been reaching for a gun when Keller got to him. If the desk drawer had been open to begin with, if Murray had been a little bit faster or Keller a little bit slower . . .

"I'm not saying it's anything to worry about," Dot said. "It's over and you came out of it okay. But you might want to think about it."

"I'll think about it," he said, "whether I want to or not."

"I suppose you will. Keller?"

"What?"

"You're fussing with your thumb."

"I am?"

"The funny one. I forget what you called it."

"Murderer's thumb."

"Rubbing it, hiding it behind your fingers."

"Just a nervous habit," he said.

"I suppose twiddling it would be worse. Look, lighten up, huh? Nothing went wrong, you went out and came back the same day, and on an hourly basis I'd say you made out like a bandit."

"I guess."

"But?"

"I was thinking about Elwood Murray."

"Never think about them, Keller."

"I hardly ever do. Murray, though, he got killed for no reason."

She was shaking her head. "There's always a reason," she said. "He pissed somebody off. Then he straightened it out, but how long would it stay that way? How long before he pissed somebody else off big-time, and somebody picked up a phone?"

"He did look like the kind of guy who would piss people off."

"There you go," she said.

CHAPTER NINETEEN

"I suppose I should be glad you recognize my voice," Dot said. "You haven't heard it much lately, have you?"

"I guess not."

"I turned a couple of things down," she said, "because they didn't smell right. But this one smells as good as morning coffee, and we're definitely the first ones called, so you won't have to be looking over your shoulder all the time. So why don't you get on a train and I'll tell you all about it?"

"Hold on," Keller said, and put the phone down. When he picked it up again he said, "Sorry, the water was boiling."

"I heard it whistling. I'm glad you told me what it was. For a minute there I thought you were having an air raid."

"No, just a cup of tea."

"I didn't know you were that domestic," she said. "You wouldn't happen to have a soufflé in the oven, would you?"

"A soufflé?"

"Never mind, Keller. Pour the tea in the sink and come up and see me. I'll give you all the tea you can drink. . . . Keller? Where'd you go?"

"I'm here," he said. "This is out of town, right?"

"It's White Plains," she said. "Same as always. A scant forty minutes on Metro North. Does it all come back to you now?"

"But the job's out of town."

"Well, of course, Keller. I'm not about to book you in the city you call home. We tried that once, remember?"

"I remember," he said. "The thing is, I can't leave town."

"You can't leave town?"

"Not for a while."

"What have you got, one of those house-arrest collars on your ankle? It gives you a shock if you leave your property?"

"I have to stay in New York, Dot."

"You can't take a train to White Plains?"

"I could do that," he allowed. "Today, anyway. But I can't take a job out of town."

"For a while, you say."

"Right."

"How long is a while, anyway? A day? A week? A month?"

"I don't know."

"Drink your tea," she said. "Maybe it'll perk you up. And then catch the next train, and we'll talk."

"I think I figured it out," she said, "but maybe not. What I decided is there's a stamp auction that you just can't miss, some stamp coming up that you need for your collection."

"Dot, for God's sake."

"What's the matter?"

"It's a hobby," he said. "I wouldn't pass up work to go to a stamp auction."

"You wouldn't?"

"Of course not."

"Even if it was a stamp you needed for your collection?"

"There are thousands of stamps I need for my collection," he said. "Enough so that I can keep busy without having to go to any particular auction."

"But if there was one particular stamp you absolutely had to have? But I guess it doesn't work that way."

"For some collectors, maybe, but not for me. Anyway, I haven't been spending that much time with my stamps lately."

"Oh?"

"I wouldn't say I've lost interest," he said, "but it sort of ebbs and flows. I subscribe to a couple of magazines and a weekly newspaper, and sometimes I'll read everything cover to cover, but lately I haven't even glanced at them. A couple of dealers send me selections on approval, and I keep up with those, but that's about all I've been doing lately. Other dealers send me price lists and auction catalogs and lately I've been tossing them out without looking at them."

"That's a shame."

"No," he said, "it's more like taking a break from it. I was worried myself, that it was turning out to be a passing fancy, but the astrologer said not to worry."

"You've been to the astrologer again?"

"I call her sometimes, if there's something that bothers me. She takes a quick look at my chart and tells me if it's a dangerous time for me, or whatever it was made me call her in the first place."

"This time it was stamps."

"And she said my interest would be like the weather."

"Partly cloudy, with a threat of rain."

"Hot one day and cold the next," he said. "Variable, but nothing to worry about. And the nice thing about stamp collecting is you can put it aside for as long as you want and pick it up right where you left off. It's not like a garden, where you have to keep up with the weeds."

"I know, they're worse than the Joneses."

"Or a virtual aquarium, where the fish die."

"A virtuous aquarium? As opposed to what, Keller? A sinful one?"

"Virtual," he said. "A virtual aquarium."

"What the hell is that?"

"It's something you can buy for your computer," he said. "You install it and the screen looks like a fish tank, with plants and guppies and everything. And you can add other species of fish—"

"How?"

"By pressing the right keys, I guess. The thing is, it's just like a real aquarium, because if you forget to feed the fish, they'll die."

"They die?"

"That's right."

"How can they die, Keller? They're not real fish in the first place, are they?"

"They're virtual fish."

"Meaning what? They're images on a screen, right? Like a television program."

"Sort of."

"So they swim around on your screen. And if you don't feed 'em, then what? They turn belly up?"

"Evidently."

"Have you got one of these, Keller?"

"Of course not," he said. "I don't have a computer."

"I didn't think you did."

"I don't want a computer," he said, "and if I had one I wouldn't want a virtual aquarium."

"How come you know so much about them?"

"I hardly know anything about them," he said. "I read an article, that's all."

"Not in one of your stamp magazines."

"No, of course not."

"If it's not stamps, what could it be? A woman? Keller, are you seeing that girl again?"

"What girl?"

"I guess that's a no, isn't it? The black girl, the one who wouldn't eat dinner. I could come up with her name if I put my mind to it."

"Maggie."

"Now I don't have to put my mind to it."

"She's not black. She wears black."

"Close enough."

"Anyway, I'm not seeing her. Or anybody else."

"Probably just as well," Dot said. "You know what? I give up. I was trying to guess why you can't leave New York, and I got stuck in a conversation about stamp collecting, and it turned into a conversation about fish, and I don't want to find out what that's going to turn into. So let me ask you what I probably should have asked you over the phone. Why can't you leave New York?"

He told her.

Her eyes widened. "Jury duty? You, Keller? You have to be on a jury?"

"I have to report," he said. "Whether I actually get on a jury is something else again."

"Many are called but few are chosen. But how on earth did you get called in the first place?"

"I don't know."

"I mean, the jury system isn't supposed to make use of people like you, is it?"

"People like me?"

"People who do what you do."

"Not if they get caught," he said. "I don't think you can serve on a jury if you've been convicted of a felony. But I've never even been charged with a felony, or with anything else. I've never been arrested, Dot."

"And a good thing."

"A very good thing," he said. "As far as anybody knows, as far as any official records would indicate, I'm a law-abiding citizen."

"Citizen Keller."

"And I am," he said. "I don't shoplift, I don't use or sell drugs, I don't hold up liquor stores, I don't mug people. I don't stiff cabdrivers or vault subway turnstiles."

"How about jaywalking?"

"That's not even a misdemeanor. It's a violation, and anyway I've never been cited for it. I have a profession that, well, we know what it is. But nobody else knows about it, so it's not going to keep me off a jury."

"You don't vote, do you, Citizen Keller? Because I thought they drew jurors from the voter registration lists."

"That used to be all they used," he said, "and that's probably why I never got called before now. But now they use other lists, too, from Motor Vehicles and the phone company and I don't know what else."

"You don't own a car. And your phone's unlisted."

"But I've got a driver's license. And they'd use the phone company's billing records, not the phone book. Look, what's the difference how they found me? I got a notice, and I have to report first thing Monday morning."

"Today's Friday."

"Right."

"Can't you get a postponement?"

"I could have," he said, "if I'd asked for one when I got the notice. But I figured I might as well get it out of the way, and things have been slow lately, and I missed my chance."

"Won't they let you off?"

"On what grounds? They used to let people off all the time. If you were a lawyer, or if you were in business for yourself. Now you just about have to tell them you're pregnant, and I'm not even sure if that works."

"They'd never believe you, Keller."

"Nobody gets out of it these days," he said. "The mayor was on a jury a couple of months ago. Remember?"

"I read something about it."

"He probably could have gotten excused. He's the mayor, for God's sake, he can do anything he wants to. But I guess he decided it was good for his image. Imagine if you're on trial and you look over in the jury box and there's the mayor."

"I'd plead guilty on the spot."

"Might as well," he said. "I wish I could take this job. I could use the work. You know what's funny? I figured, well, I'll show up for jury duty because it'll give me something to do. And now I've *got* something to do, and I can't do it."

"It's a good one, Keller."

"Tell me about it."

It was in Baltimore, so you could fly there in less than an hour or get there by train in under three. The train was more comfortable, and, when you factored in the cab rides to and from the airports, it was about as fast. And you didn't have to show ID when you got on a train, and you could pay cash without drawing a raised eyebrow, let alone a crowd of security types. All things considered, Keller figured trains had a definite edge.

There was a section of Baltimore called Fells Point, a sort of funky ethnic neighborhood that was starting to draw tourists and people with something to sell them. And—

"You're nodding," Dot said. "You know the neighborhood? When did you ever go to Baltimore?"

"Once or twice years ago," he said, "but just in and out. But I know about Fells Point from TV. There's this cop show set in Baltimore."

"Didn't it get canceled?"

"It's in reruns," he said. "Five nights a week on Court TV."

"You watch a lot of Court TV, Keller? As a sort of preparation for jury duty? Never mind."

There were, she explained, the usual conflicts that develop in a neighborhood in transition, with one faction desperate to pin landmark status on every gas station and hot dog stand, and the other every bit as eager to tear down everything and build condos and theme restaurants. There was a woman named Irene Macnamara who was a particularly vocal force for or against development, and someone on the other side had reached the conclusion that shutting her up constituted an all-important first step.

While there had been a lot of loud outbursts at planning

commission hearings, a lot of harsh words at press conferences, so far the controversy had not turned violent. So there was no reason for Macnamara to be on her guard.

Keller thought about it. He said, "You're sure they haven't called anybody else?"

"We're their first choice."

"What did you tell them?"

"That Macnamara better not buy any long-playing records, because we were on the case."

"You phrased it that way?"

"Of course not, Keller. I just put that in to brighten your day."

"Today's Friday."

"Well, I'll try to come up with something for Saturday as well. There's that page in *Reader's Digest*, 'Toward More Picturesque Speech.' Maybe it'll give me ideas."

"What I mean, today's Friday. I could go down there tonight and I'd have tomorrow and Sunday."

"Catch a train home Sunday night and you're ready to do your civic duty bright and early Monday morning."

"That's what I was thinking."

"No LP's for Macnamara, and no green bananas either. I don't know, Keller. I like it but I don't like it, if you follow me."

"I'm not sure I do."

"So I'll say two words. St. Louis."

"Oh."

"Now that was a quick one. Out and back the same day. Unfortunately . . ."

"Does this client know he can't change his mind?"

"As a matter of fact, he does. I made sure of it. But that's not the only thing that's wrong with hurrying. If you go to Baltimore knowing you've got less than forty-eight hours to get the job done . . ."

Keller got the point. It wasn't great when you could hear the clock ticking.

"I wouldn't want to cut corners," he said, "but say I go down there tonight and spend the weekend looking things over. If I get the opportunity to close the sale, I take it. If not I'm on the train back Sunday night."

"And then I tell the client to go roll his hoop?"

"No, what you tell the client is I'm on the case and the job is as good as done. Jury duty isn't a lifetime commitment. How long can it take?"

"That's what the lady in L.A. said, when they picked her for the O. J. jury."

"I'll go back to Baltimore next weekend," he said, "and the weekend after that, if I have to, and by then I'll be done doing my civic duty. Did the client put a time limit on it?"

"No. He wouldn't want her to die of old age, but there's no clause in the contract saying time is of the essence."

"So at the most we're looking at two, three weeks, and if there's any question you tell them I'm in Baltimore, trying to make sure I do the job right."

"And you could always catch a break along the way."

"A break?"

"The famous Keller luck. Macnamara could stroke out or get run over by a cable car."

"In Baltimore?"

"Whatever. Oh, and this doesn't have to be natural causes, by the way, and in fact it's better if it's not. She's supposed to be an object lesson."

"An example to others."

"Something like that."

He nodded. "I won't hurry this one," he said, "but I hope I get it done this weekend."

"I thought you liked to take your time."

"Sometimes," he said. "Not always."

The bar, called Counterpoint, was on Fleet Street, and pretty much in the heart of Fells Point. Keller got a very strange feeling walking into it. On the one hand he felt oddly at home, as if he'd spent a lot of happy hours within its walls. At the same time, he sensed that it was not a safe place for him to be.

It certainly looked safe enough. The crowd ran to twenty or thirty people, more men than women. They were mostly white, mostly in their thirties or forties. Dress was casual, mood relaxed. Keller had been in bars where you knew right away that half the customers had criminal records, that people were doing coke in the rest rooms, that before the night was over someone was going to break a bottle over someone else's head. And this simply wasn't that kind of place, or that sort of crowd. No crooks, no cops. Just ordinary folks.

And then he got it. Cops. He kept feeling as though the place ought to be full of cops, cops drinking away the tension of the job, other cops behind the bar, drawing beers, mixing drinks. It was that damned program, he realized. The cops on the program had opened a bar together, it was supposed to provide comic relief or something, and he felt as though he'd just walked into it.

Was this the very place? It wouldn't be staffed with cops in real life, obviously, but it could be where the TV crew filmed those scenes. Except it wasn't, the layout was different. It was just a bar, and an unequivocally comfortable one, now that he'd finally figured out what had seemed wrong about it.

He settled in on his stool and sipped his beer.

It would be nice to take his time. The neighborhood was the sort he would have liked even if he hadn't already grown fond of it on television. But he hoped he'd be done with this job in a hurry, and not just for the reason he'd given Dot.

Irene Macnamara might be a preservationist or a developer, Dot hadn't known which, and he didn't know either, not for a fact. But he figured the odds were something like ten to one that she wanted to keep Fells Point the way it was, while their client wanted to throw up hotels and outlet malls and bring in the chain stores. Because that's where the profit was, in developing an area, not in fighting a holding action to keep it unchanged.

This didn't necessarily mean she was a nice person. Keller knew it didn't always work that way. She could be a holy terror in her private life, nagging her husband and slapping her children and poisoning the pigeons in the park. But as far as the future of Fells Point was concerned, Keller was on her side. He liked it the way it was.

Of course, that assumed she was a preservationist, and he didn't really know that for sure. And that was the whole thing, because he really didn't want to know one way or the other. Because he had the feeling that, the more he got to know about Irene Macnamara, the less inclined he'd be to do the job.

It would be easier all around if she was off the board before he had to return to New York.

Which was a shame, because he had to admit he liked it here. It wasn't the bar from the TV series, and it wasn't a place he'd ever seen before, but he still felt curiously comfortable. He didn't have a favorite bar in New York, he didn't really spend a great deal of time in bars, but he somehow sensed that this place, Counterpoint, would suit him as no New York bar ever had. And wouldn't it be nice to have a place you came to every day, a place where everybody knew your name, and—

No, he thought. That was another television series, and it wasn't real, either.

CHAPTER TWENTY

He was back in New York late Sunday night, and at eight-fifteen the next morning he was at the State Supreme Court building on Centre Street, showing his summons to a guard who told him where to go. You had to pass through a metals detector, too. They had them in the schools now, and in an increasing number of public buildings. Pretty soon, he thought, you'd have to pass through a metals detector to go to the supermarket.

Probably necessary, though. All these kids bringing guns to class, and all these terrorists. What it did, though, was screw things up for the average law-abiding citizen. Years ago there'd been a rash of airplane hijackings. Before that you just walked onto a plane, the same as a train or a bus, but then because of the hijackers they routed you through a metals detector, and ever since it had been impossible for an ordinary citizen like Keller to bring a gun on a plane.

Well, maybe that wasn't the best example . . .

He hadn't brought a gun to court, but what he did bring was a book. He hadn't mentioned his impending jury duty to that many people——he wasn't friendly with that many people——but he'd said something to the girl who served him breakfast at the coffee shop, and to the doorman at the building next door to his, and to the guy who sold him his newspaper. They all said the same thing, and he had to wonder about the guy at the newsstand. He was a Pakistani, he'd been in the country less than two years, and he already knew you had to bring something to read when you pulled jury duty? Well, Keller told himself, the guy was in the business. He sold reading material, and maybe he had people coming in from time to time, saying they were on jury duty and needed something to read. He'd get the drift that way, wouldn't he?

Keller's novel was a thriller. The bad guy was a terrorist, but no metals detector had a chance against him, because he wasn't carrying a gun. Instead he was equipped with a sufficient supply of a new supervirus to start a plague that would wipe out the city of New York, and possibly the whole country, and not inconceivably the world. The disease was a particularly nasty one, too, and a hundred percent fatal, and it didn't just kill you, either. You bled from every orifice, even your pores, and you convulsed and your bones ached and your tongue swelled up and your teeth fell out and your hands and feet turned purple and you went blind. Then you died, and not a moment too soon.

The heroine, a special operative from the Centers for Disease Control, was beautiful, of course, but she was also resourceful and decisive and tough-minded. She kept doing stupid things, though, and you wanted to take her by the shoulders and give her a good shaking.

Keller thought the hero was too good to be true. His wife had been a research scientist with the CDC, and she'd died from a similar disease, one she'd caught from an infected hamster at the research lab. The hero was grieving manfully, and bringing up their kids, all while investigating cases for some secret arm of the Treasury Department. He helped the old lady next door with yardwork, and he coached his kids with their homework, and every woman he met yearned to sleep with him or mother him, or both. Everyone was crazy about him, everyone except the heroine.

And Keller, but that was pretty much par for the course. White knights had never appealed much to Keller.

All morning long they called names, and people went to various rooms to see if they'd be selected for juries. Keller's name wasn't called, and by lunchtime he was well into his book. On the way out of the building, a woman fell into step beside him. "That book must be good," she said. "You seemed really engrossed."

"It's okay," he said. "A maniac's going to start a plague that'll wipe out New York unless this girl finds a way to stop him."

"Woman," she said.

Oh boy, he thought. "Well, she's only six years old," he said, "so I figured it would be acceptable to call her a girl."

"She's only six?"

"Going on seven."

"And the fate of the world is in her hands?"

"It's quite a responsibility at any age," Keller said. "But it's good preparation. Fifteen years from now she might have to sit on a jury and decide the fate of a fellow human being."

"Awesome."

"I'll say."

"You like Vietnamese food? There's a place on the next block that's supposed to be good. But I didn't see it on the list they handed out."

"An unlisted restaurant," he said. "Off-limits to jurors. Let's be daring, let's check it out."

They sent everybody home at three o'clock, and by four he was on the phone with Dot. "I had something to read," he told her, "and I had a nice lunch. Vietnamese food."

"Watch it, Keller. Next you'll want to move there."

"I may just have a couple more days of this. They're picking juries, and if you don't get picked in three days there's a good chance they'll send you home."

"So don't get picked."

"So far so good," he said. "We all sit in the jury room, and every once in a while they call a bunch of names and take the lucky winners to a courtroom."

"And they're the jury?"

"They go through voir dire, with lawyers asking them questions, and they stop when they've got twelve jurors and two alternates. Then they throw the others back in the pool."

"Is that what happened to you?"

"During the morning I didn't even get out of the jury room," he said. "In the afternoon I got herded to a courtroom, and they found fourteen jurors they could live with before they even got to me."

"So they tossed you back in the pool."

"And I started paddling, keeping my head above water, and they dismissed us for the day. I'd say the odds are I won't get on a jury at all. But it's not up to me. It's up to the lawyers."

"Now there's a bad idea," she said. "You want to ruin a system, just leave things up to the lawyers. Look, Keller, I think what you want to do is be a little proactive on this one."

"What do you mean?"

"I mean you ought to be able to keep from getting chosen. There's a word I want, but what the hell is it?"

"Impaneled."

"The very word. You can make sure you don't get impaneled. When they ask you how you feel about the death penalty, you tell 'em you're unequivocally opposed to it, that as far as you're concerned it's just a form of judicial murder. The DA'll kick you out so fast you'll have boot marks on your behind."

"That's brilliant," he said.

"Actually it's pretty obvious, Keller. But it'll work. Two more days, huh?"

"That's what they tell me."

"**O**ne more day," Keller said.

Tuesday morning he had exchanged nods and smiles with his lunch companion from the previous day, and when lunch hour rolled around they fell into step and into conversation. Without either of them actually suggesting it, they walked straight to the Saigon Pearl and took the same table they'd shared the day before.

"Unless we win the lottery," Gloria said.

That was her name, Gloria Dantone. She was a few years younger than Keller, with short dark hair and a lopsided smile. She worked as a legal secretary at a midtown law firm. ("But they're never in court," she'd confided. "They do corporate real estate, they represent lenders at closings.") She lived in Inwood with her husband, an accountant who worked at the World Financial Center. ("One of the Big Four firms. When he started they were the Big Eight, and then the Big Six, and now it's down to four. They keep merging. Pretty soon it'll be the Huge Two, I guess, but it doesn't matter to Jerry. He just goes to the office and deals with what's on his desk.") Keller didn't know what she was talking about. He knew the Big Ten was a college football conference, but this had to be something else. He figured he didn't need to know more.

"Win the lottery," he said. "It's a matter of chance, all right. But look what you get if you win."

"We might get on an interesting case. Listen, it's got to be as interesting as what I do at the office. And it's not like it costs me money to be here. The company pays my salary."

"And the city pays me," Keller said.

"Yeah, all of forty bucks a day. At those prices you'd think people'd be fighting to get on a jury. You're pretty young to be retired."

"Downsizing," he said. "My job disappeared and the severance package was good, and I had money put aside. I pick up some freelance work now and then."

On the way back she asked him how he was enjoying the book. "It's okay," he said. "I had to stop myself from finishing it last night."

"She's not really six years old, is she?"

"Midthirties."

"You smartass. Of course that's just what I was being, busting you for calling her a girl. I hope I get on a case."

"Really?"

"Why not? I'm having fun."

He called Dot Wednesday afternoon. "They sent you home early," she said. "I guess that means for you the war is over."

"I got on a jury."

"You're kidding," she said. "Did you tell them how you felt about the death penalty?"

"It didn't come up," he said. "I guess when some kid runs off with a woman's purse, they don't much care how you feel about the death penalty."

"Some little bastard snatches a woman's purse, he damn well ought to get the needle. Is that the case they stuck you with? A purse-snatching?"

"No, I think it involves stolen goods. The defendant was sitting there throughout voir dire, and he looks too old and slow for purse-snatching. I'll find out more tomorrow, when we hear the opening arguments."

"You'll be up all night wondering."

"I'll be up all night finishing this book."

"The one about the plague? I thought you were saving it to read in court."

"Once you're on a jury," he said, "they make you stop reading. You have to pay attention."

"Unless you're the judge. Keller, couldn't you have done something during the whatchacallit?"

"Voir dire."

"Whatever. Couldn't you have expressed an extreme opinion?"

"I didn't really know what they would or wouldn't like," he said, "so I gave up trying to figure it out and just answered the questions. And they picked me."

"Lucky you. You still get weekends off, right?"

"Friday afternoon to Monday morning."

"Unless you get sequestered."

"The kind of trial where they lock up the jury every night," he said, "is the kind where it takes them a week to select a jury. They picked all twelve jurors and two alternates in a few hours."

"Small potatoes, in other words. How long will it last?"

"A few days. Maybe a week."

"That's not too bad."

"No."

"You'll go down to Baltimore this weekend?"

"As soon as they send us home."

"And either you'll get it done right away or you'll go back a few days later when the trial's over. I don't see a problem. Do you, Keller?"

"No," he said. "No problem."

Alone in his apartment, with nothing to distract him, he got caught up in the book. The evolving relationship of the hero and the heroine, prickly at first and increasingly romantic, left him unmoved, but there was an urgency to the rest of the plot that kept him turning pages.

And he couldn't help liking the bad guy. The author tried to humanize the villain by telling you what a rotten childhood he had, how his father abused him and his mother died and all the other bad things that happened to him. That might explain why he was the way he was, though Keller didn't really buy it. Keller liked him because he liked the way the guy operated, the way his mind worked.

Early on, there was this scene where this cute little girl is playing with her puppy, and the bad guy befriends her, and it's sweet, how he has these nice conversations with the kid. And then he tests the virus on her, spikes her milk shake with it, and she dies the way people die from this disease, bleeding from every orifice and writhing in agony.

That was to show you what a son of a bitch he was, in case you'd been harboring any doubts.

Keller didn't see it that way. The only reason the guy befriended the kid in the first place was because he intended to feed her the virus. So it wasn't as though they had a real friendship. The friendship was just part of the act.

Besides, the man was planning on killing off the entire population of New York City, if not the world. The kid would die anyway, along with everybody else. This way she'd beat the crowds, and would wind up in a hospital while there were still doctors and nurses alive to take care of her. They couldn't help her, but they could at least make her halfway comfortable.

Of course, Keller thought, he had a tendency to root for the bad guys. In books, anyway, and in movies. His favorite actors were the guys who got mowed down one after the other by Bruce Willis and Steven Seagal and Jean-Claude Van Damme. There were plenty of good Hollywood villains these days, but as far as he was concerned none of them could hold a torch to Jack Elam, possibly the greatest bad guy who ever got in front of a camera. And when did Jack Elam ever still have a pulse by the time they rolled the final credits?

He wasn't exactly pulling for this particular villain. How could you root for the annihilation of the entire human race? Even if you'd had a bad day, even if you were pissed off at everything and everybody, that had to be considered a little extreme. Still, when the golden couple succeeded in stopping him and saving the world, Keller couldn't help feeling cheated. Here was this major disaster waiting to happen, and what's the payoff? The payoff is that nothing happens. It was like lighting a firecracker and having it fizzle out.

He thought about this in bed, the book finished. He'd forced himself to stay awake long enough to finish it, and now he couldn't sleep. He couldn't afford to toss and turn, he had to be wide awake in the morning so he could sit in judgment on another human being, and—

And that was it. He was excited at the prospect. And he had to admit to himself what he hadn't admitted to Dot. He'd *wanted* to get on the jury.

Part of it, he supposed, was the impulse that made a person want to pass any test, whether or not he'd wanted to take it in the first place. Just like Charlie the Tuna, you wanted to be good enough to be Star-Kist, even if it meant winding up in the can.

So he'd done his best to get chosen. A lot of the questions had to do with the police. Did the prospective juror have any relatives who were cops? Did he believe that cops generally told the truth? Did he believe it was likely that a police officer might bend the truth in order to secure a conviction?

That suggested to Keller—and to anybody else who was paying attention—that some cop's testimony was going to be a key element of the prosecution's case, and that the defense was going to be that the cops were lying to frame an innocent man. If Keller had just wanted to answer the questions honestly, he would have had a hard time doing it. He'd had comfortingly few dealings with the police over the years, and how he felt about them generally depended on what film or TV program he'd watched most recently. He liked the cops from the Baltimore show, and he liked the fact that they sometimes had joint cases with cops on another program set in New York. In fact Munch, Keller's favorite cop from Baltimore, had now moved to New York to be on a new program about sex crimes. It wasn't just the actor who had switched, it was Munch, the character himself. Keller liked that a lot.

But there were other programs where the cops were stupid and brutal and an all-around pain in the ass, and Keller didn't like those cops. They'd stand up in court and lie their heads off, whereas Munch might introduce a lot of irrelevant stuff, blaming the system and the government and his ex-wife whenever he got the chance. But he certainly wouldn't perjure himself.

So Keller didn't follow the example of one woman who preceded him through voir dire. If cops could plant evidence in an attempt to frame a public figure like O. J., she said, then they were capable of anything. *Bang! Excused for cause.* She was followed by a man, every bit as matter-of-fact about it, who said that sometimes it was a cop's obligation to lie in court, or otherwise criminals would get off scot-free. *Whack! Excused for cause.*

Keller steered a middle course, one that made him acceptable to both the prosecution and the defense. He made the cut. He was on the jury.

And so was Gloria Dantone.

At nine the next morning, Keller was seated in the jury box, along with the other lucky thirteen. Both sides had gotten through opening arguments by the time the judge declared a recess for lunch. Automatically, Keller and Gloria drifted apart from the others in the exodus from the courtroom. Just as automatically, they went straight to the Saigon Pearl, where they both ordered the daily special.

They'd talked about the weather on the way to the restaurant, and how fresh the air was compared to the courtroom. Waiting for the food to come, they were both stuck for something to say. "We're not supposed to discuss the case," she said. "In fact I'm not a hundred percent sure we're supposed to be having lunch together."

"The judge didn't say we couldn't."

"No. Can we talk about the other jurors?"

"I don't know. We're not supposed to talk about the lawyers, or what we thought of their opening arguments."

"How about their clothes? How about their hairstyles?"

She rolled her eyes, and Keller got the message that Gloria didn't much care for the prosecutor's clothes, or the way she did her hair. The woman's hair—medium brown with red highlights, shoulder length, worn back off her face—seemed okay to Keller, and she was wearing what looked to him like fairly standard women's business attire, but Keller knew his limitations. When it came to looking at clothes and hairstyles, any heterosexual male was like a noncollector looking at a page full of stamps. He missed the fine points.

"I wonder what they talk about during those bench conferences," he said. "But I have a feeling we're not even supposed to speculate."

"A couple of times I could almost make out what they were saying."

"Really?"

"So I tried not to listen, and that's like trying not to think of something, like a white rhinoceros."

"Huh?"

"Go ahead," she said. "Try not to think of one."

There were a lot of things they couldn't talk about, but that left them the whole world outside of the courtroom. Keller told her how he'd been up late finishing the book, and she told him a story about one of the senior partners at her firm, who was having an affair with a client. They didn't run out of conversation.

At one-thirty they were back in the jury box. The assistant DA who was trying the case began presenting witnesses, and Keller concentrated on their testimony. It was close to five by the time the judge adjourned for the day.

The next day, Friday, he was sorry he'd finished his book. Everybody told you to bring something to read while you waited to see if you drew a case. What they didn't tell you was that you were just as much in need of diversion after you'd been impaneled. You couldn't read during bench conferences—it wouldn't look good if a juror whipped out a paperback the minute the judge and the lawyers got in a huddle—but there were plenty of other opportunities.

"In my chambers," the judge said around ten o'clock, and he and the two lawyers were gone for twenty minutes. A couple of the jurors closed their eyes during their absence, and one of them didn't manage to open them after things got going again.

"I think Mr. Bittner may have nodded off," he said at lunch, and Gloria said the man was either sleeping or he'd mastered the art of wide-awake snoring.

"But we're probably not supposed to talk about it," she said, and he agreed that they probably weren't.

During the afternoon there were a couple more bench conferences and one long break where the judge and the attorneys stayed in the courtroom but the jury had to leave. The bailiff escorted them to another room, where they all sat around a table as if to deliberate the verdict. But they had nothing to ponder, and they were under orders not to discuss the case, and they were seated too close together to have private conversations among themselves, so all they could do, really, was sit there. That was when a book would have come in handy.

Around four-thirty the judge sent them home for the weekend. Keller, who'd packed a briefcase with a clean shirt and a change of socks and underwear, went straight to Penn Station.

CHAPTER TWENTY-ONE

The previous weekend Keller had stayed at a hotel near the train station, but he'd come across a bed and breakfast in Fells Point that looked inviting and was certainly more convenient. He'd reserved a room the night before, and checked in a little after nine. It was almost midnight when he called White Plains from a pay phone around the corner.

"I'm in Baltimore," he said.

"That's nice," she said. "Everybody's got to be some-place. And, since you've got something to do in Baltimore—"

"Not this weekend I don't."

"Oh?"

"Our friend left town. She's on the Eastern Shore."

"Aren't we all? Isn't New York on the eastern shore, and Baltimore, and all points in between?"

It was a section of Maryland, he explained, a sort of peninsula on the other side of Chesapeake Bay. And that's where Irene Macnamara was, and would be until Monday morning.

"At which time you'll be in a stuffy old courtroom," she said. "Unless you're going to make old Aunt Dorothy very happy by telling her the trial's all wrapped up."

"How could that happen? It didn't even start until yesterday morning."

"There's always the miracle of plea bargaining. Not this time, huh?"

"No."

"Was it a purse snatcher, Keller? Are you going to make sure the little bastard gets what's coming to him?"

"I'm not supposed to talk about the case."

"Say that again, Keller."

"Is there something wrong with the connection? I said—"

"I know what you said."

"Then why did you ask me to repeat it?"

"So that you could hear it for yourself. Keller, think about what you just said and who you said it to. And think of all the things you're not supposed to do, including the one you're not going to be able to do this weekend, on account of somebody went to the Eastern Shore."

"This cop bought a VCR," he said.

"Probably a good idea, Keller. The poor guys work long hours, and sometimes they pull double shifts, so how can they be sure of keeping up with their favorite soap operas? The only answer is to tape the shows and watch them later on."

"It was stolen."

"Which means he'll have to buy another one. I hope he's got insurance."

"Look, it's late," he said. "I'll call you tomorrow."

"I'll behave," she said. "I promise. The cop bought a stolen VCR. I suppose the question is did he know it was stolen when he bought it."

"That's why he bought it. The guy who sold it to him didn't know he was a cop, and now he's on trial for trafficking in stolen property."

"Sounds open and shut."

"If the cop's telling the truth."

"What do you think?"

"I don't know," he said. "We haven't even heard the cop's testimony yet."

"You haven't?"

"We've hardly heard anything. The lawyers keep having private conversations, and I gather what they're mostly doing is arguing about what we get to hear. The way it

226

works, the people with the least knowledge of what's going on are the ones on the jury."

"Well, that's the American Way, isn't it?"

"Evidently. The judge said we could read the papers and watch TV, but if there's anything about the case we've got to stop reading."

"Or change the channel."

"Right."

"A guy got hold of a hot VCR and sold it to a cop, I don't think that's going to be the lead item on 'Live at Five.' But you're playing it safe, hiding out in Baltimore. Or are you planning on coming home early?"

"I've got the room booked. I might as well stay."

"The more time you spend there, the more attention you attract."

"I leave the inn ahead of schedule, that attracts attention, too."

"You're staying at an inn?"

"Sort of a bed and breakfast."

"Is it quaint?"

"It's nice," he said. "I'm never too sure what *quaint* means."

"It depends on your tone of voice when you say it. I'm sleepy, Keller. I'm going to bed."

He rang off. He was tired himself, and his canopied four-poster bed had looked inviting, although you wouldn't notice the posts or the canopy once you had your eyes shut.

Quaint.

He hesitated, then started walking in the opposite direction from the inn. He wasn't that tired, and he could sleep as late as he wanted in the morning. So there was no reason not to drop in for a nightcap at Counterpoint.

At lunch Monday Gloria said, "You know how I spent the weekend? You'll think I'm completely nuts."

"You bungee-jumped off the World Trade Center."

"Close. I sat on the couch watching Court TV."

"Bungee-jumping would be nuttier."

"It would also be more exciting. Like I don't get enough of this garbage during the week. You know what I was doing?"

"You just told me."

"No, what I was really up to, in my heart of hearts. It took me a while before I realized it. I was hoping I'd accidentally-on-purpose wind up watching some coverage of our case."

"Unconsciously, you mean."

"Unconsciously at first, right, and then consciously, because I saw what I was doing and went right on doing it. Of course, you know how likely it is that Court TV would waste their time on our case. It's not exactly the Great Train Robbery." She took a forkful of whatever it was they were eating. "And of course they didn't. I don't think there are even any cameras in the courtroom, are there?"

"Not that I noticed."

"When I said I'd been picked for a jury, the first thing my sister-in-law said was maybe I'd be on TV. You know, if they panned the jury. Which I don't think they're supposed to, but who cares anyway? What's the big deal about having your face on a few million television screens?"

"I think it makes it real," Keller said. "You'll see some woman, her baby gets eaten by a coyote, and some reporter sticks a microphone in her face and asks her how she feels."

"And instead of telling him to go fuck himself, like you'd think a normal human being would do—"

"She answers the question and shares her pain with the world. People think that's what they're supposed to do. They think you have to be on television if you get the chance, because it validates your experience."

"Dum-de-dum-dum. 'Deep Thoughts.' But you know what? I think you're right."

★

The next day she said, "I was talking to my brother-in-law about Mr. Bittner and how he can't keep his eyes open."

"Oh?"

"I didn't say he was on the jury, and I didn't mention his name. He said it might have something to do with Mr. Bittner being morbidly obese."

"Morbidly obese?"

"He's a paramedic, he knows all the terms."

The man was obese, Keller thought. Large enough to have his own zip code. But where did morbid come into it? Did carrying all that weight around make you think depressing thoughts? Did you spend hours wondering how many men it would take to carry your coffin?

"Maybe he's just tired," Keller suggested. "Maybe he can't sleep nights because he's weighed down by the responsibility of sitting in judgment over his fellow man."

"Or maybe he's just bored to the point of petrifaction. It's really boring, isn't it?"

"It has its moments," he said, "but they're few and far between, and the rest of it's like watching water evaporate."

"On a humid day. The lawyers go over everything until you want to scream. They ask the same question over and over. They must have a real high opinion of jurors."

"It's not like TV."

"No, or you'd turn it off. Well, take *Law and Order*. The two cops catch the guy in the first thirty minutes, and Sam Waterston puts him away before the hour's up. It takes this prosecutor longer than that to find out what brand of VCR we're talking about."

"Court TV's more realistic."

"When they're reporting live. Otherwise they just show you the part where something's happening. And even with their live coverage, they tend to cut away during the dull parts." She stirred her iced coffee. "I guess we shouldn't be talking about this."

"You can relax," he said, deadpan. "I'm not wearing a wire."

She stared at him, then burst out laughing. And put her hand on top of his.

"The cop's black," he told Dot, "and the defendant's white. I don't think I mentioned that before."

"You and Justice," she said. "Both color-blind."

"At first," he said, "we didn't know. I mean, we knew about the defendant, because there he was sitting with his lawyers, a middle-aged white guy with an OTB face and a bad rug named Huberman."

"His rug's got a name?"

"What is this, English class? You know what I meant. His name is Huberman."

"I know what a rug is," she said, "whether it's got a name or not, and I never saw a good one. But what's an OTB face? Off the books? On the button?"

"Off-track betting," he said. "There's a look horseplayers get."

"A kind of a woulda-coulda-shoulda look."

"That's the one. Anyway, you don't get to see the cop until he gives testimony, and the prosecution's case is fairly far along by then. And it turns out he's black. And the thief's black, too."

"A minute ago you said he was white."

"Not the defendant. The thief, the guy who stole the VCR in the first place and sold it to Huberman. He's a prosecution witness, and he and the cop are both African-Americans."

"So?"

"So that explains a lot about jury selection. The big question in voir dire was do we believe cops lie or tell the truth. Well, generally speaking, white people generally have more faith in the police than black people do."

"Gee, Keller, I wonder why."

230

"Right. So you'd think the prosecution would want white jurors, and the defense would want blacks."

"Got it. When the defendant's white and the cop is black, everything gets turned on its head."

"But I don't think anybody's sure just how far it gets turned. I wish I'd known all this before voir dire, because it would have been interesting to watch. See, the ideal juror for the prosecution is a black man who thinks highly of cops, and the ideal for the defense is a white man who doesn't."

"Black man, white man. Don't they have any women on your jury?"

"Seven of the twelve are women. And one of the two alternates."

"And the black and white balance?"

"Four whites and three blacks, plus both the alternates are black."

"Doesn't add up, Keller."

"Plus three Hispanics and two Asians."

"How do they factor in, as far as believing in cops is concerned?"

"No idea."

"How do you think the jury'll decide?"

"Same answer. I couldn't even guess."

"And you? How'll you vote?"

"I really shouldn't be talking about this."

"Keller . . ."

"I haven't made up my mind."

"Really? You don't know if he's guilty or not?"

"Oh, there's no question about it," he said. "Of course he's guilty. One look at him and you know he's a crook. He was probably making books on football games in high school, and he's been receiving stolen goods ever since he dropped out."

"But you just said—"

"And that's not even considering the testimony we

didn't get to hear. For example, nobody told us what they found in Huberman's apartment."

"Maybe they didn't find anything."

"Then the defense would have brought up the subject. 'Ladies and gentlemen of the jury, my client's supposed to be a receiver of stolen goods, and yet the district attorney would have you believe that the VCR identified as People's Exhibit One is the sole piece of stolen property in his possession. Isn't that an extraordinary coincidence?' But nobody's said a word about what the search did or didn't reveal, and that means they found a room full of TVs and VCRs and camcorders, and the judge ruled the search was improper and threw it out."

"Still, if you know the man's guilty—"

"But did they prove it? And was he entrapped?"

"And who cares? You know what I think, Keller? The guy's a fence, and the cop went and bought the VCR for his own personal use. And then he got mad and arrested the guy because he couldn't figure out how to program the goddam thing. Well? What do you think?"

"I think it's a shame you're not on the jury," he said.

"The cross-examination was brutal," Gloria said.

Clifford Mapes, the arresting officer, had been on the stand all morning. Keller said he kept waiting for Mapes to lose it and explode.

"What I kept waiting for was for him to burst into tears. I know, I know. Cops don't cry. But if it had been me on the witness stand there would have been tears."

"Maybe it would be a good strategy," Keller said. "Maybe it'd throw Nierstein off stride."

Nierstein was the lead counsel for the defense, a deceptively mild-looking man whose hairline had receded to complement his chin. Confronting a hostile witness, the little man turned into a bulldog.

"I'd like to see him thrown off stride," Gloria said. "Or off a cliff."

"You don't like him."

"I think he's mean."

"It's an act. 'I'm not a sonofabitch, but I play one in court.' "

"He should get an Emmy," she said, "and she should get an enema."

"Sheehy?"

"Uh-huh. You just know she's gonna bring him back for redirect this afternoon."

"She pretty much has to, don't you think?"

"I suppose. We're not supposed to let our feelings about the attorneys influence us, but how could you help it? Fortunately I dislike them both about equally, so it balances out. I don't like anybody, to tell you the truth. The rest of the jurors are jerks and the bailiff's a self-important idiot. I feel sorry for Mapes, but he's sort of a doofus, isn't he? And I feel sorry for Huberman, because he's on trial, plus he's got a family. On the other hand, the man's a crook. Guilty or not guilty, he's a crook."

"I guess you're looking forward to the end of the trial."

"And going back to work? It's a job, that's all. Believe me, it's not such a picnic at the office." She lowered her eyes. "It's not that great at home, either."

"Oh."

"Being married is like being on a jury," she said. "You're not supposed to talk about it with others. But I have to say it's not so hot."

"Maybe it'll get better."

"Yeah, right. Or I'll get used to it. Meantime, you know the one thing I look forward to?"

"The weekends? No, not if it's not great at home."

"No, definitely not the weekends. Lunch, five days a week, here at the Saigon Pearl. That's what I look forward to these days."

The prosecution rested its case late Friday morning, and when they resumed after lunch the defense moved for a directed verdict of acquittal. That was standard procedure, Keller knew, and the judge denied the motion, which was also fairly predictable. Then Nierstein announced that the defense would rest without presenting a case, since the prosecution had demonstrably failed to prove anything. The judge told him to save that for his closing argument, and told both attorneys to save their closing arguments for Monday morning. He gave the jurors his usual instructions—don't talk to anybody, don't read newspaper coverage of the case, di dah di dah di dah. Keller could have recited it along with him, word for word.

There was one addition. This time the judge suggested that they bring an overnight bag to court Monday morning. Once they began their deliberations, he explained, they would be sequestered until they reached a verdict. The city would pay for their hotel room, but the city's largesse didn't run to toothpaste and razors and clean clothes, so they ought to bring those along just in case.

"You're already packed," Gloria said, on the way out of the building. She nodded at Keller's briefcase. "I bet you've got it all in there. Socks and underwear and a clean shirt."

"And a book to read," he said. "Everything I need for a weekend away."

"A romantic weekend, I hope?"

He shook his head. "A nephew of mine's getting married. That makes it a romantic weekend for him, or at least I hope it does. For me it comes under the heading of family obligations."

He got back from Baltimore early Sunday evening and took a long soak in the tub, then called a Chinese restaurant and ordered dinner. He cradled the receiver, then picked it up again, feeling the urge to call someone. Dot?

No, not Dot, but someone.

Gloria? He couldn't call her even if he wanted to, and he wasn't sure he wanted to. Maggie? No, God, the last thing he wanted was to start that up again. He didn't want to see anybody, didn't really want to have a conversation with anybody, just somehow felt the need to check in with someone, though he couldn't think who. He felt restless, he realized, a sort of full-moon restlessness, and the moon wasn't even full, as far as he knew.

Or was it? He went to the window, but couldn't see any moon from there, full or otherwise. He could go outside and look, but he had Chinese food coming. You could probably find information like that in the Farmer's Almanac, but the only copy he had was five years old. He'd never bought it again, and couldn't recall now what had made him buy it the first time.

He'd bought a paper, but left it on the train. There was probably something in it about phases of the moon. If it wasn't in the weather report, it would probably be in the astrology column.

Louise Carpenter. That's who he wanted to call. If nothing else, the woman would know whether or not the moon was full.

Was it too late to call? He decided it wasn't, looked up the number and dialed it. She didn't answer, and neither did her machine. He tried again, on the chance he'd misdialed, and no one answered, and then the buzzer sounded to announce the arrival of his dinner.

After he'd eaten he gave his attention to the selection of approvals that had arrived several days earlier from the woman in Maine. He chose the stamps he wanted, mounted them in his albums, and wrote out a check.

He wrote a note: "Dear Beatrice, Thanks for another nice selection. I found a few I could use, and I'm happy to have them. Enclosed is a check for $72.20. I'm on jury duty, but I'm not supposed to tell anyone about the case.

235

Believe me, you wouldn't want to hear about it!" He signed his name and tucked the note and the check and the stamps he wasn't buying into the return envelope, then went downstairs and posted it in the corner mailbox. He was in the building again before he remembered the moon, and it didn't seem worthwhile to go out again and look for it.

Back in his apartment, he stationed himself in front of the television set. Around midnight he drew a tub and took another hot bath. Before he went to bed he repacked his briefcase with a fresh shirt and a change of socks and underwear.

CHAPTER TWENTY-TWO

The foreman they had selected was named Milton Simmons. He was tall, forty-five or fifty, and he looked a little like Morgan Freeman. Keller figured that was why they had chosen him. Morgan Freeman had a kind of moral authority. Whether he was playing a good guy or a bad guy, you somehow knew you could count on him.

"Well," Simmons said now, "we're going to have to figure out how to do this. I guess the question is, did the state prove their case?"

"Beyond a reasonable doubt," someone said, and a lot of heads nodded along with the phrase.

Keller felt keyed up, eager to get to it. Closing arguments had been extended, and Keller didn't think either of the lawyers was particularly good. Nierstein had led off, picking the prosecution's case apart piece by piece, switching from earnest reasoning to blistering sarcasm and back again. Then Sheehy, the prosecutor, took just as much time putting it back together again. Then, finally, the judge had charged the jury.

Keller loved the expression. He could picture the judge, lowering his head, pawing the ground, then charging the jury box like a bull, his black robes sweeping the floor.

The judge's charge had been less dramatic than that, and lengthy, and impossibly tedious. He kept saying the same thing over and over, as if they were children, and not particularly bright children, either. And finally the twelve of them had been led away and locked up together, and here they were, entrusted with the awesome responsibility of determining the fate of a fellow human being.

"It seems to me," one woman began, and left it at that

when there was a knock on the door. The bailiff entered, followed by a pair of willowy young men who moved like dancers, each bearing a tray and depositing it gracefully on the side table.

"State of New York's buying you lunch," the bailiff announced. "There's turkey sandwiches, all white meat, and there's ham and cheese sandwiches, and the cheese is Swiss. I asked before was there any vegetarians, and nobody said a word, but just in case there's a couple of peanut butter and jellies. Coffee and iced tea and Diet Coke, plus water if there's any Mormons. Enjoy your meal."

He followed the two young men out of the room. There was a silence, broken at length by Morgan Freeman. "I guess we'll eat," he said, "and talk later."

Keller had a ham and cheese sandwich and a glass of iced tea. When there turned out to be no takers for the peanut butter sandwiches, he had one of those as well. Lunch was a curious business, with all conversation suspended, and the room dead silent but for the hum of the air conditioner and the resolute chomping of twelve pairs of jaws. When they'd all finished, one woman proposed summoning the bailiff and having the rest of the food removed. Mr. Bittner, who'd brightened up considerably when lunch arrived, pointed out that the bailiff hadn't told them to do so, and suggested they leave the leftovers on the table, in case anyone got hungry during deliberations.

Keller looked across the table at Gloria, who rolled her eyes. One of the Asians said she couldn't possibly eat another bite, and the foreman said neither could he at the moment, but that wasn't to say he might not get the munchies down the line. Another woman said the sandwiches would get stale, just sitting out in the open like that, and someone countered that they were going to waste anyway, that the bailiff would just have them tossed out once they were removed from the room.

"It's not like they could take them out of here and ship

them to Somalia for famine relief," she said, and a black woman across the table from Keller frowned momentarily, then evidently decided there was nothing essentially racist in the remark and let it go.

"Is there a consensus?" Morgan Freeman asked. "Are we all agreed that we'll keep the food and drink handy?" No one said otherwise, and he smiled. "Well, we've settled the difficult issue," he said. "Now we can turn our attention to the question of whether the defendant is guilty or innocent."

"Guilty or not guilty," Gloria said.

"I stand corrected," he said, "and thank you. Judge hammered away at that one, didn't he? We don't need to believe in the man's innocence to acquit him, just so he hasn't been proved guilty. Anybody have any thoughts on how to approach the question?"

A hand went up, a Mrs. Estévez. The foreman nodded to her, and smiled expectantly.

"I got to go to the bathroom," she said.

The bailiff was summoned. He led the woman off. When he brought her back, he was accompanied by the two willowy young men, who began clearing away the leftovers. No one said a word.

"I wonder if we could go back to the VCR," Gloria said.

"My cousin had one just like it," somebody said, "and it was fine for playing movies from the video rental, but you could not get it to record a program."

"She couldn't program it," someone else said.

"My cousin's a man, thank you very much, and he programmed it just fine. It would start recording something, and then it would switch to another channel all by its own self. I swear that machine had a mind of its own."

That put it ahead of the jury, Keller decided, which at the very least didn't know its own mind, if it had one at all. They kept going off on tangents.

And now Gloria led them on a particularly oblique path. After the vagaries of VCRs in general had been explored at some length, she took up a thread the defense had pursued with some vigor. Nierstein had called several witnesses to trace the history of the VCR the prosecution had brought to the courtroom, from the moment when Clifford Mapes had allegedly purchased it from the defendant all the way to the present moment. The prosecution had taken pains to identify it as one of a shipment stolen from a Price Club warehouse on Long Island, and had produced a witness, one William Gubbins, who had acted as lookout for the thieves and had received the VCR as part of his share of the proceeds. Gubbins had testified that he sold the VCR to the defendant.

Nierstein's contention was that the chain of evidence had been corrupted, that the electronic marvel on the evidence table was not the same one that his client had allegedly bought from William Gubbins and allegedly sold to the undercover policeman.

"Remember what he asked that property clerk? Asked him if he ever took home items entrusted to his own care?"

"The man said no," said one of the Asians, a Ms. Chin.

"But Nierstein didn't stop there," Gloria reminded them. "He asked about a specific item, a video camcorder."

"Wanted to know if the guy didn't borrow it to film his daughter's birthday party."

"And he said no," Ms. Chin countered.

Keller remembered the exchange. The property clerk, who Gloria felt would cut a much more impressive figure if he lost ten pounds and shaved off his mustache, had admitted that his daughter had a birthday party on such-and-such a date, that he himself had attended, and that he had immortalized the event on tape. He had admitted as well that he had not owned a video camera at the time, and did not own one now, but he steadfastly denied that he had taken one home from work, maintaining that he'd borrowed one belonging to his brother-in-law. Sheehy had objected to the whole line of questioning, calling it irrelevant, and suggesting sarcastically that the defense might next call for the tape of the party to be played in court. That brought a reprimand from the judge, who'd evidently found the whole business absorbing enough to overrule her objections.

"Well, I don't know," Gloria said.

"We can only go by the testimony," Mrs. Estévez said. "The lawyer asked the questions and the man answered them."

Keller hadn't wanted to say anything, but he couldn't help himself. "But how did he know to ask?" They looked at him, and he said, "How did he know about the birthday party, and that the guy taped it?"

"Everybody tapes their kids' parties," somebody said.

Did they? Was every childhood birthday party captured that way, the moment frozen on time through the magic of videotape? Did anybody ever look at the tapes?

"But he knew the date," Keller said. "He must have heard somewhere that the guy borrowed a camcorder. The clerk had to deny it, it's a breach of regulations. Just because he denied it doesn't necessarily mean it didn't happen."

"It doesn't mean it did, either," a woman pointed out.

"Well, no," Keller said. "It's a question of who you're going to believe."

"But what's it matter? There's no camcorder in the prosecution's case. Just a VCR. Who cares if the guy borrowed a camcorder? Nobody was using it, and he brought it back in the same condition he borrowed it."

"It establishes a pattern," Gloria said.

"What pattern? If he borrowed a camcorder, he must have borrowed a VCR? And so what if he did? So what if he took the VCR home with him, which nobody says he did, by the way, and brought it back a day later or a week later? It's still the same VCR."

"Unless he switched it," a man said.

And now they were off and running, trying to figure out why the property clerk would borrow a VCR in the first place, and why he might then substitute another one for it. "Maybe it was like your cousin's," a man said, with a nod at the woman whose cousin's set kept changing channels for no discernible reason. "Maybe he had a lemon, so he switched it for the one in the evidence locker."

"The one Mapes bought off the defendant."

"The one Mapes *says* he bought off the defendant."

Keller looked at Gloria. She wasn't smiling, the expression on her face was carefully neutral, but he could tell that she was pleased.

"**E**ight guilty," Morgan Freeman announced. Well, Milton Simmons, Keller thought, but Morgan Freeman himself couldn't have said it better. "Three not guilty."

"That doesn't add up," someone said.

"Makes eleven, and there's one blank slip of paper. Guess somebody couldn't make up his mind." He frowned. "His or her mind. Their mind. This was just to get an idea where we stand, so your mind don't have to be completely firm to vote one way or the other, but if you can't say one way or the other at this point, that's cool. Anybody who voted not guilty want to say anything about why you voted that way?"

"Well," Gloria said, "I'm just not convinced the state proved their case. I still can't be sure it's the same VCR."

"Girl," the largest of the black women said, "is that a defense? 'That's not the stolen VCR I sold him. I sold him a *different* stolen VCR.' Stolen is stolen and sold is sold."

"What about the fruit of the poisoned tree?"

"That's something else entirely," Milton Simmons said, and explained what lawyers meant when they talked about the fruit of the poisoned tree. "If they searched the man's

242

house," he said by way of example, "and if they found a roomful of stolen goods, and if the search was ruled illegal, then everything they found and everything it led to is the fruit of the poisoned tree, and woe unto him who eats of it. Meaning it's inadmissible as evidence."

"I bet they did, too," Keller said.

"How's that?"

"Search his house. You arrest a man for receiving stolen goods, you'd search his house."

"Maybe they didn't find anything."

"Then you'd have had Nierstein crowing about it. 'And did you search my client's residence, officer? And did you find anything incriminating? So you would have us believe that the VCR allegedly sold by my client was the only piece of allegedly stolen property alleged to be in his possession?' But nobody said a word about a search, which means it was suppressed."

"Somebody screwed up the warrant," a woman said. "Fruit of the poisoned tree."

The mention of fruit aroused Mr. Bittner. "You had to go to the bathroom," he said to Mrs. Estévez. "And now there's nothing to eat."

"Hey, man, what was she supposed to do?"

"I'm sorry," Bittner said. "I have low blood sugar, I get cranky."

"Then why didn't you tell the bailiff to leave the sandwiches?"

On and on, Keller thought. On and on and on.

There was a knock, and before they could respond the bailiff let himself in. "Judge wants to know how you're doing," he said. "If you think you're getting close to a verdict."

"We're doing okay," the foreman said.

"Well, not to rush you," the bailiff said, "but it's four o'clock already, so you got an hour if you want to get home tonight. If you don't reach a verdict by five you get sequestered for the night. That means you spend the night in a hotel at the city's expense. It's a decent place, but it's not the Waldorf. My opinion, you'd probably be more comfortable in your own homes."

"What about food?" Bittner demanded.

"Meals will be provided at the hotel."

"I mean now."

The bailiff gave him a look and left the room.

"More comfortable in our own homes," said the large woman, the one who'd called Gloria "girl." "Translation: Get off your butt and come up with a verdict. Anybody think he didn't do it?"

"That's not the question," Gloria said. "The question—"

"—is did he prove it. You think I don't know that? We been saying it all day long and not getting noplace. So how about my question? Is there anybody here thinks he didn't do it?"

No one else answered, so Keller said, "Did the man ever receive stolen property? I would say yes. Did he ever sell stolen property? Yes again. Did he sell it to a cop? Did he sell this particular stolen article to this particular cop? I could believe that and still not believe the state proved its case."

"Beyond a reasonable doubt," someone murmured.

"But I don't know that I do believe it," he went on. "It comes down to the same question all the time. Do we believe Mapes?"

"Even if Mapes stretched the truth some—"

"If Mapes isn't telling the truth, there's no case. And if Mapes is lying, there isn't even a crime."

"He's a police officer," someone said, "and the ones I've known have been pretty decent and honest, but there's something about him that seems a little shifty."

"Now that's funny," someone else said, "because my experience is cops lie all the time, but he impresses me as

244

a real straightforward young man."

"That property clerk was lying."

"Yeah, I'm with you on that one."

"Took home a camcorder to tape his kid's party. That don't mean the evidence got tainted about the VCR."

"And it doesn't mean Mapes lied."

"Doesn't mean he didn't, either."

At a quarter to five Morgan Freeman polled them again, informally this time, going around the room. By the time it got to Keller there were six voting to convict and three voting to acquit. Keller figured it didn't matter, they weren't going home that night no matter how he voted, but he had to say something. "Guilty," he said.

"Not guilty," said the woman to his left.

So it evened out. Last time they'd done this, Keller had been for acquittal, the woman to his left for conviction. Now Morgan Freeman voted to convict, and they were eight to four, with fifteen minutes left to work it out.

"Okay," the foreman said. "I don't say we're deadlocked, not by any means. It's just taking us a little while to sort things out. It's whether or not a man goes to prison, and we don't need to rush ourselves. Looks like we're going to spend the night in a hotel."

There was some grumbling, but Keller thought it seemed pretty good-natured. These people were New Yorkers, after all. You had to expect a certain amount of grumbling.

CHAPTER TWENTY-THREE

The hotel was a Days Inn in Queens, not far from JFK. It looked familiar to Keller, and he realized that he'd met a client in the lounge a couple of years ago. The man had flown up from Atlanta to hand Keller a couple of photographs and an address. Then he'd caught his flight to Europe, an ironclad alibi if there ever was one, while Keller flew down to Atlanta and back again. The client was at a business meeting in Brussels when he got word that his wife had been shot dead by a burglar. He cut his trip short and went home, and four months later he married his secretary.

But that hotel had been a Ramada, hadn't it? Keller was positive of it, he remembered the client talking about the virtues of the Ramada chain. So it couldn't be the same hotel, and yet the layout was somehow familiar to Keller.

There was nothing familiar about the room they gave him, but he hadn't been in any of the Ramada's sleeping rooms, just the lounge and the lobby. He took a quick shower, then called downstairs and ordered dinner from room service, then sat in front of the television set until the guy showed up with his food. Keller signed the bill, and added a couple of dollars in cash for the waiter, who seemed surprised. Keller figured he didn't get many tips from sequestered jurors.

"I was wondering," he said. "Was this place always a Days Inn?"

"If you go back far enough," the fellow said, "it was a swamp."

"How about if you go back two years?"

"It was a Ramada." He flashed a grin. "But that was before my time, so that's only hearsay evidence."

Keller, eating his dinner, wondered how they could do that, take a hotel out of one chain and add it to another. It struck him as awfully arbitrary.

He was trying to decide whether he wanted another cup of coffee when there was a knock on his door. He checked the peephole, then opened the door. Gloria darted inside and closed the door behind her, reaching to lock it.

"It felt funny," she said, "eating alone. And instead of Vietnamese food I had a hamburger and fries and a Coke. If you want me to get the hell out, just say so."

"Why would I want that?"

"We're not supposed to spend time together, remember? Because we might discuss the case."

Her face was flushed, and she'd freshened her makeup. And had she done something different with her hair?

"You look different," he said.

"Oh," she said. "Well, I had a quick shower. So I thought I'd try my hair like this."

"It's very becoming."

"Thank you."

"I had a shower myself."

"Well, after spending a whole day in court—"

"A person needs a shower."

"Definitely," she said. She looked at him. "Well, what do you want to do? Do you want to discuss the case?"

"No."

"Neither do I. And that's good, because they told us not to. This is crazy, isn't it? I don't know what I thought I was doing, coming here."

"Don't you?"

"I mean this is so not me. After my shower I was staring at myself in the mirror. Like, you slut, what do you think you're doing? I was standing there naked, if you can imagine."

"I can imagine."

"I was thinking about this when I was in the shower. Were you? Did you have any idea?"

"I had an idea."

"Were you thinking about me in the shower?"

"Yes."

"When you lathered up—"

"Yes."

"We both took showers," she said. "Isn't that great? We're both clean." She took a deep breath. "Let's get dirty," she said.

"God," she said. "All the fantasies I had, and here we are, and it's better than the fantasies. Last night, when I packed my little suitcase? I was planning this."

"Really?"

"Oh, absolutely. When we were first sitting around the table I thought, well, we are not reaching a verdict by five o'clock. If I'm the only holdout and everybody thinks I'm an idiot and stubborn as a mule, I don't care. We're getting sequestered."

"I have to admit I was trying to drag it out myself."

"I thought you were. Your face is very hard to read, but I had a feeling we were both on the same page." She rolled onto her side, laid a hand on his chest. "You know what else I thought? I thought, if we do reach a verdict, if there's no way to stall without looking too ridiculous, then we'll walk out together—"

"The way we always do."

"The way we always did from the first day," she said, "and I had this script written. Like I go, I thought we were going to get to spend a night in a hotel. And you go, yeah, so did I. And I go, well, we still can, you know. We've even got luggage."

"I do that sometimes," he said. "Make up scenes in my head."

"Did you make any up about us?"

248

"A few."

"I don't know if I'd have had the nerve," she said. "To actually say let's go to a hotel. I barely had the nerve to come to your room."

"But you did."

"But I did. What if I hadn't? Would you have come looking for me?"

"I probably would have phoned."

"Would they have given you my room number?"

"Three-fourteen," he said. "I paid attention when you checked in."

"That's how I got yours! And you got mine the same way. So it wasn't just my idea."

"No, we were definitely on the same page."

"That makes me feel better. I never did anything like this before. God, I can't believe I said that! But it happens to be the truth. I'm a nice Italian girl, I went to parochial school, I don't do this sort of thing. I never once cheated, and believe me, I've had opportunities."

"I believe you."

"I picked you out the first day, but just because I had the feeling you'd be interesting to talk to. Then at lunch I was like, he's a nice man. And in a day or two it got to be, he's a very attractive man. By the time the trial started I was having fantasies."

"Fantasies?"

"Sitting across the table and thinking of all the things I wanted to do to you."

"Well," he said, "now you've done them."

"Hmmm."

"What?"

"Well," she said, "not quite all of them."

"Oh?"

"I have quite an imagination. Who the hell am I to even think of some of these things? I mean, I'm from Staten Island."

"I thought Inwood."

"I moved to Inwood when I got married. But where I consider myself from is Staten Island."

"I'm from Missouri," Keller said.

"You are? I thought . . . oh, it's an expression, isn't it?"

"Right," he said. "Show me."

"I guess I'd better get back to my room."

"Why?"

"Well, what if somebody calls?"

"Did you give anybody the number?"

"No. I guess I could stay, couldn't I? Do you want me to stay?"

"Yes."

"Then I'd like to, because this one night is all we're going to have. You know that, don't you?"

"Yes."

"We read the verdict and I turn into a pumpkin."

"Some pumpkin."

"Well, a legal secretary and a faithful wife. I never did anything like this before. I'm not saying I'll never do it again."

"You'll probably do it again in about twenty minutes."

"I mean after tonight, silly. With the right person and the right circumstances and the right provocation at home it might happen again. But maybe not."

"Maybe if you get picked for another jury sometime."

"Maybe. But for you and me it's ships passing in the night. I think that's the way it's got to be."

"I think you're right."

"And you know something? Otherwise we'd wear it out. I was even thinking we could stretch the deliberations so that we got to stay here a second night. But a second night wouldn't be the same, would it?"

"Not to mention the fact that the other jurors would kill us," he said.

"You don't think any of them are doing the same thing we are?"

"Well, I've got my suspicions about two of them."

"Really?"

"Bittner and Chin," he said. "A match made in heaven."

"Oh, you," she said. "I thought you were serious. What a bad boy you are. I think you'll have to be punished. Hey, what have we here? You really *are* a bad boy, aren't you? I thought I was going to have to wait twenty minutes."

"It's remarkable what a night's sleep can do," Keller said. "When I woke up this morning it seemed crystal clear to me that Huberman did everything the prosecution says he did. I don't think it matters whether it's the same VCR throughout. The man's charged with selling a stolen VCR to a police officer, and they did a good job of proving it. I think the VCR he sold to Mapes is the same one that's on the evidence table now, because a property clerk might borrow a camcorder, which is something you would use once for a special event, but who borrows a VCR and brings it back the next day?"

"Everybody's got a VCR," someone said.

"Exactly."

He went on, dismissing the defense's arguments one by one. Heads all around the table were nodding in agreement. It really was remarkable what a night's sleep would do, he thought, even though he hadn't managed more than an hour here and an hour there. It was just as well, he thought, that he was never going to see the woman again. Another such night might put him in the hospital.

"Well," Milton Simmons said, "I get the feeling our overnight stay cleared things up for everybody. Unless Ms. Dantone's still harboring some doubts."

"I guess I've known all along the man's guilty," Gloria

said, "but I wanted to be sure I was convinced beyond a reasonable doubt."

"And?"

"I woke up with better perspective," she said, "just like everybody else. And, if I had even a trace of doubt, Mr. Keller cleared it up for me."

"We could share a taxi," Gloria said, "but let's not."

"All right."

"It was a shipboard romance, and you have to know it's over the minute the boat docks. Of course instead of the Love Boat we had the Days Inn."

"It used to be a Ramada."

"Well, there you are. I'll think of you whenever I have Vietnamese food, but I'll be staying away from Vietnamese restaurants for a while. And if we're ever on the same jury again—"

"Hey, you never know."

She hailed a cab. He watched it pull away, then caught one of his own.

There were four messages on his machine, all from the same person. He called back, and Dot picked up the phone and said, "Where were you?"

"Sequestered," he said, and explained.

"So you went to court yesterday morning, and they kept you overnight at a hotel near the airport. Why the airport?"

"No idea."

"You couldn't agree on a verdict so they locked you up. Then you agreed and they let you go home. There's a lesson there."

"I know."

"But they didn't lock you up for the weekend, did they?"

"No."

"You went down to Baltimore."

"Right after court adjourned Friday."

"And came back Sunday."

"Right."

"And called me, and we had a conversation."

"No, I didn't call."

"No kidding, you didn't call. Which would have been fine. I'm not your mother, I don't get palpitations if a Sunday comes and goes without a phone call from you. If there's nothing to report, why should you feel compelled to make a phone call?"

"Dot—"

"Then Monday afternoon I got a FedEx delivery. A little package about half the size of a cigar box, and guess what it was full of?"

"Not cigars."

"Money," she said, "and that threw me, because who would be sending me money? Coincidentally enough, it was just the amount we would have had coming if you'd closed the file in Baltimore. So I took a train to the city, bought the *Baltimore Sun* at the out-of-town newsstand, and read it on the way back to White Plains. Guess what I found."

"Uh—"

"Macnamara surprised a burglar in her Fells Point home," she said, "but his surprise was nothing compared to hers when he grabbed the fireplace poker and beat her head in with it. Now this has to be news to you, Keller, because of course otherwise you would have called. So it's the famous Keller luck, right? Someone else helped us out and did the dirty deed, and we get the credit."

"I did it, Dot."

"No kidding."

"It was late by the time I got home Sunday night."

"Too late to call?"

253

"Well, pretty late."

"And it was early when you left for court yesterday."

"I was a little rushed," he said. "I had to pack a change of clothes, in case we were going to be sequestered overnight, and by then I was running late."

"And last night?"

"We were sequestered."

"They didn't let you make a phone call?"

"No telling how secure the line was."

"I suppose. But what about before you got on the train in Baltimore? Sunday afternoon, Sunday evening, whenever it was. I'd have accepted a collect call, if you were out of quarters."

"I didn't think of it."

"You didn't think of it."

"I had things on my mind."

"Like what?"

"Well, the trial," he said. "You want to know something, Dot? I had the trial on my mind the whole time. Even in Baltimore, figuring out how to close the deal and then actually going and doing it, I kept thinking about the lawyers and the witnesses and that poor jerk Huberman."

"And how did it come out? And don't tell me you're not supposed to talk about the case, because the outcome's a matter of record."

"Actually," he said, "it's okay to talk about it now. And we found him guilty."

"So he goes to jail."

"I guess so, but that part's not up to us. He's remanded to custody until sentencing."

"He'll get what, a couple of years?"

"Something like that."

"You went down to Baltimore and clipped a woman, and then you came back to New York and put a man away for a few years for selling a hot television set."

"A VCR."

"Well, that makes all the difference. Don't you see a contradiction here, Keller? Or at least an irony?"

He thought about it. "No," he said. "One's my job and the other's my duty."

"And you did them both."

"That's right."

"And we got paid, and Huberman's headed upstate."

"That's right," he said. "The system works."

CHAPTER TWENTY-FOUR

Odd, Keller thought.

He'd called his astrologer, Louise Carpenter, the night he came back from Baltimore. He couldn't remember why, something about wondering if the moon was full, and you didn't have to call an expert to determine something like that. He supposed he'd just had the urge to talk to her, and when she didn't answer he got over it.

Then a week or so later he called again, and it wasn't Sunday evening this time, it was a weekday, and normal business hours, if there was such a thing for an astrologer. Middle of the afternoon, middle of the week, and no answer. No answering machine, either.

He'd frowned, puzzled, and then he'd decided she was out of town. Astrologers very likely took vacations, just like anybody else. Maybe she was on a beach somewhere, looking up at the stars.

He'd let it go, and hadn't thought about the woman since, until the call from Dot.

He was reading a stamp magazine when she called, absorbed in a story about forged overprints on early French colonial issues. There were a lot of legitimate varieties, as well as an abundance of forgeries, and it wasn't all that easy to tell the difference. He was wondering if he had any forgeries in his own collection, and if there was any point in finding out, when the phone rang.

"Our friend's been busy," she said.

"Our friend?"

"We've been calling him Roger."

"You know," he said, "he was on my mind a lot for a while there, and then he wasn't. I couldn't tell you when

I last thought of him."

"The big question, Keller, is whether he's thinking of you."

"And the answer is yes, or you wouldn't be calling."

"He may not be thinking of you personally," she said, "because he doesn't know you personally, which I'd have to say is a good thing. But it's clear he hasn't decided to take up golf, or anything else that might distract him from his primary purpose, and you remember what that is."

"Narrowing the field," he said.

"It just got narrower. There was a job I turned down, and it's a good thing I did."

"I guess you'd better tell me about it."

"Tomorrow morning," she said, "hop on a train and come see me."

"I could come up now, Dot."

"No," she said, "wait until tomorrow. I've got some things to line up first, Keller, and then we're going to have to make some moves. We've been waiting for this clown to dry up and blow away, and it's not going to happen. Unless we make it happen."

"How?"

"Tomorrow morning," she said.

He hung up, and the first thing that popped into his head was the astrologer. He could call her, and she could give him some idea of just how dangerous a time this was. He tried the number, and this time the phone only rang once. Then a recording came on, informing him that the number he had called was no longer in service.

He tried it again, figuring he'd dialed wrong, and he got the same recording. No longer in service.

Odd.

Her apartment was clear across town on West End Avenue between Ninety-seventh and Ninety-eighth. While the West Indian driver clucked at the traffic, Keller sat back and wondered why he was making the trip. He

257

got off at the corner and found the building, but couldn't spot a buzzer with her name on it. He checked the building on either side, even though he was certain he had the right one, and he didn't see her name there, either.

He caught another cab and went home.

There was only one person he could think of who might know where Louise Carpenter had disappeared to. That was Maggie Griscomb, and he didn't want to call her.

He had to look up the number, and then he had to force himself to dial it. By the time it had rung twice he was ready to hang up, but then she picked up in the middle of the third ring. He could still hang up, and he considered it, and she said hello again, the irritation evident in her tone, and he said, "I've been trying to reach Louise."

He hadn't meant to blurt it out that way. Hello, hi, how are you, di dah di dah di dah, and *then* he could bring up the business at hand. But something had made him cut to the chase, and there was a pause, and then she said, "It's you."

What could you say to something like that? Keller was stumped, and before he could come up with anything, she said, "You've got a lot of nerve. How come you didn't call?"

"You told me not to call. Remember?"

"Vividly. And then when you didn't call—"

Because you told me not to, he thought.

"—*I* called, and I left messages, and I never heard from you."

"I never got the messages."

"Yeah, right."

Had she left messages? No, of course not. He already regretted this call, and he hadn't even gotten to the point of it yet. "I've been having trouble with my answering machine," he said, "and you can believe me or not, it doesn't matter. I've been trying to reach Louise, and—"

"Why?"

"The astrologer," he said.

"That's who. What I asked you was why."

"Why?"

"You don't need an astrologer," she said, "to know which way the stars are falling. You want her number, look it up. She's in the book."

"But that's just it," he said, and then he let it go, because he was talking to himself. She had hung up on him.

"It seems to me," Dot said, "that we've got two choices. We can wait passively for the situation to resolve itself, or we can take a proactive approach."

"That's a word you never used to hear," Keller said, "and now you hear it all the time. I know what it means, but what's the point of it? Why not just say active?"

"It sounds better."

"It does?"

"Sure. Proactive, like you're really getting off your ass and doing something, and being professional about it, too. And I would have to say it's about time. We've been taking precautions, but all that means is that Roger's been killing other people. It would be nice if one of them caught on and turned the tables on him, but he's a pro and he's active and he takes them by surprise, so what chance have they got? He just keeps on doing what he does best, and we're turning down jobs and looking over our shoulders when we do take one, and it's about time we turned that around."

"And hunted him down," he said.

"And left him with a stake through his heart, because with a guy like that you want to make sure."

"But how, Dot? How would you find him? Where would you start?"

"He has to come to us."

He nodded. "We set a trap," he said, "and draw him right into it."

"There you go."

"How? Offer him a job? He won't take it. Unless—"

"What?"

"Well," he said, "if the job was to hit a hit man, wouldn't he make an exception? I mean, he's been doing that for free, and if he was going to get paid for it—"

"I'd call him with a contract for a hit man."

"Right."

"And not just any hit man. I presume we're talking about you."

"Right."

"So I give him your name and your address and a reasonably flattering photograph of you, while you sit home in front of the TV and listen for footsteps. Do I have to explain why that's a bad idea?"

"No."

"I've been working on this for a while," she said, "so why don't I lay it out for you? What I do, I call Roger and leave word, and he picks up the message and calls back on some hi-tech untraceable line, and I run down a contract I want to give him. I give him the name and address, and he mulls it over and turns it down."

"And?"

"And I give it to somebody else."

"Me? No, that wouldn't make sense. Who would you give it to?"

"Some other pro. What I'd probably do is call another contractor and let him find somebody. Not that there are a hell of a lot of people left to be found, but whoever he picked wouldn't have to be all that slick. Once he was on the case, I'd call Roger and tell him not to worry, that I managed to get somebody else. You beginning to get the picture?"

"I think so."

"You stake out the mark's house and wait for the two of them to show up. One of them'll be a guy looking to do what he was hired to do. The other'll be Roger."

"How do I know which is which?"

"You could just kill 'em both," she said, "and let God sort 'em out, like it says on the T-shirt. But I don't think so. What you'd do is wait for one of them to take out the mark. Whoever does that, the other one is Roger."

Keller was nodding. "And once the hit's been made," he said, "he'll be ready to take out the hitter. So I follow the hitter and keep an eye out for Roger."

"When he's ready to make his move," she said, "that's when you make yours. If you can nail him before he does his thing, so much the better. If not, well, you tried. Either way, Roger's off the board."

"With a stake through his heart." He frowned. "I'd want to get him in time. Be a shame to let some innocent guy get killed for nothing."

"Innocent's a stretch, since he'd have just finished taking out the mark. But I know what you mean."

"The mark," Keller said. "I hadn't even thought of him. He was sort of hypothetical, because you don't really have a job for Roger, or for Mr. Second Choice, either. That's just a trap, but a trap has to have bait in it, doesn't it?"

"It does if you expect to catch anything."

"So who's the bait? If it's not me, who is it? Do you just pick some poor mope at random?"

"That'd be a way to do it. Keller, you look unhappy."

"The bait probably gets killed, right?"

"Since the bait wouldn't have any reason to suspect a thing, and since there'd be not one but two world-class hit men on the case, I'd have to say the bait's chances are less than average."

"Chances of surviving, you mean."

"Right. On the other hand, if you want to look on the

bright side, the bait's chances of getting killed are not at all bad."

"See," he said, "that's the part I don't like. Throwing darts at a phone book."

"Keller, you don't throw darts at a phone book. You throw darts at a map."

"How would that work?"

"It wouldn't, unless you were looking for a place to go. You throw a dart and it lands on Wichita Falls, Texas, and you go there. Eat at a nice little Mexican restaurant, buy some stamps for your collection. Maybe get some real estate lady to show you houses."

"Dot . . ."

"But if what you're looking for is a person, you don't use darts. You take a phone book and flip it open at random and jab with your finger."

"That's what I meant."

"You said darts."

"I know, but—"

"Never mind, Keller. I knew what you meant. I'm stalling, see, because this is the part I don't like."

"That's my point," he said. "Playing God, choosing somebody at random . . ."

"Not at random."

He looked at her. " 'Flip it open at random,' you just said. What do you mean, Dot? It's all karma? Written in the stars? Whatever seemingly random choices we make, they're all in tune with the purposeful design of the Universe?"

"I suppose that makes as much sense as anything else," she said, "which isn't saying much for it. Keller, I already picked somebody."

He considered this. After a moment he said, "Not at random."

"Not at random, no. No darts, no phone books."

"Some guy you know?"

262

"No and no."

"Huh?"

"Nobody I know," she said, "and not a guy."

"A woman?"

"What are you, a sexist?"

"No, but—"

"Chivalry is dead, Keller. A woman has as much right to get killed as anybody else. You've had jobs where the mark was a woman. You went and did what you were supposed to do."

"Well, sure."

"It's an equal-opportunity world," she said. "I've even heard of women hit men, except I suppose the term would be hit women, but I don't like the way that sounds. Female hit persons?"

"You hear stories," he said, "but I don't know if there really are any. Outside of the movies."

"Then it's a waste of time figuring out what to call them."

He said, "No and no, you said. Not a guy and what? Not someone you know?"

"Right."

"If it's not someone you know," he said, "then how come it's not random?"

"Give it a minute, Keller. It'll come to you."

"It's someone I know."

"What did I tell you? It came to you."

"Some woman I know . . ."

She sighed, reached for the pitcher of iced tea, filled both their glasses. "Keller," she said, "maybe it's this business with Roger, the stress of it, or maybe you've just been doing this for a long time. But lately you've been running risks and leaving loose ends."

"I have?"

"I didn't want to say anything," she said, "because your life is your life."

"Wait a minute," he said. "Be specific, will you? What risks? What loose ends?"

She extended a forefinger and touched the tip of his thumb.

"My thumb's a loose end? What am I supposed to do, cut it off?"

"I don't see that your thumb's the problem," she said. "You lived with it all your life, and it was fine and so were you, and then some dame tells you it's a murderer's thumb and you go rushing off to another dame and she tells you you're a Gemini with your temperature rising and your moon over Miami."

"Cancer rising," he said, "and my moon is in Taurus. The moon is exalted in Taurus."

"And they probably don't have to worry about hurricanes there, either. Keller, she told you all that crap, and you told her what you do for a living."

"I didn't exactly tell her."

"She knew just by looking at your thumb."

"And my chart. And I guess she more or less intuited it." He sat up straight. "She's the one you picked? Louise?"

"Keller—"

"Because they're going to have a hard time finding her. She moved, and she must have left the area altogether, because her phone's been disconnected. I suppose it's possible she left a forwarding address, and there are other ways to track a person, but you wanted to bait the trap here in New York, didn't you? If so, you can forget about Louise Carpenter."

She didn't say anything. He looked across the table at her and it dawned on him.

"No forwarding address," he said.

"No."

"She's dead, isn't she?"

"Either she's one with the Universe," Dot said, "or she's been reincarnated as a butterfly. That's how Louise herself would look at it, and who are we to argue?"

"But," he stammered. "What . . . when? How?"

"Keller," she said, "you sound like a training manual for newspaper reporters. Do you really want to know? Wouldn't you be happier just figuring it was in the stars and letting it go at that?"

"I want to know."

"You were on jury duty," she said.

"And you got someone to—"

"No. Suppose you just let me tell it."

"All right."

She drank some iced tea. "I was thinking about this for a while," she said. "Here's a woman who knows something she's not supposed to know, and how long before she says something to the wrong person? No, don't interrupt. You were going to say it's unethical for her to talk about her clients, weren't you? That occurred to me, but what people are supposed to do and what they do aren't always the same thing, or we'd both be in some other business.

"So what I did," she went on, "is I called her up and made an appointment with her."

"While I was on jury duty."

"No, long before that. I don't know where you were. At home in New York, probably, working on your stamp collection. I called her up and made an appointment, gave a phony name and date of birth, and took a train in and a cab to where she lived. Nice, if you like drapes and beaded curtains and overstuffed furniture. She sat me down with a cup of tea and we went over my chart."

"But it wasn't your chart."

"Because I made up the date of birth. You know, I realized that, but by then I was stuck. I had to sit there pretending to be impressed by how accurate she was, and it wasn't accurate, but then why should it be? It may have been right on the mark for somebody who happened to be born on the twenty-third of September. All in all, I was probably better off with a phony birthday, because it kept me from getting sidetracked by the chart, because I knew it was a lot of hooey. So I could focus on drawing her out."

"About what?"

"About you. I talked about how I went to a palmist once, and she said she knew a little about palmistry and looked at my hand, and I told her about a girlfriend of mine in high school who had an unusual thumb, and before I knew it I was hearing all about a client of hers who had a murderer's thumb."

"She talked about my thumb?"

"It doesn't necessarily mean anything," she said, "but in this instance the client with the murderer's thumb did in fact have a very real dark side. I didn't dig too deeply, but I had the feeling I could have walked out of there with your name and address if I'd really wanted to."

"That's a surprise," he said. "I thought she'd be discreet."

"She probably thought she was being discreet. She mentioned some things about your chart, but don't ask me what they were. Your Saturn squares Uranus, ooga booga dooga. You know how they talk. Keller, the woman was a loose end. She had a client who killed people for a living, and she knew it, and it didn't take a lot to get her talking about it."

"You should have said something."

"To you?"

"Of course to me. I would have . . ."

"What? Taken care of it?"

"Sure."

"You liked the woman, Keller. You talked about how maternal she was."

"I don't remember saying that."

"Well, I remember. Maybe you could have gone ahead and done it anyway, but it would have been tough for you, and it would have been a bad idea to begin with. You were a client of hers, there's a connection, so if anything's going to happen to her it should happen when you're out of town."

"So you'd have to bring somebody in," he said, thinking out loud. "And while you're at it, why not bring in Roger, too? Tie off a loose end and bait a trap for Roger, both at the same time. It makes sense." He looked up, frowning. "But it's too late for that, because she's already dead."

"I wasn't thinking about baiting traps at the time. And I wanted to leave you completely out of it, and I didn't want to wait too long, because loose lips sink ships, and who knows how long it would be before the fat lady sang to the wrong person?"

"But you waited a while after all."

"That wasn't my idea," she said. "Remember that string of jobs you had where you were back the next day? They called it off or the guy killed himself or somebody else closed the sale for you? You kept coming back before I could set things up."

"You wanted me out of town when she got taken out."

"Of course."

"So I'd have an alibi. Of course, if anybody wanted to know what exactly I was doing in Albuquerque or St. Louis or wherever . . ."

"I know, it's not much of an alibi. 'Your Honor, I couldn't have killed her because I was in Sausalito killing him.' I guess I had other reasons for wanting you out of town. I guess I didn't want you to know about it because I knew you wouldn't like it."

"You were right."

"You still don't like it, do you?"

He thought about it. "You had to do it," he said. "I would have tried to talk you out of it, or find another way, but it's over now, and I have to admit you were right. Who'd you use?"

"What's the difference?"

"No difference, I guess. When the Baltimore job came in, you figured I'd be out of town, so you booked the guy to do Louise. And then you found out I had jury duty, but that's an even better alibi than being out of town, so you let it go according to schedule. Whoever he was, he did good work. 'Death Was in the Stars'—it's a story the papers would have played up, an astrologer getting murdered. But I didn't see anything. You use this guy before?"

"Once. And there was nothing in the papers then, either."

"His trademark, I guess."

"Hers."

"Pardon?"

"Her trademark."

"The hitter was a woman? We just said there weren't any outside of the movies."

"You're the one said that, Keller. I didn't say anything."

He replayed the conversation in his head, shrugged. "Whatever," he said. "A woman, huh? And you used her before?"

Dot nodded, then raised a hand and pointed at the ceiling. Keller looked up, saw nothing remarkable but a light fixture with one of its bulbs burned out. Then he got it and his jaw dropped.

CHAPTER TWENTY-FIVE

"The old man," he said.

"Sometimes it amazes me how quick you are on the uptake."

"But that was you, Dot. He was losing it, and he was talking about hiring a kid to help him write his memoirs, and you sent me off somewhere and did it yourself."

"Sent you to Kansas City," she said. "Your first stamp auction, if I remember correctly."

"And you did Louise, too? Why, for God's sake?"

"Short notice," she said. "There was a window of opportunity, and who knew how long it would be open? And it wasn't just a matter of taking her out. It had to be quiet, so you wouldn't read about it. And somebody had to go through her files, somebody who would know what to look for. So I called her up and made another appointment."

"With him it was a sleeping pill in his cocoa and a pillow over the face."

"I didn't figure that would work with her. I thought maybe hit her over the head, make it look like a break-in that went bad."

"Makes sense."

"You get cops that way, but they start out looking for burglars, or if they smell a rat they take a good long look at her personal life. Still, who wants them looking at all?"

"You never know what they'll find."

"So I sat there, pretending to be fascinated by all of this astrological crap, all of it in a voice so sweet and gentle it could lull you to sleep, with a pause now and then so she can pop another of those chocolates. 'Those look good,' I said, and she held out the plate for me to take one."

"Oh."

"I took a couple," she said, "and I ate one, and I have to say it wasn't bad, but I'd hate to stuff myself with that crap all day long. I managed to drop the other one in my handbag. End of the session I made another appointment, and when I kept it I was prepared. 'Those look good,' I said, and when she passed the plate I made like the Great Spaldini, master of sleight of hand."

"You put back the chocolate you took the time before."

"And took a fresh one for myself, all in a single movement faster than the eye could follow. I practiced in front of a mirror, Keller. You want to feel ridiculous, that's as good a way as any."

"You'd have to be careful not to wind up with the same one you started with."

"Tell me about it."

"It'd be a hard mistake to make," he said. "I mean, you're picking up a fresh one at the same time you're planting the one you brought along. But then, when it's time to pop the thing in your mouth, you start to wonder."

"A mind is a terrible thing to have," she said. "I knew I hadn't screwed up, and even so I took a good look at the bottom of the one I wound up with, looking for the telltale pinprick."

"You used a hypodermic needle."

She nodded. "I don't know why I didn't just palm the chocolate and get rid of it," she said, "but somehow I felt compelled to eat it. I didn't see a pinhole on the bottom, so of course I decided it had sealed itself in the course of being handled. So I told myself, the hell, either it's in the stars or it isn't, and I ate the chocolate."

"Thinking it might be poisoned."

"Knowing it wasn't, but yes, thinking it might be. And wouldn't you know it had a nut in it, and I was sure I was tasting bitter almonds."

270

"You used cyanide."

"That's the thing," she said. "I didn't, I used something else, it's got a chemical name a mile long, and who even knows what the hell it tastes like? Not bitter almonds, I'll be willing to bet, but that's what I decided I was tasting, and, well, you can imagine what went through my mind."

"All while you're pretending to enjoy the chocolate."

"Smacking my lips over it. 'Oh, Louise, these are *so* good.' Which is just brilliant, because of course she offers me another. 'No, I don't dare,' I said, and truer words were never spoken. So I sat there and waited for her to pick the candy with the prize in it."

"Couldn't you just go home?"

"And wait for nature to take its course? No, because I had to search the place, remember?"

"Oh, right."

"And I also had to hear all about my boyfriend and how Jupiter trined Pluto in his twenty-second house."

"I think there are only twelve houses."

"There used to be, but then the developers came in."

"I never understood that part, the houses. Anyway, what boyfriend?"

"The one I made up. A handsome widower who had taken an interest in me. Keller, I had to have some reason to go see her again. I made up a boyfriend and made up a birthday for him, and she was doing his chart and seeing if it was compatible with mine."

"And was it?"

"We were going to have problems, and it wouldn't work out in the long run, but she felt it was worth pursuing for the time being. Of course he didn't exist and she had the wrong birthday for me, but other than that it was right on the money." She rolled her eyes. "And I'm pretending to listen to all this crap, and what I'm doing is waiting for her to pop a chocolate. But she's too caught up in what she's telling me, and when she finally stops to catch her breath and actually does take a piece of candy, it's the wrong one. Which I don't know, of course, until she bites into it and nothing happens."

"Jesus."

"What's interesting," she said, "is the way my mind worked. You know, I started out feeling sort of bad about the whole thing. She was a nice woman, and she was trying to help me out, and it was a shame what I had to do. But then, when she keeps not picking the right chocolate . . ."

"You got angry with her."

"That's right! She was making my life difficult, she was refusing to cooperate, she was not doing what she was supposed to do. Does that happen with you?"

"All the time. Like it's their fault that they're hard to kill."

"I wanted to yell at her. 'Eat the chocolate, you fat slob!' But I just sat there, and I got to a point where I almost forgot about it, and then she took a piece of candy and bit into it, and bingo."

"And?"

"It was worse than the other time. She made these sounds, got this expression on her face. Thrashed her arms around, flopped all over the place. There was a moment there when I would have stopped it if I could. But of course I couldn't."

"No."

"And then she stopped flopping and gave a long sigh and it was over. And then I didn't feel anything, not really, because what was the point? She was dead. She didn't feel anything and neither did I."

"You must have wanted to get out of there."

"Of course, but I had things to do. First I waited to make sure she was dead, and then I went on an expedition. I found a file with your name on it. It had what I guess was your chart, and some notes I couldn't make head or tail out of. I found my file, too, under the name I'd given her. I

272

took them both and got rid of them."

"Good."

"I went through her appointment book. This was my third appointment, so I was in there three times. Just a name, Helen Brown, with no address and no phone number, and nothing in her files, so I left it. It wasn't going to lead anywhere. You were in there, but so many months ago I couldn't believe anybody would check that far back. Still, I inked out your name with Magic Marker, but then I decided they'd have ways to see what was originally written there, so I just tore out the page."

"Couldn't hurt."

"I had a quick look-see through her things. That felt weird, so I didn't spend much time on it. I found some cash in her underwear drawer, a few thousand dollars."

"You take it?"

"I thought about it. I mean, money doesn't care where it came from, right? But what I did was leave all but five hundred right where I found it, and I put the five hundred in her handbag."

"So it wouldn't look like a break-in."

"Right. But that doesn't really make sense, because what burglar slips his victim a poisoned chocolate? I guess I wasn't thinking too clearly."

"If you got away with it," he said, "your thinking was clear enough."

"I guess so. I left her there and went home. I thought, should I call it in? But the people at 911 have got Caller ID, they know where all the calls come from."

"Besides, what's your hurry?"

"That's what I decided. The longer it takes before the body's found, the less likely they are to smell a rat."

"Bad choice of words."

"Bad choice of . . . oh, right. Anyway, the stuff I gave her winds up looking like a heart attack. It actually gives you one, that's how it works. Of course it would show up

273

if they looked for it, but why would they look for it? She was a good fifty pounds overweight, she led a sedentary life, she was old enough to have a heart attack——"

"How old do you have to be? Never mind, I know what you mean."

"I wore gloves all the time, like a nice little suburban lady, so there were no fingerprints to worry about. And I left and pulled the door shut, and it locked behind me, and I went home."

"Steeped in the satisfaction of a job well done."

"Well, I don't know about that," she said. "I got home and poured myself a stiff drink, and then I poured it down the sink, because what do I want with a drink?"

"You were never a drinker."

"No, but this time I had the impulse anyway, which shows how I felt. I sat there and watched her die, Keller. I never did anything like that before."

"It was different with the old man."

"Apples and bananas. He didn't kick his feet and throw his arms around and make noises. He was asleep, and I just made sure he wouldn't wake up. And you know what he was like. It was an act of mercy." She made a face. "With the star lady, it was no act of mercy. The picture in my mind, the expression on her face, mercy had nothing to do with it."

"It'll fade, Dot."

"Huh?"

"The picture in your mind. It won't go away, but it'll fade, and that's enough."

"Keller, I'm a big girl. I can live with it."

"I know, but you can live without it, too. It'll fade, believe me, and you can make it fade faster. There's an exercise you can do."

"I just hope it's not deep knee bends."

"No, it's all mental. Close your eyes. I'm serious, Dot. Close your eyes."

"So?"

"Now let the picture come into your mind. Louise in her overstuffed chair—"

"Looking overstuffed herself."

"No, don't make jokes. Just let yourself picture the scene."

"All right."

"And you're seeing it from up close, and in color."

"I didn't have much choice, Keller. I was there, I wasn't watching it on a black-and-white TV set."

"Let the color fade."

"Huh?"

"Let the color drain out of the picture in your mind. Like you're dialing down the color knob on a TV."

"How do I—"

"Just do it."

"Like the shoe ads."

"Is the color gone?"

"Not completely. But it's muted. Ooops—it came back."

"Fade it again."

"Okay."

"Closer to gray this time, right?"

"A little bit."

"Good," he said. "Now back off."

"Huh?"

"Like a zoom shot," he said, "except it's more of a reverse zoom shot, because the picture in your mind is getting smaller. Back off twenty yards or so."

"There's a wall behind me."

"No there's not. You've got all the room in the world, and the picture's getting smaller and smaller, with less and less color in it."

They were both silent for a moment, and then she opened her eyes. "That was weird," she said.

"Whenever the picture comes into your mind," he said,

"just take a minute or two and do what you just did. You'll reach a point where, when you try to picture that scene, it'll be in black and white. You won't be able to see it in color, or up close."

"And that takes the sting out of it, huh?"

"Pretty much."

"That what you do, Keller?"

"It's what I used to do," he said. "Early on."

"What happened? It stopped working?"

He shook his head. "I got so I didn't need to do it anymore."

"You toughened up, huh?"

"I don't know if that was it," he said. "I think it's more a matter of getting used to it, or maybe the exercise had long-term effects. Whatever it was, it got so the pictures didn't bother me much. And they tended to fade all by themselves. The color would wash out, and they would get smaller and smaller, until you couldn't make out the details."

The other loose end turned out to be Maggie.

He'd pretty much figured that out by himself. There was a moment, when Dot was recounting her visit to Louise's apartment, that it struck him that he, Keller, was the loose end, the string which if tugged would lead back to the big house in White Plains. He was reaching for his glass of iced tea when the thought came to him, and he put the glass down, as if it might hold the same substance as Louise's final piece of chocolate.

But that was ridiculous, he'd already drunk half the tea in his glass, and they were both drinking from the same pitcher. Besides, the whole notion was senseless. If Dot wanted to get rid of him she wouldn't do it in her own house, and she wouldn't preface it with a conversation anything like this one.

No, he knew who the other loose end had to be.

"But she doesn't know anything," he told Dot. "She's convinced I'm a corporate guy, retired now, working once in a while on a freelance basis. She thinks I fly off to Silicon Valley now and then and help them crunch numbers."

"She's the one who sent you to the star lady."

"Yes, but—"

"In fact, she's the one who told you about your murderous thumb."

"But we stopped seeing each other. She's not in my life anymore."

"When's the last time you talked with her?"

"The time before last," he said, "was months ago, and—"

"That's not what I asked you, Keller."

"Yesterday," he said, "but that's because I called her. Because I was trying to find Louise, and I thought Maggie might know if she'd moved."

"But she didn't."

"She told me I didn't need an astrologer to know which way the stars were falling."

"What was that supposed to mean?"

"I think all it meant was she was angry with me. She broke up with me, and she was angry that I hadn't called her."

"Makes sense."

"There was a call two months ago," he remembered. "I picked it up and said hello a couple of times, and the person hung up."

"Wrong number, most likely."

"It didn't feel like a wrong number," he said, "so I hit Star-six-nine, and she picked up the phone and said hello a couple of times, and this time *I* didn't answer."

"Gave her a taste of her own medicine."

"Well, I couldn't think what to say. I just hung up, and the phone rang—"

"Her turn, I guess."

"—and I let it ring, and that was the end of it. But she couldn't have been referring to that. It was something more recent, and messages she'd left for me, except she didn't."

"Except she did, Keller."

"Huh?"

"Well, this is embarrassing," she said. "When you go out of town, sometimes I check your messages."

"What?"

"Only since Roger came into our lives. I was worried about you, Keller. I have these protective Mother Hen instincts. So one evening when there was nothing good on television I called your number."

"And I wasn't there."

"Of course not, you were in Albuquerque or something. The machine picked up and I heard your recorded voice."

"And you got all misty-eyed."

"Yeah, right. I left a message, something about hoping you were having a good time, and then I decided it was stupid to be leaving messages for you. So I called back and erased it."

"How?"

"How? I called back, and the machine picked up, and I punched in the code, and when I heard my own message I pressed three and erased it."

"How'd you know the code?"

"When you buy the machine," she said, "the code is five-five-five, and they tell you how you can change it."

"And I did."

"To four-four-four, Keller."

"Well," he said.

"It wasn't the first one I tried," she said, "but it didn't take me long to get to it. I erased the message I'd left, and while I was at it I erased a message from some jerk who wanted to sell you a time-share in the Bahamas." She shrugged. "What can I say? I got in the habit of invading your privacy. When you were out of town, I checked your messages for you."

"One time *I* checked," he remembered, "and there was some kind of nuisance message, not a time-share but about as inviting, and I didn't bother to erase it. And then when I got home it wasn't there."

"It must have been one of the ones I erased. I figured I'd spare you the aggravation."

"And there were messages from Maggie?"

" 'Hi, it's me. I was just thinking of you. Don't bother to call back.' If you weren't supposed to call back, what did you need to hear it for?" She reached for her glass of tea. "That was the first one. And there were one or two others in the same vein over the months. Then when you were in Baltimore she left three or four messages, including one along the lines of 'I know you're there and you're not answering the phone and please don't pick up now because it would just make it obvious what a neurotic bastard you are.' Then a long pause, during which I guess you were supposed to pick it up, and then she called you a name and hung up."

"What kind of a name?"

"All I remember is it wasn't a compliment. Then an apology, and a request that you call. And another saying ignore the preceding message. I figured you'd better ignore them all, and I made them go away."

"And this was when I was in Baltimore."

"And while you were on jury duty."

"You called during the day, while I was on jury duty."

"A couple of times."

"Just a couple of times?"

"Well, daily, actually. At this point I was just checking for messages from her, and most of the time there weren't any, but I didn't want you hearing from her, or talking to her."

"You'd already decided she was a loose end."

"Well, it was getting obvious, Keller."

"Bait," he said.

"We'd have to take her out anyway, you know. I don't think it's something you want to do yourself, or am I wrong?"

"I went to bed with the woman," he said.

"And sent her flowers, if I remember correctly."

"I liked her, Dot. She had an interesting way of seeing things."

"The ones you pick," she said, "always have an interesting way of seeing things."

"The ones I pick?"

"This one," she said, "and the dog walker one with all the earrings. Call me judgmental, but I think we'd be safe classing them both as kooks."

"Maybe."

" 'Let's keep this superficial, so don't send me any more flowers, and we'll just meet a couple of times a month and go to bed.' "

" 'And by the way, you've got a murderer's thumb.' "

"Any more superficial, Keller, and she'd have had you stay home altogether and just send her a monthly teaspoon of sperm. I have to say she did you a favor, keeping you at a distance. It might be harder on you otherwise, closing the account."

"Bait," he said.

"The word seems to bother you. Call it sushi, if you like that better. It amounts to the same thing."

"I guess I'll get used to the idea."

"Or look at it this way," she said. "She's the lemon fate handed you. And what you're doing, you're making lemonade."

Back at his apartment, the first thing Keller did was check his answering machine. He pressed the Play button, and the robotic voice said, "You. Have. No. Messages."

And what did that mean? That no one had left a message? Or that, while he was on his way home, Dot had called and wiped the machine clean?

The first thing to do, he thought, was change his number, and to something less obvious than four-four-four. Like what? He ran three-number combinations through his head, trying to find one that was clunkier and less memorable than the others. Three-eight-one? Two-nine-four? Any number, he decided, displayed special qualities if you thought about it long enough. And, if he managed to find one that was genuinely unremarkable, one a person just couldn't hold in his mind, then how would he remember it himself?

Besides, Dot could dig it out by trying numbers at random. How many combinations were there, anyway? He seemed to remember from high school math that there was a formula for this sort of thing, but, like most of high school math, it had long since found its way out of his memory bank.

He sat down at his desk, picked up a pencil and realized you didn't need a formula. The numbers started at zero-zero-zero and ran to nine-nine-nine. A thousand combinations, that's how many there were. Ten times ten times ten, that was the formula, if formulas were important to you. It sounded like a lot, a thousand, but when you thought about it you realized it wasn't so much after all.

Years ago he'd done a job for the old man that involved a briefcase. He hadn't thought of it in years, but he remembered now that the briefcase had been locked, not with a key but with a three-number code, one of those triple dials where you had to line up the numbers correctly to get the case open. He'd used a pair of pruning shears instead, cutting right through the leather flap, but it struck him now, years and years later, that he could have opened the case without ruining it. It would have taken more time, but it wouldn't have taken forever.

281

More like two hours, he realized. Maybe even less than that. If you were systematic about it, you could easily try ten or fifteen combinations a minute. Ten a minute was a hundred minutes, and what did that amount to? An hour and forty minutes?

The pruning shears had taken no time at all. Of course it had taken him a while to find the shears, and before that he'd sawed at the flap ineffectually with a kitchen knife. But that was beside the point. A thousand combinations wouldn't take long, not with a briefcase lock and not with a telephone answering machine, either. You'd dial the number and let the machine pick up, and then you'd punch in as many of your three-number codes as you could in the thirty seconds or so that the message played. Then you'd call back and do it again. You might make a lot of calls, but so what? You wouldn't be leaving any messages. And, even if you did, sooner or later you'd get the right combination. And then you'd have a chance to erase them.

So changing his combination wouldn't help. And how would Dot feel if she called up and punched in four-four-four and nothing happened? It would be a slap in the face, and not a very effective one, either, because she could run the combinations until she cracked the code.

Of course he could tell her ahead of time. "I realized anybody could do what you did and get my messages," he could say, "so I changed the number." She'd say it was a good idea. And, if she asked what the new number was, he'd say something about it being so unmemorable he couldn't remember it himself. "But I've got it written down," he'd say, and let it go at that.

And, if she wanted to, she'd get the new number. However you looked at it, he couldn't keep her out of his answering machine. Unless . . .

Well, he could change his phone number. Get a new number, an unlisted one. With seven digits, well, that added up to ten million combinations, and it would take forever and cost a fortune, because you'd get nine million wrong numbers while you were at it.

But if he got a new number, there wouldn't be any messages to protect. Because no one would be able to call him. Including Dot, who was his most frequent caller in the first place.

Maybe he should just leave everything the way it was. Dot had probably been right to check his machine, just as she'd been right to check out the astrologer. He'd liked Louise, she was a nice woman, but if she was going to turn into Chatty Cathy the minute somebody mentioned a murderer's thumb, well, that made her a definite loose end.

And Dot had snipped her off.

Imagine that. Dot, coming down on the train, wearing gloves and a little flowered hat. She hadn't mentioned a hat, and it was hard to picture her in a hat, but it sort of fit. Gloves and a hat, and a poisoned chocolate in her handbag. And tidying up afterward, and going home.

Jesus.

Suppose she hadn't done it. Suppose she'd told him, and left him with the task of cleaning up the potential mess he'd made. Could he have taken care of Louise?

Probably. You did what you had to do. Once or twice over the years he'd made the mistake of getting to know someone he'd been hired to take out. There was that fellow in Roseburg, Oregon, set up by the government as a quick printer, secure as could be in the Witness Protection Program. Keller had liked the man, and liked the town, too, and thought about settling down there. But in the end you did what you had to do. You steeled yourself and got the job done.

He'd forgotten the guy's name. Both his names, the original one and the new one the feds gave him. Forgot what he looked like, too. Couldn't picture him.

Which was fine. The way it ought to be.

He pictured Louise as he remembered her, sitting in her

chair, the bowl of chocolates at her side. But the features were already growing less distinct in his mind, the colors fading toward gray.

Good.

CHAPTER TWENTY-SIX

Keller put his coffee cup down, and within seconds the busboy filled it up again. He'd been wondering just how long he could sit over one cup of coffee, and it was beginning to look as though the answer was forever. Because they never let the cup get empty, and how could they expect you to leave while you still had coffee in front of you?

He let the coffee cool and looked out the window. The coffee shop was at the corner of Crosby and Bleecker, and from where Keller sat he could get a glimpse of the entrance to Maggie's building. Watching it was a little like watching paint dry. No one ever went in or out of it, and hardly anybody even walked past it, as that block of Crosby Street didn't get much in the way of pedestrian traffic.

Keller drank a little more coffee, and had his cup filled again, and looked up to see a man emerge from Maggie's building. He was short and wiry, built like a jockey, and he was wearing a distressed leather jacket and carrying a metal toolbox.

He carried it to the corner and into the coffee shop, and came right over to Keller's table. "Piece of pie," he said.

"Most people say 'piece of cake,' " Keller said.

"Huh? Oh, up there? That was a piece of cake, all right, but what I want's a piece of pie. In fact"——he reached for the menu—"what I want's a meal. What's good here?"

"I've never been here before."

"Yeah, but you're here now. What did you have?"

"Coffee."

"That's all?" He motioned for the waitress, ordered a cheeseburger with fries, and asked what kind of pie they had. It was a tough choice, but he went with Boston cream.

"Here," he said, when he'd finished ordering, and put three keys on the table in front of Keller. "This here lets you into the building. Upstairs, what I did was I drilled out both locks and replaced the cylinders. Light-colored key's for the top lock, dark one's for the bottom. Turn the top one clockwise, the bottom one counter. Nothing to it, but you're gonna be disappointed."

"Why?"

"Nothing there to steal. Not that I looked around, I just did what I went there to do, but I couldn't help notice there's no furniture. No chairs, no tables, no rug on the floor. Zip, nada, nothing. It's not like they moved out, because there's papers pinned to a bulletin board and clothes in the closets. But there's no furniture. You know anything about these people?"

"I think he's an architect."

"Oh," the man said. "Well, why didn't you say so? They never have furniture. They like space. Place has got space, I'll say that for it. One big room, fills the whole floor, and there's not a damn thing in it but space."

"There must be a bed," Keller said.

"There's a desk," the man said. "Built in. Also some bookshelves, also built in. Far as a bed's concerned, well, you find it, you can sleep in it. Myself, I didn't happen to see it."

"Oh."

"Everything's white," the man said, "including the floor. Gotta be an architect. Real practical, huh? A white floor in this town?" He put down his cheeseburger, took a forkful of pie, then bit into the cheeseburger again. "I eat everything at once," he said, a little defensively. "My whole family's the same way. You're going in there, right?"

"How's that?"

"The apartment, the loft. The white space. Well, you got access. Light key's for the top lock, but hey, if you get mixed up, what's the problem? One key don't work, try the other." He picked up a french fry. "Keys are all yours, soon as you pay for 'em."

"Oh, right," Keller said. He passed the man an envelope, and the little locksmith put down his fork long enough to lift the flap and count the bills it contained.

"I always count," he said, "in case it's too much or too little. The count's off about a third of the time, my experience, and what percentage of the time do you figure it's in my favor?"

"Hardly ever."

"Bingo," the man said. "This time the count's right, and thanks very much."

"You're welcome," Keller said, picking up the keys. "And thanks for helping me out."

"What I do," the man said. "I'm a locksmith, licensed and bonded and on call around the clock. People lose their keys, I let 'em in. They never had keys in the first place, well, it costs a little more." He grinned. "You're in a hurry, and no reason for you to stick around until I'm done. I might try that pecan pie, see if it's as good as the Boston cream. You go ahead, and the check's on me. The hell, all you had was coffee. Don't forget, the bright key's for the top lock."

"And I turn it clockwise."

"Whatever." He grabbed a french fry. "You want some advice? Wear sunglasses."

It was a small commercial building converted to residential use, with an artist's loft taking up each of its five stories. The sculptor on the ground floor lived with his wife in Park Slope, and, according to Maggie, used his space on Crosby Street only for work. "He makes these massive hulking statues," she had told him, "humanoid, but just barely, and they weigh a ton, so it's good he's on the ground floor. It takes him forever to finish a piece, but he never sells anything, so it doesn't matter."

"He never sells anything?"

"I was a painter for years," she'd said, "and I never sold anything. You don't have to sell to be an artist. In fact it's probably easier if you don't."

There was a painter on the third floor, another painter on the fourth. Keller didn't know what their work looked like, or if they ever sold any of it. He knew that Maggie occupied the top floor, and that the architect on the second floor was somewhere in Europe and wouldn't be back for months.

Keller used the new keys, opened the new locks, and stepped into an enormous white room. The floor was white, as the locksmith had told him, and so were the walls and the ceiling, along with the built-in desk and the built-in bookshelves. There were windows at either end of the loft. The ones at the rear were painted white, glass and all, while the ones in the front were out of sight behind white shutters.

With the track lighting on, the whiteness of the room was enough to give you a headache. Keller turned the lights off, and the room was plunged into darkness. He tried opening one of the shutters a few inches, letting in a little daylight, and that was better.

There was furniture, he discovered, although he could see how the locksmith had missed it. White cubes, some of them topped with white cushions, served as chairs, and a big white box on one wall held a Murphy bed. Some of the cube chairs were permanently installed, but others were movable, and he carried one over to the front window, cushion and all, and sat on it.

"I don't know if you noticed," Dot said, "but the books on the shelves are white, too. They didn't start out that way, but somebody took white shelf paper and made individual covers for them."

"I know."

"You could lose your color vision around here. Between the ding-a-ling upstairs who only wears black, and this fruitcake with everything white. You want to switch? I'll watch the street for a while."

"There's somebody across the street," he said.

"Where?" She joined him at the window, squinted through the space between the shutters. "Oh, there he is. In the doorway, with the windbreaker and the cap."

"I spotted him a few minutes ago. He's just standing there."

"Well, he can't be waiting for a bus, or hoping to flag a cruising taxi. He's waiting for somebody. Have you got the binoculars?"

"I thought you had them."

"Here they are. He could look up and spot light glinting off them, if there was any light to glint. I can't really make out his face. Here, you look."

He peered through the binoculars, adjusted the focus. The man's face was in shadow, and indistinct.

"Well, Keller? Is that the guy you saw in Boston?"

"I never really got a good look at him," he said, "and I don't even know if the guy I saw was the guy who tried to kill me."

"And killed your raincoat by mistake."

"But this guy's here for a reason," he said. "He's either Roger or he's not."

"That's true of everybody, Keller."

"You know what I mean. He's here to do a job upstairs, or he's here to do a job on the guy who does."

Whoever he was, he was right there on the opposite side of a narrow street. If he had a gun, Keller thought, he could shoot the son of a bitch, and then they could go across the street and take a closer look at him.

"There's somebody else," he said. "See?"

"Where?"

"Walking down from the corner."

"Just a man walking," she said, "but that's rare enough on this street, isn't it? How about this guy, Keller. Does he look familiar?"

Keller tracked him with the binoculars. This one wasn't in shadows, but he wore a long coat and a wide-brimmed hat and a muffler and glasses, and about all you could say for sure was that he didn't have a mustache. He was on the tall side, but then so was the lurker, the guy in the doorway.

"He's turning around," he said. "I think he's looking for an address."

"And look who's coming."

"What, in the doorway? He hasn't moved."

"Coming down the street, Keller. Is that who I think it is? Dressed all in black, surprise surprise?"

It was Maggie, on her way home. She was coming from the left, and the guy with the hat and muffler was coming from the right, and the guy in the windbreaker and cap was across the street, lurking.

"This is handy," Dot said. "Everybody on stage at the same time. You want to go downstairs and handle the introductions, Keller?"

"He's crossing the street," he said. "He's walking right toward her."

"He's still in the doorway. Oh, the hat and muffler. You think he's going to do it here and now?"

"How? It's supposed to look like an accident."

"Maybe he'll throw her in front of a truck. There should be a garbage truck coming through sometime after midnight. Maybe he just wants a close look at her. No, he's stopping her."

Keller had the impulse to shout a warning. He wouldn't do that, but what was he supposed to do, just sit there and watch the woman get killed?

"They're talking," Dot said, her own voice reduced to a

whisper. "If the window was open we could hear them."

"Don't open it now."

"No. From this angle all I can see is the tops of their heads, and they're both wearing hats."

"What difference does that make?"

"I don't know. Maybe he's a friend of hers."

"Maybe."

"Maybe she'll take him upstairs. Maybe she'll do that even if he's a stranger. That'd make it easy for him, and then Roger'll be waiting across the street when he comes out. Ooops, false alarm."

Maggie was entering the building. And the man in the hat had drawn away from her and was crossing the street, moving to the right, away from the man in the doorway. He walked fifteen or twenty yards to another darkened building and stood at the door.

"He was asking directions," Dot explained. "And she pointed him over there, and that's where he's going. See? He's waiting for somebody to buzz him in. And somebody just did, and there he goes."

"And the lurker, the guy in the cap? He's not in the doorway."

"That's him two doors down," she said. "Heading to the corner. The coffee shop's still open. Maybe he's hungry."

"The locksmith seemed to like the Boston cream pie."

"I wouldn't mind a piece myself," she said. "This watching and waiting takes a lot out of you."

Around midnight, Dot took her suitcase into the bathroom and emerged wearing a flannel robe and slippers. She had trouble with the Murphy bed, but stopped Keller when he rose to give her a hand. "Wait until I take over for you," she said. "We want a pair of eyes at that window all the time."

"There's nothing happening out there."

"And how long would it take for someone to cross the

street and pop into the building? Okay, now you can get the bed down."

He knew she was right. That was the whole point of her joining him, so that at least one of them would be watching at all times. They could take turns sleeping, and one could go on watching while the other went out for sandwiches and coffee, or for a closer look at whoever was lurking in the neighborhood.

It was good, too, to have company. That had felt odd at first, because he was on a job, and he never had anyone with him when he was working. But this was a little different anyway, because his work was rarely this passive a process. There was often a fair amount of waiting involved, but you generally knew who you were waiting for, and you got to pick the time when waiting stopped and action commenced. If you were going to spend an indeterminate period of time just sitting at a window, peering through an inch-wide gap between the shutters, it didn't hurt to have someone to talk to.

She got into bed. Earlier she'd found a lamp—white, of course, with a white shade—but now she turned it out, and the sole illumination was what light came through the half-open bathroom door. "The minute you get tired," she said, "you wake me, and I'll take a turn."

While she slept, he kept an eye on the street scene. It was hard to keep his mind on what he was doing. When you stared long enough, waiting for something to change in your field of vision, and nothing did, well, your mind tended to wander. Keller, willing himself to maintain his vigil, thought of those sentries in wartime who were punished for falling asleep on duty. Like it was their choice.

Maybe it was to motivate them, he thought. Maybe the threat of execution helped them fight off fatigue. It seemed to him, though, that the best way to doze off was to struggle to stay awake. Sitting in front of the television set, staring drowsily at afternoon football, the harder he worked to stay alert, the more certain he was to drift off. His mind would slip away on some tangential thought, and the next thing he knew the Giants were trying to squeeze in a play before the two-minute warning.

This was different. His eyes stayed open without much effort on his part. But one thought would lead to another, and it was hard to pay any real attention to what was happening outside the window. Especially in view of the fact that nothing was happening. The guy in the windbreaker and cap had disappeared, and the guy with the hat and muffler had never returned, and what was the point?

They'd made a mistake early on, he realized. When Dot let out the contract, she should have specified that the job had to be done during normal business hours. Monday to Friday, nine to five. All concerned—their hitter, Roger, and Keller himself—could have the rest of the time off.

As it was, they were stuck. Not the hitter—he could return to his hotel room whenever he wanted, or kill a few hours at a movie. That was one of the nice things about the business, you could pretty much write your own schedule. There was plenty to do in New York, and time to do it. If the guy wanted to see *Cats*, say, that was up to him.

Not so for Roger, who had to be on call twenty-four hours a day. And not so for Keller, who had to be able to identify both men, and then had to be Johnny-on-the-spot when the hit happened, sitting on the hitter's shoulder and waiting for Roger to make his move.

A car appeared at the far end of Crosby Street. It traversed the block without speeding up or slowing down, then turned at the corner and disappeared from view. Across the street, a cigarette glowed in an upstairs window. Whoopee.

After a few hours he thought about waking Dot, but couldn't figure out how to do it without deserting his post. He didn't want to shout, and was reluctant to take his eyes off the street. Around four-thirty she woke up on her own and told him to go to bed, for God's sake. She didn't have to tell him twice.

"The guy over there," Dot said. "Standing over by the garbage cans, eating the sandwich."

"I think it's a hot dog."

"Thanks for pointing that out, Keller. It makes all the difference. Is he the guy with the hat and the muffler?"

"He's not wearing a hat."

"Or a muffler," she said. "Or a long coat, as far as that goes. But could it be the same guy?"

"The one who approached Maggie and asked for directions."

"And then he went across the street and into that building," she said, "and now he's two doors away, eating not just any sandwich but a hot dog. Same guy?"

"I don't know."

"Well, that's helpful."

"That was the night before last," he said, "and he was all bundled up."

"Hat, coat, and muffler."

"The best view I got of him was the top of his head. The top of his hat, actually. And the rest of the time all I could see of him was what showed between his hat and his muffler."

"I think it's the same man, Keller."

"The man I saw," he went on, "was clean-shaven. In fact that was just about the only thing I could tell you about him. He was white, and he didn't have a mustache. This one's got a mustache."

"Give me the glasses, Keller."

"You didn't see the mustache?"

"I saw the mustache. I just want a closer look at it, that's all. These aren't the greatest binoculars in the world, are they?"

"They're not the worst, either."

"No. It's a hot dog, all right, and it's probably not the best hot dog in the world, either, judging by how long it's taking him to eat it. That mustache could be a fake."

"So could the hot dog."

"Huh? Oh, you were making a joke. Aren't you clever. I think it's a fake mustache, Keller."

"Why would he have a fake mustache?"

"I don't know."

"Maybe he grew it," he said, "in the time we've been cooped up here."

"Maybe he's a master of disguise. He's done with the hot dog, believe it or not. I wonder if he's going to light a cigarette."

"Why would he do that?"

"That's what smokers do. Don't ask me why. Most of the people who stand around outside, they're smokers who aren't allowed to smoke in their offices. He's not lighting a cigarette."

"Or a pipe," Keller said.

"He's going into that building. The one he went into the other night."

"Back before he grew a mustache."

"Or pasted it on."

"The man the other night had somebody buzz him in. This fellow used a key."

"So?"

"So what is it exactly that they've got in common? The lack of an umbrella?"

"They've got the same walk," she said.

"They do?"

"It looks the same to me."

"Left, right, left, right . . ."

"Watch the window, Keller. Four flights up, second from the left."

"I'm watching it."

"See if a light goes on in the next five minutes."

He sat, waiting. The window stayed dark.

"Amazing," he said. "Can you believe it? The light didn't go on. The dark window stayed dark. You called that one, all right."

"He's sitting there in the dark."

"Maybe daylight's enough for him."

"If he put the light on," she said, "we could see him."

"See him doing what?"

"Sitting in the window. At this angle, with no light behind him, we can't see him."

"Dot," he said, "what makes you think he's there?"

"He's there."

"Why that window?"

"Because that's where he was last night and the night before."

"With the light on?"

"No, sitting in the dark."

"Then how could you—"

"Smoking," she said.

He thought about it. "A cigarette glowing," he said.

"Right."

"I noticed it once or twice. The night before last, I remember noticing it then. And maybe last night, too."

"I saw it on and off, both nights."

"You didn't mention it."

"You were sleeping, Keller."

"And I guess you were sleeping when I noticed it. It's not much to notice. If I'd had someone to talk to, I probably wouldn't have noticed it at all. There! Somebody just lit a cigarette."

"Him."

"It's always that window?"

"Uh-huh."

"So he's a guy who lives there," he said, "and he has trouble sleeping, and he sits by the window a lot."

"And smokes."

"It's his apartment. Or loft, or office, or whatever it is. He wants to smoke, it's his business."

"And it's his face," she said, "so he can paste a mustache on it anytime he wants to."

"If it's the same man," he said, "and he just happens to live there, I guess he'd either have a mustache or he wouldn't."

"My point exactly, Keller."

"He could have one and shave it off. But he couldn't not have one, and then two days later there it is." He frowned. "If it's the same man."

"Let's assume he is."

"Okay."

"He's got to be one of them."

"Our guy or Roger."

"Right."

"It would help," he said, "if we knew which."

"We just wait, and—"

"And see what happens," he said. "That's what we've been doing. And nothing happens."

"Well, if you've got a better idea . . . Isn't that your girl-friend?"

"Maggie? Where?"

"Right there."

"It's her. How'd she get over there?"

She was on the other side of the street, walking away. He waited for someone to leap out of an alleyway and strangle her, but nobody did.

"She must have left the building," Dot said, "while we were watching the glowing cigarette across the street. What's she got, a backpack? Maybe she's going away for the weekend."

"That's all we need."

"She's at the corner. She's hailing a cab. Where do you suppose she's going?"

"Read her lips, see what she tells the driver."

"Is Mr. Mustache still at the window? I don't see the telltale glow of his cigarette. No, I take it back. There it is. He's there, so he probably saw her leave."

"So did we," he said. "So what?"

"So he's not going to follow her. What about the other one?"

The man in the cap and windbreaker had been back intermittently, and Keller had spotted him that morning in the coffee shop on the corner. He'd stopped by to pick up breakfast for the two of them, and there was the guy, perched on a stool at the counter, tucking into a plate of salami and eggs.

"Salami and eggs," Keller said. "I haven't seen him since breakfast."

"Maybe he decided to catch a movie."

"Or maybe he's sitting in some other window, without a glowing cigarette to give him away. You don't think she really left for the weekend, do you?"

"Who knows?"

"The guy with the mustache has to be part of the game," he said. "How else do you explain the mustache? I mean, now you see it, now you don't."

"Either he's neurotic in a new and interesting way," Dot said, "or he's a player. Besides, didn't he stop your girlfriend on the street to ask directions? And she pointed him to the building?"

"If he was legit, he'd know where he lives."

"He wanted a close look at her," she said. "Wanted a chance to size her up."

"Why?"

"To lock in on the target, I guess. Don't you do that? Confirm the subject's identity before you close the sale?"

"I'd just as soon do it from a distance," he said. "You get up close, talk to them, it complicates things."

"You start thinking you know them."

"And you *don't* know them," he said, "not really. The

298

only reason they're in your life is because there's a contract in your pocket with their name on it. It's the job that brought the two of you together, and in the end you have to bite the bullet and do the job."

"But it's easier if you keep your distance."

"I'd say so," he said, "but maybe this guy's wired differently. Maybe he likes the idea of talking to her, knowing all along he's going to take her out."

"Sick," Dot said.

"Well, mental health's not necessarily part of the job description."

"No."

"And who says he's the one who's going to take her out? Maybe he's Roger, and the other guy's going to hit her."

"The windbreaker."

"That makes him sound like he's got gas," he said. "One of them's Roger and one's our hitter. I wish we knew which was which."

"If only," Dot said.

"Simplify things, wouldn't it? Instead of waiting around, I could just go ahead and take him out. With Roger down and out, we could call off the other guy, and everybody could go home."

"We couldn't call off our guy, Keller. He's still got a job to do, because your girlfriend's still a loose end."

He was silent for a moment. Then he said, "Maybe you could stop calling her my girlfriend."

"Sorry."

"Just to keep it simple, you know?"

"It won't happen again."

"And it'd still be good if we knew which was which, because I could deal with Roger and we could clear out. And the other guy could do what he came here to do, and we wouldn't have to sit around and watch him get ready to do it."

"Uh-huh. Have you got a hunch?"

"As to which is which? I've got two hunches, and I'm pretty sure one of them is right."

"Narrows it down."

"On the one hand," he said, "the guy with the mustache is Roger, and that's why he's at the window all the time, puffing away on a Marlboro Light. Because why else would he need an observation post? If he's just there to fulfill a contract, all he needs to do is a little reconnaissance. But if he's Roger, waiting to hit the hitter, he's got to spot the other guy and know when the hit goes down."

"Makes sense."

"On the other hand," he said, "what's with the mustache? Why does he need to change his appearance?"

"To keep from being recognized."

"Who's going to recognize him, Dot? Maggie? She saw him once, when he stopped her on the street, but she never has to see him again. The other hitter? The other hitter doesn't know anything about Roger. He's here to do a job and he's got no reason to think it's going to be complicated."

"On the one hand he's Roger," she said, "and on the other hand he's not."

"There you go," he said.

"I had this thought," he said.

"Care to share it?"

"I could just do them both, you know? Instead of waiting, because we could sit here forever. She's out, and God knows when she's coming back, and nobody can do anything until she does. Unless our hitter tailed her, but he wouldn't do that, would he?"

"Two things I told him," she said. "It has to be in her loft and it has to look like an accident."

"So it won't happen until she comes back, but what do we need her for? I go across the street and up four flights and take out the guy with the mustache. Then I come down and hit a few doorways until I bump into the guy with the windbreaker, and I do him."

"Kill 'em both and let God sort 'em out."

"We might never know which was which," he said, "but what difference would it make? The thing is, I'd be killing an innocent man."

"How do you figure that?"

"The guy you hired. He comes to New York to do a job and gets killed by the people who hired him."

"He's here to kill a girl, Keller. Don't you think it's a stretch to call him innocent?"

"You know what I mean. I'd be killing him for no reason."

"Suppose someone hired you to kill him."

"Then I'd have a reason."

"But this way you don't."

"Not in the same way, no. But it's a waste of time talking about it. I mean, who even knows for sure that it's narrowed down to those two guys? Maybe somebody else is Roger, somebody we haven't even noticed yet."

"It's possible."

"So it'd be nuts, taking them both out. Anyway, it was just a thought."

"Keller, I had the same thought."

"Really?"

"And the same objections, plus an extra. We'd still have that dame to worry about. Your girlfriend, and I'm sorry, I was going to stop calling her that."

"Well," he said.

"I suppose we could burn that bridge when we came to it," she said, "but I think what we've got to do is stick with the original plan. I just wish I'd realized there was going to be so much waiting involved. I'd have set it up differently."

CHAPTER TWENTY-SEVEN

"Keller!"

He was dreaming, and yearned to sink back into the dream, but she said his name again and he shook it off and got out of bed. "Quick," she said, and he hurried over to the window in time to see a woman leaning against the side of a cab while her companion counted out bills and paid the driver. The cab pulled away and the two of them stood in the middle of Crosby Street. The woman was Maggie, but who was the man?

He wore jeans and a beat-up leather jacket, and for a minute Keller thought it was the locksmith, but this guy was bigger. Of course, he thought, the little man could have put on a few pounds by now. Boston cream pie will do that, but would it make you taller, too? Maybe if you stood on it . . .

Maggie pulled the man into an embrace, and Keller felt as though he shouldn't be watching this. "Her latest superficial relationship," Dot said dryly. "We haven't seen him before, or have we? Help me out here, Keller."

"He doesn't look familiar."

"He's certainly getting familiar with her, though, isn't he? Has he got his hand where I think he does?"

"I think she's bringing him in the building."

"I knew that when the cab drove off, Keller. Although for a minute there I thought they were going to do it in the middle of the street. No, don't say anything. Just listen for a minute. There!"

"What?"

"They're on the elevator. Noisy contraption, isn't it? Slow, too. Now it stopped, they must be at her place. Did you get a good look at his face, Keller?"

"Not really."

"Neither did I, and by now she's probably sitting on it. Use the binoculars. Do you see either of our friends out there? The mustache or the windbreaker?"

"No."

"See a cigarette in the usual window?"

"No."

"The guy she was with. Could it be one of our two guys?"

"I don't know," he said. "I don't think so. She left earlier, she walked to the corner and caught a cab, and haven't we seen both of our guys since then?"

"We saw Mustache. Did we see Windbreaker? I can't remember."

"You think one of them figured out where she was going and hooked up with her there and got to go home with her?"

"The hard part would be figuring out where she was going. Nobody tagged her to the corner, and she got a cab right away. I don't see how she could have been followed."

"It's probably just some guy she picked up."

"Met him at a party and dragged him home. That's how you wound up with her, isn't it?"

"It was a gallery opening."

"Trees," she said. "It all comes back to me. Maybe he's Mr. Goodbar, maybe she picked him up and he's a homicidal drifter and he's gonna kill her."

"Yeah, right."

"Tell me it couldn't happen, Keller."

"It could," he said, "but don't count on it."

"No, but if it did . . . He just lit a cigarette."

"How on earth . . . oh, across the street."

"Who did you think I meant?"

"The homicidal drifter upstairs. But if that's Mustache puffing his way toward emphysema, then it couldn't have been him in the cab with her."

"Good thinking, Keller."

"But it could still be Windbreaker. I wish we could see him."

"The only reason we can see Mustache is he smokes. And we're only guessing that's him. He could have rigged up a night-light on a timer."

"Just to fool us."

"Right. Keller, nobody's about to arrange an accident for her as long as she's got company up there. By the time Mustache finishes his cigarette he's going to come to the same conclusion. He'll go to sleep, and I bet Windbreaker's been asleep for hours already. Why don't you go back to bed?"

"I don't think so. You go if you want to."

"I'm not tired. I should be but I'm not. You hungry?"

"No."

"Because there's some of that pizza left."

"I'm not hungry."

He stayed where he was and thought about the dream he'd been having. He rarely remembered dreams, but he'd been in the middle of this one when she woke him up, and it was still vivid for him. He'd bought someone's stamp collection, picked it up cheap, and he kept finding things in it, valuable and desirable stamps he hadn't known it contained. He drew out prize after prize, remounting his finds in his own albums, and he'd already taken out stamps worth ten or twenty times what he'd paid for the whole collection, and still there were more wonders to be found, and . . .

"Keller!"

"That was really strange," he said. "I was remembering my dream, and all of a sudden I was back in it again."

"Well, are you awake now? Because that's the elevator."

"Going up or down?"

"That's all they do, they go up and down. I can't tell

which, all I can tell is it's running. But since it was last on the top floor—"

"You think he's leaving. But it could be somebody who rang for it downstairs, and in a minute we'll hear it heading back up again."

"It's almost four in the morning, Keller."

"So?"

"So it's late for somebody to be getting home."

"Or to be going out," he said. "These people are artists, Dot. They don't punch a time clock. They—"

She silenced him with a hand on his arm, pointed out the window. A man in a leather jacket emerged from the building and walked to the curb. It was the same man they'd seen a couple of hours ago, paying the cabdriver, then pulled into a public embrace by Maggie. But had they seen him earlier? In a windbreaker, say?

"He's our guy," he said, suddenly certain.

"He's Roger?"

"No, he's the guy we hired. Look at him, he's looking to hail a cab."

"Then he'd better walk to the corner. The only traffic on this street is the garbage truck, and it's through for the night."

"That's the point, he doesn't know the neighborhood. He picked her up, he came home with her, and he killed her. She's dead and he's on his way home. How am I going to follow him? He gave up on the cab, he's walking away. If I miss him, and if Roger picks him up . . ."

"Harlan!"

He stopped in midsentence, even as the man outside stopped in midstride.

"She speaks up nicely for a dead girl," Dot said. "I guess his name is Harlan."

"You forgot this," Maggie called down. Then something sailed through the air and landed at the fellow's feet. He bent down and retrieved it.

"Thanks!" Harlan called out, and put it in his hip pocket.

"His wallet," Dot said. "He forgot his wallet."

"Why would he take it out of his pants in the first place?"

"Maybe it fell out," she said, "when he took off his pants in a hurry. Or maybe there was something he needed up there, something a man might carry in his wallet."

"Oh."

"The whole thing," she said, "was just what it looked like. She picked him up, brought him home, took him upstairs, and then sent him on his way. Go back to sleep."

"I'm awake now."

"What were you dreaming about, anyway?"

"My stamp collection."

"You dream about it?"

"Evidently."

"Well, maybe you can drift off counting stamps jumping off envelopes. She's probably back in bed now, and he's on his way home. Why didn't she let him stay the night?"

"How do I know?"

"I was just making conversation, Keller. We're the only two people in the world awake at this hour, I figured we could talk to each other. I thought—"

"We're not the only two people awake."

"You're probably right, but—" She broke off the sentence, looked where he was pointing. "You're definitely right," she said, "unless our friend learned to smoke in his sleep. There he is, puffing away."

"Still up at this hour, and watching the street."

"I think we should do the same," she said. "I think something's about to happen."

The first thing that happened was that the man in the fourth-floor window finished his cigarette, or at least took it out of view. Then, a few minutes later, he stepped out of his front door. He was wearing the hat and the muffler, and

306

it was hard to say whether or not he had the mustache.

"Gloves," Dot noted. "And not because it's cold."

"He doesn't want to leave prints."

"If he was just going out for another hot dog," she said, "he probably wouldn't care. Here he comes."

He crossed the street, walked their way, and entered the building.

"I got a look," she said. "The mustache is gone."

"I noticed."

"I don't hear the elevator."

"He's probably taking the stairs."

"It's the middle of the night. Will she let him in?"

"He'll have a story."

"Suppose she doesn't buy it. What kind of locks has she got?"

"I don't remember."

"You don't remember?"

"I was just there a few times," he said, "and I didn't think I was ever going to have to break in, so why should I pay attention to the locks on her door?"

"I wonder how long it'll take him."

"Not long."

"He has to make it look like an accident."

"That's easy enough."

"Will he leave right away? With the astrologer, I couldn't seem to get out of the apartment."

"You were searching the place."

"I guess that was part of it."

"All he has to do is set the stage and leave," he said. "And he's a pro, he'll get out of there as quickly as he can. I don't have time to waste."

"Where are you going?"

"Outside," he said. "I want to be out there waiting when he hits the street."

"Roger's probably watching the building. He'll see you leave."

"Can't be helped. If he leaves first, how am I going to follow him?"

"Just be careful," she said.

If Roger was out there, in his cap and windbreaker, Keller couldn't spot him. He tried to scout around as much as he could without being obvious about it, then took a position in a doorway midway between Maggie's building and the coffee shop on the corner. Maggie's light was on, and he took that to mean that the man with the hat and muffler was in there with her. Of course she could have had the light on anyway, she could have been sitting up reading a book or making jewelry, but the odds were that the guy was in there with her.

Matter of fact, she was most likely dead by now. Once he was in the door, well, her life expectancy went way down. He wouldn't have to confirm the identification, because he already knew what she looked like, he'd spoken to her on the street that first night. So he'd just do it. Loop that muffler of his around her throat, say, and make it swift and silent.

Well, maybe not the muffler. Hard to do it that way and make it look accidental. But there were plenty of ways, all of them quick and quiet and deadly.

Unless he was the kind of guy who liked to take his time. There were people like that, Keller knew. You didn't find too many in the professional ranks, but there were a few. He'd heard stories.

He found himself remembering things about Maggie. The way she had of cocking her head. Other winning little mannerisms.

No choice, he thought. Couldn't be helped.

He pictured her, looking sweet and saucy and desirable, and he willed himself to do the little trick he'd taught Dot. He turned the color level down, faded it all the way to black and white, then muted the contrast until it became shades of gray. He shrank the picture, moved it farther and farther away so that the image got smaller and smaller.

He was holding it in his mind like that, just a blur, really, invisibly small, when Maggie's light went out.

Keller let out a breath he hadn't realized he'd been holding. For a moment he felt a slight sense of loss, but it gave way to anticipation. He was just about done with waiting. Now he was going to have a chance to do something.

He drew back into the shadows and kept his eyes on the front door, waiting for the killer to emerge. But something made him look up, and he saw a faint red glow in the top-floor window, saw it brighten as the man drew on his cigarette.

He was having a smoke, taking a long look out the window. Did he have the sense that someone was outside waiting for him? Keller figured he himself was invisible, but what about Roger? Was he around? Could the killer see him?

And had Roger noticed the glow of the cigarette?

CHAPTER TWENTY-EIGHT

The killer had a cigarette going when he emerged from the building. The same one, Keller figured. It was evidence, and he wouldn't want to leave it behind. He flicked it at the curb, and sparks danced when it hit the pavement.

The man looked both ways, then turned toward Keller. As soon as he did, Keller left the shelter of the doorway and walked on ahead of the man, leading him, turning left at the corner, walking toward oncoming traffic. He hailed a cab and got in front, next to the driver, who gave him a look, then asked the destination. Keller didn't say anything until the killer came into view, then pointed him out to the driver.

"See that man?" he said.

"Guy with the hat?"

"That's the one. He's going to get a cab, and we're going to follow him."

"This a gag?"

"I beg your pardon?"

"*Candid Camera*, something like that? And I got news for you, he's not even trying for a cab. He's walking."

"Follow him."

"Follow a guy that's walking?"

"Slowly," Keller said. "Don't get too close."

The man walked east for three blocks, setting a brisk pace. Keller followed him in the cab, trying to ignore the driver. Then the man turned, heading north on a street that was one-way southbound.

"Shit," Keller said, and paid off the cab. He got out on the opposite side of the street from his quarry and scanned the area, trying to determine if either of them was being followed. He couldn't see anybody, but that didn't necessarily mean there was nobody there.

They walked for a couple of blocks, Maggie's killer on the left-hand side of the avenue, Keller on the right. Then, at the corner of a westbound street with a fair amount of traffic, the man stepped to the curb and held up a hand. Keller did the same, and snatched the cab the man had been trying for. This time he got in back and leaned forward, pointing out the man to the driver.

"He was tryin' to flag me," the driver said, "but you were first. You want to give him a ride?"

Keller was tempted, but only for an instant. "No," he said. "I want you to wait here, and when he gets a cab I want you to follow it."

"Good tip, right?"

"Fifty bucks."

"Plus the meter?"

"You drive a hard bargain," Keller said. "Here we go. No, hang on. Wait a minute."

A cab had stopped, but pulled away after a brief conversation. "Maybe he didn't like the guy's looks," the driver suggested.

"Why not? He's dressed decently."

"So maybe your guy didn't like the cabby's looks. Maybe the cab's a mess, maybe some drunk puked in it."

"Maybe he wanted to go to the airport," Keller thought aloud.

"No," the cabby said. "Brooklyn, maybe. Here's another one stopping for him. Well, it's his lucky day. He's getting in."

"Don't lose him," Keller said, "but don't get too close to him, either."

"You got it."

Keller sat forward, his eyes on the cab in front of them. After a moment he said, "Why not the airport?"

"No luggage."

311

"Maybe he travels light."

"You figure he's going to the airport?"

"It's possible."

"Which airport, you happen to know?"

"I could narrow it down to three."

"La Guardia and JFK's okay, but I get double the meter if it's Newark."

"Double the meter," Keller said.

"For out of town."

"Plus the fifty we agreed to."

"Plus the fifty, and plus the tunnel toll."

Keller was silent, watching the cab in front of them, and the driver took it for resistance. "You want a cheap ride to Newark," he said, "they got a bus at Port Authority'll take you there for ten, twelve dollars. No tip and no tolls, but don't point out some asshole with a hat and expect the driver to follow him for you."

Keller told him the money wasn't a problem. Anyway, it didn't look as though they were headed for Newark. They were on Eighth Avenue now, headed uptown, and they'd passed the turnoffs for both the Holland and Lincoln Tunnels. If the killer's destination was one of the other two airports, what was his cab doing this far west?

"Here we go," Keller's driver said, slowing to a stop. "Hotel Woodleigh, a touch of Europe in Old New York. Didn't I tell you he wouldn't go to the airport without luggage?"

"Your very words," Keller said.

"He'll be out in a minute, carrying a suitcase. Or more likely it'll have wheels on it and he'll be rolling it. Those Rollaboards are taking over the world."

"He's paying off his cab."

"So?"

"So I think he's got the right idea," Keller said, and drew three twenties and a ten from his wallet. The cabby seemed satisfied—he damn well ought to be, Keller thought—but

312

would have preferred to stick around for the rest of the operation.

"He'll be out in five minutes, and you'll wish you had me waiting," he said. Keller figured he was probably right, but all the same he got out of the cab and walked into the hotel lobby.

He found a chair where he could watch both entrances and the bank of elevators, but barely got settled into it before he sensed that someone was taking an interest in him. He looked around and caught the desk clerk looking his way.

A few hours from now, he thought, a man like himself, presentably dressed and groomed, could sit for an hour with a newspaper without attracting any attention. But at this hour, with the sky still dark and the city as close as it got to sleep, he was conspicuous.

He walked over to the desk, took out his wallet, flipped it open as if to show a badge. "Fellow who just came in here," he said. "Had a hat on."

"You know," the clerk said, "I had a feeling about him."

"Where'd he go?"

"To his room," the clerk said. "Well, to somebody's room. He went right up on the elevator. Didn't stop at the desk for his key."

"You happen to know the room?"

"Never saw him before. I wasn't on when he checked in. *If* he checked in." He leaned forward, lowered his voice. "What'd he do, anyway?"

He killed a friend of mine, Keller thought. "I'll just have a seat," he said. "I don't know how long he'll be, but I wouldn't want him to slip past me. You don't have newspapers for sale, do you? So I don't look too obvious sitting there."

The papers hadn't come yet, but the clerk managed to find yesterday's *Times*. Keller didn't offer to pay for it, figuring a cop wouldn't. He sat down with the paper and tried to look interested in it.

At first there was no activity at all, but then as dawn approached, the elevator would open every few minutes, and someone would emerge from it and head for the desk to check out. Some looked tired, others looked wide awake, but none looked like the man who had paid Maggie a visit. He kept an eye on the hotel entrance, too, and now and then walked out onto the street for a quick look around. One time he saw a fellow in a cap and windbreaker, caught a quick glimpse of him entering a deli across the street.

Roger, he thought, and tried to position himself so he could watch the front door of the deli and still keep an eye on the hotel lobby. His eyes darted from side to side, it was like watching a tennis match, and then the man in the cap and windbreaker came out of the deli with a plastic bag in each hand, and a frontal view made it clear it wasn't the man he'd seen on Crosby Street. This guy was shorter and heavier, with a big gut on him, and Keller had a hunch the shopping bags each held a six-pack.

He returned to the lobby, settled in with the paper. And, just a few minutes later, he almost missed the guy in the hat.

That's because the sonofabitch wasn't wearing a hat this time. Four men got off the elevator, all bareheaded, all wearing suits and ties, all carrying briefcases. One walked to the desk, while the other three headed for the street. Keller looked down at his newspaper, then looked up suddenly. He hadn't recognized the man, but he recognized the walk, the way the guy moved. He went out after him, and there he was, getting into the first cab at the taxi stand. No hat, and he was wearing the mustache again, and his hair was blond and shaggy.

He was leaning into the cab, and Keller got so close he could have reached out and touched him. He had the momentary urge to do just that, to spin him around, grab hold of his necktie and throttle him with it. The impulse startled Keller, and of course he didn't act on it, nor did it keep him from hearing what the man told the driver.

Keller watched the cab pull away, then got into the one next in line. He got in back, made himself comfortable. "Newark Airport," he said. "Continental Airlines."

Newark was a hub city for Continental, and the airline had a whole terminal for itself and its code-share partners. Keller sort of liked the idea of partner airlines, hanging out together like the costars of a buddy movie, sharing a secret code. What he liked less was the number of gates Continental had. He didn't see his man in the ticketing area, and had to assume he already had his ticket and had proceeded directly to the gate.

But which gate? There were dozens of them, and it wasn't as if he could page the guy. He had to go from gate to gate until he spotted him.

The woman in front of him at Security kept setting off the metals detector, and the delay, only a matter of seconds, drove him nuts. It had been a mistake, he told himself, to give the cabdriver the destination and let it go at that. He never should have let the man out of his sight. Of course it was easier this way, and they might very well have lost the other taxi in the tunnel traffic, but now he was scurrying from gate to gate, scanning the passengers, trying to move as quickly as he could without making himself conspicuous, and where the hell *was* the sonofabitch, anyway?

And he almost missed him again. Because he wasn't a blond anymore, he had short dark hair, and the mustache was gone. And he'd taken off his tie, which meant Keller could forget about choking him with it, and instead of the suit jacket he was wearing a windbreaker.

A windbreaker! But this one was black, not tan like Roger's. He wasn't Roger, for God's sake. Still, he managed to look different every time Keller saw him, and was it even him this time? Could he be sure?

He was in a flight lounge waiting for a flight to Jacksonville. He still had the briefcase, and Keller wondered what it held. So far the man had dispensed with a hat, a long coat, a blond wig, a muffler, a suit jacket, and a necktie. They couldn't all be in the briefcase, which meant he must have abandoned various articles along the way. That seemed to Keller like an awfully complicated aftermath to a fairly straightforward assignment. He'd been hired to kill a woman in a loft on Crosby Street, and had been instructed to make it look like an accident. He'd spent a long time looking over the scene, sitting in a window across the street and working his way through a carton of cigarettes, and—

That's what he had in the briefcase. Cigarettes. Packs of them, Keller figured, and he couldn't smoke a single one of them, not in the airport and not on the plane. And his flight didn't leave for an hour and a half. Poor bastard would be chewing his nails by the time he got to Jacksonville.

Was that where he lived? Jacksonville? Dot hadn't known anything about the guy, booking him through a broker, and with this fellow it stood to reason that the broker didn't know where he lived, either. Wherever it was, Keller would be willing to bet it wasn't Jacksonville. Everything he'd done so far suggested the guy would change planes three times before he went to ground.

Maybe, Keller thought, just maybe the guy was on to something. Maybe he himself had been altogether too casual about his work. He generally just flew in, did the job, and flew straight home. He'd been a little more circumspect lately, but that was because he had Roger to worry about. But this clown didn't know about Roger, and certainly didn't have a clue that he'd been the bait designed to lure Roger into the open. It stood to reason, then, that he took precautions of this sort all the time, and Keller had to say he was impressed.

The killer might not know about Roger, but Keller did. And, because they'd both been in the corner coffee shop at the same time, he'd managed a good look at Roger's face.

He looked around now, trying to spot it.

He was also keeping an eye open for a cloth cap and a tan windbreaker, but he didn't really expect to see that outfit again. That had been Roger's street attire, designed to render him inconspicuous in a shadowed doorway. For an airport, he'd choose a tie and jacket.

Of course, the hitter had chosen a windbreaker for his airport appearance. So, for all Keller knew, Roger might show up in a clown costume, or a suit of armor. He wasn't in the Jacksonville flight lounge, Keller made sure of that, and he wasn't lurking nearby, either.

Had the hitter lost him? It had been well past midnight when the boyfriend du jour left Maggie's loft and the hitter came over to take his place. Climbed all those stairs, probably took them two at a time, eager now, champing at the bit. The way he smoked, you'd think he'd be winded by the time he got to her floor, but not this son of a bitch, not with the adrenaline pumping through his system. Then he knocked, and Maggie opened the door. Maybe she checked, and couldn't see anything because his hand was over the peephole. She asks who it is, can't make out his intentionally muffled reply. And it occurs to her that she shouldn't open the door, it just crosses her mind for an instant, but no, it has to be the boyfriend returning, coming back for something else he'd forgotten, something besides the wallet, or coming back because he couldn't get enough of her and wants to take her in his arms one more time, and then, once she's unlocked the door, it explodes inward and a stranger bursts in, one gloved hand over her mouth, the other reaching for her throat—

Whoa!

Keller got hold of himself. The question, he reminded

317

himself, wasn't how the killer had gotten into her loft, or how she'd reacted, or any of that. He'd been pondering whether Roger had been on the scene at the time, or whether he'd been cooped up somewhere, getting some sleep.

He decided there was no way to tell, short of running into the bastard. All he could do, really, was stay where he was until they called the Jacksonville flight for boarding. Once the man who'd killed Maggie got on that flight, he was out of harm's way. Keller could only conclude that Roger had dropped the ball somewhere along the way, which was beginning to look more and more likely. If he'd been sleeping while the hit went down, well, he wouldn't know about it.

So what would he do? He'd show up on Crosby Street, Keller decided, finding another doorway to lurk in while he waited for something to happen. In fact, if Keller went back right now, or as soon as the Jacksonville flight was in the air, he stood a fair chance of finding Roger on the scene, and this time he'd know the guy was Roger. He wouldn't have to wait for him to make a move. Instead, Keller could make the move. "Say, do you happen to have the time?" "Sure, it's . . . arrrggghhhh!" Just take him out right there on the street and be done with it.

But sooner or later there would be cops called to the Crosby Street loft, and then you could forget about finding Roger anywhere in the neighborhood. He'd realize he'd missed his chance and he'd get the hell out of there. So the thing to do was go back right now and hope to surprise him there before the cops showed up.

He'd wait, though, until the Jacksonville flight left. Just because he couldn't spot Roger didn't mean the man hadn't found his way to the airport. Suppose he were Roger. Would he hang around the departure gate while the minutes crawled by? Not a chance. He'd show up at the last minute, ticket in hand, and board the flight just before it pulled away from the gate.

So what Keller would do was stay right where he was, keeping an eye out for last-minute travelers, and if Roger turned up . . .

Then what? If Roger turned up he'd have a ticket and a boarding pass, and he'd get on the plane, and what the hell was Keller going to do about it?

Or suppose Roger was being ultra-cute, which was entirely possible. Suppose Roger had spotted the hitter early on, and had tagged him back to the Woodleigh. How hard would it have been for a resourceful guy like Roger to get into the guy's hotel room? Say he found a ticket there, knew where his quarry was headed and what flight he'd be on.

Wouldn't he be tempted to catch another flight, an earlier flight, so he'd be waiting at Jacksonville Airport when the man arrived?

As far as Keller could make out, there was only one way to play this.

CHAPTER TWENTY-NINE

The flight was sold out in coach, but they had a couple of seats left in first class. They boarded the first-class passengers ahead of everybody else, along with the passengers requiring special assistance and the small children traveling alone. You didn't have to board ahead of the others, you could bide your time, but Keller didn't see the advantage. Keller was in the third row. If Roger was there, if he boarded now or at the last minute, he'd have to pass Keller to get to his seat.

Unless he was flying the plane, or artfully disguised as a stewardess.

The passengers filed onto the plane, and Keller checked them out as they came into view. His eyes widened when the man in the black windbreaker appeared, and then he reminded himself that he shouldn't be surprised to find Maggie's killer on board. He'd already known the guy was going to be on the flight, and that was why Keller himself was on it.

Keller was somewhat surprised to find out the man was also flying first class, and close enough so that Keller could almost reach out and touch him. Keller was in 3-B, on the aisle, and Maggie's killer was in 2-E, one row up and on the other side of the aisle.

Suppose they'd been seated side by side. Suppose the guy turned out to be chatty.

That seemed unlikely, but you never knew. But Keller's seat mate was a woman, middle-aged, and she was already engrossed in the book she'd brought along, and it looked thick enough to see her through a couple of flights around the world. She seemed happy to ignore Keller, and Keller felt free to ignore her in return.

The plane left the gate on schedule. There was one empty seat left in first class, but Roger didn't show up at the last minute to claim it. Keller leaned back in his wide, comfortable seat, stretched out his legs, and relaxed.

It wasn't the first time Keller had ever flown first class. He generally avoided it, because the price was ridiculous, and, really, what was the point? You had a wider seat and more legroom and a better meal, and the drinks were free. Big deal. Everybody got there at the same time.

And didn't it make you more conspicuous? The flight attendants gave you more attention, so wouldn't they be more likely to remember you?

Keller kept glancing across the aisle, taking the measure of the man in 2-E. Did the son of a bitch fly first class all the time? Keller supposed he could afford it, there was enough money in a job to cover a lot of overhead. He couldn't remember what they'd arranged to pay this master of disguise to kill Maggie, wasn't even sure Dot had mentioned a figure, but it stood to reason that it was comparable to what Keller got, and that was enough to pay for a lot of airline tickets.

Son of a bitch liked to spend money, didn't he? Bought hats and scarves and jackets and just left them behind. Wasn't it risky, strewing the landscape with your castoff clothing? Well, maybe not, Keller decided. If you bought new items and discarded them when you were done with them, there'd be no laundry marks, nothing that led back to you. Besides, you wouldn't be leaving anything at the crime scene. If someone found your hat or your jacket, nobody would rush it to a forensic laboratory. It would just get tossed in the trash, or wind up in a thrift shop.

Where this bird would never see it again. Because he wasn't the type to walk into a thrift shop, was he?

The man was no stamp collector.

Keller grinned at the thought, figuring it put him right up there with Sherlock Holmes. The man flew first class, the man bought and discarded great quantities of clothing, the man spent money like he didn't know what to do with it. Therefore he wasn't a stamp collector, because a stamp collector always knew what to do with money. He bought stamps with it. Keller, faced with the choice of tourist and first-class air travel, couldn't help doing the math and translating the difference into potential philatelic purchases. The difference on this flight, for instance, would pay for a couple of mint high values from the set Canada issued in 1898 for Victoria's jubilee. Keller, given the choice, would have taken the less comfortable seat and the stamps. The murderer across the aisle wouldn't have any better use for those stamps than to paste them on a letter.

Keller looked at him again, saw he was wearing a black silk sleep mask. Had his head back, his hands in his lap. He'd killed an innocent girl, and he was sleeping like a lamb.

One thing Keller realized—he was glad the bastard wasn't a stamp collector.

When they served the meal, the man across the aisle had a good appetite. The murder he'd committed on Crosby Street didn't seem to have put him off his feed. Keller, fiercely hungry himself, couldn't fault the guy on that score. For that matter, had he ever had trouble eating after a job?

Not that he could remember.

And the meal they served you was certainly better than what the peasants were making do with in the back of the plane. They even gave you real glasses and china and silverware instead of that plastic crap you got in coach. Well, not silverware, he thought, although people called it that. *Stainless,* he read on the back of the fork.

Stainless. Were there bloodstains in Maggie's loft on

322

Crosby Street? Had he shed her blood? It was supposed to look like an accident, but there were all kinds of accidents, and some of them broke the skin.

What difference did it make? Why was he even thinking about it?

He looked across the aisle. The killer had polished off his food and was sipping his wine. They gave you a half-bottle of wine in first class, red or white, and Maggie's killer had gone for red. He'd had a drink before the meal, too, a scotch on the rocks. Well, why not? His work was done, he was heading for home, and he didn't have any reason to think he needed to have his wits about him. He didn't know about Roger.

Keller, who wasn't crazy about wine in the first place, had turned it down, and for a drink before the meal he'd settled on orange juice. He knew this didn't make him morally superior to the other man, but that's how he felt, sitting there, eyeing the fellow, watching him smack his lips over the blood-red wine.

In Jacksonville, Keller managed to be the first one off the plane. He led the way, scanning the gate area for a sign of Roger. He was looking for a tan windbreaker and a cloth cap, but he was also looking for the face he'd seen in the coffee shop.

No sign of the man.

There was a video monitor with a list of upcoming departures, and he pretended to study it while the hitter got off the plane, then tagged him all the way to a Delta gate, where a flight to Atlanta was scheduled to depart in a little less than an hour.

Keller's heart sank as he watched the man step up to the desk and show his ticket to the clerk. There were plenty of nonstops from New York to Atlanta, so getting there by way of Jacksonville was taking the long way round, clearly designed to throw a pursuer off the trail. And, he thought, if you were flying first class it was an expensive way to do it. Whatever they were paying this bastard, it was going to have to stretch to cover the kind of overhead he was piling up.

And Keller was certain Atlanta wouldn't be the end of the line. Atlanta was a hub city for Delta, and the hitter would hop off the plane there and hop on another, and who knew where he'd wind up?

It had been easy enough to tail him to Jacksonville, but it wasn't going to be that simple from here on. The flight to Atlanta might very well be sold out in all classes. Even if there was room for Keller, he couldn't reasonably expect to set foot on the plane without drawing the man's attention. If the guy was taking all these precautions, he'd certainly look around for a familiar face. Wherever Keller sat, in first class or in the last row in coach, the odds were he'd be spotted.

So? Wherever Roger was, he'd obviously lost the scent. If he hadn't turned up by now, he wasn't going to be lurking in a flight lounge in Atlanta or Des Moines or Keokuk, or wherever Mr. No-Hat-No-Muffler decided to go next. There was a slim chance that he'd somehow managed to learn the hitter's name and address, as he'd evidently done with some of his previous victims. That would explain Roger's disappearance—he'd go home for now, and in a week or a month he'd pay a visit to the hitter's hometown and take him out at leisure.

Nothing Keller could do about that. What was he supposed to do, track this murderous bastard back and forth across the country until he finally pulled into his own garage? Even if there were some way for him to do that, then what? He pictured himself holed up on the hitter's back porch, waiting patiently for Roger to show.

Time to pack it in, he told himself. Time to find the next flight to New York and buy a ticket. In coach this time, because he'd already spent enough money on a comfortable seat. He had better ways to waste his money.

Speaking of which, weren't there a couple of stamp dealers in Jacksonville? He didn't have his catalog with him, but he always had a few checklists in his wallet, so that he could tell what stamps he needed from those particular countries. He could check the Yellow Pages, drop in on a dealer or two before he caught a return flight to New York. No reason why the trip had to be a total loss.

So what was he waiting for?

Whatever it was, it kept him close to the gate for the Atlanta flight. He was still there when the man who'd killed Maggie went up to the counter for a brief conversation with the clerk, then walked off in the direction she'd indicated.

Where was he headed? Not the men's room, it was directly opposite the gate, and clearly marked.

Oh, right.

Keller tagged along in his wake, stopping at a newsstand to buy cigarettes. If he'd guessed wrong, if the man's destination wasn't what he thought it was, well, he was out the price of a pack of Winstons. But no, there was a sign for the smoking lounge, and that's where the man was headed.

He slowed down and let his quarry get settled in. The man was puffing away by the time Keller opened the door and slipped inside. It was a glassed-in area, the furnishings limited to a double row of couches and a generous supply of standing metal ashtrays. The killer was at one end of the room, and two women were over at the other end, barely visible through the smoke, heads together, chatting away. And smoking, of course. No one would come to this foul little room except to smoke.

Keller shook a cigarette out of his pack, put it between his lips. He approached the man, patting at his pockets, reaching into the breast pocket of his jacket. "Excuse me," he said, "but have you got a light?" And, as recognition came into the man's eyes, Keller said, "Say, didn't I see you on the flight from Newark? I don't know what the hell I did with my matches."

The man reached into a pocket, came out with a lighter. Keller bent toward the flame.

CHAPTER THIRTY

"Keller," she said. "I swear to God I was sure you were dead."

"Dead? I just talked to you on the phone."

"Before that," she said. "Well, don't just stand there. Come on inside. What the hell happened to you, Keller? The last time I saw you, you were walking north on Crosby Street. Where have you been for the past four days?"

"Jacksonville," he said.

"Jacksonville, Florida?"

"That's the only Jacksonville I know of."

"I'm pretty sure there's one in North Carolina," she said, "and there are probably others, but who cares? What the hell were you doing in Jacksonville, Florida?"

"Nothing."

"Nothing?"

"I went to the movies," he said. "Dropped in on a few stamp dealers. Watched television in my motel room."

"Call a realtor? Look at some houses?"

"No."

"Well, that's something. I don't want to sound like your mother, Keller, but how come you didn't call?"

He thought about it. "I was ashamed," he said.

"Ashamed?"

"I guess that's what it was."

"Ashamed of what?"

"Ashamed of myself."

She rolled her eyes. "Keller," she said, "do I look like a dentist?"

"A dentist?"

"So why does every conversation with you have to be

like pulling teeth? Of course you were ashamed of yourself. A person can't be ashamed of somebody else. Ashamed of yourself for what?"

Why was he stalling? He drew a breath. "Ashamed of myself for what I did," he said. "Dot, I killed a man."

"You killed a man."

"Yes."

"Keller, do you want to sit down? Can I get you something to drink?"

"No, I'm fine."

"But you killed a man."

"In Jacksonville."

"Keller," she said, "that's what you do. Remember? That's what you've been doing all your life. Well, maybe not all your life, maybe not when you were a kid, but—"

"This was different, Dot."

"What was different about it?"

"I wasn't supposed to kill him."

"You're not supposed to kill anybody, according to what they teach kids in Sunday school. It's against the rules. But you haven't lived by those rules for a while now, Keller."

"I broke my own rules," he said. "I killed somebody I shouldn't have."

"Who?"

"I don't even know his name."

"Is that what bothers you? Not knowing his name?"

"Dot," he said, "I killed our guy. I killed the man we hired. He came to New York to do a job, a job we hired him to do, and he did everything just the way he was supposed to do, and I followed him from New York to Jacksonville and murdered him in cold blood."

"In cold blood," she said.

"Or maybe it was hot blood. I don't know."

"Come on into the kitchen," she said. "Have a seat, let me make you a cup of tea. And tell me all about it."

★

"So that's basically it," he said, "and one reason I stayed there in Jacksonville was I wanted to figure out why I did it before I came back and told you about it."

"And?"

"And I still haven't figured it out. I could have stayed there for a month and I don't think I would have worked it out."

"You must have some idea."

"Well, I was frustrated," he said. "That was a part of it. How many months have we had Roger to worry about? This was supposed to smoke him out, and it did, I even got a fairly close look at him, but then he slipped away. Either he got wind of what was going on or the man who killed Maggie gave him the slip, but either way I'd missed my chance at Roger."

"And you just had to kill somebody."

He thought about it, shook his head. "No," he said. "It had to be this guy."

"Why?"

"This is crazy. I was mad at him, Dot."

"Because he killed your girlfriend."

"It doesn't make any sense, does it? He pulled the trigger, except it wouldn't have been a trigger, because he wouldn't have used a gun, not if he was making it look like an accident. How did he do it, do you happen to know?"

"Drowning."

"Drowning? In a fifth-floor loft in lower Manhattan?"

"In her bathtub."

"And it looked like an accident?"

"It didn't look much like anything else. Either she passed out or she slipped and lost her footing, hit her head on the edge of the tub on the way down. Went under the surface and took a deep breath anyhow."

"Water in the lungs?"

"So they said."

"He drowned her," he said, "the dirty son of a bitch. At least she was unconscious when it happened."

"Maybe."

"How could he do it if he didn't knock her out first?"

"It's too late to ask him," she said, "but if he knocks her out first then he has to undress her and put her in the tub, and he might leave marks that wouldn't be consistent with the scene he's trying to set."

"What else could he do?"

"How would you do it, Keller?"

He frowned, thinking it through. "Hold a gun on her," he said. "Or a knife, whatever. Make her get undressed and draw a tub, make her get in the tub."

"And then hold her head under?"

"The easy way," he said, "is to pick up her feet. Lift them up and the head goes under."

"And if the person struggles?"

"It doesn't do any good," he said. "He might splash a little water around, that's all."

"Wrong pronoun."

"Well," he said.

"I remember a few years ago," she said. "A job you did, but don't ask me where. A man drowned."

"Salt Lake City," he said.

"That how you did it? Hold a gun on him?"

"He was in the tub when I got there. He'd dozed off. I had a gun, I went in there to shoot him, but there he was, taking a nap in the tub."

"So you picked up his feet?"

"I'd heard about it," he said, "or maybe I read it somewhere, I don't remember. I wanted to see if it would work."

"And it did?"

"Nothing to it," he said. "He woke up, but he couldn't do anything. He was a big strong guy, too. I wiped up the water that got splashed out of the tub. I guess he would have done the same thing on Crosby Street, took a towel and wiped the floor."

"He left the tub running."

"And what, it overflowed? You couldn't tell there was a struggle, not if the tub overflowed."

"And?"

"And what else would it do?" He thought about it. "Well, it would make it look as though it happened while the tub was filling. She slipped getting into the tub, knocked herself out, and drowned before she could wake up."

"Or drugs. She got in the tub while it was filling and passed out from the drugs she'd taken."

"What drugs?"

"She was an artist, right? Lived in SoHo?"

"NoHo."

"Huh?"

"SoHo is south of Houston," he explained. "That's where the name comes from. Where she lived is a couple blocks north of Houston, so they call it NoHo."

"Thanks for the geography lesson, Keller. Look, she just went out to a bar, picked up some stud and partied with him. I'd say there's a fair chance she provided herself with a little chemical assistance along the way. But it doesn't matter. We're getting off-track here. Where'd the water go?"

"The water?"

"The water. Where'd it go?"

"All over the floor," he said.

"And then?"

"Oh."

"Right, and the people downstairs banged on her door, and when that didn't work they called the cops. It's a way to let the client know the job's been done. You don't have to wait for the smell to tip off the neighbors. You should have thought of that in Salt Lake City."

"It wasn't a consideration," he said. "Besides, it was a house in the suburbs. The tub overflows, the water winds up in the basement."

Dot nodded. "Could run for days before anybody noticed."

"I suppose."

"Waste all that water. Bad enough anywhere, but in Salt Lake City? That's the desert, isn't it?"

"Well," he said.

"Right," she said. "Who cares? All water over the dam, or through the floorboards. How'd we get on this, anyway? Oh, right, you wanted to know how she died."

"What I wanted," he said, "was to kill the man who killed her. And that doesn't make any sense, Dot. If you look at it in a certain way, *I* was the person who killed her."

"Because if you never got involved with her . . .'"

"It's more direct than that. I was the client, I ordered the hit on her."

"If you want to be technical," she said, "I was the one who ordered it and set it up."

"Maybe deep down I was angry at you," he said, "and at myself, but that wasn't how it felt. I sat there in the plane and I hated the guy, Dot. Him and his toupee and his fake mustache and his costume changes. He did just what I'd wanted him to do, what we were paying him to do, and I hated him for it."

"I sort of get it," she said.

"And the other one, Roger, had given us the slip. We went through all this and Roger slept through it, or whatever he did, and he's still out there for us to worry about. Maybe he was lurking on Crosby Street when the neighbor called the cops, maybe he saw them bring her body out. I didn't have a shot at Roger, but I had a shot at this bastard that I hated. So I took it." He shook his head. "Roger's home by now, cursing his luck. He doesn't know I did his dirty work for him."

"How'd you do it, Keller?"

"Followed him to the smoking lounge and stabbed him."

"Stabbed him?"

"I leaned forward so he could light my cigarette, and I had a knife in my hand, and next thing you knew it was in his chest."

"A knife."

"Right."

"How'd you get it through airport security?"

"It was already there."

She looked at him.

"I had to fly first class," he said, "and they serve you a real meal there, as if you were in a restaurant. Cloth napkin, china cup and plate, and metal utensils. When I was done eating, I put the knife in my pocket."

"You were already planning to do it."

"What struck me," he said, "was this was a way to arm yourself after you had cleared the metal detector. At this point there was still a chance I'd find Roger waiting for us at Jacksonville."

"And you could attack him with your butter knife."

"It wasn't a butter knife."

"No, it was just the sort of thing Davy Crockett killed a bear with."

"It had a serrated edge," he said. "You could cut meat with it."

"My God," Dot said. "And they let just anybody have these lethal weapons? You'd think they'd fingerprint you before they passed them out."

"Well, it worked just fine," he said. "Went between the ribs and into the heart, and he wouldn't have died any faster if I'd used a twelve-inch Bowie. There were a couple of women yakking away at the other end of the smoking lounge, and they didn't notice a thing."

"And you got rid of the knife."

"And the cigarettes."

"And spent a few days in Jacksonville, thinking about it."

"That's right."

"Didn't pick up a phone."

"I thought about it."

"Well, that's the next best thing, isn't it? If thoughts had wings, I could have heard them flapping. Instead I figured you were dead."

"I'm sorry, Dot."

"I figured Roger got you and the hitter both. Figured the bastard turned the hat trick."

"The hat trick is three," he said.

"I know that, Keller. The old man was a hockey fan, remember? Knew the names of all the Rangers back to the first year of the franchise. I used to watch hockey matches with him."

"I didn't know you were a fan."

"I wasn't. I hated it. But I know what a hat trick is. Three goals in one game, all scored by the same player."

"Right."

"So I figured Roger got the hat trick."

"Roger got shut out," he said. "Roger sat in the doorway with his thumb up his ass while I took out the hitter for him. But even the way you figured it, it wouldn't have been the hat trick. If he killed me and the hitter, that's two. Who's the third?"

"Your girlfriend."

"My—you mean Maggie?"

"That's right, I wasn't supposed to call her your girlfriend. I keep forgetting."

"Roger didn't kill her."

"You sure about that, Keller?"

He stared at her, tried to read her face. He said, "Dot, we saw what happened. She brought a guy home and he left and our hitter went up, and *he* left, and a little while later the painter on the fourth floor had water coming through the ceiling."

"Right."

"The guy she brought home," he said. "If that was Roger . . . but it couldn't have been, because we saw him. And she was still alive when he left, remember? He forgot his keys, and she threw them down to him."

"His wallet."

"Whatever. Roger didn't do anything except lurk in a doorway and eat at a lunch counter, and that's the one good thing to come out of all this, Dot. Because I got a good look at him. I didn't know who was who at the time, but I do now, and I can recognize him when I see him again."

"The man in the cap and windbreaker."

"Right, Roger."

"You'd know him if you saw him again."

"Absolutely."

"Maybe you would," she said, "but we'll never know. Because you'll never see him again."

"What are you talking about?"

"Keller," she said, "you'd better sit down."

"I *am* sitting down. I've been sitting down for the past twenty minutes."

"So you are," she said. "And it's a good thing. And don't get up now, Keller. Stay right where you are."

It was just as well that he was sitting. He didn't know that what she told him would have knocked him off his feet, but he didn't know that it wouldn't, either. One thing he could say was that it was hard to take it all in.

"He was Roger," he said.

"Right."

"The guy in the hat and muffler. The guy who sat upstairs across the street, smoking one cigarette after another."

"Most smokers do it that way, Keller. They smoke them in turn, rather than all at once."

"The guy who went upstairs to Maggie's loft. If he was Roger, why would *he* kill Maggie? He wasn't getting paid for it. He turned down the assignment, remember? And came in on the sly so he could have a chance to kill off the competition."

"That's right."

"So he was watching the building, waiting for the hitter to make his move. Did he think the guy she brought home was the hitter? No, he would have seen what we saw, her throwing his wallet down to him. He knew she was alive when he went up there."

"And he knew she was dead when he left."

"Thus depriving himself of the chance to draw a bead on the man who had a contract on her. So he threw away his hat and went home."

"With you in hot pursuit."

"Why would he leave New York without killing the man he came to kill? And why do the hitter's work for him? What was he trying to do, make him lose face and kill himself? That might work in Japan, but—"

"He already did it, Keller."

"Did what?"

"Hit the hitter. And we can stop calling him that, incidentally. His name was Marcus Allenby, or at least that's the name he was registered under."

"Registered where?"

"The Woodleigh," she said. "And he had a couple different names on the ID in his wallet, and Allenby wasn't one of them, and he'd hanged himself with a sheet from the bed, and it was all dramatic enough to get his picture in the *Post*. The picture didn't show the cap or the windbreaker, but it was the same guy."

"Roger drowned Maggie," Keller said, working it out. "And then he went to the Woodleigh, went to Allenby's room—Allenby?"

"Got to call him something."

"Forced his way in, strung the guy up, and left."

"I think he went to the Woodleigh first. Followed Allenby there, got into the room by posing as a cop or a hotel employee. That part wouldn't be hard. Then he caught Allenby off guard."

"And killed him? Then why did he come back after he killed Maggie?"

"Maybe he left Allenby trussed up," she said. "And then, after he'd killed her and left the tub running to establish the time of death, he went back to the Woodleigh, took the Do Not Disturb sign off the knob, let himself in with the key he'd taken from Allenby on his first visit, hanged the poor bastard with a sheet from his own bed, and wrote out the note."

"What note?"

"Didn't I mention that? A note on hotel letterhead. 'I can't do this anymore. God forgive me.' "

"Allenby's handwriting?"

"How would anybody know?"

He nodded. "The drowning looks like an accident," he said, "but the client who ordered the job—"

"Which is to say us."

"—knows it's a hit, and figures it was one job too many for Allenby, and the guy's conscience tortured him into ending it all. Either he left Allenby alive while he went down and did Maggie—"

"Risky."

"—or he killed him the first time, figuring nobody was going to discover the body, and so what if they did? But by coming back he could make a phone call from the dead man's room, and the phone records would establish time of death regardless of the forensic evidence."

Keller frowned. "It's too tricky," he said. "Too many things could go wrong."

"Well, he was a tricky guy."

"Speaking of tricky, didn't you say he hanged him with a bed sheet? That's what guys do in prison, but would you hang yourself with a sheet if you had other things to choose from?"

"I wouldn't hang myself at all, Keller."

"But a sheet," he said. "Why not a belt?"

"Maybe Allenby wore suspenders. Or maybe it was part of the game Roger was playing."

"He liked playing games," he agreed. "The whole thing was a game, wasn't it? I mean, chasing around the country to murder other people in the same line of work as yourself. The idea is you increase your income that way, but do you? What you really do is use up a lot of time and spend a ton of money on airfare."

"Not a good career move, you're saying."

"But it made him feel smarter than the rest of us. Smarter than everybody. Switching clothes, pasting on a mustache and peeling it off. All that phony crap. You'd expect it from some jerk in the CIA, but would a pro waste his time like that?"

"He wasn't perfect, Keller. He killed the couple in Louisville that wound up in your old motel room, and he popped the guy in Boston who stole your coat."

"I was lucky."

"And he was a little too cute for his own good. I guess he spotted Allenby easily enough. Well, so did we. Allenby wasn't worried about being spotted by anybody but the designated victim. And then I guess he got tired of waiting. Well, I can understand that. We were getting pretty sick of it ourselves, as I recall. You even said something about killing them both and getting it over with."

"I remember."

"Once he spotted Allenby, why wait? He could just follow him home and take him out, and he did, in his hotel room."

"He didn't have to kill Maggie," Keller said.

"But the contract was always carried out, remember? That was Roger's trademark, he bided his time until the hitter got the job done, and then he did a job of his own on the hitter. This time the hitter was out of the picture early, so Roger felt it was up to him to do the job. Maybe he thought it was part of being a pro."

"Maybe."

"And it got him killed."

He sat there for a while. She went on talking, going over it, and he let the words wash over him without taking in everything she was saying. He'd avenged Maggie, which had seemed important at the time, for reasons that made no sense at all now. He tried to picture her, and realized that her image was already fading, getting smaller, losing color and definition. Fading into the past, fading the way everything faded.

And Roger was gone. He'd been looking over his shoulder for months, stalked by a faceless killer, and now that threat had been removed. And he'd done it himself. He hadn't known that was what he was doing, but he'd done it anyway.

"If I'd done the right thing," he said, "he would have gotten away."

"Roger."

"Uh-huh. I'd have turned around and gone home, convinced that Roger wasn't going to show. And I'd have been letting the real Roger off the hook, and we wouldn't know anything more about him. Not his name or where he lived. We wouldn't know any of those things."

"We still don't," she pointed out.

"But now we don't need to."

"No."

"The broker who found Allenby for us says we owe the balance."

"What did he get, half in advance?"

"And the rest due on completion, and the guy's point is the job was completed. Woman's dead and it goes in the books as an accident, so we should be satisfied, right? If Allenby gets pangs of conscience afterward and decides to kill himself, well, what does that have to do with us? He offed himself without blowing the Crosby Street hit, so we got what we ordered."

"What did you tell him?"

"I wasn't about to explain what really happened."

"No, of course not."

"He thought I had booked this on behalf of a client, and that the client should pay. And I told him I agreed, but on the other hand we both knew the money wasn't going to Allenby, because Allenby wasn't alive to collect it."

"The broker would keep it."

"Of course. So I said, 'Look, your guy killed himself, and that's a shame because he did good work.' "

"All he did was stand in a doorway."

"Let me finish, will you? 'He did good work,' I said, 'but he's dead, and you're not gonna pay him, and I'm not gonna give my client a refund. So what do you say we split it?' And I sent him half of the half we owed."

"That sounds fair."

"I'm not sure fairness has anything to do with it, but I could live with it and so could he. Keller, we're out of the woods. The loose ends are tied off and Roger's dead and gone. You take all that in yet?"

"Just about."

"You did the absolute right thing," she said, "for the wrong reason. That's a whole lot better than the other way around."

"I guess so."

"It wasn't that girl, you know. That's not why you wanted to kill him. That's what you told yourself, but that wasn't it."

"It wasn't?"

"No. Be honest, Keller. You don't care about her, do you?"

"Not now."

"You never did."

"Maybe not."

"You sensed something about that guy. You didn't know he was Roger, you really thought he was our guy, but you picked up some vibration. And you didn't like him."

"I hated the bastard."

"And how do you feel about him now?"

"Now?" He thought about it. "He's gone," he said. "There's nothing to feel."

"Same as always, right?"

"Pretty much."

"Maybe it's your thumb."

"Huh?"

"Your murderer's thumb, Keller. Maybe it gives you good instincts, or maybe it's just good luck. Either way, I think you should keep it."

He looked at his thumb. When he'd first become aware of its special quality, he'd gotten so he didn't like to look at it. It had looked weird to him.

Now it looked just right. Not like everybody else's thumb, maybe. Not even like his other thumb, for that matter. But it looked as though it belonged on his hand. It looked right for him.

"You buy some stamps in Jacksonville, Keller?"

"Some."

"Paste them in your album yet?"

"You don't paste them," he said. "You'd ruin them if you pasted them."

"You told me once what it is you do. You mount them, right?"

"Right."

"Like you'd mount a horse," she said, "except different. Did you mount these yet?"

341

"No, I didn't have a chance."

"So you've got stamps waiting to be mounted. And there's probably mail that came while you were gone, too."

"The usual."

"Magazines and catalogs, I'll bet. And what do you call it when they send you stamps and you get to pick and choose?"

"Approvals."

"Any of those come?"

"There was a shipment, yes. From a woman in Maine."

"She's going to stay in Maine, right? And you're not going to run up there for a visit."

"Of course not."

"So you can go home and work on your stamps."

"I could," he said. "I guess that's what I'll do."

"I think that's a good idea," she said. "And take good care of your thumb, okay? Dress it warm and keep it out of drafts. Because Allenby's dead, and so is Roger, and so are all the people good old Roger put out of business. Which means there are fewer people than ever doing what you do, Keller, and I can't see the volume of work shrinking."

"No," he said, and touched his thumb. "No, I don't think that's anything we have to worry about."

342